Shadow's Curse

Book Two in the
Imnada Brotherhood Series

ALEXA EGAN

D1560297

Pocket Books
New York London Toronto Sydney New Delhi

Pocket Books
A Division of Simon & Schuster, Inc.
1230 Avenue of the Americas
New York, NY 10020

First Pocket Books paperback edition October 2013

POCKET and colophon are registered trademarks of Simon & Schuster, Inc.

For information about special discounts for bulk purchases, please contact Simon & Schuster Special Sales at 1-866-506-1949 or business@simonandschuster.com.

The Simon & Schuster Speakers Bureau can bring authors to your live event. For more information or to book an event contact the Simon & Schuster Speakers Bureau at 1-866-248-3049 or visit our website at www.simonspeakers.com.

Manufactured in the United States of America

10   9   8   7   6   5   4   3   2   1

ISBN 978-1-4516-7292-3
ISBN 978-1-4516-7295-4 (ebook)

*For Do & Maggie, who help me find the words
and always share their snacks*

1

LONDON, MAY 1817

The man stood over his victim, knife flashing in the dim light of Silmith's round yellow moon. The scent of blood and urine hung on the stale breeze, and the clink of a money pouch echoed in the quiet of the alley. David hung back in the shadows, awaiting his moment. The thief would have to pass by him to reach the street and disappear into the warren of dockside wharves and warehouses. When he did, David would pursue. It was a tactic he'd perfected over the course of the past year.

Not once had he allowed his prey to escape his particular brand of justice. Not once had he been caught or even seen except as a ghostly shape, an enormous dark shadow with glowing gray eyes. Some called him a demon or a monster—the newspapers who prospered from his exploits and those who worked the darkness for their own gains. But those who'd been saved by his intervention labeled him a guardian angel, a mysterious hero.

He was neither. Merely bored.

And angry.

Very, very angry.

If any member of the five clans of shape-shifting Imnada were to discover he spent the time between sundown and sunrise saving the lives of humans, they'd deem him mad. Not that he cared what they thought. He was *emnil*, dead to his clan. An outcast and an outlaw.

And while he was no longer condemned to pass his nights in his clan aspect of the wolf, having escaped the clutch of a curse that forced him and his friends to shift, these short, vicious hours had become a solace; these cluttered, squalid alleys and dark, twisted lanes his personal hunting ground. If he couldn't spend his rage upon those who'd banished him to this tormented existence, he'd turn it on the villainous cutthroats and slimy pimps who prowled the stews in search of victims. Not that he cared overmuch about the men and women he assisted, but few questioned the deaths of thugs or mourned the loss of murderers. Only the Fey-bloods might realize the truth behind the monstrous beast prowling London's stews, but that only added to the knife-edge thrill he craved like an addict—an existence he knew all too much about these days.

The clouds passed over the full moon, the breeze kicking up in starts to ruffle the fur along his back, the bristly ridge at his neck. He lifted his face to it, felt it curl over his muzzle, bringing with it the salty tar-laden stench of the Limehouse docks. Just then the victim moaned and stirred as he regained consciousness. His hand groped feebly for the knot at the back of his head. Shoving the money pouch in his coat pocket, the assailant lifted his knife with deadly intent. Theft soon to become murder.

Thought fell to instinct, and, with fangs bared in a vicious snarl, David sprang.

Callista rubbed a cloth over the last silver bell before returning it to its case alongside the other two. Closing the lid, she secured the lock with a roll of her thumb over the circular tumblers. But instead of tucking the mahogany box upon the high shelf beside her bed, she remained at her desk, the box in front of her. Her finger followed the familiar loops and swirls decorating the lid. Her mother's box. Her grandmother's. Her great-grandmother's.

Necromancers, all.

The power to journey into the realm of the dead and speak to those who walked its paths had been gifted to the women of her house, stretching back beyond anyone's memory. At least that's what Mother had claimed. Callista couldn't know for certain. She'd never met any of the women of her house except Mother to ask them.

Now she couldn't even ask Mother.

Callista slid open the top desk drawer, removing a bundle of yellowed letters wrapped in a frayed ribbon. The wax was dried and crumbling, the writing smudged and faded. Mother had kept them all, every single missive she'd sent to her family that had been returned unopened. The prominent Armstrong family of Killedge Hall never forgot or forgave the shame of their daughter's elopement.

Callista pulled free the top letter, reading the

words, though she knew them by heart. A cheerful letter, despite the anguish and the dread prompting this last desperate attempt to reconcile. Mother had died a month later.

Mother's letter had been returned a week after the funeral.

Every time Callista walked into death, the urge to summon her mother's spirit almost overcame her. And yet, she held back. Refused to trace the symbols that would bind her mother to her. Callista couldn't bear to let her see how far her only daughter had fallen, trading her power for coins like a huckster at the village fair alongside the dog-faced boy and the bearded lady. To her mother, the gift of necromancy had been a sacred trust. To Callista, it had become a trickster's ploy.

The door behind Callista opened, a breeze stirring the hair at the back of her neck, raising gooseflesh over her arms. As she slid the packet of correspondence back into the desk drawer, she felt Branston's thunderous stare bore into her, his fury like a shimmer of red behind her eyelids.

"Running away again, sister dear? You should know by now, Mr. Corey has eyes and ears all over London. There's nothing happens in this town he doesn't know about."

Callista shuddered with loathing for her half brother's new business partner but wisely kept her opinion to herself.

"I almost wish his men hadn't found you in time for your appointment," he said. "Better to postpone the summoning than have poor Mrs. Dixon's hopes dashed so cruelly."

"Your concern for the grieving mother is touching," Callista answered wearily. "I'd not have taken you for a sentimentalist."

"What I am is a businessman and you, my dear, are the business. A fact you keep forgetting."

She rose to confront Branston. His small, washed-out blue eyes narrowed, his nostrils flared as if he smelled something rank. "That's where you're wrong. I know it all too well. You haven't let me forget for one moment in the past seven years."

His hands flexed and curled into fists, his well-fed body wired with tension. "Is that what your sulks are about? Your feelings are hurt? You don't feel appreciated? Is that why you decided to dash a grieving mother's hopes by telling her you were unable to speak to little Jonny?"

"It's not right to take these people's money without offering them comfort in return."

Shoving his hands in his pockets, Branston shrugged away from her. "We offer solace. Reassurance. Hope. Worth it at double the price," he said, in the same tone he used to hawk her skills during their years traveling town to town and fair to fair. "We're the only link to their loved ones beyond the grave, to the infinite knowledge of the future the spirits can offer us."

"Yes, if I'm able to find the spirit they seek and the client's questions are answered. But I never found that woman's son. I walked as far as I dared into death. I tried every path I knew. I couldn't lie to her."

"Perhaps you need to delve farther? Walk paths you've yet to explore?"

"I'm not trained for the deeper reaches. Mother died before she could teach me those lessons, and without the proper instruction, it's too dangerous to attempt."

"I don't bloody care." He spun around, jaw clenched. Brotherly concern, obviously a pose too difficult to maintain. Not that he'd ever tried very hard. Perhaps if they'd been closer in age or she'd been born a boy or if he'd not been an ill-tempered, spiteful, good-for-nothing sod.

"Do what you need to do to satisfy the customer, Callista. If you won't risk it, then lie. If you'd done that tonight, the old cow would have left here pleased as punch, thinking little Jonny was with dear old Dad doing ring-the-rosy in heaven. She'd have been happy to be comforted in her time of grief. I'd have been happy to relieve her of her money."

"We've only begun to recover after the fiasco in Manchester. Do you want to be arrested this time? Or worse? Mother always said—"

"What I want, Callista"—he slammed his hand upon the table—"is for you to do as you're told. I don't give a damn about your bloody bells or your Fey-born gift or your sainted mother. She's long dead, and if it weren't for me, the only gift keeping you from starvation would be the one between your legs. So, you'll tell these sniveling, drippy, hand-wringing women with their sob stories whatever they want to hear, because if you don't"—he shoved his face close enough for her to smell the whisky on his breath—"I'll make you very, very sorry."

She refused to cower before him, though she knew it only made him angrier. Instead she locked her knees, forced her shoulders square, and met him glare for glare. "You're no longer my guardian, and I won't be forced to act as your circus sideshow any longer."

His gaze grew icy, a wicked smile dancing over his mouth. "The next time you leave, I've told Mr. Corey he can return you in any condition he chooses. I'm sure he'd be more than willing, and, knowing him, any struggle on your part will only increase his ardor. You suppose that high-flown aunt of yours you're always running on about will take you in once you're ruined and stuffed with a bastard child?"

"You wouldn't dare." Cold fear splashed across Callista's back, nearly buckling her knees. Aunt Deirdre, her mother's elder sister, resided in Scotland as a priestess of High Danu. Callista had never met her, but for seven years, she'd dreamed of traveling to the convent at Dunsgathaic. Of finding a home with her long-lost relative. Of finally escaping Branston.

"Wouldn't I?" Branston grabbed her, his fingers digging into her upper arms until tears burned in her eyes. "You'll do as I say. No more arguments. No more running. Do I make myself clear?"

"Completely," she answered, forcing a calm she did not feel.

He released her to pat her cheek, an unpleasant smile stretching his wide mouth. "You make it so much harder than it needs to be. I'm only looking out for your best interests. Haven't I always been there to take care of you, unlike those high and mighty relatives of your mother's?"

She crossed her arms over her chest, eyeing him like the disease he was. "Your persuasive abilities continue to amaze me. It's no wonder none of your schemes pay off."

Annoyance flickered in his gaze. "Get some rest. We've two appointments tomorrow, and I want you at your best. I'm going out. Mrs. Thursby will be here if you need anything."

Hardly a comfort. The old bawd acting as Branston's housekeeper was another of Mr. Corey's associates. Since they set up shop in London six months ago, their household had slowly been taken over by the ruthless gang lord and his underlings. But why? What really lay behind his continued and growing interest in them?

"Where are you going?" she asked.

Branston chucked her chin as if she were ten years old. "Worried for me? Don't be, dear sister. I'll always be here to look after you. Always."

She crossed to the hearth, though no warmth touched her frozen, shivering skin. Always was what she most feared.

No matter how many times he did it, David St. Leger always hated this part.

With held breath and steady hand, he eased the silver-bladed knife across his opposite palm, wincing as blood welled behind the thin cut. Holding his hand above the glass he'd prepared earlier, he waited as three large drops fell into the viscous slime-green liquid, then snatched up a napkin to wrap around his wound. The initial sting became a steady throb as the silver's poison moved up his arm into his head until spots bounced in front of his eyes and his stomach squirmed ominously.

Swirling the liquid around as if he were appreciating a fine brandy, he raised the glass to his lips, closed his eyes, and downed the vile, greasy brew in one shuddering swallow. It had been almost two years since the dying Fey-blood had spat his evil curse over him. A few months since the discovery of the draught that prevented his unnatural shift from man to beast with each setting of the sun.

David wasn't sure which was worse—the cure or the curse.

Leaving the glass on a nearby table, he sank into an armchair, leaning his head back against the cushions, until the dizziness passed and the potion took hold. The clock struck the hour. A log in the grate fell apart in a shower of sparks. Rain pattered against the window.

And then there were the sounds that didn't belong. A far-off click of a latch. The brush of a boot against carpet. A rattle of a knob. Not a servant. He'd sent the last one to bed on his arrival home an hour ago.

Taking up his knife once more, David waited—and listened. He'd take no chances. Not with the Imnada's brutal Ossine enforcers searching for any shapechanger suspected of going against tradition to seek an alliance with the Fey-bloods. The rebels claimed it was their only chance to save the race from extinction. The Ossine called it treason.

David might be innocent of insurrection, but he was still *emnil*, exiled from his clan and labeled a dangerous rogue. That was an engraved invitation to any enforcer who sought to cleanse the clan once and for all of his corrupted bloodline. None would question his death . . . after all, within a wolf pack, the crippled and the sickly were the first to be eliminated. Within the five clans of Imnada, those same laws applied.

But David would not be taken down without a

fight. The Ossine enforcers would not lay their hands on him again.

Ever.

The sounds came closer. David hung back, the knife ready, every muscle tensed for the attack. The door opened and a shadow fell across the floor. Unhesitating, he lunged, his arm sweeping out to catch the intruder. A shout erupted. Glass shattered. A knife flashed. The intruder's neck ended trapped in the crook of David's elbow, his back arched against the silver blade pressed to his kidneys.

"Are you barking mad, St. Leger?" the man growled from between clenched teeth.

David closed his eyes on a string of profanity. Dropped his arm and his blade.

Captain Mac Flannery.

"Is this how you greet all your guests?" Mac snarled, his cat-slanted green eyes narrowed in fury.

"Only those who sneak in like thieves," David quipped with a smile, despite the renewed rush of dizziness spinning his head. He tossed the knife with a clatter onto a nearby table.

"I knocked, but I expect your housekeeper's retired for the night."

David cast a glance at the mantel clock. "It's two in the morning. Of course she's retired." He poured himself a drink. On an afterthought, poured one for Mac, who was straightening his waistcoat. "What the hell are you doing here at this godforsaken time of night anyway? Shouldn't you be home making mad passionate love to your new bride?"

"I wish. I came to let you know there's an enforcer skulking around London."

"Let him skulk. I'm not up to my neck in traitorous revolution like some I could name." David settled into a chair. It felt good after the busy night he'd had. He tossed back the whisky, feeling the burn all the way to his toes. "Much as I appreciate the warning, couldn't it have waited until morning?"

"I didn't want an audience for my arrival . . . just in case."

"Does Gray know about this meddlesome Ossine?"

"Gray's gone north to Addershiels. I haven't heard from him in weeks. I'm starting to worry."

"And well you should. If the enforcers discover his involvement with the rebel Imnada and their Fey-blood conspirators, he'll end in pieces and us right alongside him."

Mac rubbed his temples as if staunching a headache. "I know, but Gray doesn't listen. I think this whole uprising is his way of getting back at his grandfather."

Among British society, the Duke of Morieux was known as a shrewd and cunning aristocrat with the wealth to buy a nation and the influence to rule it, though he chose to spend most of his time and attention on his vast Cornish estate.

Among the Imnada, the heavyset bear of a man with his shock of white hair and the ice-blue eyes of a hawk was known simply as the Morieux, hereditary leader of the five clans, whose word was law.

David simply called him a fucking mealymouthed cocksucker.

"Do you blame Gray?" David asked. "His grandfather could have saved him. He could have saved all of us. But if Gray wants revenge, a nice blade between dear Grandpapa's ribs would be a hell of a lot easier than a revolution."

A tense silence sprang up though neither strove to break it. The three friends had reached a tacit agreement. They never spoke of the last chaotic days of war and a dying Fey-blood's vicious spell that had trapped them all within the prison of the curse. Nor did they talk of the cure that fast became a deadly addiction. They could not stop; they could not continue. Either choice brought sickness and finally death. In their struggle to free themselves of the spell, they'd ended trapped and tainted by the magic of the Fey—again.

Mac found solace from his pain in love; Gray in revenge.

David found it at the bottom of a whisky bottle.

"Your message has been delivered, Captain. Care for a drink—or three?" He started to rise.

"There's another . . . small matter."

David sighed, dropping back into his chair. "There always is."

A shuffling step sounded from just outside the door, followed by the click of a heel on the parquet. David snatched up his blade and was halfway to the door before Mac grabbed him. "Wait."

David swung around, eyes wild. "What the hell—"

"Caleb!" Mac called. "Show yourself. It's all right."

A thin man with a long, pockmarked face and dingy brown hair stepped into the study. His eyes darted around the room as if gauging safety.

"St. Leger won't harm you. Will you, David?"

"That depends on who the devil he is." He turned once more to the sideboard. Mother of All, but he needed another drink.

"This is Caleb Kineally," Mac began. "He's—"

"Imnada." David finished Mac's sentence at the first mental brush of shapechanger magic against his mind. "I take it he's one of Gray's rebels."

Mac ran a hand over his haggard face, and for the first time David noticed the waxen pallor of his friend's features, the smudges hollowing his eyes. "Aye. He needs to lay low while the enforcers are close. I want you to look after him."

"Me?"

"While Gray's away, you're the only one I trust. Bianca's been through enough. I can't place her in danger again. Not with a baby on the way."

David's resolve wavered at mention of Mac's out-clan bride, but he shoved his better nature aside. Mac had asked for trouble when he'd bought into Gray's mutinous rhetoric. It wasn't David's problem nor his cause.

"Just until things quiet down," Mac pleaded.

"You and Gray are deluding yourselves if you believe you'll make our lives better by defying the Ossine. You'll end up dead. But you won't take me with you."

"We're dead either way, though, aren't we?" Mac answered. The simple truth of those words hit David like a kick to the stomach.

So much for delusions.

"Please, David."

He'd never heard Mac beg. Not in Charleroi with battle looming and the Fey-blood's spell singeing their veins like acid. Not when he'd been brought in chains before the stern-faced clan Gather to have the sentence of *emnil* pronounced. And not even when they'd burned away his clan mark, leaving his back a charred wreck and making death seem like mercy. Mac did not beg. He suffered. He endured. It was what David had always admired about his friend.

"You once told me the dead were the only ones who might make a difference," Mac said. "You once believed in the cause as much as any of us."

"Did I? Must have been drunk at the time." David tossed back his whisky. Was this his third or his fourth? He'd lost count.

Mac eyed him over the glass with a last-throw-of-the-dice look on his face. "The Ossine on Kineally's trail is a man by the name of Beskin."

David's back twitched with remembered pain, the whisky turning sour in his gut. Eudo Beskin remained in his head as a brutal nightmare from which there was no waking. If keeping Kineally safe thwarted the dead-hearted bastard, David would do it gladly, but he glared at Mac for playing his trump. "He can stay. But that doesn't make me one of you."

Mac smiled his success as he placed his glass upon a sideboard. "Scoff all you like, St. Leger." He tossed a newspaper on the sofa open to the headline "Monster of the Mews Prevents Malicious Murder." "But you're one of us whether you admit it or not."

The man sat at his usual corner table, his plate emptied of dinner, a brandy before him. Those in the crowded chophouse who noticed him at all dismissed him without a second glance. Just as he'd planned it when he set the spell in motion that repelled eyes and minds, allowing him to disappear while remaining in plain sight. A useful gift. In his early days on the street, it had kept him alive in the brutality and chaos of London's fetid alleys and dank winding passages, when finding food had been his primary goal. But as his skills grew, so did his ambitions. After all, why be given such a talent if it wasn't to be used?

". . . big as a bear with teeth like a lion and claws like the barber's razor. Seen it myself . . ."

". . . this before or after you'd spent your week's pay on blue ruin . . ."

". . . found old Moseby last week, gutted like a mackerel in an alley near the steelyard . . ."

". . . wager his old woman did him in rather than some slavering monster . . ."

The nearby conversation grated on his already strained temper. He'd not come to hear gossip from two red-nosed drunken knaves with less in their heads than they had in their pockets. He checked his watch, sipped sparingly at his drink. Half his success came as a result of keeping a clear head among a rabble of half-soused alley scum.

The door opened and Branston Hawthorne scrambled in as if he had a constable on his tail. Out of breath, he darted his suspicious eyes round the room before sidling over to slide into the seat opposite. "So sorry," he wheezed. "A group of us were meeting to discuss these rumors about the Imnada. Hope you weren't waiting long."

"*What* are Imnada?" Victor Corey sipped unconcernedly at his brandy. It wouldn't do to show too much interest. Keep them guessing. Keep them off their stride. Never show your hand. That had always been his way.

"You don't know about the shapechangers?" Hawthorne asked, disbelief creeping into his voice.

"Damn your eyes! Would I ask the question if I knew?"

Corey hated that he must rely on fools like Branston Hawthorne to instruct him in a magical world that should have been his birthright. He hated that the knowledge this boot-licking poltroon took for granted, Victor Corey, king of the stews, scrabbled to grasp. But grasp it he would. It had taken years to fully understand his power, both its limits and its possibilities. The results had gained him wealth and influence, if not admiration. No matter. The world might not respect him, but it feared him. An emotion that served him twice as well.

Nervousness flickered now in Hawthorne's gaze. Corey relaxed back in his seat, taking a sip of his brandy. "Who or what are Imnada? They must be important if they kept you from our meeting."

Hawthorne licked his lips and rubbed the side of his nose with one pudgy finger. "Yes . . . I mean no . . . I mean of course. I'm happy to explain. The Imnada are shapechangers. Used to be plentiful as grass on a hill until they betrayed Arthur at the last battle. Their war chief cut the king down where he stood"—he snapped his fingers—"just like that. But the Other paid them back for their treachery—"

Corey scowled. "*King* Arthur? Is that the Arthur we're talking about?"

"Aye, last great king of our kind, old Arthur was. Said to be more Fey than human. But it didn't stop the Imnada from doing him in. He bled same as anyone with a sword stuck through his gut. Afterward, the shifters were hunted down, the whole monstrous lot of them. Killed in droves like vermin until none were left . . . or so we thought, the sneaky buggers. It's said they've returned bold as brass and twice as dangerous."

Corey leaned back in his chair. "They change shape? Into what exactly?"

Hawthorne sighed as one might when confronted with a small child's incessant questions. But his long exhale was choked off at a single cold stare from his host. "They shift from man to ruthless wild beast. As soon kill you as look at you. The Other are organizing. We'll not be taken unawares by a bunch of dirty shifters."

"Pitchforks and torches?" Corey said smoothly. "I'd love to see a mob like that parading down Bond Street amid the hoity-toities. Give them a good scare." He held Hawthorne's gaze long enough for the man to move uneasily in his seat before glancing away with a lift of a shoulder and a wave to the barman. "Enough about your bogeymen in the night. I invited you here to find out what you plan on doing about your sister's continued defiance. I don't appreciate being made a fool of and I'm sure you don't want me to change my mind about our arrangement."

He regarded Hawthorne's unease with satisfaction. "No, of course not, Mr. Corey. You've been more than generous with your offer and I'm indebted to you for your patience in the matter."

"You're indebted to me for far more than that, Hawthorne. And I expect payment in full. The girl or the coin. Which will it be?" Though he already knew the answer. He'd made sure Hawthorne was up to his neck in debt with no hope of repayment. Not that it had been difficult. The man had the business acumen of a babe in the cradle.

Hawthorne straightened in his chair, his chubby face breaking into a smile. "You'll have Callista, Mr. Corey. No worry on that score. I've given her a good dressing-down. There won't be any more of her foolishness." He took a long greedy swallow of his wine, dabbing at his mouth with a napkin, unaware of the red drops flecking his neck cloth. "She can be a handful at times, but a stern husband should settle her down right quick."

Corey smiled. Oh, he'd settle Miss Callista Hawthorne down all right. Once tamed, she'd make good bed sport. The woman was ripe for a man's attentions. All she needed was the right man to show her the way.

But while he would enjoy introducing her to the pleasures of the flesh, it was Callista's gift of necromancy he truly desired. She was his key in to death. And when one possesses the key, one controls the door—both who goes in and, more importantly, what comes out.

The realm of Annwn was full of dark spirits bound to the underworld's deepest paths. Dark spirits who only needed a guide to lead them up to and through the door separating life and death. Once that door was breached, Branston Hawthorne with his round little body and unctuous pandering would be the first to die. And from there, who knew . . .

With an army of the underworld at Corey's command, his grip on London would tighten like a noose. They already called him a gang lord and a prince of thieves.

Soon they'd call him mayor.

Perhaps in time they'd hail him as king—or better. Arthur might have been the last great king of the Other. Victor Corey could be the next.

Some thought him mad to take a dowerless nobody as his wife, but he knew better. Callista Hawthorne would bring him the world as her marriage portion.

2

The gang closed in on the woman from two sides, leaving her nowhere to run but toward the alley. False hope, for that way ended in a brick wall. Too high to jump, and while the stones of the empty tenement backing onto the passage were held with barely more than plaster and a promise, no slip of a female would be able to bring them down and win a way out.

Alone, she was as good as caught, and judging by the ripe odors of alcohol and brutality rising from the men, she'd be lucky to escape with her life, much less her honor. She must have known it, too, for she grabbed up a broken plank, holding it in front of her like a sword. Or like someone who'd never handled a sword might hold one. She whipped the board from side to side, her eyes darting between her captors as they circled.

David slunk from his position in the lee of St. Martin's Lane, threading the mews, coming up behind the old tailor's shop. Then through the broken crawl space under the abandoned brewery before arriving at the other side of the wall. Six and a half feet straight up.

His fur rippled with excitement. A growl vibrated low in his chest.

Too high for the woman.

An easy leap for a wolf.

He took a short approach before curling his back legs under and vaulting skyward with every ounce of force, front paws stretched for the ledge. A momentary scramble, and he was up.

His gaze moved slowly over the tableau spread beneath him. The woman backed against the wall, her cloak thrown off her shoulders to reveal a heavy satchel dragging her off-balance, her arms wobbling under the continued weight of the plank as her attackers chortled and swaggered with their success. The fizz and burn of Fey-blood magic jangled at the base of his brain, crawled over his skin. Which one of the group bore the blood of the Other in their veins? David tried focusing on the source, but he was interrupted by the woman's scream as one of her attackers slammed her against the bricks. His mates cheered him on as he tore the plank from her hands and pressed against her, groping his way under her cloak to squeeze her breast.

"How dare you!" She lashed out, her palm connecting with his cheek.

"Spitfire, this one is."

"Don't let Corey see ya pawing the girl, Bates. He'll cut your dick off and shove it up your arse."

"Just softening 'er up is all." Bates released her with a shove, but his lecherous, wild-eyed look remained. She scrambled for the plank, but he kicked it to the side and out of reach. "Your brother's worrit sick about you, he is, miss. Wouldn't want somethin' to happen to ye alone in the big city at night. Mayhap you'll run

into a fella who'd want to stuff his cock into ye . . . or
mayhap a whole group of fellas with stiff cocks. What-
cha think of that?"

The others sniggered.

A mite early for gloating. David's lips curled back
in a toothy grimace, a low snarl rolling up from deep
in his throat to bounce eerily between buildings. Immediately, what had been an easy abduction erupted
into chaos. They looked up, freezing under the inhuman stare from the enormous black shadow, their
frightened shouts warming his heart, his laughter
sounding as another low, frightening growl.

In one flowing move, David leapt from the wall and
sank his teeth into Bates's arm. The blood leaked hot
into his mouth, bones cracking under the pressure.
The man's face went chalk-white, his mouth opening and closing in a silent scream. Shaking him from
side to side, David thrilled at the man's choking gasps
and jerking blood-spattering twitches before he went
silent and then limp. Passed out? Dead? David didn't
care. The vile filth had been a rapist and a murderer.

". . . monster from the papers . . ."

". . . Devil of Dawlish Street . . ."

David lifted his head, lips pulled back from his
fangs in a dripping gruesome smile. Hadn't heard that
one before.

The remaining men retreated, their shouts and
panicked cries better than a Beethoven symphony.

"Hold your ground, boys," someone shouted. "We
ain't gonna let no ruddy animal scare us off."

The panicked men rallied under the newcomer.
A knife sailed past David's face to clang against the
bricks. Then a broken bottle.

So much for easy.

David lunged for his nearest attacker, savaging him with a rake of his claws. Tearing clean a chunk of thigh. Breaking an ankle between his jaws. The man screamed, hunched and shaking against further attack. A bullet smashed into the wall above David's head. He whipped around in time to catch another murderous bastard aiming a long steel knife. One focused, ruthless look from David was all it took for the rascal to flee in a mad scramble for safety, his shoes ringing loud against the cobbles.

One more murderous gang of cutthroats to spread the word of the mysterious monster prowling the midnight streets. One more victim saved by the ghostly beast of the night.

He turned his head for his first real look at the woman when a sudden burst of pain ripped through his skull and his brain exploded with a dazzle of fireworks. His gaze narrowed on the upraised plank gripped in the woman's shaking hands. The plank swung down, the fireworks became a bomb blast, and darkness rose up like a wave to swallow him whole.

"Wake up. Please wake up," Callista whispered as she shook the man by his shoulder.

He groaned, blinking bleary, unfocused eyes. "Go 'way, Mac. Head's splitting. Whisky . . . too much . . ." Then he slumped back against the wooden post he'd been lashed to, wrists taut behind him.

She pulled her shawl tighter around her shoulders against the attic's chill and shook him again. "I'm not Mac, but please, you have to wake up."

Even though long familiar with the otherworldly, what she'd seen back in the alley still seemed unbelievable. The strange blurring of air around his prone body as a swirling wind burned against her face, the prick and sting of unfamiliar magic up and down her arms as wolf gave way to naked man. Her shock lasted mere seconds, but it had been enough time for Corey's men to return. She struggled as they grabbed her, but it was no use. She and the unconscious stranger had been brought back to the house.

She'd been locked in her bedchamber. She'd not seen what they'd done with their prisoner. Not until a jimmied lock and a quiet search had ended here in the attic among dusty trunks and broken furniture.

She shook him once more, trying very hard to keep her eyes on his face and off the rest of him, which remained as he'd been found—very, very naked. Not that it was difficult to keep her stare fixed above his shoulders. He was the most exquisite man she'd ever seen. A face like a fallen angel, all chiseled angles and stern lines, a stubborn chin, a straight nose, and a sinfully full mouth. His blond hair curled against his neck, slightly longer than fashion allowed, but obviously cut by a very good barber. In fact, even without clothes to label class or rank, it was easy to perceive he was no Whitechapel thatch-gallows. From the impossibly broad shoulders to the well-defined, muscular body, the man oozed elegance and the confidence that comes with wealth. Hard to manage being nude and trussed like a Christmas goose awaiting the farmer, but the gentleman did it in spades. The only incongruity was his back, which bore horrible scars as if he'd been through a war—or two. Still, that only added to the raw physicality of the man. If that were possible.

Her gaze snapped back to his face and off his . . . "Can you hear me? Please say something." Who knew how much time she had before Branston checked on her—or the prisoner. She needed to speak with the man first. She needed to find out who he was.

She needed to find out what he was.

He opened his eyes, the vacancy now replaced with a razor-keen stare. He jerked, coming up hard against his bonds, his gaze flicking down over the silver chain interlacing the thin cord at his ankles. "Fucking bollocks," he grunted. "Damned bastard Fey-blood."

He might look aristocratic Mayfair, but his vocabulary came straight from the St. Giles stews. "Can you hear me?" she asked again. "Do you know who you are? Do you remember anything?"

"Of course I bloody well hear you." For the first time, he seemed to take her in, that frightening, steel-edged gaze raking her like a sword point. "You're the minx that clobbered me over the head."

She slumped, her breath heaving out in a sigh. "I'd hoped you might not remember that part."

"Do you always bash in the heads of your rescuers?" He worked at his wrists before leaving off with a small moan that might have been frustration or pain. He looked pale, great shadows pooling beneath his eyes, his chest heaving in short gasps. "Fuck all," he muttered. "Bloody silver. No wonder I feel like shit on a stick." His gaze flicked back to her. "Here to smash another great piece of wood down on my skull, Fey-blood?"

She frowned. "Why do you keep calling me that?"

"It's what you are, isn't it?" He snorted, once more working at his wrists. "Caught by a damned Other," he muttered under his breath.

"You were coming to my rescue?"

He paused to scowl at her. "That was the idea. Seems you weren't in as desperate straits as I thought. Maybe those bastards had a perfectly legitimate reason for cornering you. If I were untied, I might throttle you myself."

She shuffled another arm's length away. The knots held for now, but who knew—he might be strong enough to free himself or turn back into a wolf and gnaw his way out.

"Where am I, Fey-blood?" the man asked, glancing about the sparse attic.

She didn't like his tone, but then, she couldn't fault him for being angry if he had in fact been trying to rescue her from Corey's villainous crew. "You're in a house just off Queen Street in Soho—for now."

A corner of his mouth curled up in a grimace, dimple flashing. "Wondering what to do with me?"

She sat back on her knees, arms folded in her lap. "If I know my brother, he'll know exactly what to do with you."

"Why is that not a comfort?" He closed his eyes, sagging back against the beam. By now, his skin had gone clammy, and shudders ran through his body. Was he ill? Had she hit him harder than she thought?

"May I ask you a question?" she ventured.

"Turnabout's fair play," he answered without opening his eyes. "Go ahead."

"Who are you?"

"The name's David. Anything else?"

"What are you?"

This time a dry snort of laughter broke from his chapped lips, and she was once more subjected to a stare that could melt steel. "Didn't take long to get round to that. I assumed you'd know exactly what I was—hence the bash over the head and the silver chains." He shot a look at his ankles, which by now had swollen and turned an ugly shade of purple.

"What has silver to do with it? Or you?"

"You really don't know?" He laughed again, though it no longer held the angry edge of earlier. Instead it was almost with pride that he said, "Just my thrice-damned luck. Clubbed over the head and lashed to a post by a Fey-blood who's never heard of the Imnada."

"But shifters died out ages ago. How have you managed to hide from the world without anyone finding out?"

Interesting. Fey magic fairly shimmered off her, yet she gazed on him with wonder rather than revulsion. In fact, her power seemed to shine right through her skin and gilded her dark brown hair with strands of butter yellow, auburn, and burnished copper. David had always enjoyed beautiful women, and this one, while not his typical style—her chin was a little too narrow, her mouth a little too generous, and her eyes a muddy hazel without even the flecks of gold that typically signified one with the blood and magic of the Fey—still possessed a certain quality that held his eye and piqued his interest.

That or he was still reeling from the effects of a blow to the head.

Perhaps this was all part of an extremely elaborate dream in which he chatted with a lovely young woman about the Imnada clans while chained nude to a post. Not actually the strangest dream he'd ever had, but certainly the most vivid. Though he supposed if he were dreaming, her gaze would not be locked on his face as if her life depended on it, and her hands would not be white-knuckled in her lap. Instead, she'd be . . . He smiled. And her hands would be . . . His groin tightened.

"Why would you hide?" she asked earnestly, tearing through the shreds of his fantasy.

He sighed while envisioning glaciers, icebergs, his housekeeper's warty bulldog features, all in the hope of reducing his burgeoning erection. This situation was awkward enough without humiliating himself.

"Hiding is easy. The human race tends to ignore what they can't explain. The Imnada don't fit into their neat and tidy view of the world, so we don't exist."

She cocked her head and continued to eye him the way he imagined a botanist might look at a particularly odd new species of fungus. A change from the usual practiced flirtations and seductive half-smiles offered by the typical females of his acquaintance. He knew how to behave around those women. This one didn't play by the rules. Instead, she stared at him as if she wanted to understand him, not undress him. Not that she needed to. He was already as bare-assed as the day he was born. Still, she piqued his interest, awakened a long-dead curiosity. And, fuck it all, few things did that these days when life had narrowed to drunken carousing and unemotional coupling with women chosen for nothing more than their easy virtue.

"If we're going to continue this scintillating discussion, do you mind . . ." He motioned with a jerk of his chin and a lift of his brows.

Her eyes snapped back to his face after another surreptitious perusal of his nether regions, her face coloring to a blotchy red. "Oh, right. Of course." She leapt to her feet to rummage in a nearby trunk, pulling out a length of moth-eaten pink wool. "Will this do?"

"Not my color, but I'll endure." She hesitated for a moment before quickly draping the fabric over his midsection. Thank heavens his Arctic imaginings seemed to have succeeded, though he remained uncomfortable in the extreme. "Much better. Thank you."

She knelt once more, though he noticed she maintained a discreet arm's-length distance, as if afraid he might snatch her. If only he could, but the knots held and the silver sapped his strength with every painful breath.

"You said the world doesn't see what it can't explain, but the Other would believe. After all, we're as impossible and out of the realm of normality as you."

"You're why we hide—Fey-bloods."

"You mean the Other? Why would you want to hide from us?"

"You don't know the legends?"

"Of course, but that was all so long ago. Surely, the shifters no longer fear the Other. We're not killers."

"No? I'm a prisoner in the attic of a Fey-blood who bashed me over the head. Forgive me if I remain skeptical." He glanced briefly at his fetters. "Perhaps if you loosened the cords round my ankles and wrists, I'd look on you with more charity."

Alarm flickered across her face. "I can't. I'm not

even supposed to be up here. If my brother catches me, there'll be hell to pay. If Mr. Corey finds me . . ." She shuddered, throwing a glance at the door.

"Coward," he murmured.

"I'm not." Her eyes cut once more to the door. "It's complicated."

"Ahh, well, guess I'll catch some sleep while I can." He slumped back against the post, closing his eyes. Immediately, his thoughts turned to Kineally. Would his fugitive houseguest wonder what had happened when he didn't return home? Enough to contact Mac and set the wheels of rescue in motion? Recalling the spring-loaded tension of the man, David doubted it. He was on his own.

"Wait. You haven't told me how you've survived so long," she said. "For heaven's sake, I don't even know your last name or anything about you. That's not fair."

"Neither is trussing your knight in shining armor to a pole, but there you are."

"I didn't truss you. My brother did."

"But you can untruss me."

She looked torn. A hopeful sign. Escape might be only a little more charm and persuasion away. "I would, but—"

The approaching heavy tread of boots up the attic stairs interrupted her explanation. She threw herself to her feet, alarm replacing her earlier curiosity as she scanned the room for a place to hide.

The latch turned, and a chubby, rumpled fellow stood upon the threshold. "What are you doing up here?"

So much for charm and persuasion.

*   *   *

There were two of them: a tall shadowy figure by the door, and a second, shorter, plumper, shifty-eyed chap sitting in a chair drawn up close, though not too close, as if he feared David might escape and rip his throat out.

If only he could.

But after endless hours of the silver's poison seeping into his system, his head pounded, his muscles stiffened in painful spasms, and every breath felt as if his lungs were being chewed through slowly. Even if he did escape, he'd barely have the strength to drag himself across the floor, much less tear his captor's head off and shove it up his ass.

"Extraordinary," the man in the chair said for a third time, shaking his head. "Absolutely amazing." He eyed the silver laced cords with another shake of his head. "The silver's working just like they said it would, Mr. Corey. Can you believe it? Sickened by the mere touch of the metal. It's extraordinary."

The figure in the doorway stepped into the light of the lamp. Dressed in an immaculate tailcoat with a diamond winking in the folds of his starched cravat, the man looked as if he'd just left Almack's. Any matron's dream for her daughter, but for the emptiness of his eyes and the scar twisting one side of his mouth into a strange parody of a smile. "This is the monster terrorizing London, Hawthorne? One of these dangerous Imnada demons you told me about? He looks more like a little mouse to me." He reached out with a gold-knobbed cane to prod David's side. "A naked little mouse caught in my trap. What should we do with you, mouse?"

"Send me happily on my way?" David ventured.

The man's laughter was as empty and frightening as his eyes.

David had heard of Victor Corey, of course. One couldn't read a newspaper without some mention of the London street urchin who'd begun his career picking pockets and ended up with enough ill-gotten wealth to finance a small country. The man had a finger in every pie and owned half of Parliament; it was whispered that the Prince Regent himself owed Corey a tidy fortune.

"You said they were supposed to have died out over a thousand years ago, Hawthorne. Perhaps we should help this one back into extinction." The cane poked David's ribs again, this time leaving a bloody scrape.

"An admirable sentiment, Mr. Corey, certainly, but perhaps . . ." Hawthorne let his words trail off enticingly as he scratched at his chin. "We might turn this to our advantage. After all, it's not every day one's handed an opportunity like this." He turned his attention to David. "Where are the rest of your kind, shifter?" he said, enunciating every syllable at a roof-rattling volume. "Tell me and we will let you go."

"I'm neither deaf, foreign, nor stupid. If you want us, find us."

"Cheek for someone in your position," Corey said as he smashed his cane against David's ribs, eliciting a hissed indrawn breath. "Show a little respect."

"Respect's not my strong suit."

"What did you want with Callista? What did my sister tell you?" Hawthorne asked.

"Is that the pretty Fey-blood's name?" David asked.

Hawthorne stiffened. "What did you call my sister? How did you know about that?"

"About the power in her? She fairly glows with it." He lifted his eyes to the ceiling. "Callista. A beautiful name for a beautiful woman," he mused aloud.

"You'll keep your tongue between your teeth about my betrothed or I'll cut off your tail, little mouse." Corey's cane found David's shoulder, his thighs, aimed for his crotch, but David arched away before it did any permanent damage.

"Stop. Stop," Hawthorne whined. "Don't you see, Mr. Corey? This creature could make us our fortune."

"What do you want to do? Sell tickets? Look at him, Hawthorne. He's naught but a man. Who'll pay to see that? I say we take him apart in pieces."

"He may look human, but he's far more. He's Imnada. A shifter. You heard the men that brought him here. He can become a wolf with a snap of his fingers. People will definitely pay to see that. You give me twenty-four hours and a loan of a hundred pounds, and I'll double—mayhap even triple—your initial investment in a week."

"You'll not wriggle out of our deal so easily. Callista's still mine."

Hawthorne rose from his chair. "Of course—wouldn't hear of backing out of that part of the agreement; but there could be more. The scope staggers. Twenty-four hours for me to make some inquiries about our friend here. If I can't make the creature pay in spades, you can feed him to the fishes."

Corey grunted his reluctant assent, and with a final painful smash of the cane upon David's stomach, the two of them departed.

The scrape of the key in the lock grated against his nerves. The thump of their boots on the stairs echoed in the pounding of his heart. Alone, he fought like a wild man, writhing against his bonds. Back and forth he sawed until blood oozed hot over his fingers and his breath came broken and ragged, but the silver drained his strength even as it held him fast in his human form. He could not shift. He could not escape.

He was fucking trapped.

David St. Leger was still very, very angry. But he definitely wasn't bored.

3

"Come along to the dining room, Mr. and Mrs. Hopewell. Some tea will help you gather yourselves together." The grieving couple followed Branston out, she dabbing at her nose, he pale but collected.

Branston closed the door behind him, leaving Callista alone to recover from her journey into death. A few deep breaths to steady the fluttering of her heart. A shot of brandy to warm her chilled and stiffened limbs. A long, unblinking stare into the heart of a candle's bright flame to break her free of the horizonless shadowy landscape that was Annwn. These were the techniques Mother had shown her to ensure her spirit's full return.

A missed step, and who knew what part of her soul might remain lost within the maze of paths that led always downward into the realm of Lord Arawn, ruler of the underworld. Even Branston respected the ancient rituals enough to leave her in peace as she collected herself.

"Fools and their money, eh, Callie?"

Unfortunately Mr. Corey proved less considerate. He swaggered from behind the heavy velvet curtains drawn on rods all the way around the small room they set aside for appointments. The thick blue fabric muffled sound and light, making for better spectacle as well as simplifying her search for the border into death.

"Good trick. Giving them a song and dance about dear little Joe and his dear little pony. Almost made me want to blubber—or puke."

She swallowed the lump in her throat. This was the third time in a week she'd been asked to find a child. She hated these requests the most. Not only were children difficult to summon but they were notoriously hard to bind long enough for conversation. And they were such delicate fluttery bright little things. She always felt as if she'd captured a firefly in a jar, its tiny body flinging itself against the glass, desperate to escape. Little Joe Hopewell had been no exception, barely offering his bereft parents a spark of comfort before he slid from her grip, to be lost within the tangle of roads leading to deeper reaches where she dared not trespass.

But it had been enough. She'd seen that as soon as she passed back through the door and into her body to find Mrs. Hopewell snuffling into her handkerchief, Mr. Hopewell's eyes suspiciously bright.

"You shouldn't be here," she said, picking up the first and largest of the three bells to polish it. Key had an ebony handle engraved with the sword and cauldron of Arawn. Its deep, solemn tone paired with her tracing of the proper symbols freed her powers to unlock the door between the realms of the living and the dead. Allowed her to pass through into the vast frozen tangle of paths where cold sapped the strength from her body and deadened her aching limbs. Mother had warned her never to stop moving once she entered death and never to tarry lest the demons and dark spirits find her and take advantage of her weakened state.

Unfortunately, she'd never told Callista how to avoid the monsters within her own house.

Corey came up behind her and put his hands upon her shoulders, fingers digging into her skin. "I like to watch you do your hocus-pocus act." He leaned down to whisper in her ear, his breath hot against her cheek. "Better than a night at Vauxhall. You've the gift of the actress. A real showman, you are. Had them eating out of your hands."

"Well, the show's over."

Doing her best to ignore him, she placed the bell in its case and picked up Summoner, the next in size and the one whose higher strident ring called and bound the spirits to her so that she might speak with them. With the pad of her thumb, she caressed the four faces carved into the ash wood handle: the maiden, the warrior, the innocent, and the priest. Ran the cloth over the aged sheen of the silver before placing it, too, in the case.

Lastly, she wiped clean Blade, the smallest of the bells but the most deadly, and her only weapon against those creatures that made the underworld their home. Its hawthorn handle was always warm to the touch, its call sharp as a soldier's sword. If only its power to banish and disrupt worked on the living.

"You'll find my brother in his office counting his

coins," she said. "Why don't you go gloat over the misery of others with him and leave me alone?"

Corey spun her around to face him, leaning in close. She could smell a mix of cloves and brandy on his breath. "You think you're better than me, don't you? I have news for you, you're nothing but a sideshow freak. The same as that chap locked upstairs."

The man upstairs. David.

The name suited him. Strong yet with a touch of upper-class panache.

Unfortunately, knowing the prisoner's name only made her feel worse about knocking him over the head and dragging him into this mess. Not to mention that had she accepted his help as it was meant, she might have made her escape. She might even be aboard a northbound coach by now. Free and clear. On her way to Scotland and Aunt Deirdre.

Safe.

"All of our kind are afflicted with powers that make us strange and different. Make us more than human." Corey looked past her and muttered a few words of household magic, causing the candles upon a side table to burst into flame and the fire in the hearth to roar to life. "It's what we do with them that's the key."

"Just because you use your powers to swindle and scam doesn't mean I should do the same."

She winced as he turned the same intensity of expression on her that he'd used to kindle the candles. "Those powers were all that kept me from starving when my pa chucked me out. Six years old I was, and lucky he didn't have me tied in a sack and drowned in the river for being a monster. But I didn't starve, did I? I succeeded. Got rich. And made sure the old man knew it, right before I gutted him like a market hog."

She tried to edge away from him, but the table dug into her back, the chair cutting off her escape. "I didn't know."

His scarred face twisted in a cold look of fury. "Of course you didn't. You think I go about advertising what I am or where I come from? You think you're something special, but you're not. You're a dealer in dreams just like I'm a dealer in goods. We each use what we have the only way we can to get ahead and to hell with the stupid prats who don't have our advantages. They deserve to be swindled."

She dropped her gaze to her hands, the truth of his words more painful than the grip he had on her chin. "That can't be all there is. Or the only reason for our gifts. I won't believe it."

"So grand and selfless, but the world doesn't bow to the meek and the righteous. It's power and money that make men respect you." He smiled, licking his lips, undressing her with his eyes. "Another few weeks and you'll belong to me. Together we'll show the world what *monsters* can do. We'll show them *real* power."

"What do you mean?" Callista asked, though she knew already she'd not like the answer.

"Hasn't Branston broken the news? Your brother has accepted my very generous offer. You and I are to be married by special license in a few short days."

She wanted to be sick. "I'll never marry you. You may dress like a dandy and ape the manners of a gentleman, but you're nothing more than a common street thug."

Corey grabbed her, his fingers digging into her

upper arms until tears burned in her eyes. "I'll have you if I have to drag you bound to the altar and afterward I'll show you just how common I can be."

Before she could respond, he clamped his mouth on hers, shoving his tongue between her teeth while his free hand fondled her breasts. She struggled, but it only made him press his body closer to hers, his excitement shoved between her thighs. She couldn't breathe. His hand pinched at her nipple until tears stung her eyes. The case fell with a clang of spilled bells to the floor, their ring sizzling along her bones, the paths into death opening like a tumbled knot in her skull, her spirit lifting away from her.

He bit her lip, blood mingling with his spit, and she was yanked back into her body in time to slam her knee into his groin.

"Bitch!" he shouted, releasing her with a shove that sent her hurtling backward to trip and sprawl on the rug near the fallen bells.

She wiped her mouth on her sleeve, eyeing Corey with disgust and loathing.

He loomed over her, fury making him seem even larger, his scar white against the scarlet of his flushed complexion. "I'll show you what kind of proper gentleman I am and not take you on this floor here and now. You can play the simpering innocent, but not for long, my darling Miss Hawthorne. Not for long."

"You're a pig."

He smiled as he bent, placing a hand around her throat, his fingers gently squeezing. She tried to pull away, but his grip tightened. She couldn't swallow, couldn't breathe. Madness flickered in his gaze. "I'm going to enjoy our wedding night. Pain can be such an aphrodisiac, did you know?" She clutched at his hand, trying to loosen his hold before she passed out. "So, if you want to keep all that lovely pink flesh intact, you should be very careful how you speak to me from now on."

He released her, straightening to adjust his cuff, pluck a hair from his sleeve.

Callista scrambled to her feet, her chest heaving as she sucked in great lungfuls of air. If he had hoped for screams or sobs, he was disappointed. She glared at him, fury hazing her vision. "Why me? You could buy any woman in London for your bride."

His eyes slid casually over the bells scattered on the floor before returning to her face with a blaze of triumph. "Because I'm a businessman, Miss Hawthorne. And I know a bargain when I see one."

Before she could respond, voices sounded in the corridor: ". . . must have dropped it in the room . . . go and have a look . . ."

Mrs. Hopewell.

Callista didn't think twice. Leaving her bells behind, she ducked between the curtains where a hidden door led to the dining room. Fumbling with shaking hands for the handle, she yanked it open, tumbled inside, and threw the latch behind her. Fleeing up the stairs, she slammed her bedchamber door shut. Not that it would keep anyone out. Corey had been right on one point. She and David did have much in common.

They were both prisoners whose time was fast running out.

By the gods, he was dead.

Pocketing the key filched from Branston's office, Callista rushed to David's side. He remained as she'd left him twenty-four hours earlier, knees drawn up, eyes closed. But now all the color had drained from his skin and long purple streaks inched their way up from his bound ankles. Matching ugly patches of red stretched from the ropes at his wrists almost to his shoulders. Unthinking and in a panic, she knelt, placing her cheek upon his bare chest, praying for a heartbeat.

"You smell like cabbage."

The deep voice rumbled against her ear, throwing her back onto her haunches. "You're alive."

A corner of his mouth curled up in a tired smile. "Really? What gave me away?"

"I didn't sense death like I usually do right here"— she tapped her breastbone, then added with a frown as she realized he was joking, not actually asking for an explanation, "Do I really smell like cabbage?"

"Good, comfortable smell. Reminds me of the army."

She gave herself a surreptitious sniff. "I've been in the kitchen assisting Mrs. Thursby. She needed someone to keep her gin glass filled."

"Knew a soldier in the Forty-third. Killed a man over a plate of boiled cabbage. Shot him right between the eyes."

"That's horrible."

He chuckled, his smile widening to a boyish grin. "You didn't taste the cabbage."

Feeling herself blushing, Callista hid her discomfiture in a quick scan of the room. A nearby trunk looked her best bet. Dragging it over, she rummaged through old magazines, a moth-eaten fox muff, and a set of mildewed cravats. "I suppose I should be relieved. If you're well enough to tease, you're probably not in imminent danger of expiring."

He gave a gruff bark of laughter. "You're not like most women, are you?"

She paused, every sense on alert. "What makes you say that?"

"Most women, upon being told they smell like boiled cabbage, would fly into the boughs over the insult." Even now, a spark of impish mischief lurked in his bleary, bloodshot eyes. Did he never take life seriously? She thought of her own predicament. Did he never despair?

She shrugged and continued to search through the trunk. "You'll have to do better if you're going for outrage. I've grown a thick skin over the years."

"Actually, I was going for compliment. Illness has affected my aim."

"But obviously not your tongue."

"Minx," he muttered.

She withdrew an old velvet frock coat and draped it over his midsection. He didn't seem to be cold, but he was definitely, awkwardly, very . . . very . . . male.

"Glad to see you safe, Fey-blood," he said, licking some moisture back into his chapped lips. "Worried you caught trouble sneaking up here last night."

"You're a prisoner, tied up and half-dead, and you're worrying about me? That's rich."

"What, this?" He shifted, wincing as he did so, a quick indrawn breath between gritted teeth. "Minor setback. Hardly worth mentioning."

She eyed him speculatively. The bone-white pallor of his body worried her. His gaunt, sickly features scared her to death: eyes sunk within deep hollows, lips tinged blue. Had she waited too long? She'd batted her idea back and forth all day and seen no other alternative. But now the reality of the plan seemed ludicrous. Even if she didn't sense the presence of imminent death, he was clearly unwell. But was that her only reason for second-guessing herself? Or did it have more to do with his quicksilver charm and his stomach-fluttering stare?

She'd no experience with men of his quality. She felt like a child as she struggled to counter his witty banter and a fool as she melted at his enticing smile. But better a live fool than a dead bride. If anyone could help her escape Branston and Corey, this man could. He was her best—and maybe her last—hope.

"I have a proposal for you."

"Really?" The smile vanished. She caught a glimpse of the dangerous beast she'd watched savage Corey's hired killers and was oddly reassured. "Go on."

"If I help you escape, you agree to take me with you."

His brows inched skyward. "You're more brazen than you look."

This time she refused the blush stealing up her neck. Yes, she was proposing a very unorthodox idea to a nude man, who even sick as death looked like your average Greek god, but it was that or marriage to Corey. Embarrassment was nothing compared to what awaited her at his hands.

"I need an escort to my aunt in Scotland. You need the knife I have secreted in my pocket. I think we can help each other."

"What about your brother?"

"He doesn't want . . . that is . . ."

"Scotland is your idea. Not his."

"I'm of age. He has no legal right to keep me here."

"Why doesn't your aunt come and collect you?"

"The particulars of my dilemma aren't your concern."

"It's my concern if I'm carting you all over the countryside with an irate brother after me."

"Your choice is simple, Mr.—"

"David."

"It's simple . . . David; escape with me or rot here alone."

"You drive a hard bargain, Callista."

She straightened, chin up. "Miss Hawthorne to you."

Amusement flickered in his eyes. "When?"

"Now. My satchel is packed, my brother won't be back for hours. Mrs. Thursby is downstairs sleeping off her gin. Hold still." Sliding the knife between the rope and his ankles, she began sawing until the cords gave way in a ravel of frayed ends. She pulled it free while unwinding the thin silver chain, revealing ugly black welts where the silver had rubbed his skin raw.

"Is the housekeeper our only watchdog?" he asked.

She moved behind him to cut the ropes at his wrists. "I heard Mr. Corey telling my brother he'd left two men to guard the house. They don't trust that I won't attempt to escape again."

"Again?" Freed of the ropes and the silver chains threaded through them, he slowly rolled his shoulders, rubbed at the deep black welts encircling his wrists.

"Three attempts. Three failures."

"Four times the charm?"

"Let's hope so. Are you sure you're fit to travel? You don't look well."

"The silver weakens me. I'll recover—sooner or later."

"Hopefully sooner rather than later. We don't have all night."

"Haven't left the attic, and you're already nagging me? Here we go."

With a deep gulping inhale and a few expletives, he shoved himself to his feet, dragging the blanket with him. Callista stood poised, waiting for him to topple over or faint dead away.

"Mother of All, even my hair fucking hurts," he grumbled while casting her a swift measured glance as if gauging her reaction. When she said nothing, he gave a good-natured snort and a shrug. "You really aren't like any woman I've ever met."

"Another compliment?"

"Most definitely." He tugged at the coat wrapped around his hips. "Did you bring me clothes?"

"I thought you'd . . . that is, that you might just . . ."

"You thought I'd shift?" He grinned. "I like how your mind works, sweet Callista."

She opened her mouth to protest. Snapped it shut with an audible click.

He agreed to her scheme. He was helping her escape. He could call her anything he bally well wanted.

The shirtsleeves stretched only as far as David's fore-arms and the boots pinched his feet, but the breeches fit, and the three-caped greatcoat Miss Hawthorne had purloined from her brother's closet was voluminous enough to hide any style faux pas as well as the death-on-a-stick pallor he was currently sporting. "What do you think?"

Callista threw a darting glance over her shoulder before turning around, though personally he thought it was a bit late for modesty on her part. There wasn't an inch of his body she hadn't already seen. "Oh dear." A tiny smile curved the very edges of her mouth, her eyes crinkling with unvoiced laughter.

He ran a preening hand down his shirtfront. "That bad?"

"Absolutely horrid." She sobered. "Are you certain you can't just . . . you know . . . change? It might make our escape easier."

"The word is *shift*, and no, I can't." He inhaled his first comfortable breath since she'd cut his bonds. Not a deep breath yet—his lungs still ached too much for that—but since breathing at all was a minor miracle, he'd not complain. "Three days of silver poisoning my body, you're lucky I'm upright." When her brows began to draw together in a frown, he grinned. "No worries, Fey-blood. I'm not completely without resources."

Clearly unamused, Callista pursed her lips and gripped the handle of her satchel as if she might swing it at his head.

This only caused him to grin wider. He'd always been perverse that way.

"Can we leave now?" For the first time, David sensed the rising panic in her voice. It was obvious that the potential dangers Callista Hawthorne faced by escaping with him paled in comparison to the definite dangers she faced if she remained here.

"We made a bargain," he said, placing his hands on her shoulders, forcing her to look up at him. "Trust me."

Drawn to her eyes, he found himself focused on the strange shimmering intensity he saw there, an almost hypnotic sweep of storm clouds flickering across her gaze. The longer he looked, the more dizziness set the room around him swaying. But instead of narrowing, his vision expanded until it felt as if he might walk directly into her mind. Images flashed in front of him: a woman kneeling, her hair falling to shield her face, a man's broad form rising behind her, a dagger clenched in his bloody fist.

David dragged a horrified breath from his lungs, bowels cramping in terror.

"Trust you? I've heard that line before," Callista said quietly. "Forgive me if I remain skeptical."

She blinked, long black lashes sweeping down over the rose of her skin, and his odd light-headedness receded. Even so, he kept his hands upon her shoulders a moment longer, just to reassure himself he wouldn't fall over when he let go and undermine all his encouraging words.

They had been this close only once before, during the time she took to cut his bonds. Or should he say, Callista had only allowed herself to get this close to him that one instance. Since then, she'd maintained a civil but definite distance. But now, he felt the warmth—and the tension—of her body where his fingers rested. He noted the soft roundness of her cheeks and the fullness of her coral lips, but there were also deep smudges beneath her eyes and a tightness to her mouth. Whatever experiences pushed her to seek his help also hardened her expression to wary suspicion and made her seem older than her years. But for that one small half-smile, quickly snuffed, he'd have said she was incapable of anything less than a scowl.

He took her skepticism as a personal challenge. The doubt he saw in her face made him want to prove himself. But it was the dimple at the edge of her lips and the clean linen scent of her hair that drove him to kiss her.

That or he was a whole lot woozier than he thought.

As kisses go, it was less than spectacular. In fact, it was a bloody great failure. Instead of melting against him, eyes fluttering closed in sweet surrender, she went rigid as a tent pole, shock in her gaze, lips pressed tight. The farce ended when she jammed her bag up between them, catching him a blow to the ribs with one brass-reinforced corner.

He stumbled backward with a gasp and a curse. Nearly tripped over a hassock and fell arse over end. Not the reaction his advances usually caused.

"That is not part of our bargain," she said, fairly quivering with rage.

"So I surmised," he wheezed as he rubbed his chest. So much for breathing easily. "What do you carry in that damned bag? A pair of anvils?"

She merely tightened her arms around the valise. "If you're ready, we should go. I want to be far away from here before Branston comes home."

"Fine, but this long trip to Scotland just became a hell of a lot longer."

She eyed him with another of those world-weary stares that, for some reason, made his chest bunch with a strange, unexpected ache.

"Agreed," was all she said before she turned away.

As they crept downstairs, David used his study of the floor plan to keep his mind from the throbbing in his head, the churning of his stomach, and the bone-deep ache of his body. His former army scout's eye absorbed details such as number of rooms, position of stairways, and points of entry and egress. And, along with the strategic intelligence he gathered, he couldn't help but notice how the spartan shabbiness of the upstairs chambers gave way to an over-the-top vulgar elegance as they descended to the first floor's public rooms.

Every window and doorway was draped in heavy dark velvet and gold cord. Ornate chairs upholstered in damask and silk sat beside gilded and veneered tables more appropriate to a ducal household than a down-at-heels town house in Soho. The walls were plastered floor to ceiling with paintings in every period and artistic style as if someone had purchased them en masse from a Petticoat Lane market stall. And hanging above it all like a sickly-sweet fog was the cloying odor of dying flowers.

"What the bloody hell kind of business are you in?" he whispered, trying to breathe without gagging.

She shot him a sidelong glance even as she surprised him by taking his hand in a firm clasp and tugging him toward the door. "We need to hurry. I don't know how long Mrs. Thursby will stay asleep."

The entry hall lay wrapped in flickering shadows from a lamp set upon a side table. A clock ticked the turn of the hour. No sign of an irate housekeeper or either of the guards supposedly stationed on the premises, though loud snoring issued from the front parlor. He raised his brows, signaling his question. She shrugged in response, then pointed once at the front door and once behind her at the passage to the kitchens.

He eased back the bolt and turned the latch, cracking the door an inch while he scanned the street, stretching with every Imnada and human sense for the telltale footstep, the betraying scents of sweat and gin and human flesh, even a revealing stir of the air or unexplained shadow.

Nothing.

Shoving the door wide, he stepped out on the stoop. Lifted his head, eyes swiftly adjusting to the darkness. Body drawn taut against any hint of danger.

Not a whiff of minion anywhere. The way seemed suspiciously clear.

Where were Corey's men hiding? And why? He'd have felt better had they leapt from the bushes, guns blazing. This eerie calm rippled fear over his skin and tensed already painful muscles.

He jerked his head toward the street. "There's a hackney stand at the end of the block. If anything happens, don't stop and don't look back. Tell the driver to take you to Cumberland Place. I'll find you."

She gave a last frightened shift of her eyes before nodding. For some reason he reached for her hand again, but she avoided him by drawing her hood over her hair and adjusting her grip upon her satchel. He dropped his arm to his side, unsure why her continued rejection disappointed him but dismissing the brush of emotion with practiced ease.

Before he could whisper the order to go, she scurried out into the street and he'd no recourse but to follow.

One street down.

Five hundred miles to go.

4

Stunned at the ease with which they'd made their escape, Callista sat ramrod straight on the seat of the hackney carriage, her bag perched on her lap, her gaze traveling between the window and the man sprawled in the seat across from her.

No. She needed to stop thinking of him as *the man*. He had a name—David.

David . . . ?

Heat crept into her cheeks. Heavens. She didn't even know his last name . . . or really anything about him at all. She was placing her trust in a man she'd known for a few short days.

A man who, according to every book on the subject, wasn't supposed to exist. The heat sank into her stomach, quivered between her legs. A man she'd kissed.

All right, if she were to be strictly accurate, he had kissed her and she had startled like a scared deer—or a silly little girl—and nearly ended her escape before it had begun by knocking him unconscious.

But he'd caught her off-guard. Never in a million years would she have imagined he'd lean down, his breath warm against her cheek, and press his lips to hers. She'd been stunned. Not just that he'd taken such a liberty—after four years living within the rough-and-tumble world of traveling players, churlish drovers, and itinerant chapmen, and the last six months avoiding the odious Mr. Corey and his gang of hired thugs, she knew more than she cared to about men's base urges. No, it wasn't his kiss that had surprised her. It was the fact that for a split second she'd almost enjoyed it. Her knees had nearly gone weak, her stomach had just about flipped, and her chest had more or less fluttered like she'd bats beneath her ribs.

Either she'd almost enjoyed it, or she was coming down with the flu.

"I don't know your full name," she blurted, trying to fill the silence with something beyond her turbulent thoughts.

"No," he replied, "you don't."

She waited a moment. "Is it a secret? Are you a wanted fugitive?"

His lips twitched. "I am now." He leaned his head back against the seat and closed his eyes. "No secret. I just enjoy hearing you call me David. You say it with a bit of a shameful breathlessness."

"I do no such thing."

He smirked, and she made herself look out the window lest she clobber him with her bag—again.

Still, it wasn't long before she found herself casting swift glances his direction through downcast lashes. There was just something about him that drew her eye. Something beyond the golden Adonis looks, though these were sadly dimmed after days locked in the attic. His face flashed in and out of shadow as the hackney passed the occasional streetlamp or lit doorway, but the grim angles and deep gorges of illness were abundantly obvious, as was the greenish-gray cast to his damp skin. Each breath was an ominous wheezing rattle, punctuated now and again by a hacking cough. In fact, one could definitely say the man looked and sounded sick as a dog.

Seeking reassurance, she opened herself to the power within her, but there was no twinge along her bones to indicate death loomed near. The man might resemble a walking corpse, but he was very much—and very disturbingly—alive.

She stifled an almost-hysterical bubble of laughter. Now, not only had she called him *the man*, but she'd likened him to a dog. A more than apt simile as it turned out.

She continued to sneak glances at him in between adjusting her cloak or shifting on her seat. Strange, how human he looked. In fact, as humans went, he was a breathtaking, heart-stopping specimen of one. Or would be once he recovered. No doubt women fawned for a single glance from those steel-gray eyes and simpered for the mere touch of his lips upon the backs of their lily-white hands. If they only knew that their knight in armor was a wolf in disguise.

Which went against every nursery tale known. The wolf in those stories was the villain. Not the hero.

Which would David turn out to be?

"Have I a boil on my neck or a carrot sprouting from my ear?"

Her fingers tightened on her bag, but she refused to be intimidated. "You don't look well."

"I once had three bullets pulled from my body with a rusty fork." He sucked in a breath through clenched teeth as the hackney swung round a corner, throwing him against the side of the carriage. "That, Miss Hawthorne, was a walk among the daisies compared to this. Are you afraid I'll die and not keep our agreement?" The corner of his mouth curled in a mocking smile.

She wasn't used to humor from men, either. It unnerved her almost as much as his unearthly good looks, and that shocking kiss, and . . . well, everything about him unnerved her.

"It had crossed my mind," she answered sharply.

He chuckled—actually chuckled. But while Mr. Corey's chuckle sent ice water rushing through her veins, David's low, quiet laughter buzzed her insides and made her pulse race.

Score a point for the truthful woman.

By the gods! Those words had not come from his mouth. She'd been staring at those full, perfectly formed lips curled in a sly smile like an addle-pated debutante, and they had definitely not moved. No, those words—by gads, even his amused and cynical tone of voice—had appeared in her mind.

"You're a telepath?" The realization chilled her to her core, making her jerk halfway from her seat, the bag tipping from her lap.

Between one breath and the next, David reached out, grabbing the handle before the bag struck the floor, the discordant clang of a bell rattling her already rattled nerves.

"What the hell is in here?" he asked. "The family silver?"

She grabbed the satchel, resettling it on her legs, wrapping it even more tightly to her chest. "I asked my question first."

He shrugged, the effort drawing a fleeting grimace. "Fair enough. I'm a path. Not a reader, Fey-blood. Your thoughts are yours to keep. Couldn't read you even if I wanted to. It's your turn. What's in the bag?"

She felt her chin rise in automatic defiance. "I didn't take anything that wasn't mine, and my reasons for leaving my brother's house are too numerous to mention."

"I'm a good listener."

She shot another nervous glance out the window. So far, there had been no sign of Corey's henchmen in hot pursuit, but she'd be a fool to think he'd give up without a fight. He'd not risk such a loss of face as to have his intended bride slip her leash. She tried not to recall the feel of his hand closing around her neck as he issued his vicious threats. To do so would shatter her fragile nerves. She needed to remain calm and in control if she wanted to win her way to freedom. She forced herself to take a slow relaxing breath. "The man you saw with my brother—they call him the king of the stews."

"I know Victor Corey. Aside from his criminal empire, the villain holds markers from half the *ton*. He's got ministers, MPs, and more than a few peers in his pocket. Your brother plays with dangerous friends."

"He's not a friend. Branston borrowed heavily when we first came to London. Far more than we could ever pay back, even should we have made a success of the business."

SHADOW'S CURSE

"So Corey decided to accept your maidenhead as compensation. Crude but not surprising, given the man's past. That still doesn't answer the question. What's in the bag? And what business are you in?"

She fiddled with the leather strap, shifted upon her seat. "These are my bells. I use them in my work."

"Which is . . . ?" He motioned with his hand.

"People come to me after a death."

"You're a gravedigger?"

"They come for solace, not for spades."

He lifted a brow. "Now I am intrigued."

She pinched her lips together in a frown. What was it about their every conversation that left her flushed and flustered? Annoyed with herself, she blurted, "Pull your mind from the gutter. I'm a traveler into death. A summoner of souls. A necromancer."

There was no time to pursue what had suddenly become a very interesting conversation. The slam of a pathed sending ripped across David's mind—a scream of terror, a plea for help.

Shit. When it rained, it bloody well poured.

He rapped on the roof, signaling the driver to pull over. "Stay here, Miss Hawthorne. Sit tight. Say nothing."

"Where are you going?" she asked.

But he'd already swung from the hackney, only a slight hitch in his stride as he hurried toward Cumberland Place, senses on alert for any possible trouble.

Carriages jammed the street and men and women crowded the flagways; laughter and conversation floated on a damp spring breeze. Lamps blazed from

the windows and above the door of No. 3, while liv-
eried footmen stood at attention on either side of
the marbled steps leading to the fan-lit entryway. Of
course. The Fowlers' ball was tonight. He'd been sent
an invitation. In fact, Lady Fowler had brought it to
him herself, stayed far longer than was necessary, and
returned home much happier than when she'd arrived.

A smug smile curled his lip. The woman was
wasted on that dottering old baronet she'd married.

"What's going on?"

David whipped around to find Callista standing
behind him. "I told you to stay with the carriage," he
growled.

"You didn't think I'd let you sneak off that easily,
did you?"

"I'm not sneaking."

"You certainly look as though you're sneaking."

He closed his eyes on a deep calming breath before
he answered. "I'm reconnoitering. You really don't
trust me, do you?"

"No," came her curt response, but there it was
again. A tiny curve of her lips, a brightness to her eyes.
She needed to do it more often. It smoothed years
from her face. Unfortunately, the current situation
didn't exactly seem well suited to smiles and laughter.

He shook off the distracting thought and bent all
his attention back to the problem at hand. The sending had stopped abruptly, the mental shout of surprise
and then alarm had fallen silent. "Something's not
right."

She peered over his shoulder at the aristocratic
throng clogging the pathways and making their way
up the wide steps. Tilted her head, a look of intense

concentration on her face, eyes locked on an invisible distance.

"My house is just there." He motioned to the far end of the crescent. "It seems quiet, but—"

Callista's body jerked as if she'd been struck, her eyes wide and midnight black in a face drained of color. "The door into death is open," she said in a shaky voice.

"What the hell does that mean?"

She flashed him a determined glance. "It means someone's died. Violently, by the feel of it. " She grabbed his hand and tugged him back toward the hackney.

Questions fired like gunshots through his frazzled brain and his body ached with every second he couldn't lie down and collapse in a heap. He dug in his heels. "Wait. If we're going to make it farther than Islington, I need money and clothes."

David swung around, the blood draining from his head into his ankles in one vicious rush. On the front steps of his house stood his worst nightmare in the flesh. Cold, empty eyes, a lipless slash of a mouth curled at the edges into a permanent snarl, and a whippet-thin body that nonetheless bore the strength of the strongest of beasts—Eudo Beskin. *I know you're out there, St. Leger. The traitor Kineally's dead.*

The enforcer's sending threw David back in time to the moment two years ago when the Ossine had come for him. He had explained. Then he'd pleaded, and finally he'd fought. But there had been no escape. His stomach clenched as memories of pain churned his insides and sizzled like fire along his limbs.

He sent up a prayer for Caleb Kineally. There

would be no funeral pyre. No rites or rituals to help his soul pass through the Gateway to the land of their ancestors. As punishment for his crimes, he would be buried in the ground, staked with silver through the heart to hold his spirit fast to the earth for all eternity.

Should have known you were involved with these rebels, Beskin continued. *Should have killed you when I had the chance.*

David took Callista's arm. "We need to get out of here now!"

She took a few scrambling paces after him until she dragged to a halt. "Stop! Those men that just rounded the corner. I recognize the tall one. He's Mr. Corey's lieutenant. They must have followed us."

Two men strolled up the flagway as if out for an evening walk. Nothing in their outward appearance spoke of murderous intent, but David knew dangerous men when he saw them—the way they carried themselves, the expressions in their eyes. Neither had come here tonight looking to dance.

"Come," David said in a hushed voice. "I have an idea." Outflanked, he made the only move he could in this deranged chess match. He dragged Callista Hawthorne through the jewel-encrusted perimeter of the Fowlers' guests.

"Hey, now!"

"The nerve of some people."

"He's ripped my train with his big feet."

"Oof! How dare you, sir!"

David and Callista elbowed their way to the top of the steps, where Lady Fowler welcomed her guests. Her eyes lit with delight when she saw David coming toward her, and she spread her arms as if she meant to crush him to her ample bosom. "Mr. St. Leger! What a lovely surprise."

Damning the woman's big mouth and parade-ground bellow, David cringed as all eyes swiveled in his direction. Revealing no hint of the growing anxiety tightening viselike in his gut, he bent over Lady Fowler's outstretched hand, hoping his knees didn't give out and send him straight into her lap. "You're a vision as always, Lady Fowler. The belle of the ball."

She gave a coquettish laugh and smacked him playfully with her fan. "You're such a tease, sir. I'm merely the evil stepmother tonight." She leaned close, her lips brushing his ear. "God, but I'm wet for you, my darling man."

David snapped to attention, yanking Callista up the final step to stand beside him. "I hope you don't mind that I brought my . . . second cousin with me. She's from . . . uh . . . Dorset. Turned up out of the blue today. Couldn't leave her at home all alone. You understand. Family duty and all that."

A frown creased Mrs. Fowler's penciled brows and pouted her full red lips while she eyed Callista as one might a stray puppy. "I certainly understand the odious pressure of family responsibility." Her narrowed gaze moved from Miss Hawthorne's thick woolen travel cloak and leather satchel to David's odd, haphazard attire.

He grinned. "I apologize, my lady. I came straight from 'dress like your favorite dustman' night at my club. Silly, but then, you know what revels go on at these places. Bad as the old school days."

"Yes, of course," she answered smoothly, her wary expression growing more than appreciative as her

gaze leveled off somewhere south of his waist. "If only
our local dustman had your masculine attributes, sir,"
she purred.

Out of the corner of his eye, David saw Corey's men
approach, though the press of Mayfair's finest held
them back from making a full frontal assault. Beskin,
on the other hand, crossed the street like a hound on
the scent, his sneer positively fiendish. David doubted
a minor obstacle like a mob of mere humans would
stymie him for long.

"Yes, well, I'd love to chat, but is your daughter
within?" He edged Callista and himself around Lady
Fowler and ever closer to the door. "Such a sweet girl.
Full of . . . verve."

"Really? I don't remember your ever noticing Har-
riet. She's just inside by the—"

"No worries. I'll find her myself." David made a
final storming of the breach, dashing past the proud
mother and into the entry hall.

"What are you doing?" Callista hissed.

"Saving our asses," David answered. "No one will
risk barging into the Fowlers' drawing room after us."

"We barged in."

"But we—or at least I—was invited. That's different."

"Fine. So, we're in. How do you propose we get
out?"

"Just stay close, follow my lead, and try not to draw
attention to yourself."

Callista pinched her lips together. "A bit late for
that advice, wouldn't you say—Mr. St. Leger?"

He acknowledged the hit with a smile and took
her hand. Together they shoved through a gaggle of

girls in virginal white hovering by the stairs, a cluster of rowdy young men by the punch table, and a row of stern matrons overseeing the couples on the dance floor like high court judges. Most were too caught up in their own amusements to notice an oddly dressed couple scurrying through the crush. And the few who recognized David and raised a voice in friendly greeting were left behind with a tossed grin and a wink. Luckily, Callista didn't seem to notice the appreciative nods or knowing nudges.

"We're almost there," David encouraged. "Freedom is through those terrace doors and across the garden to the mews beyond."

"Then what?"

"Damned if I know."

"Oh, Mr. St. Leger!" toodled Lady Fowler above the din. "We need to speak."

That was one raised voice that would not be so easily fobbed off.

"Bugger all. Quick. In here." David dragged Callista through the closest curtained archway into a tiny alcove full to the brim with wraps, coats, hats, umbrellas, and cloaks. Trapped. No other way out. They were pressed together on the six inches of floor space not taken up with cast-off outerwear, Callista's body snug against his.

"Is this supposed to be better?" she asked, her breath whispering against his throat.

"Much," he answered as her warmth, combined with the tingle of Fey-blood magic, shivered over his skin.

"Mr. St. Leger? I have some lovely etchings I want to show you," Lady Fowler's voice sounded from just outside their refuge, a slight predatory edge coloring her tone. "I think you'll find them exquisite."

"Etchings?" Miss Hawthorne scoffed. "Really?"

A ringed hand gripped the curtain to draw it aside.

Frantic, out of ideas, and because, damn it, this whole horrible mess could be laid squarely at Callista Hawthorne's door, David kissed her—again.

No sooner had David's lips touched hers than Callista's spine stiffened with instinctual fear and her stomach clenched in knots. No, not David. His name was Mr. St. Leger. A very proper and formal address to stop the wild quivering up her spine.

Follow my lead.

The words flickered to life in her mind, but so, too, did the deep velvet of his voice, roguish amusement coloring even his mental touch.

He slid an arm around her resisting body, crushing her against him just as Lady Fowler dragged the curtain back. Light blazed into every corner of the dim cloakroom, and Callista quickly shut her eyes, trying to look like a woman enjoying the attentions of a man.

Trouble was, she didn't know what that looked like. She placed a tentative hand upon his waist, but that seemed so intimate somehow. So possessive. Not that lips were less intimate, but somehow offering him encouragement made it real and not the act it was.

"Oh!" Lady Fowler exclaimed waspishly. "Second cousin indeed."

This was where St. Leger would break away to offer his apologies or make some flippant joke to turn the woman's wrath aside. Callista would be left to gather her damaged pride and her shattered nerves.

Instead, his hold on her tightened, his free hand cupping her cheek to tip her face up to his, the kiss spinning deeper.

Relax, Fey-blood.

Relax? She was trapped against his chest, the heat off his body singeing her insides as his lips moved warm and soft against hers. Yet her shoulders did seem to be inching down from around her ears with every second they remained locked together, and that strange influenza-like fluttering had begun again in her stomach. She didn't seem able to help herself. It was as if her body had mutinied. It knew what it wanted, and what it wanted was more of this delicious heat worming its way through her until even her toes curled with delight.

She found herself answering the slow movement of his mouth, and her hand moved from his waist up his ribs to his shoulder and then to the stubbled strength of his jaw. She'd never felt a man's face before. It was so different from a woman's. All hard bony angles and jumping tension.

Through the roaring in her ears, she heard Lady Fowler's snappish voice turn suddenly muted. In the dim recesses of her captive brain, she knew the curtain had dropped back in place, and the two of them were once more alone, the immediate danger passed. But the kiss didn't stop. David cupped her face gently in both his hands as she melted into him, her knees now dangerously weak, her heart drumming. His tongue slid along the seam of her lips, and she felt herself unconsciously opening to him; letting his tongue dip within, slide against hers in a teasing, tasting dance she found herself answering. Her breasts tightened as the fluttering in her stomach sank between her legs, and she tilted her head back as his kiss deepened and grew more powerful, almost hungry. The hand that had caressed her cheek dropped to trace the length of her throat, glide along the collar of her gown, brush her painfully sensitive nipples through the serviceable fabric.

This was nothing like the rushed groping of the fair men she'd spent years dodging. Nor was it the crude ugly fury of Corey. This was a shimmering tingling buzz of anticipation. This was light and fire and joy and laughter. As natural as breathing.

"Beautiful Callista. *Theosai nostimmeth*," he murmured as his kissed moved to her cheeks, her eyelids, behind her ears.

"David . . ." Her voice barely more than a gasped breath.

Her grip on the bag unclenched. It slithered off her shoulder toward the floor, and before her mind even registered what her body was doing, her eyes flew open and she jerked loose of his embrace. The bag hit the floor with a startling clanking thud.

And the moment ended.

"I'm sorry. I don't . . . that is . . . I never . . ." She inhaled a shuddery breath, confusion stammering her words.

David knew exactly how she felt because he felt the same. Off-balance. Bewildered. His mind topsy-turvy. He chalked up his reaction to the continued debilitating effect of the silver. Heart palpitations, shaky-kneed weakness. That had to be the reason. He'd kissed hundreds of women and never experienced these odd, yet not completely unpleasant, sensations before.

He opened his mouth to confess his confusion when she glanced up at him through the frame of her lashes. Her great dark eyes swam black as sin, an infinite emptiness without light or warmth. He tried to look away, but her gaze trapped and held him fast, visions flashing across his mind. He smelled the tang of pine, the crisp clean of new snow, and the sharp odor of rabbit as he hunted in the form of his aspect, his pack lifting their voices in unison with him as they ran the deep mountain trails. He tasted blood on his muzzle and the crunch of bones between his teeth, and later took his pleasure with a lithe young female, both as wolf and then again as man, beneath the bright round moon of Silmith. He felt silver burning like acid against his bare skin and the Ossine's flames searing his clan mark from his back with the stink of charred flesh. He heard himself screaming as if he were being cleaved in two before his agonized shouts died away to slow gulping moans, whispered pleas for mercy, and finally begging for death.

Darkness and a frozen, knifing cold pierced every part of David as he was buried beneath an avalanche of happiness and heartbreak. On and on it went, tumbling him breathless, lifting him high only to crush him with a mountain's weight of raw emotion. He felt the earth-shattering passion of a marriage bed, moonlight gleaming in a pair of dark eyes as his bride took him inside her and he marked her forever as his chosen mate. He tasted the salt of her skin and the wine upon her tongue and the sweet lush heat of her woman's place as she gasped her release. He smelled the powdery fresh scent of a child's hair and the starch of clean linen as he held the precious bundle in his arms. He heard the cries of a new mother and the squall of an angry infant and the soft voice of a young girl calling for her father to read her a bedtime story and chase away the bogeymen.

A tremor racked his body, and he gritted his teeth until the battering storm of sensation passed. Not memories this time; not shades pulled from his past. He would call them dreams, but somehow he knew better. They held too much power, buried themselves too deep into his brain. This was Fey-blood magic at its most potent and most prophetic. But did Callista realize what she'd done? What he'd seen?

He squeezed his eyes shut, but not before a final horrible image passed like a shadow over his heart. "David?" A hand touched him, heat where there had been only cold. It filled the emptiness, tore through the dark like a blade through a curtain.

He opened his eyes to see Callista watching him carefully, worry in her gaze, but nothing else. Her pulse beat wildly in her throat and her cheeks were flushed pink.

"Did I do it right?" she asked. "Do you think we convinced her?" Her head tilted like a bird's as she awaited his answer. Nothing but innocence in her expression. She was either unaware of what he'd seen or a damned good actress.

He shoved the darkness away and forced a weak smile. "Covent Garden cyprians couldn't have been more convincing."

A line appeared between her brows. "Is that supposed to make me proud?"

"Only if you appreciate what skilled professionals they are."

She gave a tiny shake of her head, almost but not quite reaching for him. He wouldn't have even noticed the slight movement except they were still crushed against each other amid the mountain of discarded coats. She offered him a quick smile, here and gone between one breath and the next. "I'll assume you know all too well, so I shall take it as another compliment."

She looked as if she wanted to continue the conversation, but he forestalled her by taking her arm and leading her back into the crowded corridor. The last thing he wanted to do while he remained off-kilter and dazed was to talk. Who knew what foolishness he might utter?

By now the guests had thickened to an outright crush. None would notice two more amid the cacophonic mob of rich and titled packed into every square inch of breathing room. Holding his head above the swarm and gripping Callista's hand in his, David bulled his way through to the French doors fronting the gardens, an instance where his sheer mass was an advantage.

The terrace was nearly deserted. Fairy lanterns strung between the trees glimmered down on only a few strolling couples. The press of humanity had not yet reached this far.

"We're almost there. The mews is through that gate. We can be away before our pursuers realize what's happened."

They crossed the lawn to the back wall in silence. David shoved hard on the gate, hinges giving way with a spine-sizzling rusty screech. Then they were through, lights and laughter left behind as they made their way through the heavy gloom of the narrow mews.

"You call yourself a soldier, St. Leger? My granny could foil a scent better than you." Eudo Beskin's voice oozed like slime as he stepped out from the shadow of the stables.

Once the Ossine discovered that David was living under the shadow of a Fey-blood's curse, his sentence of exile had been returned quick as a headsman's ax. If only the punishment had been so clean and swift. Instead, it had been a drawn-out torture by inches meted out by the enforcer now standing a few feet away, eyes glowing in his pale face. David had spent the past two years dreaming of the day he would exact ruthless vengeance on the man who'd stripped him of his clan mark and then his dignity; who'd stolen his life but never once offered him the death he craved.

Here was his chance and yet fear stole his breath and his will. Faced with the moment of reckoning, he couldn't move, his brain thick with fog. Despite all his preparations, he froze, drowning beneath a flood of paralyzing memories no amount of whisky had been able to obliterate.

"Caught in the act with a pretty little Fey-blood whore," Beskin sneered, his eyes raking Callista with one disparaging glance. "Do you whisper Imnada secrets in her ear while you're stuffing her? Does she pretend to enjoy it as she wheedles information out of you?"

Beskin drew his sword from a heavy leather sheath. The moon's faint shine glinted down the length of the blade.

Silver.

No wonder David wanted to be sick.

Trained over a lifetime of service to withstand its effects, all enforcers carried such weaponry as part of their arsenal, though they rarely resorted to it. Silver didn't affect humans or Fey-bloods, the Imnada's normal enemies. It was a dangerous sign of the times that Beskin carried such a sword. More so, that he seemed so comfortable attacking one of his own.

"Hand over the book, St. Leger, and I might spare the Fey-blood's life," Beskin said in a smooth, cold voice. "Of course, I might have to remove her tongue first. Can't have her blabbing about our little encounter to her *Other* friends, can I?"

"David, what's happening?" Callista's frightened voice finally jarred him free of his demons.

"What are you talking about?" he asked. "What book?"

"Don't play the fool with me," Beskin snarled. "Kineally stole it. Sir Dromon and the Ossine want it back."

Immediately, David began to regroup. Plan. Scheme. Plot. He was a soldier, damn it. Beskin might hold all the cards—and a silver sword—but there was no fucking chance David would lie down and make it easy. He might play the fool these days, but he still knew how to outsmart an enemy.

He snatched up a discarded shovel and the lid from an empty grain bin. Hardly knightly sword and shield, but in a pinch, they'd do. "I don't know what you're talking about. I don't have a book, though if I did, I sure as hell wouldn't give it to you."

"Maybe not voluntarily." Beskin's slash of a smile

widened, fangs extended and gleaming like knives. "But by the time I'm finished with you, you'll be begging to tell me where the book is, along with the names of your dirty traitor friends. It will all come spilling out of you along with your bloody entrails."

David swallowed down the sour bile clawing its way up his throat. Slammed his mind against the images of his vicious punishment at the hands of this man ready to stun him into frozen panic once more if he let them.

"Tough talk from a coward whose opponents are usually chained and helpless," he snarled.

Beskin lunged, his sword striking David's makeshift shield. Again the enforcer thrust and again David countered. Attack and parry over and over, David giving ground as he struggled to keep the silver blade at bay. As weak as he was, it wouldn't take but a scratch to bring him down. The sword flashed, Beskin bringing it up and under David's guard. He threw up his shovel handle in a last-ditch effort to keep the blade from taking him in the ribs. But Beskin's strength and the force of his blow proved too much. The handle splintered, the flimsy wood unable to withstand a determined effort to crush it. David threw himself sideways to escape the sweeping follow-through edge of the silver blade from opening his unprotected gut.

"Give me the damn book!" Beskin snarled.

"Fuck you!" David replied through a clenched jaw. His muscles screamed in protest. Sweat rolled down his face, damped his shirt to his back. He rolled up and onto his feet, but he was trapped. There was nowhere to escape and no weapon at hand, not even a stray piece of planking.

Beskin closed in, triumph glittering in his eyes. "Tell Kineally I said hello when you see him in hell."

"Leave him alone!" The satchel came from nowhere and struck Beskin square on the side of the head. The man crumpled dazed to his knees, his sword clanging to the cobbles.

David immediately grabbed it up, his hand falling easily into the grip's well-worn grooves. He stood over the enforcer, fury and vengeance eating through him. Hazing his vision. Vising his chest. His lips pulled back in a low snarl from deep in his chest, his own fangs extended, the beast prowling close to the surface. "Tell Kineally yourself, you fucking bastard."

Pounding boots rang on the cobbles. Raised voices bounced off the close walls of the narrow mews. "There they are!"

"Stop! Corey wants you!"

David couldn't fight. He was too weak. Too slow.

With a muttered oath, he tossed the sword away, shot a last rage-filled glance at Beskin, and, grasping Callista's hand, fled into the dark.

5

Mac wasn't at home. Of all the possibilities David had envisioned, that one hadn't even entered his mind. Mac was always at home. The man barely budged from his hearth these days. He and Bianca had been married for almost six months, and though David assumed the novelty of a bride would have worn off by now, Mac seemed content never to leave the side of his new wife unless absolutely necessary. Now that she was breeding, he was practically glued there.

Except for tonight, the one night David needed his help . . . urgently and without delay. "You're certain he didn't leave word telling you when he would return home? Or where he was going?"

Bianca eyed him with a look of waning patience. "Would you please tell me what's going on, David? I've seen that ghastly death-warmed-over look before. Something bad has happened, hasn't it?"

Despite the late hour, she'd welcomed them attired as if she'd only just arrived home. And perhaps she had. He remembered vaguely reading about her most recent role as Desdemona at Covent Garden. She must have performed tonight, though he personally couldn't imagine Hamlet's suicidal girlfriend played by a woman as round as a pudding.

"It's nothing," he hastened to reassure her. "At least, nothing to do with Mac. That is . . . not directly." He was babbling but couldn't seem to stop.

Bianca gave him her famous ice queen stare, the leveling power of a firing squad behind her Arctic blue eyes. "Don't treat me like a child, David St. Leger," she snapped, strain edging her words. "Miss Hawthorne, do you know what this is about?"

"I'm as clueless as yourself," Callista answered.

Though not for lack of trying. She'd peppered David with questions every time they'd slowed to catch a breath. Which in his present state had been frequently. He'd dodged her pointed interrogation with a rambling monologue about the three faces of the Mother Goddess and a long roundabout legend involving Idrin the Traveler and a ship that sailed among the stars. At least, he told himself that was the reason for his meandering, one-sided babbling. In fact, he might have just been entering the final stages of delirium right before complete collapse. He couldn't be certain.

Bianca gripped a chair back, fear overtaking her anger. "If Mac is in danger, so help me God, David, I'll—"

"You'll what?" came a deep voice from the doorway. "Send out the cavalry? Storm the fortress with sword and buckler? Claw your way to my side like the Valkyrie you are?" Mac Flannery entered the drawing room, flapping the water from his dripping greatcoat.

"All of the above." Bianca swung around to greet her husband, but not before David caught the fleeting look of complete and utter relief cross her face.

"Bloody spring weather," Mac grumbled as he accepted a kiss from his wife, dragged off his coat, and ran a hand through his wet hair. "Halfway up Bond Street, it began pouring like the second flood."

David sent up a silent thank-you to the Mother of All. Hopefully, the downpour would erase any scent trail Beskin might follow. The last thing David wanted to do was to lead the enforcer straight to Mac and Bianca.

Mac's gaze traveled over Callista before settling on David, his expression sobering, though David caught the shock that passed across his face.

He rose to meet his host, though his legs didn't seem to want to hold him, and he had to grab the chair back to steady himself. "We need to talk."

Mac lifted his brows in an obvious question. David answered with an almost imperceptible shake of his head and a slant of his gaze toward the women. Events had grown too complicated, and he was far too tired to path his explanation. The look, the gesture; both were enough. Mac nodded in understanding. "My study."

"Mac?" Bianca said. "What's going on? David refuses to explain."

Mac shot David another cautious glance before turning to his wife. "I'm sure it's nothing."

Bianca placed her hands on her hips, her pose one of imminent argument. "Cormac Cuchulain Flannery . . ."

Mac wrapped an arm around his wife's waist, whispering a few quiet words in her ear. Whatever he said seemed to mollify her for now. She offered David a sharp nod and, with the bustling maneuverings of the soon-to-be mother, took Callista in hand. "I'll find Miss Hawthorne some supper and a place to sleep." Just before she left the room, she turned one last spearing gaze his direction. "But don't think I'm through with you, David St. Leger. You've got some definite explaining to do."

Once the women were gone, David motioned with a wave of his arm. "After you, Captain."

Only after he'd spoken the words did he realize how often over the years that phrase had left his lips. They had fought together from Lisbon to Waterloo, but it had always been Mac who'd been the first to volunteer, the first to leap into any situation no matter how dangerous, the last to retreat no matter how impossible. If David had to describe his comrade, the words *duty*, *honor*, and *courage* would have come first to mind. Followed by *stubborn*, *single-minded*, and *a pain in the ass*.

But *friend* would have been emblazoned at the top of the list.

It had begun as a company of four. Adam, Mac, Gray, and David. Infantry scouts. Imnada clansmen. They had quarreled, teased, laughed, and loved like brothers. The friendship had frayed after the Fey-blood sorcerer set his curse upon them in the chaotic days before Waterloo, but it had never unraveled completely. And when Adam had been murdered last year, it had been his tragic death that finally reminded the remaining three of that unbreakable bond.

Oh, they still quarreled. David thought Gray a self-righteous prig and Mac a besotted fool, but he'd lay down his life for either one of them. It was as simple as that.

Mac closed the study door behind them. "You can collapse now if you like. There's none to witness it."

David's legs gave out as if his strings had been cut. Only Mac's quick shove of a chair in his direction kept him from falling to the floor in a heap. He closed his eyes, a shudder running through him as he fought the teeth-chattering cold that overcame him all at once. Even breathing was almost too much effort, but he managed to squeeze out, "Kineally's dead."

David heard Mac take a seat at his desk. He could picture the spark of tamped fury in his pale green eyes and the battle tension tightening his shoulders. Mac might have sold his commission, shedding his scarlet tunic and gold braid for more sober attire, but he would always be pure soldier. Never happier than with a weapon in his hand and an enemy in his sights. Always had been. Only now, his was a war of secret meetings and quiet conspiracies. What he needed was a good, solid, face-to-face, till-the-death, fight-to-the-finish brawl.

"He was a good man," Mac said quietly. "He'll be mourned."

David snorted his cynicism. "By who? Not his family or his clan. To them, his treason placed him lower than the lowest dung bug."

"He chose to join our cause, David. He wasn't forced. You see now how great the Ossines' power has grown. They send enforcers into the heart of London to seek us out. They're no longer merely defenders of the clans. They bring the battle to us."

David forced his eyelids open to meet Mac's sober gaze. "Who says this was initiated by the Ossine without the Gather elders' approval? Perhaps the Duke of

Morieux has given the enterprise his personal stamp of approval."

While each of the five scattered Imnada clans as well as the Ossine shaman had a seat at the Gather council, the Duke, as hereditary ruler, remained the final arbiter of clan law. Gray's grandfather had always been a thoughtful if somewhat cautious leader. A man who wielded his position lightly, though none had ever been in doubt that he was in charge. That had changed with his son's untimely death, and after Gray's disgrace and exile, the old duke had grown increasingly frail, his hold on the Gather progressively more ineffectual.

Mac gave a sad shake of his head. "The Duke is near death. Few but Sir Dromon Pryor have even seen him recently. The Arch Ossine controls all access to His Grace. He's the real authority these days."

"What of the N'thuil? Pryor may be head of the Ossine but, bound to Jai Idrish, old Tidwell must have some say in clan matters."

They called the faceted crystal sphere the Imnada's heart, but Jai Idrish might be more correctly called the shapechangers' soul. It had come with Idrin the Traveler when the Imnada first arrived on this world. Some said the sphere had guided them here, laying a path through the Gateway from their old dead world to this new one burgeoning with life and hope. Some said when the time was right, it would show them the way back. David didn't know if that was true, but the power contained within Jai Idrish was supposed to be as vast as the universe the Imnada once navigated. All of it contained and focused by one person, the N'thuil, the voice and vessel of Jai Idrish.

It was said that the N'thuil's body was flesh and bone, but his heart was pure crystal. In Muncy Tidwell's case, it was more like mountains of blubber surrounding a heart soft as his fat head.

"Tidwell does as he's told," Mac explained. "Besides, Jai Idrish hasn't made itself felt for centuries. Not even the oldest clan members remember a time when it spoke its will. The position of N'thuil is barely more than one of figurehead these days, and that's just how Tidwell prefers it." He made a useless gesture with his hands. "No, David. Pryor's unchallenged in his bid for control of the clans. And as long as Gray remains in exile, leaving no obvious heir to the Duke, the Arch Ossine's grip on power will remain unbreakable. Any hope for a reconciliation with the Fey-bloods will be impossible."

"You're awfully conversant with internal Imnada politics these days."

"We have to be."

David struggled to sit up. His chills were being overtaken by a feverish heat that damped his already clammy skin. "Damn it, I don't care about the Duke or the N'thuil or who's fucking in charge of the Ossine. Because of you, Beskin believes I'm in league with your rebels and that I'm carrying some blasted book. He wants it back and he's determined to add my head to his trophy wall to gain hold of it."

Mac didn't flinch. Hell, he didn't even bat an eye. "I'd think you'd be used to pursuit by those with murder in their hearts. How many outraged husbands and scorned mistresses have queued up to put a bullet through you? There must be scores by now."

"Flannery . . ." David said with an impatient growl.

Mac shoved himself to his feet and walked around to lean against the desk, a sly smile creeping over his face. "Where does the woman come into it?"

"Her name is Callista Hawthorne."

"No wonder Beskin believes you guilty of treason. She reeks of Other magic, or hadn't you noticed?"

"Of course I bloody well noticed," David growled. "If I'd known what she was at the time, you can be sure I'd have run the other way as fast as four legs could carry me."

"At the time?" Mac's face cleared to one of dawning comprehension. "You played your avenger act again in some slimy back alley, didn't you? What happened? Did you save her from a tragic fate worse than death, only to find yourself stuck with her?"

"You've got the stuck bit right." David slumped farther into his seat. "But the humiliating truth is . . . she saved me. Twice."

"Here's a nightgown, Miss Hawthorne. It should be about the right size. I wore it pre-belly," Bianca Flannery said with a grimace and a pat of her rotund midsection, though she looked anything but unhappy at her growing bump.

Callista had seen the famous actress once before, back when she was still Bianca Parrino and London theater's darling. She could never in a million years have imagined one day she'd be standing in the woman's guest bedchamber borrowing nightclothes. But why had David brought her here? It was obvious he knew Captain Flannery and his wife. But did that mean . . . could it be that the captain was one of these

Imnada as well? Could both husband and wife be shapechangers? Or was it just the opposite and Mrs. Flannery had no inkling of her husband's powers?

"I'll have Molly bring you some supper. You look completely done in."

A minor understatement. Callista would gladly have crawled between the covers of the bed behind her, turned her back on the plague of unanswered questions, and slept for a month.

"I've some cold chicken and biscuits and there may even be a bit of cake left."

Callista's stomach gave an embarrassing growl.

"Yes, definitely supper," Bianca Flannery affirmed. "And two slices of cake."

"It's not what you think," Callista blurted "That is, David . . . I mean, Mr. St. Leger and myself aren't what you think . . ." Her words trailed off into an embarrassed silence and her face grew hot, almost unbearably so. Mrs. Flannery looked up from turning back the bedcovers to regard her with a mix of compassion and kindness; two emotions all but unknown in Branston's household.

"That is to say"—Callista scrambled to fill the silence—"we're merely traveling in company. Not as a couple . . . or . . . anything scandalous."

Though it *was* scandalous, disastrously so. It didn't matter if they never did more than spend time in a closed carriage together. Just the fact that she was an unmarried female in the company of an unmarried male was enough to ruin her. Would it be enough for Mr. Corey to break off the engagement? Perhaps if she was very lucky. But would it also be enough to keep Aunt Deirdre from taking her in?

In Callista's haste to escape, she'd not thought that part through. Or if she had, she'd pushed it to the side as a future problem she'd sort out once the more immediate problems had been dealt with. It had been enough just to escape Branston. She had the entire length of the country to worry over minor technicalities like David's awkward presence.

Perhaps she could pass him off as a footman or a . . . a cousin on her father's side. Someone harmless and innocent and free of nefarious motivations.

Right. The man was about as harmless and innocent-looking as the wild beasts in Exeter Exchange.

Seeming to understand the welter of emotions chasing their way through Callista's brain, Bianca guided her down onto the edge of the bed with a comforting pat. "There's no need to say any more, Miss Hawthorne. Not to me," she said reassuringly.

Such a small gesture, but Callista hadn't had anyone offer the small gestures since her mother's death. A strange lump caught in her throat and her eyes stung, which is probably why she couldn't read the expression on her hostess's face, though she definitely felt her tremble when she touched her arm.

"You've been very kind," Callista said, blinking the mist from her eyes.

Bianca's gaze softened. "It's obvious something has happened to throw you and David into the sauce together. I'm more than familiar with the sort of impossible tangles one can find oneself in, but I'm certain there's nothing unseemly between you."

"You are?"

"Of course. Call it woman's intuition, or perhaps just knowing David like I do. He has a penchant for leaping in and out of scrapes and loving every minute of it. But if it were that kind of trouble following you, I doubt he'd have brought you here to us. He's far more surreptitious about his light o' loves." She smiled another one of those disarming sisterly smiles that made Callista want to cry or throw herself in her arms or confess the whole horrid story. Maybe all three. It had been so long since she'd had anyone to confide in.

"Besides," Bianca Flannery added, "you look far too clever to fall for David's practiced scoundrel's charm. And he tends more toward blond, plump, and brainless. Easier that way, I suppose."

Lady Fowler's round china-doll face and Rubenesque body sprang to mind. Callista should be relieved her reputation remained intact. Instead it just irritated her.

Bianca gave her one final pat on the shoulder before she headed for the door. "I'll go see about supper while you try and get some rest. And don't worry. Whatever has happened, you can be sure David and Mac together will sort it out."

But was she as convinced as she tried to sound? Or had Callista stumbled into deeper troubles than she'd left behind?

"Scotland? Are you insane? That's an entire country away." Mac paused in his pacing to spear David with a gaze of complete disbelief.

"Thank you for pointing that out, Mac, but I'm well aware of the mileage."

"And you agreed to take her?"

"What the hell else could I do? I was hardly in a

position to haggle. I figured I'd purchase her a ticket
to Edinburgh on the Royal Mail and be done with
it—with her. I didn't realize I'd be dragging her across
London with murderous Ossine on my tail."

"So much for best-laid plans," Mac quipped.

David cast him an evil look as the room began to
sway alarmingly and spots formed at the edges of his
vision.

Mac folded his arms across his chest, his grim stare
dropping David's heart into his shoes. "I have the book
Beskin is after."

David sat up. "You? I should have bloody known."

"Kineally was supposed to hand the book over to
Gray. His death and Gray's unexpected trip north to
Addershiels have thrown those arrangements out the
window."

"A shame the poor man's murder complicated
your treasonous plotting. Damn it, Mac. My life was a
shambles already. The last thing I needed was another
shovelful of shit making it worse."

Ignoring David's outburst, Mac tapped his chin in
thought. "You can't go home. And with Beskin nosing
about, you're not safe in the city."

"Thank you for stating the obvious."

"Why not take over Kineally's assignment and deliver the book to Gray?"

Forget heart in his shoes; David's heart plummeted
through the floor and into the basement. "Are you mad?
Beskin will be on me faster than a vulture on a carcass."

Mac ticked off his reasoning on his fingers. "Gray
needs the book. I can't leave Bianca. And you were
headed north anyway. It's the perfect solution to both
our problems."

"It'll take days to reach Scotland with Miss Hawthorne."

"I thought you'd count that a bonus." Mac leaned against the mantel, a boot propped upon the fender, his gaze lost amid the flames. "She already knows you're Imnada."

David's gaze fell to his hands. He noted with curiosity that they were shaking. Barely, but enough. "That may be, but she doesn't know about *me*. About the curse."

"Why should she, if you continue to take the draught?"

David fisted his hands, forcing them to still. "Because the damned draught is back at my house. Because the need grows ever greater as the effects grow ever shorter. You must have noticed it too."

Mac nodded. "I'm lucky if I can squeeze a fortnight out of a single dose."

"The other symptoms grow stronger as well. The dizziness, the fatigue, the headaches."

Worry darkened Mac's catlike green eyes. "Bianca tells me I should quit taking it. Let the Fey-blood's curse take hold once more. She thinks that will end it."

"You haven't told her everything?"

Mac squeezed his eyes shut, shoulders hunched. "How do I tell her that it wouldn't make any difference? That either way, she's married to a dead man? I can't. It would destroy her and I've put her through enough as it is."

"She's your wife, Mac. She has a right to know."

Mac's fury blazed in his face. "What would you know about husbands and wives?"

David shrugged. "Enough to recognize that falsehoods have a tendency to turn around and bite one in the ass. I'd not want Bianca angry with me. That cool façade hides a dangerous streak."

Mac gave a dry bark of laughter. "A fair enough reading." The laughter died in his eyes. His neck muscles taut with some deep inner turmoil, he sucked in a quick painful gasp as if just speaking the words pained him. "We made so many plans, David. We had so many dreams. And now . . ." He opened his hand in a gesture of futility, myriad scores crisscrossing his palm, the marks of his own fight to keep the curse at bay.

"Now it hangs by a thread unless we find a cure for our cure? Should have known it had been too easy."

"Everything hangs by a thread. Not just our future but the future of all the Imnada. I won't have my youngling hunted down by the Ossine as a half-blood freak to be exterminated."

Mother of All, would the Ossine really do that? Kill a child simply for bearing mixed blood? Had things come to such a desperate pass?

Mac looked up. "Will you do it? Will you take the book to Gray?"

David sighed. "Do I have a choice?"

"That's the spirit. Who knows? Maybe there's hope for you yet."

David slanted Mac a disbelieving glance. "Hope? What's that?"

Mac shoved his hands in his pockets with a small shrug and a weak smile. "It's all we have left."

Leave it to Mac to get the final word in.

*   *   *

Callista stood at the window, looking down upon the dark street. Despite the late hour, a few carriages still rattled their way past, on their way home from some fancy ball or extravagant musicale. And once or twice she caught a glimpse of a shadowy figure making his way north toward Cavendish Square to the comfort of a warm, snug bed and a good night's sleep.

A warm, snug bed waited just behind her. But the good night's sleep she'd found to be impossible.

Her thoughts ran in too many circles, and so she watched the waning crescent moon hover in the west, its light barely enough to penetrate the heavy coal-fired haze. Berenth, St. Leger had labeled it; the crone face of the Mother Goddess. This period fell between the full moon of Silmith, when the goddess looked down on the clans as both fertile lover and mighty warrior, and Morderoth, when death took the moon and the skies were absent of her light until reborn as the maiden at Piryeth.

All this and more David had imparted as they fled from his house in Cumberland Place to the Flannerys' on Holles Street. By the time they'd climbed the front steps, he was babbling sixteen to the dozen and barely able to point both eyes in the same direction.

Surely he should have improved once she'd removed the silver chains that poisoned him. Instead, he seemed to worsen, as if his body were slowly crumbling to bits in front of her eyes. Her last sight of him as Captain Flannery led him away had truly frightened her.

What would happen if he became too ill to escort her to Scotland? What would happen if he died? Callista had thrown all her eggs into his basket. If his

assistance was lost, she'd be once again at the mercy
of strangers—or worse. The captain and his wife had
been more than kind so far, but she couldn't count
on them once they understood the threat Mr. Corey
posed. Captain Flannery seemed capable of handling
any danger, but why should he bother when handing
her over to Branston would be so much easier?

No. David couldn't die. It was as simple as that.

Her fingers tightened on the curtain. Simple? Who
was she trying to fool? She, better than anyone, knew
death was never simple. And cheating it, impossible.

As if conjured from her worries, heavy footsteps
sounded outside her door. Not Captain Flannery. He'd
retired over an hour ago. She'd heard him pass her
room. Heard a low, urgent conversation with his wife
just before their door shut. So, this was David . . . Mr.
St. Leger . . .

David.

The steps were slow but steady. They paused, and
Callista felt her breath still in her chest. Would he come
into her room unasked? And then what? Take her in
his arms and kiss her as he'd done in the Fowlers' alcove? The idea prickled along her skin and shimmied
like lightning up her spine until she squashed it flat.

No, David might tease her with his banter and his
quick, sly glances, but she knew, without quite knowing how she knew, that he'd never press his attentions
where they weren't wanted nor take a woman unwilling. He might bend rules, but he respected boundaries.

After a long moment, the steps resumed. Five . . .
six . . . seven. Then came the snick of a latch and the
quiet bump of a closing door.

She let out her breath in a whoosh of slumped

shoulders before a frown pinched her mouth and a new more troubling thought burrowed its way into her heart.

How completely selfish could she be? David was ill, and it was her fault. She'd been the one to drag him into this predicament in the first place. He'd come to her rescue and she'd thanked him by bashing him over the head. She should have insisted on making sure he was being attended to. She should have asked after his welfare. For heaven's sake, she should have thanked him—just once.

She'd done none of those things. No wonder she paced the room sleepless and guilt-ridden. She'd go to David first thing in the morning. As soon as she saw him, the first words to roll off her tongue would be *Thank you*. Not difficult at all. Two little syllables and she'd no longer feel like an ungrateful wretch.

Satisfied, she lay down on the bed, pulled the covers up to her chin, and closed her eyes. Waited for sleep to catch up with her. But still her brain whirred like a top and David's face hovered against the backs of her eyelids like an accusation. Apparently good intentions weren't enough. She huffed a frustrated breath.

If she couldn't sleep until she'd spoken to David and assured herself he was not about to expire, then that's what she'd do. A niggling voice warned of what befell women who visited men in their bedchambers. Callista chose to ignore it. Despite her babbling justifications to Mrs. Flannery, it was obvious her reputation couldn't sink any lower.

Before the voice grew more insistent, Callista slipped from her room, padded the few paces down the corridor, and lifted her hand to David's door; stopped just before her knuckles gave a sharp rap. What if he was asleep? She didn't want to wake him. She'd simply sneak in, take a peek, and, if he was asleep, leave. No harm done. No questions asked.

She turned the latch, cracked the door, and stepped a pace into the room, and stopped dead.

He definitely wasn't asleep.

"David?"

He spun around, dagger gripped in one hand, the other fisted tight, blood oozing from a deep cut across his palm. By now pain chewed at his muscles and silver-blue flames crowded his vision. The last thing he needed was an audience.

"Dear gods, what are you doing?" Callista demanded.

"Swooning?" he said as his legs buckled.

Before he hit the floor, a shoulder propped him up and an arm came round his back to edge him unresisting down on the bed. "You're burning up with fever. Is it the silver?" she asked. "Is that what's wrong?"

He snatched up a cloth, winding it tight around his hand, and glanced down at his naked torso. Not that Callista hadn't already seen him in every way, shape, and form, but somehow this was different. The silver's poison was an external weakness. But the curse's slow destruction was his own body betraying him. A death best endured alone.

"You shouldn't be here."

"I'm sorry," she answered caustically. "Should I leave so you can drop dead alone?"

He winced as he shifted on the bed, putting a few

crucial inches between them. "You're the necromancer. Can't you just fetch me back?"

"It doesn't work that way." She started to rise.
"Should I get the captain? Perhaps he—"

"No!" David grabbed her back. "Let him sleep."
He drew a shuddering, painful breath. His strength
waned with every moment he delayed. He needed to
either toss her out or ask for her assistance, and he
didn't have the energy to toss her out. "Just hand me
the . . . the cup over there. I don't think my legs will
carry me that far."

She did as he asked, giving the contents a wary
sniff before she handed it to him. "Ugh, what is it? It
smells horrible and looks worse."

"Life." He brought it to his lips with a held breath.
Sucked the contents dry. Then closed his eyes on a
weary sigh. "Thank you."

"That was supposed to be my line," she answered
quietly.

He opened his eyes and looked at her, really looked
at her, for the first time since she entered his room. She
was dressed for bed, the ribbons of her nightgown tied
at her throat, the sash of her robe cinched tight. But her
dark hair hung loose and shining down her back, her
toes peeked endearingly from beneath her hem, and
her Fey-blood aura shone under her skin like a lamp.
Hard to reconcile this slip of a woman with the shadowy powers he'd experienced while trapped within her
gaze. Even harder to reconcile his unexpected attrac-
tion to her. She was Other. He'd been taught from birth
to despise her kind. To fear and loathe her magic. To
kill or be killed. And yet something about her called to
him in a way he'd never experienced.

"Did you risk scandal by coming to my room simply to offer your gratitude?" he asked.

She dropped her gaze to her lap and her hands threaded tightly there. "I couldn't sleep. I was worried about you, and . . . well . . . I wanted to say thank you for all you've done."

"Almost getting you gutted like a fish?"

Her eyes flew to meet his. "No. For . . . for not . . ." She paused. Drew a breath and started again. "For helping me escape."

"Did I have a choice?"

Her expression seemed to close, any hint of what she was thinking wiped clean.

He tightened his bloody hand on the cloth. Already, the draught moved through his system, repairing, maintaining. He would not shift. He would not die.

Not today.

"Consider us even, Miss Hawthorne. Bloody hell, more than even, in fact. I still owe you one. You've a hell of a brutal swing. Give you a cricket bat and you'd be unstoppable."

She offered him the makings of a smile before rising to pace halfway to the door, hands fisted at her side, hips swaying ever so slightly. He thought about calling her back, but he was tired, plague-sick, and what would he say to her anyway? He didn't know, which was a first. Normally the witty patter came without effort. Not tonight. Not with her.

She placed a hand on the doorknob. Paused for a long moment before swinging around and returning. Surprised him by seating herself back on the bed beside him, legs drawn beneath her.

"Forget something?" he asked.

Her sharp gaze traveled over his bare chest before locking on his face. "You look terrible."

"Thank you."

She frowned. "You know what I mean. Is it the silver?"

He couldn't help it. A laugh escaped him, rough and painful as it ripped up through his aching chest. "No, Callista. Not this time."

Her scowl deepened, and he realized he'd called her by her first name. He waited for her to scold him for his presumption, but she merely gave a slight shake of her head, her hair falling forward to shield her expression. "But you won't tell me what it is."

"It's a long, dull tale. Hardly bedtime story fare."

He sensed her watching him. Sensed the questions on the tip of her tongue. The clues were there in the taut way she held herself, the hesitation in her breathing, her hand splayed palm down upon her leg, nails digging ever so slightly into the fabric. He should insist she leave. Pretend this inappropriate visit never occurred. It was the smart thing to do. The proper thing to do.

But he didn't. For some reason, he didn't want to be alone. Not with time to think. Time to rage.

Still, if she was going to stay, he needed to make at least a cursory bow to propriety. He hefted himself to unsteady feet long enough to retrieve his shirt and drag it over his head.

"Very well," she said, breaking the silence between them as she tucked her hair behind her ear. "At least tell me who that man was tonight and why he wanted to kill you."

"Us."

"Excuse me?"

"Beskin wanted to kill *us*," David clarified. "Me for treason. You for being . . . you. A Fey-blood. The enemy."

"I'm not an enemy."

"Your kind is. The Other have been the enemies of the Imnada for a thousand years and more."

"So I've put you in danger."

"No, Callista," he replied with a weary shake of his head. "I was an outlaw to my people long before I met you. You're the excuse, but not the cause."

"What's the cause? What's happened to exile you from your own kind?"

Exile. *Emnil.* The word turned like a knife in his chest. Just as it had done since it had been pronounced over his bowed head within the Gather's circle. Under other circumstances, he'd have laughed away the feeling, his expression one of bland amusement. But tonight it was impossible. Tonight every nerve had been stripped raw and he ached with more pains than he could count. He shuffled to the window, drawing back the curtain, using the dark street and the setting moon to hide the gnawing pain at his heart. And said nothing.

"It's bound up in this illness, isn't it?" she asked.

"You're perceptive," he said without turning around.

He heard her moving behind him. The creak of the bed. The swish of fabric. His body tensed as he half expected, half hoped she would lay a hand on his shoulder or brush fingers over his arm. "No, just observant. It helps in my profession. I know without asking what my clients truly need from their visit."

"And what do I need?" He spoke without thinking,

then clenched his jaw tight, wondering what truths she might peel free from the dark places where he kept them locked away. "Wait. Don't answer that. I don't want to know."

Awkward silence threatened until Callista's voice broke through the rising tension, her tone uncertain, her words breaching the stone round his heart. "You don't have to pretend with me, David. I know what it is to be alone."

"You have a brother and an aunt."

"You have a clan."

His back twitched in remembered agony. A vise clamped his skull as he fought back the ghosts of those horrible days caught in Beskin's brutal care. "To my clan, I'm a traitor and a rogue."

"To my family, I'm an embarrassment and a disgrace," she whispered. "We're more alike than you realize."

He left the window to sink into a leather armchair, closing his eyes on the lingering sway of the room. The draught worked, but slowly. "We'll leave at dawn tomorrow."

"You can barely stand."

"As long as I continue to take my medicine, I'll be fine."

"That horrid potion? Is that what . . . is that why your hand . . ." Before he knew what she was about, she'd grabbed his wrist, forcing him to open his fingers, revealing the open cut across his palm, the myriad silver lines marking his earlier dosings. "You work powerful magic, David. Powerful Other magic."

A ghost of a smile curved his lips. "Not powerful enough."

Callista scowled, eyes fierce with shock, cradling his hand in one of hers, the tips of her fingers brushing over his palm. She leaned over him, so close that her hair fell against his chest and he could lean up and kiss her lips. She smelled of mint and lavender and something else, something earthy and sweet that filled his head. His stomach tightened, his body alive with her closeness.

Her gaze locked with his. He forced himself to meet her stare, though fear curdled his insides at what he might see within the midnight reaches of her eyes. Yet no pit opened beneath him to send him spiraling down where his darkest memories lay like serpents and the future gaped like a wound before him. Instead, he sensed the heat of her flesh even through the layers of fabric and the telltale tremble in her fingers as they cupped his hand.

Her voice slid soft as silk over his skin. "Why take the risk, David? You're free now. You could simply turn your back on our agreement. Pretend it never happened. Put me on a northbound coach and assume that made us even. Why do you help me?"

Which is exactly what he'd planned to do; get rid of her and pretend it never happened. Pretend his life was just as he preferred it. But who the hell was he kidding?

He shrugged. "When one can't help oneself . . ." he murmured, "what else is there?"

6

"I knew it. Damn it, I knew that shifter would be worth a fortune and now he's gone!" Hawthorne paced the study feverishly, jowls quivering, his face a dangerous ruddy shade.

"Sit down," Corey ordered. "You're giving me a headache."

Hawthorne collapsed into an ornate velvet chair, pudgy fingers drumming on the carved arm. "There's no telling what the fiend has done with Callista—or *to* her. These Imnada aren't like normal men, Corey. They have appetites . . . hungers."

"According to my men, Callista looked a willing partner rather than a kidnap victim, and the knife cuts to those ropes bear this out. I'd heard St. Leger had the women of London eating from his hands, but thought your prunes-and-prisms sister was made of sterner stuff."

Hawthorne sat up, eyes wide. "You know the shifter's name?

Corey smiled. "Why do you think I let them slip

away so easily? I wanted to know where the man went . . . who he was . . . what made him tick. Now I know that and far more. David St. Leger is a former decorated army captain. Sold his commission after Waterloo. He's currently the pet of every discontented wife and the nightmare of every overprotective father. He's a rogue, a gambler, a pink of the *ton*."

"He's a damned shifter is what he is."

"Just so. But one so distinguished will find it hard to remain hidden forever. He'll turn up, and when he does—"

"When he does, we hold him," Hawthorne interrupted. "Wrap him in silver and cage him behind steel bars if need be. He's our route to the top. Having him under our control will be like having the Bank of England printing us money."

"So you claim, but is your source trustworthy?" Corey's gaze fell once more on the withered, pock-faced man huddled in the corner of the room. He crouched fearfully, his rheumy eyes darting here and there over the elegant furnishings of Corey's private study as if he'd never seen any room so grand. Doubtless he never had. The man was as flea-filled as a bag of cats, his clothes gray and stiff with dirt, and the smell coming off him was pungent enough to make one's eyes water. Where Hawthorne had dug him up, Corey couldn't imagine.

"Are you certain you're not being taken for a fool?" he asked.

Hawthorne shook his head. "Pearne here looks a sight, but he belonged to the Amhas-draoi before he was kicked out for rape and murder. If any living know about the Imnada shifters, it's the brotherhood."

Corey eyed the man like a disease. "This bag of chattering bones was one of the famed guardians of the divide?"

The Amhas-draoi devoted their lives to protecting the realms of man and Fey, mostly from each other. Nothing passed over the walls separating earth from the summer kingdom of Ynys Avalenn that they did not allow. Great warriors and powerful sorcerers, the brotherhood founded by the Fey battle-queen Scathach stood for honor, justice, and integrity. For those in need, they were a bright sword against the dark. For those who undermined their supremacy, they were a cold blade in the back.

"Look, he bears the mage marks of the Amhas-draoi." Hawthorne shoved up the man's sleeve, where swirling inked tattoos of purple encircled his arm from wrist to elbow. "He's got no reason to lie."

"Step forward, old man," Corey instructed.

Pearne downed his glass of wine before he crossed the floor, fear rising like a stench from his unwashed skin.

"Is it true? Did you once belong to Scathach's mage-born army?"

"Aye, m'lord, though it's been years since I trod the ramparts of Dunsgathaic as one of the battle-queen's best. Kicked me out, they did. Tossed me aside as if I was nothing. The girl was willing enough, sir, I swear it on my honor. Her father had no right to accuse me of aught else and so my dagger told him."

"I don't give a damn about some peasant slag you raped. What of the Imnada? Is their blood as potent as it's rumored?"

Pearne held out his empty glass. Corey pressed his lips together but stepped forward with the bottle.

The man swallowed, wine trickling down over his greasy beard and onto his shirtfront. He smacked his lips, wiped his mouth with his sleeve. His gaze seemed sharper, his mouth curled into a clever leer. "Aye, so the ancient scrolls say. A drop is said to restore a man's life after even the gravest hurts. Ten such can turn back time. Immortality contained within their very arteries."

"But have you seen it for yourself? Can you prove it?"

"The shapechangers are dead, sir. Killed off for their treachery after the murder of Arthur. The devils were sent to hell with spear and blade and arrow until none remain. It's naught but writing on an old tattered scroll now."

"Not so dead as the Amhas-draoi thought." Corey turned to Hawthorne. "So, we capture St. Leger and . . . what? Siphon him off a teaspoon at a time? Is that your plan?"

"Who wouldn't pay for the most powerful medicine? A cure for the plagues of aging? We could ask any price we wanted. It dazzles the mind with possibilities."

Corey ran a hand over his chin as he mulled this over. "Why come to me with this proposition, Hawthorne? What do you get out of it?" He stiffened. "Your sister is mine. I don't care if she's rutted with a bloody barnyard bull. She'll marry me. That was our deal."

"Of course. And generous it is of you, to take her still. No, I came to you because I need your network to help me find the shifter. You need me to help you find Callista. It's a business arrangement. Fifty-fifty."

"Eighty-twenty if it's my carriers doing the hunting."

"Of course, Mr. Corey. That sounds fair. Are you in?"

Corey shrugged. "Why not? We'll be shedding his blood anyway. Might as well see if the beggar's claim is valid."

Hawthorne stuck out his hand and Corey shook it. "Where is she, then?"

"Callista has an aunt on the Isle of Skye; a priestess at the *bandraoi* convent there. I'd wager all I have that my sister heads for Scotland."

"You wagered once and lost. Are you certain you wish to roll that die again?"

"I'm sure of it. There's nowhere else for her to go. She has no other family. And when we find them, St. Leger will pay for taking Callista away. And if he . . . if the two of them . . . if he's soiled her . . ."

"I'll send men out tonight. Immediately."

"Make sure they know to take St. Leger alive. He's no use to us dead."

"Nor is your sister."

"Oh, her . . . well, of course . . . goes without saying . . ."

Did it? Corey thought not. Hawthorne cared nothing for his sister now that he had the potential for untold riches in the shifter's blood. Eighty-twenty. A decent split if the old beggar spoke true, but Corey liked a sure thing over a long shot. Better yet, he liked to rig the odds so that no matter how he chose, his success was ensured.

He slid open a desk drawer, pulled free the pistol he kept there. "On second thought, why share the wealth when I can have it all for myself?"

The bullet took Hawthorne in the face, blood and

brains exploding out the back of his skull, his body still twitching as it dropped to the carpet. Pearne, despite his age and infirmity, was quick. He dashed for the door, his fingers scrabbling for the latch. Corey's knife took him in the back. It didn't kill him outright, but it slowed him enough for Corey to rise, cross the room, yank the blade free, and slide it across the man's throat from ear to ear. The man jerked and gurgled, and was still. So much for Amhas-draoi prowess.

Wiping the blade clean on a handkerchief, he rang for a footman to clean up the mess, his mind already pondering how to turn this new development to his best advantage.

The world as his domain or immortality? Why choose when he could have both?

True to his word, David rose in the morning well enough recovered to set out as planned, though not before he and Captain Flannery spent hours behind closed doors. Callista couldn't make out what the two men were saying, but judging by the volume of the discussion, it wasn't an amiable chat over tea and toast. By the time they stood on the front steps saying their goodbyes beneath a drizzling leaden sky, the two men looked haggard and tight-jawed. Only Bianca's intervention smoothed their final moments. Rising on her toes, she pressed a kiss upon David's cheek, whispering, "Mac doesn't know I know. He'll tell me when he's ready."

The comment made no sense to Callista, but David seemed to understand. He offered Bianca a sober smile as he glanced at her growing belly. "I've said it before, Mrs. Flannery, you're no shrinking wallflower."

She turned to Callista. "You'll be safe with David. He's tougher than he looks and smarter than he acts."

David laughed. "High praise indeed." He assisted Callista into the coach before mounting a big-muscled bay that arched its neck and raked the cobbles in anticipation. His hands fisted the reins as he held the horse still and settled a long serious look on Flannery. "You can count on me, Mac. I'll see the package gets safe to Gray."

The captain gave a nod. "See you get yourself there safe and I'll be satisfied."

They left London amid a steady rain that turned the roads to mud and wearied horses and passengers alike. Despite the weather, David chose to ride rather than travel inside the coach with Callista. She felt an uncomfortable mixture of guilt and relief as she watched him hunched in his sodden coat, squinting into the wind, water streaming down his face. She needed time alone. Time to forget the few desperate moments in his bedchamber when she'd ached to feel his arms around her and his mouth moving against hers in a kiss as scandalous as it was powerful.

It worked.

After two long days of cloud-heavy skies and drenching downpours that perfectly matched her mood—during which time David had been nothing but breezily charming or ominously silent—she woke on the third day to blue skies, green meadows, and a somewhat restored equilibrium. There had been no repeat of the uneasy conversation and neither of them had brought up the matter again.

It was as if it had never happened.

With the return of the sun, their pace increased,

and soon they were bowling along the wide road, slowing only for the occasional tollgate or village crossroads. Every mile behind them eased Callista's fears of pursuit. She no longer jumped at every sound of hooves and harness or shrank into her cloak at every stop to keep from being noticed. Still, she'd not feel truly safe until the gates of Dunsgathaic closed behind her. Only then would Branston's reach recede and Corey be naught more than a bad dream.

They had just passed Grantham, the afternoon well progressed and dusk only now darkening the skies to the east when, drowsy with the motion of the coach, Callista put aside her book to lean against the window, head resting on her hand. More often than she liked, she found her gaze straying to David riding a little ahead of them, his horse tossing its head in the wind.

Where before she'd pitied him as the rain lashed his face and dripped under his collar, now she envied him the freedom and pleasure of the wind against his cheeks and the sun warm on his shoulders. She admired the easy way he handled his horse; the straightness of his back and the gentle touch he maintained on the reins. But she also noticed the experienced way he scanned the landscape for trouble, the flexing of his hand upon his thigh as though it sought the reassurance of a sword, and the grim set of his chiseled jaw.

Bianca Flannery was correct. He might play the pleasure-loving town dandy, but there was a dark heart hidden behind the quick smile and the twinkling eyes.

At one point, he looked back over his shoulder, and Callista drew into the shadows of the coach, a wild tingling deep in the pit of her stomach, her hands sweaty within her gloves. For a moment, she found

herself back in the musty dim corner of the Fowlers'
entry hall, shivers of unexpected pleasure trilling up
her spine as David's lips moved slowly over hers in a
kiss of tender seduction. What would it be like to feel
his body pressed skin on skin against hers? To explore
the hard planes of his chest and the rippled muscles of
his stomach in a slow and sinful trail southward? To
hear him plead her name as he buried himself inside
her? As he possessed her body and soul?

The carriage lurched, breaking into the wild spin of
her thoughts before the lush, wanton heat coiling up
from her center overcame her completely. She shifted
uncomfortably until the impetuous sensations faded.

So much for her equilibrium.

She snatched up her book, burying herself in the
prose. This trip was fraught with enough perils. She
didn't need to add to them with silly girlish fancies.
There was no real bond between them. David St. Leger
offered his protection, but he had not done so out of
honor or chivalry or for any tender emotion. They had
made a bargain. And he was as much a fugitive as she.

He gave a shout to the postillion. Lowering her
book for one last swift glance out the window, Callista
saw David tether his horse to a sapling and disappear
into the line of trees close to the road, a flash of sunlight off steel as he drew his knife.

Her tingles turned to knots. Hard and tight, they
jumbled her insides as her mouth went dry. But there
were no shouts or signs of trouble, the coach rumbled
on, and soon the horse and the wood were lost around
a bend.

Another mile and still no sign of David. She
clutched her satchel to her chest, running her finger

back and forth along the latch to calm her nerves. He was fine. There was nothing wrong. He would appear any minute.

As she fretted, the trees gave way to wide hedge-rowed fields and a low arched bridge, then a hill leading down into a long green meadow. Hundreds of feet had beaten the grass flat and churned great muddy swaths between a few scattered tents. Where the river looped away from the bridge, a group of four garishly painted wagons clustered together, mules hobbled to graze nearby. Two men worked to bring down a large blue-and-yellow-striped pavilion. Ropes coiled at their feet as they folded great swaths of canvas. A woman threaded past carrying a bucket of water, and a bearded giant strode from the nearest wagon, shouting orders, arms gesticulating.

Her finger stilled upon the metal clasp. She recognized that tent, that man.

Sam Oakham.

It was said that Sam could shoot the wing from a fly at a hundred paces and split a strand of hair from twice that distance. But it was his fists that earned him his bread and butter as he traveled from town to town offering to bare-knuckle fight any comers. For two long years after Mother's death, Branston and she had made their lives among the itinerant players and fairfolk. Then Sam had asked for her hand in marriage following her seventeenth birthday. Her brother had refused the proposal, and soon after, they had left the road for lodgings in Bath. She'd not seen the fighter since.

A face appeared in her window, nearly stopping her heart in a wild moment of panic.

Dirt-smudged and rumpled, David leaned down in the saddle. "Miss me?" He grinned, though Callista noted that the smile didn't quite reach his eyes, which remained troubled.

"Where did you go? I was worried sick."

He shrugged. "When the need arises . . ."

But Callista had seen the knife, caught the intent in David's eyes. Something more than the call of nature had lured him into those woods.

He motioned toward the empty meadow. "Looks as though we missed all the fun. Fair's over and packed up."

She turned to fling one last sidelong glance out at the pavilion and the wagons and the man in his shirt-sleeves bellowing orders. "I've not missed it at all," she murmured.

"More wine?" David held the bottle over Callista's glass.

She looked up from her dinner of stringy beef and burnt potatoes. They had decided to stay at this shabby down-at-heels tavern on the edge of town rather than the more comfortable posting inn near the market cross. Less traffic to notice them. Easier to escape should difficulties arise. Even so, the taproom was full, and David had offered the barman extra coins for a private room and his silence.

"It's no Clos de Vougeot, but it's better than the beer—barely," he said.

She placed her hand over the rim of her glass. "If I didn't know better, I'd say you were trying to intoxicate me."

"With this? Doubtful." He leaned back in his chair. Poured another glass for himself. That had to be the fourth or fifth. He didn't seem any the worse for wear, and after years spent living with Branston, she definitely knew the signs. Still . . .

"Should you be drinking so much?" she asked.

His eyes locked on hers, and she cringed. *Haunted* didn't begin to describe the shadows filling his storm-gray stare—an expression replaced so quickly with his usual scoundrel's twinkle, she couldn't decide if she'd seen it at all. "I'm in a ramshackle tavern on the edge of some godforsaken town, being hunted by Ossine enforcers and dangerous Fey-bloods." He lifted his wine to his lips as if he meant to toss it down in one gulp, then slowly placed it back on the table. "Probably not."

"This isn't a lovely spring fete for me, either," she replied. "I'm just as uncomfortable and just as hunted. At least, if they catch us, you'll only be killed. *I'll* have to marry Victor Corey."

For a moment he stared at her as if unsure how to respond. Callista's nerves jumped and she dug her fingers into her skirt, wishing she'd kept her mouth shut. It wasn't like her to talk back. She'd learned long ago to keep her own counsel and let none see what she truly felt. It must be fatigue and the awful weight of her fear making her waspish and presumptuous.

He continued to eye her, but she sensed no anger in his expression. If anything, it was amusement. Laughter lurked in his gaze and his mouth twitched. "Point well-taken, Miss Hawthorne." He reached once more for his wineglass, but at a stern look from her subsided. "You win. No more wine."

Instead, he pulled a chunk of wood from his coat

pocket, a knife from a sheath at his waist. Slowly, he drew the blade across the wood. A long, thin shaving fell away. Then another. And another, the delicate curls falling on his lap and at his feet.

"What are you doing?" she asked, pushing her plate aside to lean her elbows on the table.

He looked up, a corkscrew curling up over his palm, knife stilled in his hand. "Not drinking."

"I mean with the wood. Are you . . . whittling?"

He lifted his brows and a smile crooked a corner of his mouth. "Can't pull the wool over your eyes, can I?"

He continued to shave at the wood, a little thinner at one end, rounder at the other.

"Where did you learn to do that?"

"The army," he answered without looking up. "Moments of sheer terror. Months of complete boredom. My friend Adam kept a journal to pass the time. I'm not nearly that scholastic."

She leaned forward, amazed at his deft skill. For some reason, it was hard to equate this artistic aptitude with his muscular warrior's build and predator's stare. "You're quite good."

His lip quirked in a smile. "I spent a very long time in the army."

Callista watched as he shaped and honed, pausing now and then to study the piece before he laid knife to wood once more. He'd shed his jacket early on during the meal. Now he sat with his shirtsleeves rolled back, his cravat wrinkled and barely knotted. Most men would have appeared disheveled and scruffy. David looked mouthwateringly stylish. Blond hair fell across his forehead as he bent over his work. He shoved it off his face with a quick scoop of his fingers. His eyes flickered up to hers, then dropped once more to the carving.

"Tell me about this aunt of yours," he said.

She'd been so absorbed in the quiet intensity of the knife's flicking in and out and the way his large, blunt-fingered hand cradled the wood in his open palm that she jumped at the sound of his voice, her cheeks burning as if she'd been caught at something wicked. She smoothed her hands down over her skirts and shifted in her seat. "What do you want to know about her?"

"Her name for starters. And where she lives. Scotland covers a lot of ground."

"Her name is Deirdre Armstrong," Callista said slowly, gauging his reaction as she spoke. "She lives on . . . Skye."

"Mother of All!" He nicked his thumb. Sucked at the bloody gash, his eyes wide and accusing as they flashed to meet hers. "The Isle of Skye? She's a damned Amhas-draoi, isn't she?"

"Aunt Deirdre lives at the convent there," she fought to explain. "She's a priestess of High Danu."

"Witch or warrior—does it make a difference?" he argued. "Either one would mount my head on the wall without blinking an eyelash."

"Aunt Deirdre wouldn't do that. Not if I tell her what you've done for me. How you've helped me."

"Right. That should do it. A thousand years of hatred wiped out in five minutes of hurried explanation."

"You promised to escort me to my aunt. You can't go back on your word now."

"You lied to me."

"I didn't lie."

"A lie of omission . . . my dear."

He had a point, which only made her feel worse and thus angrier. "I knew you wouldn't agree if I'd told you the truth, and I was desperate. You said yourself Victor Corey is a dangerous man."

"Right, while the brotherhood of Amhas-draoi are a cozy basket of kittens."

She forced herself to remain calm despite an overwhelming urge to weep or shout or both. This wasn't how and when she'd meant to tell him. She'd wanted to be closer to the border. Farther from London. "And if I'd told you? If I'd explained the whole situation and relied on your sense of honor to convince you? Are you telling me we'd be sitting here having this conversation? I don't think so. I think you'd be floating in the Thames and I'd be . . ." She couldn't finish.

He snorted, his expression still thunderous, but he took up his knife again and began to whittle, the long spirals falling faster, his mouth pressed into an angry line, his jaw tight. "Is your aunt a necromancer as well?"

"I . . . I don't know," she answered, tensing for another explosion. She wasn't disappointed.

"What do you mean you don't—" His face was a mask of shocked disbelief. "You've never met the woman, have you?"

She looked down at the table, suddenly very interested in her empty plate, refolding her napkin. "It doesn't matter. She's—"

"A complete stranger and a witch." She could almost hear his teeth grinding as he fought to keep his temper. "Does she know you're coming?"

Callista's face must have belied her attempts to remain composed. David gave a hard brittle laugh, tossing the knife and the carving on the table with a clatter.

"Hell and damnation! You've never met the woman and she has no idea you're headed her direction with a villainous mob hot on your tail. You don't even know if she'll take you in. It's just as likely she'll hand you back to your betrothed with a wink and a smile."

Anger and embarrassment crawled hot over her skin. "Aunt Deirdre is the only family I have left. She won't turn me away. Not when I tell her I want to join the sisterhood."

That seemed to startle him. "You, a *bandraoi* priestess?"

"I'll be safe at Dunsgathaic."

"Locked away in a fortress on Skye forever? That's your idea of freedom? To trade one prison for another?"

"What would you know of prisons and free will? You're wealthy. You're a man. For heaven's sake, you're a shapechanger who can turn into a wolf at will. You've never known anything but freedom and choices. You've never suffered or been trapped with no way out."

He lurched to his feet, eyes blazing in his face. "Is that what you think? Truly? You have no bloody idea, Callista. None at all."

With another muttered oath, he grabbed up the wine bottle, swung on his heel.

"Where are you going?" she asked, afraid of the answer.

His smile was cold, but his eyes held heartbreaking sorrow. "To get pickled drunk."

Rather than storming out in a temper as Branston would have done, David offered her an oh-so-formal courtier's bow and departed in ominous silence.

Should she chase after him or give him space to work off his temper? Would he return or did his rigid back and clenched fists signal the end of their tenuous alliance? She rose from her chair, grabbing her shawl from a hook by the door. Got as far as laying a hand upon the latch before she changed her mind. David would stay or he would go. It would hardly be the first time she'd placed her trust in someone and been disappointed. If she woke to find herself on her own, she would manage. Freedom was what she'd wanted. She'd not shrink from it now that it stared her in the face.

Despite David's accusations, she knew without a doubt that her deception had been necessary. If what he'd told her about the violent animosity between Other and Imnada was true, there was no way he would have agreed to her proposal if he knew what he was agreeing to exactly. And as for writing to Aunt Deirdre, well . . . she *had* begun half a dozen letters, all of them ending in the fire. It seemed so much easier to show up unannounced, leaving her aunt no opportunity to come up with excuses to turn her away. Once on her doorstep, Callista could plead her case in person. Her aunt would have to acknowledge her. She would have to let her stay.

Callista rubbed at her temples, which had started to throb. Her eyes were tired and achy, her body sore from the days cramped in the coach. She rose from the table, catching back a gasp when her gaze fell on the half-whittled piece of wood David had abandoned. Even rendered in the quick sharp strokes of a blade, the similarities were uncanny. The high bones of her cheeks. The deep-set eyes.

It was *her* face David had carved.

A frisson of delicious excitement shivered up her spine.

Perhaps she hadn't completely ruined everything. Perhaps there was still hope—but for what?

David lingered in the stable's doorway, the untouched wine bottle resting at his feet. He didn't have the stomach for even a sip. No light shone from the tavern's windows, and even the most thorough of drunkards had already stumbled to bed. A far-off clock tower struck the half hour. He was alone with nothing but his thoughts and a bony cat for company.

He'd half expected Callista to come running after him with apologies spilling from those completely kissable lips, that wild riot of dark hair tumbling loose from its pins to cascade over her shoulders like a cloud.

He shook his head in hopes of dislodging that uncomfortable image. Callista's hair, lips and every other luscious part of her were no concern of his. Once they reached Gray at Addershiels and David handed over this blasted book, he'd pack her onto a convenient mail coach and send her on her merry way north. Bargain or no bargain, he wasn't about to traipse into the heart of Fey-blood power to have his head whacked off by an overzealous Amhas-draoi.

Surely by the time they reached Northumberland, Callista would be safe from pursuit. Victor Corey was hardly likely to spend so much energy chasing after a reluctant bride. And that pudgy brother of hers couldn't be much danger.

A small niggling voice whispered that she trusted

him to see her safely to her aunt. That he'd made a promise. That she needed him.

That he might need her.

It was a voice he squashed ruthlessly and efficiently.

Rage was his armor, apathy his shield, and drink his balm. Take any of the three away and he was left with nothing but despair and desolation.

He bent to retrieve the wine bottle. Eyed the contents. Sweet oblivion for an hour . . . perhaps two if he was lucky.

"Should you be drinking?"

He closed his eyes, remembering her solemn stare as she said the words; the concern in her tone. He gripped the neck of the bottle. Smashed it against the wall, glass and wine exploding over his clothes, the heavy aroma burning his nostrils. Ducking into the stable, he pulled off his boots. Shirt and breeches followed. The night breeze cooled his naked body. Trailed like a lover's fingers over his skin. The moon was a narrow crescent low in the sky. The period of Berenth, when shifting grew more difficult and dangerous, was well advanced. But he needed to escape this form before he went mad . . . before absent thoughts became painful regrets. Before dark memories tore his mind apart.

Rolling his clothes in a ball, he shoved them behind the grain bins. None to notice until the grooms appeared to feed and water in the morning. By then, he'd have long since returned.

He smiled as he left the guttering lamplight to wrap himself in shadows, the magic moving within him like fire in his blood, transforming him, freeing him, returning him to the night where he belonged. Hunter, not hunted.

Back arched, the bony cat hissed in panic before racing for the safety of the darkest corner of the barn, but the wolf, eyes cutting the darkness like two flames, never looked back. And he smiled, knowing that those indoors huddled closer to their fires when they heard him lift his voice to the wind in a lonely call to a family who would never answer.

7

Callista's heart lurched. Her eyes flew open. She tried to scream—or breathe—but a hand clamped tight over her mouth. A harsh voice sounded low in her ear, breath hot on her cheek. "Don't make a sound."

She nodded, her heart galloping like a runaway horse.

The hand retreated, but the figure remained poised above her, silhouetted in the gray predawn light seeping round the edges of her bedchamber curtain. She sat up, drawing the sheet close around her neck. A threadbare piece of linen was the only barrier between herself and humiliation. "Are you mad?" she hissed. "You scared me to death."

He put a finger to his lips. "*Shhh.* They've found us." David's words hit her like a punch to the stomach. "I didn't expect Corey's thugs to be so skilled, but even a rabid hound can track a scent once in a while."

"You saw them?"

"Four men. London accents. Weapons out of sight, but close to hand. They just rode in. There's few people awake yet. It's early. But soon the tap will be full and the maids up and about. It won't take these chaps long to find someone willing to trade our whereabouts for a purse full of coins."

"I thought you'd left me."

"I should have. It seems I really *am* a gentleman. Who knew?"

Gentleman was hardly the sobriquet she would have used. His shirt was wrinkled and smelled like horse, his breeches were the same, and his boots bore a bog's worth of thick black mud. She gave a surreptitious sniff. No smell of alcohol on him, and his eyes shone clear and bright, without a drunkard's stare. In fact, not just clear and bright but glittering with wide-eyed excitement.

"Prove your gallantry." She swung her feet onto the floor, dragging the sheet with her. "Turn your back."

"Excuse me?"

"Turn your back while I dress. I can't very well escape in nothing but a chemise."

"Is that all you have on under that sheet? I'm not *that* much of a gentleman."

Under his scrutiny and with the sheet wrapped tight around her, she sidled over to the chair where her gown and petticoats lay draped. "Please, turn around."

"You have a delightful waddle," he commented.

"Thank you. Please?" She made circling motions with one hand.

He offered her a rogue's smile before he swung his back to her, arms folded, eyes trained on the opposite wall. "Like a goose on her way to the pond."

With shaking fingers, she dropped the sheet to fasten her corset before slithering into her petticoats. "You're enjoying this, aren't you?"

"What?" he said without turning around. "Staring at this horrid painting of a field full of sad cows? Not particularly."

"I mean being one step ahead of the chase . . . the trap closing . . . the thrill of outsmarting an adversary . . . you like the excitement, don't you?"

"No, I just dislike being dead. Are you done? We need to move now if we're to outdistance them before the sun rises."

One more layer complete. One less chance for him to see the trembling in her knees or notice the flush of her skin. He'd think it was on his account and he was vain enough already. "Have you arranged for the coach—"

"No coach. Ordering the horses harnessed would give us away. They're not fools. It's shank's mare for now."

"We can't walk to Scotland."

"Not if you keep chattering on, we can't." He swung back around as she struggled with her gown. Crossed the room in three ground-eating strides to take the collar of her dress in his hands.

"You said you were a gentleman," she gasped.

"This isn't a ravishment, Miss Hawthorne. I'm fastening your buttons."

"Oh," she muttered, her face growing as hot as the rest of her body.

"Unless . . ." He drew out the word, leaning forward. He was so close she could smell the scent of him and feel the tension smoldering just under his skin.

She jumped and spun, nearly knocking him in the face with the top of her head. "What of Corey's henchmen?"

"They can get their own women."

"You're mad."

He grinned, the gleam of it positively fiendish. "You're only now realizing that?" He shrugged. "Perhaps when the dogs aren't howling at the door and we can take our time."

Her gaze swept up to his face, but he'd already turned to swing his saddlebag over his shoulder, his face lost in shadow, and she couldn't read his expression nor tell from his tone whether he was joking.

The passage was dark, save for a shuttered lamp at the top of the stairs, though every second the light increased. Soon it would be dawn and impossible to slip away unnoticed. She hoisted her satchel more firmly on her shoulder and started for the stairs, but David restrained her. "Not that way. We use the kitchen stairs and the gate leading into the alley. Once we reach the road, we'll cut into the wood and travel east and south a bit. That should throw them off."

The wood. The road south. It was a risk, but an acceptable risk. "We're not walking to Scotland."

"So it would seem. You do realize we're in a bit of a hurry."

"No, I mean we don't need to walk anywhere. We can hide from Branston *and* travel to Scotland at the same time."

He cocked a head, his eyes sharp and bright as knives. "Do tell."

She took his hand. It was warm and felt far too perfect fitted against her own. That scared her and she would have pulled away, but he tightened his grip, trapping her beside him.

She swallowed down the flutters in her chest, gave a deep breath, and said, "Follow me."

*   *   *

Sam Oakham was enormous. He towered over David, muscles bulging, fists like hammers. He scowled out from behind a thick, wiry beard and lowered bushy brows and stood with legs wide and shoulders braced in a pose meant to intimidate. No doubt, most people cowered before this shambling mountain. David stood his ground, stepping closer to Callista and spreading his fingers to touch the small of her back, as if marking her as his own.

The man's eyes narrowed in understanding, and his scowl deepened. "Why should I? What's in it for me?"

David felt a shiver race up Callista's spine before she stiffened, her sharp chin lifting. "I can pay my way. You don't have a fortune-teller, do you?"

Oakham tugged at his beard. "We had Old Polly and her crystals, but she died winter before last."

"Then I'll take her place. Any coins I collect are yours in exchange for our bed and board."

"I don't know . . ." Oakham hedged, though David saw an avaricious gleam light his expression. From the ramshackle look of the wagons and the scrawniness of the mules, Oakham could use any moneymaking leg up he could acquire.

The sun hung tangled within the eastern woods, throwing long morning shadows across the churned field of drying mud and crushed grass. Three days ago the wide meadow and the fields surrounding would have been clogged with stalls and booths. Now all that was left of the army of peddlers, drovers, farmers, musicians, acrobats, puppetmasters, quacks, and freaks who'd collected for the sheep fair were four gaudy wagons, each blazoned with *Oakham's Follies* in particularly repellent shades of crimson and green.

"Please. I need your help." Callista paused. "We were friends once, Sam, you and I."

Oakham turned his head and spit. "We were never friends, Cally girl. I wanted you for my wife."

A failed suitor? This was Callista's idea of salvation? David wished she'd made mention of the situation before he'd introduced themselves as lovers fleeing north for a hasty illicit marriage. Not that she'd liked the idea very much, but it was the first story that had popped into his head.

"You knew Branston would never agree," she explained.

Oakham snorted his disdain. "That simpering brother of yours never scared me. And had you favored my suit, I'd have shown that little pea-wit what for and married you anyway."

"I'm sorry I hurt you, Sam. I never meant to."

He continued to scowl down on them like a pirate eyeing up his next plank walker. This plan had disaster written all over it, but with Corey's minions watching the main roads, there were few better alternatives. Alone, David would have melted into the countryside like a phantom, leaving them chasing their own tails. And why he hadn't done just that, he still didn't know. He'd registered the danger, and his first instinct had been to wake Callista and get the hell out. Upon seeing her in a scanty nightgown, tousled and heavy-lidded with sleep, his second instinct had been to climb in bed beside her and take his chances.

Then he recalled her violent way with a valise and his first instinct won.

"You think *he's* going to marry you?" Oakham interrupted David's train of thought with a jerk of his bearded chin and another spit. "More like bed you and bruise you and fill your belly with his brat before he takes his leave. I know his sort. That's what his kind do."

It was David's turn to stiffen. "Watch your step. My kind doesn't tolerate insult. And my sort is like to prove it by thrashing you to within an inch of your life."

Callista backed up, her foot coming down hard on his instep in painful warning. "It's good of you to worry over me, Sam, but there's no need. David loves . . ." He felt her stumble over the lie, her shoulders tense. "David loves me."

Oakham's ham fists flexed as he took a menacing step forward. "You think you're so much better than me, don't you, pretty boy? But I know you for what you truly are, a weak-kneed lickspittle that will take Cally's maidenhead for sport and laugh about it later with your mates round your poncy drawing rooms."

"Sam! Stop it! It's not true!" Callista scolded, her face scarlet.

"If you know what I am," David snarled, "you'll know I could rip your head off and shove it up your ass with one hand tied behind my back. My mates would find that hilarious."

"You are not helping, David," Callista snapped.

No? It was helping him tremendously. For the first time in days, he felt a lessening of the tension eating away at his nerves. As if now that his rage had found a target, it no longer sought to consume him. "Oakham started it," he said.

"Are you five years old?" she groused. "What kind of excuse is that?"

"One hand, pretty boy?" Oakham jeered. "Let's see you test that mettle." His gaze shot sparks, his body quivering with fury.

"Any time, any place, old man."

Callista grabbed his arm. "We need his help, David."

He shook her off. "I'm tired of running like a rabbit. Oakham will learn the wolf doesn't turn his back on a fight."

"The wolf is trying to get me to Scotland, not kill himself," she hissed.

"He has to hit me to kill m—"

Oakham's first blow nearly took off David's head. Only a split second's warning kept his teeth in his mouth. Even so, the blow clipped his chin, sending him lurching backward. He recovered his balance, gathered his strength, and plunged forward, landing a vicious crack to Oakham's jaw, another brutal punch to his stomach. Oakham laughed, blood streaming from his nose down over his beard to drip on his vest. Then he launched himself at David, and the vicious scrum began in earnest.

Back and forth they struggled, matching blow for blow until David's right eye had swelled shut and Oakham was smiling through a broken front tooth, blood spattering his clothes. Callista's shouts were drowned out by the drumming of David's heart. His attention was all for his adversary. On keeping his feet in the mud. On judging where the next blow would come from and on pushing forward when the advantage was his.

By now a small crowd had gathered to watch and shout encouragement. David doubled his efforts, his feet always moving, his body darting and sliding in and out of Oakham's reach. The giant lunged, his arm reaching out with an enormous swipe that would have knocked a smaller man—or a slower one—into the dust. David used Oakham's momentum to slide under his guard and land him a sickening fist to his kidneys, knocking the bastard to his knees. He followed it up immediately with a second hit that sent Oakham reeling onto his back.

"What's going on?" A woman's voice broke through the ringing in David's ears. "Samuel Oakham, have you taken leave of your senses?"

David blinked, trying to wipe the sweat and blood from his eyes, his gaze drawn to the furious woman striding toward them. A moment's lapse, but long enough for someone to toss Oakham a dagger.

The man caught the blade and, with a flip of his wrist, immediately hurled it at David, who intuitively lunged to the left as it passed. Ha! Missed him.

He'd barely regained his breath and his balance when Oakham bulled into his midsection and knocked David flat into the dirt, the wind driven from his lungs, his ribs grating up into his spine. He fought to breathe, but Oakham gave him no time, his attack coming fast and furious.

A normal human would have begged for mercy or been broken under the unceasing violence.

The wolf did not beg.

Nor did it surrender.

Rage boiled up from the corners of his soul; rage and brutality and a desire to rend his enemy limb from limb until victory was assured. Muscles tightened, and his blood ran hot and fast through his veins. As his aspect fought to break free, his vision narrowed, time stretching, pain receding, his mind aflame. Oakham became Beskin. And this time David would finish what he started. He would kill the man who'd taken his life from him with fire and sword and left him with nothing but a slow, excruciating death, exiled from his own kind.

With a savage cry ripping up through his throat and a twist and a shift of his weight, David slammed Oakham facedown in the dirt, bending his arm so far behind him that he could feel Oakham's tendons grinding and bones creaking. "Mother of All, I'm going to enjoy killing you, Beskin, you son of a bastard."

"There won't be any killing this morning." A cold blade touched David just beneath his chin. The prick of it shocked him back into himself, and the wolf fled as if it had never been, leaving him shaky and sick.

"Nan? I'll not have you interfere," Oakham gasped.

Oakham, David remembered . . . not Beskin. This was not the enforcer struggling against a quick snap of the neck. David had come close to committing murder, blind to all but his own vengeance. Was this what he'd come to? Is this how far he'd fallen in the years since his sentencing? The wolf was his aspect; he wore its shape and possessed its soul. But it did not control him.

He was not the monster the Other labeled him—yet.

"I'm saving your life, you stupid git," the woman scoffed.

Oakham spat, but the woman's blade held firm and David rose slowly to his feet, pulled back from the brink by the veriest hairsbreadth.

Callista tried to lead him away from the crowd, but he stood with his hands on his knees as he sucked in air, hoping to calm his raw nerves. The woman knelt by Oakham, her long black hair caught up in a scarf, her stomach distended in late pregnancy.

"You should thank me, Nan," Oakham whined as she helped him to his feet. "One less girl will have her heart broken by the likes of pretty boy here."

"That's for Cally to decide. It's her heart." She focused her ire on David. "And you—I know my brother has the thick skull of a dumb bear, but you? What's your excuse?" She didn't wait for an answer. "Cally, you can put your things in the wagon there. We'll share what we have in return for your help, and we can always use another strong back for the heavy lifting."

David felt blood seeping down his collar where the girl's blade had broken the skin.

"Thank you, Nan. I can't tell you how grateful we are," Callista answered.

Nan's hand curved unconsciously around her swollen belly, her contemptuous gaze leveled on David. "I told Sam it was your business, but you take care, Cally." She lifted her knife. "If this fellow hurts you, I just might finish what I started."

"Hold still."

David flinched as Callista dabbed at the cut above his eye. "It hurts, damn it."

"That's because you're not holding still," she answered impatiently.

Callista had dragged him away from the wagons, following a narrow track down a hill and into the wooded copse. They walked until the only sounds that met the ear were birdsong and the chuckle of a lazy creek. David had allowed himself to be led, but she knew he remained on edge. She felt the coiled tension in his body as he knelt, the hard set of his jaw beneath her fingers as she angled his head and pushed the hair back from his forehead to better attend to the long, ugly gash.

If Nancy Oakham hadn't interfered, how far would the fight between the men have gone? David had come away with a few cuts and bruises, but Sam, whose mastery of knife and pistol was dwarfed only by his prowess with fists, had stumbled like a drunkard to his wagon, shaking his shaggy head as if unsure how he'd ended in the dirt at a pretty London boy's mercy.

Callista could have told him.

She had seen the moment when David had become more than a man and less than completely human. She'd stood transfixed as the mask was peeled away to reveal the dangerous Imnada soul beneath the human exterior. Animal bloodlust burned hot and cruel in his steel gaze, his movements too quick for Sam to follow, his strength too great for Sam to withstand.

Yet when it was done and David stood, out of breath and blood dripping, there was nothing left of the feral viciousness but a grim press of white lips and fists clenched and bruised. Then he looked up, their eyes met, and his torment shone clear in his hunter's stare. It lasted but the space of a breath before vanishing, but it was more than long enough for Callista to recognize his suave care-for-nothing attitude as a ruse. She was a necromancer. She understood ghosts.

He sucked in another breath, trying to pull away, but her fingers tightened on his chin. "If you stopped moving about, this wouldn't hurt so much."

He offered her an indignant stare. "If you wouldn't keep jamming that cloth into my scalp, it wouldn't hurt at all."

"Are you always this whiny?"

"Are you always this tyrannical?"

"You'll have to ask my brother."

"I'd rather not. Our last conversation was bad for my health."

Refusing the smile hovering at the edges of her mouth, Callista dipped the cloth back in the stream, wrung it out, and continued cleaning dirt from the bloody gash.

"I don't know if you've noticed, Miss Hawthorne," David said, "but the longer I'm with you, the longer grows the list of people who want to kill me. Where does it end? In my grave?"

"Stay away from Sam, and we'll be fine."

"And if he insults you again?"

"I lived for seven years at the mercy of a brother who hated me from birth. Insults mean nothing to me, but your dying will."

"You really do care." A smile lit his eyes.

She sighed and sat back on her haunches. "There. I think you'll live."

He pulled himself up on the stream bank. Stalked a few paces away before he clutched the tail of his shirt in dismay. "Brilliant. I have one shirt left and it's covered in filth. This trip just gets better and better."

"The mess we're in, and you're concerned about a soiled shirt?" He looked like such a pouty little boy, she couldn't help herself. She laughed.

"Glad you find it so amusing," he said, sulking.

"I find *you* amusing. Thank you."

He watched her with those piercing gray eyes that seemed to cut right through to her very thoughts. "Has it been so long, then?"

"Long?"

"Since you laughed."

She tried shrugging off his question, though he'd cut closer to the mark than she appreciated. "I haven't had much reason for laughter."

"Then I'll have to give you one, because your whole face lights up and your eyes sparkle. You're very beautiful, Callista Hawthorne"—he grinned—"for a Fey-blood."

Backhanded or not, butterflies swooped around her stomach at the unexpected compliment. Before she could think of a witty reply, David knocked her for a second loop by shedding his boots, tossing his shirt onto the grass, and wading into the stream up to his waist. The water lapped low against his hips and the rippled muscles of his abdomen. Even sporting an ugly collage of purple and black bruises, he managed to exude enough raw sensuality to turn her insides to warm mush.

"If you drown, I won't come fish you out," she called, praying he didn't notice the scorching heat burning its way into her cheeks.

He gave her another toothy smile and dropped beneath the surface like a stone. She counted off the seconds until he emerged with a splash and a wet flick of his hair off his face. Water sluiced over his broad shoulders, trickled against his neck, skimmed down his muscled torso. Drops clung to his golden skin and slid like tears over his stubbled cheeks.

Like an addlepated twit, she couldn't tear her eyes off him. The air grew hot and thick. Her body was one galloping heartbeat from complete collapse.

"Wake up!" David slapped at the water, splashing her hair and gown.

Startled, she jumped back before answering his attack with one of her own. He laughed and smacked the water again, catching her in the face. Wiping her eyes, she let out a cry, scrambling up from the riverbank as he waded toward her with a menacing smile.

"Don't you dare, David St. Leger," she shouted.

"Or what?" He took another step toward her, the sculpted curve of his hips emerging from the river as he approached the shore.

"Or . . . or I'll scream."

He grinned. "Hoping Sam Oakham will come to your rescue? I've thrashed him once. I'll do it again."

By now the water lapped around his knees and her heart drummed against her chest, her mouth dry. She swallowed, but her feet wouldn't move. She could only watch as he came closer, striding onto the bank. As he took her hand in his own, fingers threaded, the palm rough. He was inches away, and when she lifted her eyes, she saw how fast his own pulse beat in the hollow of his throat.

"You're not screaming," he murmured.

"No," she said, her voice barely a whisper.

He reached out to touch her temple, a curl of hair behind her ear, a finger tracing the line of her cheekbone. His eyes pulled her in, pushed her under, drowned her. She tried to breathe, but he seemed to suck the very air from her lungs.

He didn't pull her close. He never moved beyond that tentative study of her face with one finger, but every part of her burned, and she knew he felt the same blood-sizzling need. It was there in his eyes and the way he stood and the very aroused bits of him she was doing her best *not* to see. This not touching slid like wildfire against her nerves and made her gasp with every shivering trace of his finger. He skimmed the bones of her cheeks, the fullness of her lips, along the line of her jaw, down the taut length of her throat and the edge of her collarbone to the valley between her breasts. One wayward finger, but it was more than enough to send coiling spirals of raw lust straight to her center. She was damp with wanting him, her knees barely holding her upright against the wickedly erotic assault.

"But you aren't smiling, either," he said, his voice silken and deep—and solemn.

She gave the smallest shake of her head, all she could manage while caught in this web of volcanic desire.

His expression hardened and his hand dropped back to his side. "What's happening to me, Fey-blood? Why do I feel this way when I'm with you?"

"What way is that?"

"Confused. Out of my depth. As if I need to run as far and as fast as I can away from you lest you destroy me."

She chewed her lip, her body aching in ways she'd never felt, a shivering need floating across her damp skin like a chill. "How could I destroy you? My powers aren't dangerous. They're barely useful, except as a way to comfort bereft widows or grieving parents. I'm a trickster. A showman."

His face held a weariness and a sorrow, the same look she'd last seen the night at the Flannerys' when the sickness gripped him. "And yet I see my death when I look into your eyes."

She gave a small sound in the back of her throat, barely more than a breath or a sigh, tears taking the place of river water on her cheeks, and her lashes fluttered down as she looked away. "I can pass through into death. I cannot foretell it. It must be Arawn's shadow you see—the mark borne by all his descendants. That's all."

His lips curved into a smile that did not quite reach his eyes. "Perhaps. A relief if you're right. It was not a peaceful death."

Footsteps and the crunch of bracken and twigs snapped David's head up. He stepped back while Callista broke away, embarrassed.

Nancy Oakham emerged from the trees, a bitter smile curving the corners of her mouth as she took in David's near nudity. "I've convinced my brother it's in our best interest to have you join us. So, if you still need a lift, best hurry up or be left behind."

David dragged his shirt over his head and sat down to pull on his boots. "How can we refuse such a gracious invitation?"

Nancy's gaze flicked over Callista before raking David with a long, appraising look. "Remember what I said, St. Leger. We're letting you stay on for Cally's sake. But watch your step or watch your back." With a dark scowl, she departed, the shuffle of her boots through the fallen leaves seeming loud in the silence that opened like a chasm between them.

David rose to his feet, a rakish smile tilting one corner of his mouth. "I don't know about you, but I have the distinct feeling we've gone from frying pan to fire." He held out a hand. "Come, my lady, our chariots await."

She gave a jerk of her head, motioned him on. "Go on. I just need . . . need a moment to wash up."

His gaze dimmed briefly, then with a last flash of his scoundrel's grin, he followed Nancy up the path toward the waiting caravans.

Callista knelt to splash water on her heated cheeks before staring into the river, seeing the reflection of trees and sky and a bird sitting high in a nearby pine. A breeze ruffled her damp skirts, but it was not the icy cold of death. She felt no tug upon her chest as the door cracked open.

What had David seen when he looked into her eyes?

"I wish you were here, Mother. I have so many questions. So many things I don't understand," she said to the breeze and the sky and the rustle of leaves.

A crow flew down to settle a few feet away, its beady eyes fixed upon Callista.

"The bird of death. An appropriate companion for a daughter of Lord Arawn's line," she said, rising to her feet with a deep, restorative breath.

The bird ruffled its shiny black feathers and squawked before shuffling a few steps closer.

"Can *you* tell me what I want to know?" she asked.

With a last squawk, the bird flew off.

Death. Death. Death, rang in Callista's head.

But, as a necromancer, had she expected anything else?

David stood just beyond the flickering glow of the fire studying his new traveling companions.

Edward Perkins and his wife, Lettice, performed a magic show together, though David felt no trace of Fey-blood powers from either one of them. Clearly, there was little of magic and much of show about their act. Then there was Big Knox, a juggler and acrobat who spouted Shakespeare while he capered and leapt and spun plates on sticks. Pretty, blond Sally Sweet worked as a dancer, though David would wager she made more money on her back than she ever did on her feet. Finally there was Sam Oakham and his sister Nancy. Despite her brother's loud, bullying leadership, Nancy appeared to be the real glue that held this motley troupe together. Beneath her hard-bitten façade, she seemed to have a way of handling people, including her brother, that relied less on bluster and more on charm. Too bad she was a female. She'd have made a brilliant general.

Big Knox leaned over and tossed another log onto the blaze. The flames shot high into the air, sparks flying, resin snapping. David stared into the heart of the pyre, watching the twist and curl of the flames as they danced within the circle of stones, feeling the heat against his face even here, where he stood among the trees.

His grandmother had always warned him that he'd end as the main act in a mummer's show if he wasn't careful. If he didn't follow clan law. If he didn't hide what he was from a dangerous world. What would she say if she knew he was traveling to the Isle of Skye in company with a Fey-blood as a member of Oakham's Follies? He chuckled, knowing exactly. She'd call him a hen-witted fool and a brainless bag of hammers. Would she be far wrong?

He followed the track of the floating sparks up and up into the sky to be lost among the distant stars on their way through the Gateway.

Gran had passed beyond. He'd been ten when she'd died and his family had returned with her body to the ancestral clan holding in Wales, where her spirit was released with fire and wind. Father and Mother had seemed completely out of place among the Imnada clansmen gathered to assist in the rites and offer their prayers. It was the first time David had realized the difference between his family and the shapechangers who stayed hidden behind the Palings shield wall. The children had called him *avaklos*, meaning "one who lives beyond the wall," and mocked his London clothes and his city ways. They had split his lip and shoved him down on the rocks and he'd cried to his mother, who wiped his tears and soothed his fears.

Better a brave avaklos *than a craven* andala *who cowers within his holding and prays that the Fey-bloods pass him over. The Palings serve a purpose, but we cannot cower behind them for all time. Look at the Duke of Morieux. He understands this. He does not wrap himself in mists and shadow and pretend there is no world beyond. He strides out boldly and unafraid. He knows that sometimes the best hiding place is right under your enemies' nose. You are the wolf and your bloodline lies*

*deep here in Wales, but the wolf does not burrow into
the ground like the badger. And when the battle's joined,
he does not run and he does not hide. Remember that
always, David.*

He and his father had returned to the holding in
Wales only two years later, and this time there was no
mother to soothe his hurts when the taunts began, but
he'd grown larger and prouder, and this time he did
not need assistance. He stopped them on his own and
called himself *avaklos.*

Funny, he'd not thought of those visits to Wales in
years. Nor spent more than a passing thought now
and again for his gran or his mother. But the spirits
seemed to hover closer these days and memories he'd
fought to lock away pushed to the surface of his mind.
Was it Callista and the power she possessed who
caused this dwelling on people long dead and events
best forgotten? No, as he'd told her once before, she
was the excuse, but not the cause.

He'd been feeling this way since Adam's murder last
year. The first of the brotherhood to fall, though not
the last. Each of them faced a painful death, and all
knew there would be no funeral pyre lit in their honor,
no gathering of clan and kin to speak the words and
send them back to the stars. They would be bound to
the earth to rot, their souls trapped and unable to re-
join their families beyond the Gateway. Exiles even in
death.

But how long until there were no Imnada left? A
generation? Five? Already, the magic of the Palings
waned, the holdings became vulnerable, and elders of
the five clans far outnumbered the younglings born
of the blood. Under siege from Fey-blood and human

alike, what chance did the clans have? None. Not with
the Ossine's clamp on power holding them captive to
the outdated ways of *andala* isolation and men like
Beskin hunting down the few who spoke out against it.

He rubbed his face. Shook off the oppression with
a shrug of his shoulders and a crack of his neck. What
he needed was a damn drink. A nice big whisky or a
pint or two . . . or ten. Surely one of these men possessed enough alcohol to wash away a lifetime of
sorrows, though he doubted any would offer him as
much as a sip and risk Oakham's anger.

It would be water or cider, if he was lucky.

"Are you waiting for your valet to bring you dinner, St. Leger? Better eat. Breakfast will be bread and
cheese. We won't have time to stir up the fire so that
you can dine on sausages and tea."

Nancy Oakham had joined him under the trees,
her chin thrust in a challenge, her expression a mixture of bravado and suspicion. She held out a plate of
stew, the smell enticing. He accepted it with a nod, but
she didn't withdraw. Instead, she followed the track of
his gaze, her lips pressed tight.

"I still can't believe Cally's here. She's the last person I ever thought to see again. And in company with
a fancy man like yourself." She gave a bark of laughter.

"Desperate times call for desperate measures."

"She must be extremely desperate to turn up asking Sam for help after the way things were left between
them."

"You've met Branston Hawthorne. What do you
think?"

"The man was a slug and a bully." She cast him a dubious glance. "But can you tell me you're any better?"

"No, but I can say I'm definitely no worse."

"Hawthorne should have accepted Sam's suit. He'd have made a good husband for Cally," she said pointedly.

"Perhaps he wanted more for his sister than a traveling player, no matter how good a man he was."

She gave a lift of her brows and a quick sniff in response. "Then why are *you* running?"

"Anyone ever tell you it's not polite to pry into other people's business?"

"As long as you're traveling with us, you and Cally *are* my business."

"Let's just say that if Branston Hawthorne wants his sister back, he'll have to go through me." A corner of his mouth twisted in a humorless smile, almost wishing Hawthorne would appear to give him an outlet for the frustration boiling just under his skin.

"Tough words for a London gent"—Nancy folded her arms over her chest—"if that's what you really are."

Every muscle wound to spring, fire chewing up through his belly. "What else would I be?"

"That's the question, isn't it?" she answered coolly.

He forced himself to relax, even give a nonchalant shrug and a quick practiced grin. "No mystery. I'm just a pretty boy fancy man, Miss Oakham."

"You're more than that. Nobody bests Sam who isn't a notch above." As if hearing his name, her brother eyed them grimly from his seat by the fire.

"I told you," he said. "I was a soldier."

She continued to eye him suspiciously. "Mm-hm. That's what you said. But I've known soldiers before and I think there's more to you than mere training at drills and guns. I saw it in your eyes when you were fighting. And the way you moved. It was different somehow. Better."

"I was a very *good* soldier."

"Just remember, St. Leger. I've got my eye on you. Cally's had her share of trouble. I don't want to see her hurt. And I'm not nearly as easy to best in a fight as Sam. You'll never know what hit you. You got that?"

"A threat, Miss Oakham?"

"Plain speaking. I protect my own and while Cally travels with me, she's family."

"I'm traveling with you."

Her lip twitched with reluctant amusement. "You look plenty able to protect yourself."

"I'm feeling hungrier already." He scooped up a forkful of stew, but Nancy refused to take the hint and leave. Instead, she seemed determined to remain, her stance unyielding, expression dogged.

So be it. Two could play at question and answer. He'd see how she liked being interrogated. "Who was your fancy man, Nancy? Was he a soldier too?"

She stiffened, but he noticed her hand drop to the apron spread across her growing stomach. "I don't need your pity, St. Leger. I'm not a softheaded maiden and I knew even as he was whispering sweetness in my ear that he'd leave sooner or later."

"Why is that?"

She glanced to the fire, where Callista sat chatting with Sally Sweet, and back to David, suspicion once more shrouding her face. "Because no gentleman is going to marry a peddler's daughter, no matter how much he says—or doesn't say—he loves her. Is he?"

8

Victor Corey pulled on his gloves and accepted a walking stick from his valet; selected more for the heavy knob of its handle than for the elegance of its design. One good swing could crush a man's skull like a ripe melon.

His coach stood waiting. A footman to open the door; another to carry his bags. A third waiting to place a hamper of food upon the seat beside him for the long trip. Hell, if he snapped his fingers, he could have a damned footman wipe his arse . . . or kiss it. All it took was coin, and he'd plenty of that. Enough to make this journey north both pleasant and fast.

He sat back against the cushions, tapping his fingers against the knob of his cane, impatient at the congested streets that held his progress to a minimum. Once clear of the city, they could fly, but now there was little he could do but dwell on the failures that had led to this unwanted journey. It should have been easy. St. Leger's height and looks should have drawn every eye. The man had a rugged soldier's build, and a face women wept over. He was everything Corey had ever dreamed of being—handsome, charming, sophisticated.

And it was all a lie.

Beneath that polished façade lay a savage beast. A predator that would rip your throat out or leave you bleeding entrails like snakes.

Corey knew all about monsters that dressed in silks and sported with princes.

He was one.

Perhaps he and the shifter were more alike than he thought.

He'd fix that easily enough.

He'd show the world what monsters were made of. A knife blade to the eye would destroy that golden beauty easily enough. A few broken teeth. Smashed fingers. A shattered knee. As long as he didn't kill the shapechanger, the blood would flow as readily from a grotesque as it would from a prince.

He could almost thank the shifter for making it so easy. For, once the Imnada was his, Callista Hawthorne would see what happened to those who disobeyed him. She would watch him cut her lover down to size and she would not attempt to flee again. Not if she didn't want those same knives to carve his initials into her even as he placed his ring on her finger.

She would take him as her husband.

She would open death for him.

She would summon him an army from the grave.

Or she would watch St. Leger hacked apart bit by bit, his screams the last to die.

The traffic moved more quickly, houses and shops

giving way to trees and fields. His coachman set the horses to and the world was a rattling blur of green and brown.

He had salted the roads with men and news of the shifter's supposed crimes. But, to be certain of his success, he'd decided to travel north himself.

He would be there ahead of them. His quarry would see the walls of Dunsgathaic rising up before them. They would believe they were safe.

And that's when he would spring his trap.

He rubbed a finger over the knob of his cane. One good swing to crush a man's skull—or a wolf's.

Nothing and no one would stand in the way of his destiny.

Callista sat beneath the shade of a spreading ash tree, finishing her lunch of cheese and bread and a few shriveled apples washed down with a bitter frothy beer passed freely among the company.

"Where's St. Leger?" Sam barked, wiping his hands on a cloth as he came from the wagons. "He's needed to help Big Knox mend that back wheel on the Perkinses' wagon. I'll not carry deadweight. He does his share or he leaves."

Sam hadn't stopped goading David since their arrival, offering him naught but barbed words and grueling work. David merely smiled and did as he was told, but Callista sensed the rein he barely maintained on his temper. Should he lose it, there would be more than a few blows exchanged. It would take only a trigger to unleash the shapechanger's lethal ferocity. Sam would be dead before he hit the ground.

"Maybe Pretty Boy got lost on his way to take a piss." Perkins guffawed at his own joke.

"Sam wishes," Big Knox cracked with a gap-toothed grin. "At least we know one place he ain't. Cally's right here with us. Otherwise, I'd say he was taking a few minutes to dip the wick."

"I don't think our little runaway would know what to do with a wick if it jumped up and bit her," Sally said with a wicked smile, fanning herself from a blanket under a nearby tree. "Look at her, just talking about it has her pale as a wheel of cheese."

"Maybe they had a lovers' quarrel," Lettice sighed, a hand over her heart as she turned doe eyes up at her husband. "And Mr. St. Leger's gone off to drown his sorrows."

"Wherever he is, it's none of our business," Nancy said, abruptly ending the conversation, though she directed a long, thoughtful stare in Callista's direction. "St. Leger works hard and doesn't complain . . . unlike some I could name." Thankfully, her gaze widened to scour the men and Callista no longer felt like a bug under glass. "He'll turn up."

"Like a bad penny," Perkins added.

Sam growled and stalked off toward the wagons, though not before raking Callista with a greedy stare that made her shiver. It was not the first time he'd looked on her like a starving man eyeing a three-course meal. Obviously five years had done little to ease Sam's desire for a wife. She pinched the bridge of her nose against a sudden headache.

"Did St. Leger tell you where he was going, Cally?" Nancy asked, maneuvering her bulk as she sought to stand.

"No," Callista answered with a sigh.

She'd seen him disappear, but one look at the expression on his face and she hadn't dared ask where he was going.

Nancy mumbled something under her breath and gave an exasperated shake of her head before heaving herself to her feet.

"I'll find him." Sally Sweet stretched and rose from her blanket like Venus rising from the sea. "He might be . . . hungry." Her eyes rested for a brief, challenging moment on Callista. "As far as I can tell, he hasn't been *eating* very well lately."

Callista smoothed a hand over her skirt to keep it from slapping the tart's face.

David might not be hers in truth, but she wasn't about to let a hussy like Sally get her claws into him. Not without a fight.

It wasn't that she was jealous. That was absurd. Jealousy implied a relationship, and there was nothing between David and her but friendship and a deal brokered out of desperation. Once she reached Skye, their arrangement would be completed. David would depart. She would move on. No more rambling conversations or teasing laughter. Never again would she look across a fire and meet his eyes in a look of shared amusement or feel his steady presence beside her across the endless miles.

"Enough, Sally," Nan snapped. "Take the bucket there and fetch some water for the washing-up." To Callista she said, "If you're finished eating, go find your fancy man and tell him we can't leave till he sees to that wheel."

Glad for an excuse to escape, Callista got to her feet

and followed the path into the trees that David had taken an hour earlier.

The track wound up from the road, a difficult rocky climb, and by the time she reached the summit, she had to stop to catch her breath. She stared out over the landscape of hills, stretching unbroken to the north and west. A flock of crows rose into the air from a thick stand of trees, and Callista shivered, her thoughts darkening.

Death, the crow had warned.

"I see my death in your eyes," David had explained.

As a necromancer, a daughter born of Arawn's seed, she stood within both worlds. Was it any wonder David would see shades of that truth in her gaze? Or that she might imagine a harbinger of the Lord of Annwn would offer answers to her impossible questions? There was nothing sinister about it and she jumped at shadows for nothing. Yet she was suddenly frantic to find David. She abandoned her study of the far distant hills and her own churning thoughts to continue across the ridge of the hill.

The track wound down into a hollow, the warmth of the open fields giving way to a cool dampness within the shade of the thick stand of oak. By now a stitch cramped her side, and her breathing came raspy from a throat gone tight and dry. Where could he be? Had Corey found him? Had he finally had enough of Oakham and decided to abandon her? Questions swirled as she hurried down the path. Perhaps she should retrace her steps in a different direction. Just one more corner, and she would call out, praying he answered.

Her strides lengthened until she was running, the

undergrowth reaching for her as the path narrowed. It swung past an old tumbled sycamore, crossed a dried streambed, and then . . .

Thank the gods.

She dragged to a stop, knees quivering. He was here. He was safe. She was being completely ridiculous.

She opened her mouth to speak. Thought better of it.

David sat upon a boulder, his back to her, head bowed. His left elbow was propped on his left knee. His left hand was spread as he drew a silver-bladed knife blade across his palm, the flesh parting in a thin crimson line, blood welling to slide over his open fingers. His shoulders jerked in a flinch of pain and she heard him catch back a gasp before muttering a muffled "Fuck."

Beside him on the log rested a cup, a handkerchief, and a leather wallet unrolled to reveal a few small vials and a flask. As she watched in horrified silence, he tilted his hand over the cup, the blood sliding into it one sickly drop at a time.

"As always, your timing is perfect," he said without turning around. He reached for the handkerchief, closed his hand around it.

Skin crawling, she took a step forward as blue and silver light rippled like shadows over David's body. "I thought silver weakened you and made you ill."

He slid the blade into a heavy leather sheath, rolled it into the wallet. "It does, but it's part of the spell. The draught doesn't work otherwise. Not that it works very well anyway."

"I can feel the magic," she said. "It's dark and reeks

of evil." A twinge creaked her sternum. "Not death but the Unseelie void, the pit where the blackest demons lurk."

"Funny. If you ask the Fey-bloods, they'll tell you that's where I come from." He turned toward her, and she saw his drawn face and hunched shoulders. "It's vile, filthy muck but it's the only thing keeping me alive—to a point."

"I don't understand. You said this magic was bound up with your exile and part of the reason that man tried to kill you in London."

"Beskin's his name."

She made an impatient gesture, angry at herself for worrying over him. Angry at him for keeping secrets. No good reason for feeling either emotion, but still her words came shrill as fear slithered up from her stomach into her chest. "I don't care a fig for his name, David. I want to know why he's hunting you and why you're ill and what's going on."

"Is it any of your business?"

"We're friends. Of course it's my business."

He gave a humorless, almost angry laugh. "Friends? Is that what you're calling it?"

"What would you call it?"

He stood, the bandage round his palm drawing her eye. Then he moved, and the strange blue and silver light fell across his face and shimmered against his skin, turning his gray eyes to silver. Her heart twisted uncomfortably, her body taut with a different emotion than worry, though one just as useless. As she had already concluded, David was not hers to claim or lose.

"I've never had a female friend before."

"We're just like males but we don't slap one another

on the back, consider bodily functions humorous, or discuss sporting events ad nauseam."

"You do have a dim view of the male species, don't you?"

"David," she repeated, hating the crack in her voice. "Please."

He hesitated for only an instant, but when he spoke, it seemed to her there was as much relief as there was sorrow. "Very well. You want the whole rotten stinking horrible truth? I'll tell you. I'm cursed, Callista Hawthorne. Cursed by a Fey-blood's spell. And death is the only thing to save me from its grip."

The wheel was fixed amid much grumbling, and the wagons moved ponderously back onto the roadway. David held the reins loosely in one hand, though he could have thrown them completely away and still the mules would have placidly followed the wagon ahead. The plodding, unwavering gait and the warmth of the afternoon eased the pounding in his chest that seemed to vibrate out along his ribs until his whole body felt squeezed by a giant's grip. He'd taken the draught, so it wasn't the curse that clawed at his innards and throbbed at his temples. It was the woman seated beside him, hands folded, body swaying with every bump and shimmy of the wagon.

Friends, she'd called them. That was rich. Friends implied trust, reliability, constancy, honor. By that definition, he was the epitome of enemy. Would she still consider him a friend when he bundled her into a coach bound for Edinburgh and told her to have a nice life? Probably not. But then, that whole plan held less and less appeal as the miles rolled on. Would she be all right on her own? Would her aunt take her in or would she refuse to acknowledge the relationship, leaving Callista without a place to stay or family to protect her from Corey and that odious brother of hers?

Did it matter? She wasn't his problem. She wasn't his responsibility. And she sure as hell wasn't his friend. He had friends, and he'd never felt about Mac or Gray the way he felt about Callista.

"You've stalled long enough, David. Are you going to explain what's going on?" She gave him a long look that allowed no vacillation. She would have the truth, and—Mother of All, friend or no friend—he wanted to tell her. The words seem to claw their way up his throat, hot and furious. He could no longer choke them back. Instead they spilled from his lips in between gulping breaths as if he were running, his hands tight on the reins.

"There were four of us," he said. "We fought together during the war. We were comrades . . . brothers."

"Was Captain Flannery among them?" she asked.

"Yes." David recalled the house outside Charleroi, the long golden fields alight in the afternoon sun, the bloody bodies scattered among the yard, the Chevalier d'Espe in his study, face aflame with vengeance made real.

"There was a Fey-blood. He recognized us as shapechangers. I don't know how nor what black arts he used to force the shift upon us, but he did. We retaliated as we'd been taught from the cradle. Fey-bloods are the enemy. And a Fey-blood who learns of our existence must die."

Her flinch was noticeable, but she continued watching him with those great dark eyes, shadows lurking within the murky depths.

"With his last breath, he cast a spell upon us. It corrupted our powers. Tainted our lives. We were no longer acceptable to the clans." He shrugged away from the memory, his back and mind on fire with a phantom pain. "We became *emnil*. Rogue. Less than the dirt upon the road or the smallest ant. We became nothing."

If the silence had been tense before, now it thickened like a blanket of ice. She no longer looked at him, but down at her hands in her lap. He sighed, ran a finger along a stain on his breeks, and wished for a bottle of his best burgundy.

"Is there nothing that can be done? No Other that can undo this spell?"

He snapped the reins, the mules breaking into a trot for a few lazy steps, a grim smile curling his lip. "I can't very well go about asking, can I?"

He didn't fear dying. He'd begged to be killed once until his voice had become a mere croak from parched lips. And since he'd begun taking the draught, he'd always thought he knew how his death would come.

Until Callista.

Within her gaze, he had witnessed a new and infinitely more horrible demise. One he could never have imagined in a million years. One he prayed was wrong—for both their sakes.

"Perhaps my aunt or one of the sisters at Dunsgathaic can help."

"Or perhaps they'll lop off my head and tar it for their ramparts. I suppose, either way, my problems will be solved." He heard the bitterness in his voice, and pressed his mouth shut. None of this was Callista's fault. And really, if he had to be running for his life, he was oddly pleased that she was the one he was running with. Perhaps that was the definition of a friend.

The wagon might have looked ungainly and enormous from the outside, but the interior was far smaller than Callista could ever have imagined. She stepped inside, the door banging her rear as it shut, cutting off the dancing light from the cookfire. Down the left wall ran a long, cluttered counter, shelves beneath. To the right trunks and boxes held props and costumes, and one larger than the others seemed to double as a table. A newspaper lay spread beneath a dirty plate and a stool was drawn up beside. Above, a soot-blackened lamp hung from a chain.

Big Knox was not exactly a superior housekeeper.

At the back of the wagon was a bunk on a raised platform, a curtain on rings that could be drawn for privacy. Callista's eyes settled on the thick mattress, scattering of pillows, and rumpled sheets before her eyes slid away, her stomach flipping as wildly as any of Big Knox's juggling plates.

She undressed quickly, afraid David would come barging in. Lay down on the bed, sheet drawn to her chest, wondering why he didn't. Had he decided to sleep outside again tonight? Had he disappeared into the countryside, his body sliding from man to beast beneath the light of the setting moon? Did he find her ugly, skinny, nosy, irritating? Would he rather curl up with a pillow for a rock than join her in this closet on wheels?

Doubts slammed her from every side, or maybe that was her heart, beating wildly and out of rhythm. Impossible to say.

Outside, the rest of the company retired for the night. Conversations waned, then ended. Doors closed. The fire was doused, its flickering glow no longer splashing pink and orange over the far wall. Silence, but for the creak of the lamp upon its chain. She felt herself drifting to sleep, eyes fluttering closed, mind rising out of the lumpy bunk to inhabit a dreamworld where she could arrange things just as she wished.

In this fantasy, David lay beside her, his body almost feverishly warm. He cradled her against his side, his breath soft on her cheek, his heart beating steadily beneath her palm. A kiss brushed her brow and she curled closer. Since her mother had died, she'd not had anyone to kiss her good-night. It felt good, like coming home after a long journey.

"*Ormeko mineai a'sitha*. Sleep well, lovely dreamer."

She frowned, her hand caressing the hard chiseled planes of a very male torso. Definitely not her mother.

A gasp caught in her lungs as she realized her dream had been anything but. David lay beside her on the bed—and not just beside her. She had curled into the crook of his arm, a leg thrown across his thighs as if she owned him.

She snatched her hand away, scrambling back as far as she could before she bumped into the wall.

A rumbling chuckle oozed through her like warm honey. "Ease yourself, Fey-blood," David said. "I may bear the soul of an animal, but I've not yet sunk to taking a woman unwilling. You're safe from my dishonorable intentions."

"You kissed me without my consent."

"You're safe from *most* of my dishonorable intentions. But see, both my hands are present and accounted for and all useful bits are tastefully covered."

She relaxed at the tartness of his tone. He certainly didn't sound like a man bent on seduction. Still, her skin prickled all over and a tugging ache stirred low across her belly.

"You did realize we'd be sharing the wagon, didn't you?" he asked.

"Of course," she replied, trying to feign calm. "I was standing right beside you when Big Knox made the offer. Though it's been almost a week. I suppose I assumed you didn't . . . that is, that you'd . . . sleep on the floor."

But there was no floor. Or rather, not enough of one after all the clutter to accommodate David. Only a very narrow, very tight-fitting bed where even the air seemed at a premium.

"Our companions were growing suspicious about our sleeping arrangements. Lettice kept asking if we'd had an argument, and Big Knox warned me that if this was how things stood before the wedding, it would be ten times worse after you had a ring on your finger. And I won't even tell you what Sally said, except to say I had to scrub afterward." He shuddered. "Personally, I think Big Knox only offered us his wagon to bait Oakham, the sneaky pot-stirrer."

"It worked. Sam looked as if he'd swallowed a mouse." She giggled.

"Poor bugger. He does have it in a bad way. Is there no hope for the poor bastard?"

She turned to face him; his eyes shined like silver

pools. "Five years ago, I might have said yes, if only to escape Branston. But now . . . he's too late."

The two of them lay quiet in the dark with the night sounds beyond the tiny window, the bed curtain drifting in and out with every little breeze. She rested beside him unmoving, his arm touching her arm, his leg touching her leg. She'd never been so intensely aware of the scratchiness of his linen shirt or the softness of his leather breeches or the smoky, soapy man scent of him in her nose.

How different this silent solidarity was from Victor Corey's vicious arrogance, his bruising touch and ugly words. Cold washed over her skin to replace the heat of David, and a small sound escaped the back of her throat as if the terror of that afternoon finally caught up with her now, days later. "If it weren't for you, I'd be married already—to Corey." She shuddered.

"Dreadful thought." His voice was quiet, but she knew he hadn't been asleep. There was a waiting in his body, a coiled tension.

"He's a dreadful person," she said. "He once claimed that together we would show the world what 'monsters' were capable of."

"What did he mean by that?"

"I have no idea, but with him anything is possible. He's obsessed with proving himself to the world. He thinks respect comes through fear and he uses his Other powers for his own criminal ends. Twists them and makes—"

David rolled up onto one elbow. "Other powers? The man is a Fey-blood?" The tension exploded into irritation and frustration.

"Didn't you know?"

"How the hell should I have known that? I never saw him except with your brother and I thought . . . Shit all!" Now the quiet was anything but comfortable as David's expression hardened. "Let's examine this," David mused aloud. "Corey wants a wife, but instead of buying himself entrée into respectability with some aristocratic daughter whose family's on their knees in debt to him, he chooses a dowerless, friendless nobody with the power to journey into death."

"I would be insulted by that remark if my intended groom were anyone other than Corey."

He grimaced. "The delivery was faulty, but the question remains. Why does he want you so badly that he sends his network of carriers all over England to drag you back?"

"You think it's because I'm a necromancer?"

"It makes sense."

"But I was already working for him—or as good as."

"But you weren't completely under his control. What if you wed another? Or left for your aunt's? There was always a risk."

"A slim one, as you've just pointed out. What man in his right mind would want me with nothing but the clothes I stand up in? "

The trees outside scraped and creaked, an owl called. David continued to watch her, his gaze as potent as a touch against her cheeks, her lips, her throat. "I can think of one."

"Sam?"

A pause. A breath. "That's right. Sam."

Why did she have the feeling a moment had passed her by? That something precious had slipped away to be lost forever?

He lay back down, his mouth kissably close, his eyes like new steel, burning almost silver in the darkness. Tiny shocks ran up her nerves to slam against her heart. She curled her fingers into her palms to keep from reaching for him. She licked her lips, afraid to breathe lest she surrender to the impulses firing like fireworks.

David chuckled quietly and she gasped, terrified he had somehow read the thoughts quickening her blood.

"Would you believe that a week ago, I was at a dinner with the Duke of Melksham, Lord and Lady Braunton, and Mr. Wissett from the Prime Minister's office?" he said.

She let out an enormous breath. "Yes, I would. You may dress like Sam and the others"—her gaze flicked over his clothes—"but there's no way you'd be mistaken for one of us. Your breeding is stamped all over you as clearly as if you had it written across your forehead."

"What if I let my beard grow, shunned all combs and brushes, and kept bathing to once a month, needed or not?"

"Not even then."

He huffed. "Killjoy."

A rush of laughter added to the fires already licking along her body. "It just occurred to me that I said the very same thing to Victor Corey once. You took my opinion far better than he did."

"I certainly hope so." As he sighed and moved beside her on the mattress, his arm brushed her ribs, his shoulder knocked against her elbow.

"Is something wrong?"

"Definitely. I'm lying in bed beside a beautiful woman and . . . chatting. It feels decidedly odd."

"You don't chat?"

"I usually find far more entertaining ways to pass the time with a lady."

"Perhaps none of those women were friends."

"Diamond-encrusted pit vipers would be more accurate, and no, I wasn't attracted to them for their sparkling conversation."

"Again, I think I'm being insulted."

Callista was crushed against him with nowhere to go. Her arms were folded against her chest, but that wasn't what made it so hard to breathe. Instead it was the light caress of his fingers as he pushed her hair off her face, the intensity of his gaze as he watched her, the slide of his hand down her bare arm raising shivers of gooseflesh.

"Not at all. In fact, I could learn to like this friendship thing," he murmured.

"You said I was safe from any dishonorable intentions." She tried to sound flirtatious, but it came off strained and awkward.

"Did I say that?" David cupped the curve of her hip, but he did not pull her close, merely touched her. His fingers were warm and strong through the fabric of her gown, and she ached without quite knowing what she ached for. "Then it must be so."

"What if I don't want to be safe?" she whispered, just a breath, soft and trembling.

"Wanting and having are two very different things," he answered. "I know that all too well. Good night, sweet Callista."

She rolled over to face the wall, rigid and hot, but now with embarrassment. "Good night."

*   *   *

He came awake with a gasp, his body crackling with unfilled desire, every inch of him painfully aroused. It had been so real. The scent of her in his nose and clinging to his skin, her body beneath him, writhing with need, her voice soft and urgent in his ear as he took her. But that was not what had roused him, heart racing and sweat crawling cold down his back. No, the dark images that had shocked him awake had followed after like a cloud across the face of the moon. Even now, they clung to his mind like damp streamers of fog.

Callista had been part of them as well, though there was nothing of passion in her presence then. Only heartbreak, pain, blood, and loss . . . and a void more infinite than forever.

He ran a hand over his face as his breathing and heartbeat slowed, the dream seeping back into the shadows that had conjured it. With all thoughts of sleep at an end, he rose stiffly. The night called to him, and perhaps if he couldn't shake the dream, he might outrun it.

"David?" Callista's quiet voice in the darkness tightened his already cramped muscles. "Where are you going?" she asked.

Desire lifted the hairs at the back of his neck on its way down his spine, and he fought the urge to pull her close and plunder her mouth with kisses, cup the firm round breasts beneath her gown, slide a hand under her skirts to touch the silken flesh of her calf, her thigh, the hot sweet junction between her legs. She would not cry out or push him away. He knew how to gentle a woman until she matched his urgency. Until she moaned soft and breathless. Until she guided him inside with her own hand.

Only afterward would she have hated him for it.

No, Callista was no bored matron or practiced seductress, and he'd not fallen so far as to seduce maidens—despite his reputation. His cock hard and throbbing, he forced his breathing to a slow even pace and did not answer. For while the vision of her tantalized, the darker dream burned like acid on the surface of his mind. And he would not take a chance on its coming true.

Friends was all well and good, but he would not fall in love.

He would not die knowing he'd failed her.

9

The book was old. Mildew stained the cover with green, fuzzy splotches, the binding hung by a few ragged threads, and it smelled as if it had been lying in a cave for a million years—not exactly out of the realm of possibility. David ran one finger over the four interlocking circles burned into the leather, then cracked open the pages. One drifted free to spill across the floor. He bent to scoop it up, scanning a few lines as if somehow that might explain its importance to Gray.

Ha! Who the hell was he fooling?

The writing, if it could be called that, had faded almost to invisibility. Columns of odd scratches and dashes, squiggles and dots, twisted and looped down the page before ending in a mouse-nibbled edge. He ran a confused eye down the page, stabbed one symbol among the dozens with a finger—a double crescent. The mark of the Imnada.

The door opened on a squeak of hinges. "David? Sam needs you to help with the mules. You'd better come—"

He shoved the pages back into the binding and slammed the book closed with a puff of ancient dust.

"What have you got there?" Brows crinkled in curiosity, Callista shut the wagon door behind her, eyeing the book with interest.

"I have no idea."

She clearly didn't believe him. Her gaze moved from the book to his open saddlebag to his face and then down to the floor. She bent and pulled a paper from the floor caught between a cupboard and the wall. "Is this writing or some wild, ugly artwork?"

"Again, I have no idea."

Now she regarded him with a mix of confusion and exasperation. "If you don't want to talk about it, just say so. You don't have to be deliberately obtuse."

"I'm not. I truly don't know. I told you, my friend Adam was the scholar. Mac was the soldier. And then there was Gray, who kept us all in line and out of trouble . . . well, mostly out of trouble."

She hesitated before taking a seat on the one and only stool as if sitting beside him might be dangerous. "Where did you fit into the mix?"

"I didn't." He cocked her a grin. "Still don't, though this"—he held up the book—"is their latest and most impressive attempt at persuasion."

"Persuading you to do what?"

"Make war. Make peace. I'm not sure anymore. Maybe they aren't, either. But this book has cost at least one man his life. I'd rather not be the next one to die for a few moldy, illegible pages."

"Die? Why would . . ." She frowned, her gaze locked once more on the book. "This is what Beskin wanted, isn't it?" she said. "He was after this book."

"Beginning to wish you stayed in Soho and took your chances?"

Her head shot up, mouth a firm determined line. "No."

He laughed before running a hand over the book's cover, feeling the burnt pattern in the leather rough under his palm. His expression darkened with his mood, a roiling twist of emotion rising up from his gut to tug at his chest. "The Fey-bloods know we exist, Callista. What they do with this knowledge is still anyone's guess, though if your brother and Corey are any indication, it won't be pretty. And what are the fucking Ossine doing while danger to the clans looms? The whoreson bastards are hunting their own people down and slaughtering them. The Fey-bloods won't need to lift a finger. We'll destroy ourselves."

His fingers dug into the book, frustration and fury crowding his vision.

"But, David, if Beskin is willing to kill for the book and you have the book, do you think he's still"—her gaze shot to the door—"following us?"

He took a deep breath, focused on the worry lines wrinkling Callista's brow, the shine of her hair in the light of the lamp, the hollows and curves picked out in the flickering light. It helped to ease his rage, but his frustration doubled. "Eudo Beskin is one of the Ossine's most brutal enforcers, but he's a scavenger. He prefers to finish the nasty job others have started for him. On the run, I stand at least a fifty-fifty chance. Seventy-thirty, hidden among Oakham's motley band of misfits. But it should be only a few more days. I've sent a message to Gray."

"And once the book is delivered, will you finally be safe?"

"There is no safe for me. No forever. The curse took that away." He shoved the book back into his saddlebag, buckled the flaps, and placed it back within the cupboard among Big Knox's painted silver plates and blunted steel knives. Flashed her a bright smile, only slightly ragged at the edges. "And on that happy note, I'll go face Oakham and his mules."

She grabbed his arm. "That's it? You just give up hope? Surrender without a fight?"

He slammed to his feet, the bed behind him too big, too soft, too close. Callista looked up at him with challenge in her eyes. What would she do if he took her up on her dare? It was a question he'd asked himself every night since they began sharing this rolling cupboard, lying side by side in a purgatory of sweet-smelling skin, soft curling hair, and luscious curves. Then he would close his eyes, the dream would come, and his answer would be clear as the death he saw over and over.

"Do you think I just rolled over and accepted my fate without a whimper? Damn it, I fought tooth and claw with every power at my command, Callista, and yet every night the curse overtook me just the same, twisting me against my will from man to wolf. And every dawn, blue and silver flames torched my flesh, and I shifted back. Dusk and dawn relentless, unstoppable."

"But the draught . . . it's a cure . . ."

"It's a temporary stay of execution, that's all. I take it because to stop is to die more quickly and more painfully. All my raging and all my struggle did nothing but tighten the noose about my neck."

She was either courageous or foolish, but she didn't shrink from his anger. Instead, her gaze burned brightly and she lifted a hand to his face, her touch cool on his fevered flesh. "Mac and Gray . . . your friends . . . have they given up hope? Or could this be the answer? This book you're carrying?"

"Mac and Gray are revolutionaries and dreamers. I'm a pragmatist. I play the odds and face the facts. I don't hope." He gripped her fingers, pulling them away from his face. When had this damn wagon grown so small? He could barely breathe. His skin prickled and danced in the presence of her magic. He felt battered and bruised, with nowhere to run and no way to avoid her barrage of unanswerable questions.

"What a horrible way to live," she said simply.

He offered her a gallows smile and a lift of his shoulder. "Yes, but definitely a far easier way to die."

Just before nightfall they'd drawn up on the windy brow of a long sloping hill north of town. By tomorrow, the place would be a crush of humanity as rowdy crowds moved through the maze of stalls and booths to gawk at the minstrel shows and wild-beast menageries, the fortune-tellers, chapmen, quacks, and cookshops. Already the place teemed with activity as farmers and herdsmen mingled with peddlers and prostitutes, and Oakham's faded and careworn caravans were forced to set up shop in an out-of-the-way corner behind the farthest sheep pens.

There had been a few hours of frantic activity as mules were hobbled and set to graze, water was fetched, and supper set to simmer over a hasty cookfire, but with the hour growing late, the troupe had settled into a state of resigned readiness for tomorrow's performances.

Callista sat with Lettice, the two discussing the latest fashions from London, the best way to scrub stains from muslin, and whether a husband's snoring could be grounds for murder.

"It's the most horrendous noise imaginable. I wake afraid I'm about to be devoured by wild animals," Lettice complained as she pulled another shirt from her pile of mending.

"You're the magician. Can't you just cast a spell on him?" Sally had joined them, her tone insolent, her manner sinuously attractive.

"I'm the magician's *assistant*, and no, I can't," Lettice sniffed, simultaneously threading a needle and shooting Sally dirty looks.

"Seems to me wives do nothing but complain," Sally said, dripping contempt. "If they were smart, they'd not wed in the first place. It's the first step to utter boredom."

"And what do you suggest? As if I didn't know."

Sally's sloe-black eyes snapped. "Criticize me all you like, but I make them pay for the privilege. A man appreciates what he has to lay out good coin to have."

By now Lettice looked ready to shove her needle into Sally rather than the shirt. "And when that beauty of yours turns to dross? You won't be young forever."

"I won't be spreading my legs for drunken fairgoing culls forever, either. I've got plans. I'm going to find me a wealthy man, one who'll set me up in a house and buy me a fine carriage and fancy clothes. He'll give me whatever I want for the pleasure of my cunt. And when he's ready to move on, I'll make sure he pays for that pleasure too. When I'm tired of doing for myself, I'll start up my own house, have girls who work for me. I'll be a grand lady then."

"You're mad. It'll never happen."

Sally squared her shoulders as if preparing to challenge Lettice to pistols at dawn. "You don't think so? I'll wager you're wrong and I'll back it up with a night's till."

Shirt finished, Lettice pulled out a pair of breeches with a hole in the seat. "That's nonsense. Am I supposed to wait twenty years to see if you find yourself some fancy protector who'll lavish gifts on you?"

"You don't have to wait. Cally can tell us. She's the fortune-teller." Sally swung an arch gaze toward Callista. "So, little runaway, will I find a wealthy handsome man and be treated like a queen forever after?"

Sally shot a hungry look toward David, who lurked just beyond the firelight, tinkering with the wagons, checking the mules, always moving, always apart. Callista had not been alone with him since their conversation in the wagon. If she didn't know better, she'd say he was avoiding her.

"It's the spirits that see the future, not I," she answered.

Sally sank down on the ground beside them. She even sat gracefully, her long legs folding, her blond hair gleaming in the firelight. "Spirits? You mean like spooks?"

"They show me things if I ask them, but it's not always the future. It can be the past or the present. And sometimes they only show me glimpses of their life; a snippet of memory they've clung to even in the afterlife."

"Yes, yes." Sally rolled her eyes. "I didn't ask for a lecture. Can you or can you not tell me my fortune?"

"I don't—"

"Go on, Cally," Lettice urged. "Show her. I could use a new gown with all that money she's bringing in."

Cornered, Callista had no choice. "All right. I suppose I can. Come into the wagon."

Sally made a brisk motion with her hand. "No, we can do it here. I want everyone to hear my glamorous future."

From the corner of her eye, Callista caught David giving her a searching look, but before she could give in to the urge to go to him, he had already turned away. "Very well. I'll just be a moment."

Retrieving her box from the wagon, she tried not to hear Sally's excited comments as she roused the others to the game. There was a grumbling murmur from Sam, a few interested side wagers between Edmund and Big Knox, and by the time she returned, the group had gathered and a crate had been upended for her use.

Opening the mahogany box with a set of the tumblers, she removed and placed each bell in order from largest to smallest; Key, Summoner, Blade. Then, taking a steadying breath, she traced a pattern on the crate, all just as her mother had taught her. The symbols swam in her head, the power behind them pushing out from her heart with every calm beat and every rise and fall of her lungs. She picked up Key, swinging it in a slow circle, the clapper's strikes vibrating along her bones and pushing the symbols ever outward, until her body buzzed with the strength of her mage energy. Frost chilled her skin. It glittered on her arms and steamed her breath while a numbing cold cramped her lungs.

She took up Summoner, the bell's metal glowing softly blue, the carvings within the bone handle smoothed with years. This she rang once, tracing the same symbols in the air. Her heart sped up, and she shifted on her seat to return feeling to her legs. Replacing Summoner, she took up her smallest and most powerful bell, Blade. She'd never had a problem, but caution had been drilled into her along with the stories of past necromancers who'd not walked the paths well armed or well prepared and paid the price for their arrogance.

By now the world had faded away like mist hitting the sun. Ahead, a path of tidy brick lay spread out before her, unrolling toward a far gray horizon. She stepped out boldly, feeling the moment she passed from life into death as an uncomfortable buzzing up her spine into her brain, where it prickled behind her eyes and made her teeth ache.

Trees lined the brick path, straight, sturdy limes like parade ground soldiers marching onward into Annwn. They wore summer's leaves, though steam curled from her mouth with every breath and her hands cramped with cold, the knife holding a patina of frost in just the few moments since she'd passed through the door.

Between each tree stood a statue of black stone, creatures grotesque and beautiful, horrifying and breathtaking. On and on they ran as the path continued for what seemed like miles. A house stood off in the distance, a great stone structure as gray and unwelcoming as the empty garden and the cold path. But no matter how far she walked, it remained always out of reach, a promise that was never fulfilled.

A glimmer of light flashed at the edge of her vision, all the more conspicuous within this gray world. She rang Summoner, its peal high and clear. The glimmer erupted into a burst of crimson and gold, purple and green, as the spirit responded to the bell's call. Trapped by the echo, its presence beat against Callista's mind, seeking escape.

"Who have I called?" she asked, tracing a third pattern in the air.

The glimmer lengthened and stretched until it touched the path, its form flickering and wavering but coalescing before her eyes. A female's form. Tall and slender and dressed in the hooped petticoat and bustle of a hundred years ago. "You speak to Violeta who was," she answered. "A spirit who is." The voice was as shimmery as the figure, sounding like the dying chime of a cymbal. "What would you have of me, walker of the paths, summoner of the dead?"

"I wish to see what you see."

The spirit glistened like beaten gold, the light impressing itself on Callista's eyelids so that even when she blinked, the figure of the dead woman shone bright as the sun.

"I see only death," the spirit answered, gliding forward until she overlapped Callista, hand over hand, heart over heart, two perfect puzzle pieces fitting one in the other. Locked in this twinship of spirit and flesh, Callista saw through Violeta's dead eyes, felt with her dead fingers, ached with a horrible empty pain that seemed to be constant with these restless spirits, as if their insides were nothing but yearning for the life they had lost.

Images flickered past like beads upon a string; a woman holding a fan of black lace across her mouth, her face round and pink-cheeked; a man with dark curls dancing in a room ablaze with candles; a bed surrounded by worried faces and hushed whispers, screams as if someone were being cleaved in two and then the piteous weak cries of a blue-faced child.

"Your past you have shown me. Now I wish to see a future. I wish to see what lies in the years beyond your living."

Callista opened wide her eyes as the ache blossomed in her chest to an agony and the world tipped and spun in a silver wash of stars. Her vision settled. A woman knelt, head bowed, hair a dark ripple down her back. A man approached her from behind, his face lost in the encroaching shadows, but the knife he gripped in a white-knuckled fist flashed silver. He reached for the woman as if he meant to embrace her, the knife sliding across her throat in a gleaming arc.

Callista gasped and lurched free of the spirit's aura, breaking the connection, dissolving the vision.

"I see only death," the spirit of Violeta repeated.

Shaken, Callista rang Summoner again, freeing the spirit from her prison. It hovered for a moment still in the form of a woman before shrinking down to a diffuse glimmer of light and flitting off across the gray lawn toward the dark house.

Callista watched the spirit glide away, wanting to chase it down, force it to show her a different future, a different vision. But a sound brought her head up in a swift catch of cold breath.

It came again, a lone, fearful howl that chilled her already frozen skin.

She retraced her steps, the tidy brick path of her arrival now a tangled, root-strewn track of beaten earth through dense briars and across shallow streams of sluggish gray water. Only the statues remained, their faces twisted in agonies, their bodies ripped and slaughtered. She sensed the buzzing, spine-snarling magic of the door, traced the final pattern in the air with hurried strokes of her tired arm, and she was through.

A warm spring breeze melted the frost upon her shoulders and in her hair, the fire snapped and crackled, throwing a rosy glow over the faces around her, and the raucous sounds of fiddle, squeeze-box, and drum from somewhere in the fair grated on her ears. She stared into the dancing flames. Took a sip from the cup someone had placed at her elbow, the burn of gin sizzling its way into her belly.

"You can't be finished already," Sally whined. "You just sat down."

Callista's fist wrapped round the handle of the bell, her fingers numb. "Time is . . . different in death."

"Whatever you say," Sally answered with an impatient flick of her fingers, "but what did you see? Am I covered in jewels and riding in a fine carriage? Does Lettice lose our wager?"

"You are . . ." Callista shivered. "That is, I saw . . ." She closed her eyes, trying to re-create the vision in her mind, to see it clearly, the hair—"an expensive carriage"—the way she knelt—"a fine house"—the way she cupped her outstretched hands—"and a man as rich as Croesus." Her voice shook. "I saw all of it."

Sally crowed her delight, but Callista barely heard her over the drumming of her heart as she sought David out. He had to be here. She needed to speak to him. Instead her eyes took in Lettice's miffed disappointment, Big Knox's wide-mouthed laughter, and Sam's always hungry stare, but David had vanished.

With trembling hands, she placed her bells back in their box, rolled the tumblers shut, and rose, hoping her legs held her upright. It couldn't be. She'd made a mistake.

"Are you all right, Cally?" Nancy asked softly. "You look as if you've seen a ghost."

She had seen one. And it had shown her, not Sally's future, but her own.

David reclined against a log, short stubby branch in one hand, knife in the other, no real purpose to his whittling but a way to pass the time and relax the knots squirreling his gut. The fire had long since burned down to a few glowing embers, but it was more than enough light for him to see by.

Callista slept a few steps away. He pictured her soft lips and soft skin. Every cell in his body burned with the image. He'd thought Beskin's sadistic methods had been agonizing, but the rat bastard had nothing on Miss Callista Hawthorne. Mother of All, but Gray couldn't reach them fast enough.

He slid the knife forward, shaving off a long peel of wood in a tight curl that fell on the crumpled map at his side; a map he despised with every fiber of his being. By its reckoning, they were still a good hundred miles from Addershiels. They'd been lucky so far, but luck was a fickle friend. Soon or late, she'd turn her face against them and danger would strike. The only real question in his mind was, who would find them first?

Another slide of the knife against the wood. Another moment to gather his thoughts and make his plans. Another moment he didn't have to be cooped up beside Callista with her hair tickling his chest and her body's curves melded against his own. He drew the blade toward him with a flick of his wrist and a brace of his thumb and swore silently at the first stirring of hairs at the back of his neck and the quickening of his pulse. He adjusted his grip on the knife, ready to spring before turning the move into a stretch, as Sam Oakham plopped himself down across from him with a drunken belch and a black stare.

"That's a good way to get yourself killed," David commented, itching for a fight to ease the tension crackling along every nerve.

The man grunted, drizzling the last of his flask into the fire in a burst of alcoholic flames. "By you, pretty boy? Not bloody likely."

"Throw a punch. I dare you," David challenged, a wild recklessness twitching his muscles and firing his brain. "Hell, I'm begging you to do it. Just one. That's all I'm asking."

Oakham snorted, his dark eyes boring into David. "I don't know who you think you are, but if I didn't fear being strung up for murder, I'd put a bullet in your brain and be done with it."

David refused to be intimidated. Instead he gave a bark of humorless laughter, his expression hard. "I'm sorry for Nancy's predicament, but don't confuse me with the horse's ass that abandoned your sister."

Oakham jerked, his great bulk almost coming off the ground and across the fire in a wrestler's throttling move. "Don't even speak of my sister, you poncy son of a bitch. You're not good enough to wipe the muck from her boots."

Here was his perfect excuse to be offended, to beat the crap out of a man who'd made his life miserable for over a week, and to work off his edgy nerves at the same time. Not that it would solve anything. He'd be as trapped, frustrated, and cheesed off as ever. And Oakham would hate him even more—if that were humanly possible. Instead, David drew his knife in another long slow peel of the branch, letting his fury run off him like water. "Nancy's a woman grown, Sam. She made her choice."

"What do you know of it?"

"I know she's been hurt by a bloody little shit, and I know you want to murder the weasely bastard. I would, too, if she was my sister. But I'm not the guilty son of a bitch, so don't push me unless you want to be knocked on your backside again."

Oakham folded his arms over his chest and stared into the fire, his voice laced with simmering belligerence. "Men like you think it's all a lark, a quick bit of fun when you're bored and looking for some sport. But it's not you that has to clean up afterward, is it? You just run off to the next party, the next bit of fun, the next woman to lift her skirts for you. You don't see the tears or suffer the cruelties when people talk."

"Nancy's strong," David replied.

"Nancy's blasted ruined!" Oakham shouted. "She's got a babe on the make and no man to wed her. And Cally's next. I ain't blind, St. Leger. I can see what's happening in front of my own nose. You're not running to Gretna Green to marry Cally. You aren't even thinking about marrying her."

David let the branch lie forgotten in his lap, the handle of his knife digging into his palm. "Cally's a woman grown as well. And she, too, made her choice."

"Aye," Oakham snapped, "but if she knew the truth, would her choice be the same? Answer me that."

David wanted to refute him. Hell, he wanted to plant his fist in the smug asshole's face—repeatedly—but Oakham was right . . . or would have been at one time. David had played for years with no thought to consequences. As an Imnada, he was bound by clan law to accept the bride picked for him by the blood scrolls. The strength and purity of the race depended on it. And after . . . his back twitched, his stomach knotted in memory . . . after he was pronounced *emnil* and cast out, broken in mind and body, what was the point? The curse had taken it all away.

The knife handle snapped. Blood trickled between David's white-knuckled fingers. "And if I did want to stay with her forever, but couldn't? If it was impossible? What would you say to that?"

Oakham spat. "I'd say you were lying through your teeth."

"Then you know less than you think, Sam Oakham."

David tossed away the wood. It had failed him. He was more wire-taut now than ever. He rose to his feet, mouth dry, need terrible. To hell with his promises—to Mac, to Callista—he would drown them all.

David strode the town's high street in search of a tavern. Or rather, another tavern. The first one had shown him the door after a brawl involving broken bottles, a smashed window, and three broken bones—

none of them his. It wasn't his fault. The three who'd accosted him had been looking for a fight. He'd been more than happy to oblige.

But now his buzz was wearing off. He needed more whisky to deaden his last remaining nerves. For that, a bathtub full might be about enough.

David snorted his disgust. What was wrong with him? He'd promised to get the girl to Skye. Nothing more. Once she was taken behind the gates of Scathach's fortress, he would return to London. Take up his life, take out his rage. And be taken in turn when the curse finally destroyed him.

End of story.

Callista was one of many. Nothing special. Nothing to turn him from his path.

And yet, when he closed his eyes, the dream was always there. A dream where she was everything to him, and his path lay strewn with blood and fire and crow-pecked corpses; where only his death remained constant. That never changed, waking or sleeping.

He drew up in front of a three-story, half-timbered building of mullioned windows, various levels of mossy roof, and smelly, gurgling drains. A battered, illegible sign hung from one rusty chain, but the stench of stale beer and tobacco smoke was unmistakable.

Success.

The scruffy interior held all the welcoming ambience of a murderous thieves' den, though it didn't seem to affect business. Crowds packed the place, peddlers and drovers mixing with farmers and fairgoers.

David waded through the hanging pall of smoke to take a seat at the counter between two bleary-eyed gaffers working on their gin blossoms. Accepted a whisky and a helping of greasy stew of nameless meat and gritty potatoes from a taciturn barman. He must have spoken. Words must have been uttered, but David heard nothing. Instead, he stepped around the counter and ripped the nailed broadsheet from the wall behind the bar.

"Somethin' wrong?" the barman asked, his words finally penetrating.

From the tone of his voice, the nervous expression, and the militant way the man gripped a heavy pint glass, David's shock must have showed on his face. The gaffers muttered between themselves, one getting to his feet as if in solidarity against a common enemy.

"Why, David. I thought that was you. You're just the person to see me safely back to the fairground." Looking like the cat that's caught the canary, Sally linked her arm with his. She nodded to the men. "Good day, gentlemen," she said as she guided David unresisting from the tavern.

Outside, he shoved the notice in his coat pocket, his brain turning over this new wrinkle, adjusting plans, picking through alternatives. Unfortunately, his whisky fog made that difficult.

"I'd stay out of town if I were you, Mr. St. Leger. You've done a fair job at hiding yourself, but you're not exactly inconspicuous, are you?"

It took a moment for her words to sink in. Then he stopped, pulling her to a halt beside him. "What do you know?"

"Only what's on that paper you tried to hide. You're not just haring off to the north to get hitched, are you?"

"You're a bright girl, Miss Sweet."

"I've had to be, sir."

"So what do you plan on doing with this newfound information?"

"You want to make it worth my while to keep my gob shut?"

"It could be arranged," he answered.

She ran a hand down his chest, gazing on him with undisguised lust. "And what did you have in mind?"

He ignored her hand and her invitation. "Once we reach Scotland . . ."

"*If* you reach Scotland. If the road north is plastered with those placards, it's doubtful you'll reach Newcastle without them catching up to you. I'd rather take my payment now, if you don't mind."

"I have a little money. Not much, but—"

"Who said it's money I'm looking for?" Her hand dropped lower as she leaned in. Her breath smelled of onions, her body of sweat overlaid with heavy perfume. He thought of Callista's subtle but pleasing scent and his chest tightened on a hitch of breath.

Sally reached up on tiptoe. "Come to my wagon tonight. I'll make sure Nancy's gone. You come see me and my lips are sealed about that little bit of paper there. Never saw it. Don't know nothing. Deal?"

An easy way to keep her silence. A simple choice. There was no reason to feel guilty or disloyal to Callista. Sally's fingers slid beneath his waistband, her tongue sliding over the curve of his ear. His stomach rolled in response as if the entire day's alcohol intake were about to end on his boots. He grabbed Sally's wrist, sweat curling down his spine. "Your price is too steep, Miss Sweet. I'll have to take my chances on your better nature."

She wrenched her arm away, her winsome smile turned ugly, eyes hard and lip curling. "Your loss, St. Leger. In more ways than one."

10

Callista came awake as soon as David pulled the blanket over the both of them, her body going instantly rigid, a hitch in her breathing. "Where have you been?"

"Out," he growled. "I know we're feigning an elopement, but you're not my wife yet."

"What's that supposed to mean?" She rolled over and sat up. "Have you been drinking?"

"Yes, but not nearly enough."

"What's wrong? Why are you so angry?" As she'd done earlier that night, she reached out to touch him with a hand that would be cool on his fevered skin, a hand that would make him yearn for more than this ridiculous fantasy they'd embroiled themselves in. But this time he flinched and she withdrew, her fingers tacky with his blood.

"You're hurt—again." She sat up, throwing her legs over the side of the bunk. "One would think you seek out trouble."

He sank back on the bed, closing his eyes. "I was

managing fine until someone we know took a board to my skull."

"So you just happened to be in that alley, David St. Leger? Or should I call you . . . Monster of the Mews?"

He opened his eyes to see her staring down at him, hands on her hips. "Figured it out, did you?"

"Two and two . . . I've always been good at sums. But why?" she asked. "Suppose someone caught you?"

"Someone did."

"Exactly. Why would you put yourself at such risk for complete strangers?"

"Why does anyone do anything, sweet Callista?" he answered. "It seemed like a good idea at the time. Much like this . . ." Before he could think better of it, he rolled up and off the bed to cradle the back of her head as he kissed her. She jerked once in his arms but did not run. He ran the tip of his tongue across the tight seam of her lips until she slowly relaxed into his embrace. He felt the mix of fear and want within her but carefully, delicately, he teased her into compliance. Her body slackened, her lips parted to allow his tongue to plunder the velvet within. Edging closer, he reached to palm the luscious curve of a breast—and gasped as a hot slash of pain sizzled down his arm to his fingers.

She jerked away, dazed but quickly refocusing. "I knew it was more than a scratch. Let me take a look."

"I'm fine," he said, though the wagon did seem to be pitching and rolling more than it ought—or was that his stomach? Difficult to tell after the insane amount of gin and whisky he'd poured down his throat, not to mention a disgusting brew that tasted like turnips but carried the devil's own kick.

"I'll be the judge. Let's go outside where I can see"—her gaze swept the cluttered wagon's interior—"and we have some space to breathe."

He sighed. So much for his famed prowess with women. He'd hoped for a courtesan and had gotten a nurse. He closed his eyes, jaw clamped tight, nostrils flaring in a huff of ironic laughter. Best to surrender to her ministering and get it over with.

Outside, the sky shone black as ink, stars high and cold. She sat him down beside the smoldering gray ash of the cookfire, whispered words under her breath as she fed it kindling and stoked it with the end of a burnt stick until the flames burned bright, dancing in her eyes.

Better flames than death.

"Do you have a healer's magic as well, Fey-blood?" The sarcasm was unwarranted, but his body throbbed from temples to toes, an effect that hours in the single-minded pursuit of inebriation had done little to curb.

"No, but you can't just let it fester. You'll sicken."

Before he could argue, she had his shirt off with only the slightest hesitation. Her expression grim and businesslike, she dabbed at the long, shallow gash just below his collarbone. The bleeding had stopped, but a thin trail of it remained smeared across his chest, the trail of her finger easily visible even in the thick gloom. "How did it happen?"

"The particulars are vague, but if memory serves, there was a drag hook involved. Must have been baited to catch fox."

Her body stilled, her breath catching in a ragged gasp as she clutched the rag, eyes locked on the gash with new intensity. "Fox . . . or wolf?"

He lifted her chin with a finger, forcing her to meet his gaze. "It was a coincidence, Callista. That's all. I should have been paying closer attention. Now that I know the lands hereabout are well guarded, I'll be more careful."

"Being careful would mean staying close to the wagons and staying human," she scolded.

He gave a bleak smile, his pleasant fuzziness fading as if it had never been. But that was always the way. He could run from the ruin his life had become, but it always caught him up in the end.

"I'm not human, Callista . . . not completely," he answered.

He covered her hand with his own, felt her soft skin, her fingers trembling. Lightning licked along his blood, shooting southward to his groin. There were only inches separating them, inches that closed as he leaned toward her, waiting for her to pull back, to stop him, to run for the safety of the wagon and lock the door behind her. She did none of those things. Instead, she swayed toward him as if strings holding her taut had been cut. Her lips parted, a sigh escaping as he kissed her brow, her temple, her cheek. He turned over her hand and kissed her palm and the underside of her wrist where her pulse fluttered.

"*Psiyo kr'ponelos toro.*"

"What did you say?"

"I called you a tall, cool drink of water. Something I'm in desperate need of right now."

"Come inside. I'll pour you a glass and tuck you into bed."

Now, there was a loaded suggestion fraught with possibilities, all of them out of bounds. But, Mother of

All, he was more than willing to indulge. Already he was rigid as a tent pole. "I think I'll just sit out here for a bit and, uh . . . whittle."

She folded her legs beneath her, a clever smile on her face. "Then I'll keep you company."

"Is this your friendly way of keeping me sober or keeping me safe?"

She cocked her head with a quick look of amusement. "Too late for both tonight, but we'll reset the clock and begin fresh from now." She paused, the smile dying. "Why do you drink so much, David?"

"It keeps me from thinking . . . or feeling. At least for a little while."

"But don't you pay for it afterward?"

He shrugged. "A price I find tolerable. Besides, I could guzzle a trough and it would barely affect me. It's one of the so-called advantages of my shifter blood. A head like a rock."

A dimple quirked a corner of her mouth, her eyes bright with laughter. "You said it, not me."

He drew a deep breath. The gash on his chest stung, but it was the throbbing between his legs that nearly brought tears to his eyes. He'd desired women before but never like this. Never with such a visceral yanking of every heartstring in his body. It made no sense. She was pretty, but not beautiful. She was smart, but no bluestocking. She was funny, but hardly a drawing-room wit. So, what was it that made him want to reach out and hold on with both hands? Her courage? Her patience? Her artlessness? Her smile?

"Are all Imnada like you?" she finally asked, breaking into the endless spin of his thoughts.

"Do you mean incredibly virile or breathtakingly

dangerous?" he asked with a rakish arch of his brows and a sly curl to his lip—a move that made the typical women of his acquaintance flutter their eyelashes at him in blatant invitation.

Callista laughed and tossed a pebble at him. "Odious man. How about exquisitely conceited?"

The curl of his lip broadened into a genuine smile. "Guilty on all counts."

An owl called from a nearby tree and sheep murmured in the pens behind them. He leaned back, a hand behind his head, and watched the crackle and dance of the flames. He'd done this earlier, but damn if Callista wasn't better company than Sam Oakham.

"I just mean that you seem so much"—she paused as if searching for the right word—"so much more than normal humans, or even the Other. Larger than life almost, as if you know a secret the rest of us don't. As if you possess some great knowledge none of us can even fathom."

"Perhaps we once did. It's said we were here long before the Fey. We don't have their magic, but we tend to be faster, more agile, quicker to respond to danger and quicker to heal when injured."

"And yet there are so few of you left."

"We bleed. We die. In the end, disguising what we were was the only way left to us."

"We're taught to hide our gifts as well. We learn early how to mask our talents and pass as nonmagical Duinedon." Was it a trick of the flames or did she shudder, her gaze growing distant, her face heartbreakingly sad?

"Or make money from them?"

Her eyes snapped to his face with a noticeable

wince of her shoulders. "That was Branston's idea, though it never made him the fortune he imagined it would. We always seemed to be one step ahead of constables and moneylenders as we traveled from town to town and fair to fair."

"No wonder you knew how to escape Corey. It wasn't the first time you'd slipped the net."

She made a small gesture, as if shaking off this uncomfortable train of thought. "Enough about my disreputable family. What of yours? Is there a gaggle of equally imposing brothers and sisters out there?"

"No. No one."

She waited. He could feel her held breath, her expectant silence.

Once remembered, Mother's words seemed to haunt him with their truth: "The wolf does not run and he does not hide."

He'd been doing both for the last two years. Hiding from his past. Running from his fate. It had availed him nothing but exhaustion.

"When my parents died," he said, his throat tight as the words moved like boulders up from his chest, "my uncle was technically in charge of my well-being, but he was an infantry lieutenant and barely around. When I told him I wanted to join the army, he was pleased as punch to arrange my commission. He died later in Portugal."

She drew her knees to her chest, the flames picking out the hollows beneath her eyes and the kind set of her mouth. "It sounds lonely."

"The clans never allow one of their own to be alone. The bonds are too strong between kin and holding. And each of the five clans is in constant communica-

tion through our *krythos*, disks that amplify our pathing far beyond their normal range."

"And you said you possessed no magic."

"They're not magic, or not as the Other define it. I
can't explain the *krythos*. They just have always been."

His hand still unconsciously reached for his far-
seeing disk, though less so now than in the first terrible weeks after he'd destroyed it with a well-aimed
swing of a hammer, gratified at the lovely crunch of
shattering glass. Unfortunately, it had been a short-
lived satisfaction. Much like whisky and women.

And even those two palliatives were losing their ef-
ficacy.

A lot like the damned draught, come to think of it.

"Between the bloodline ties and Gather law, even
the lowliest orphan is surrounded and supported by
family and clan. No one is left behind," he added.

"No one but you."

He reeled as if slapped, the breath knocked out of
him in a gasp, which he transformed to a quick bark
of cynical laughter. "Me? I'm constantly in company.
Either at my club, parties, dinners, balls, breakfasts,
salons, luncheons, and shopping. You name it. I'm
surrounded by people."

She ran her hands one over the other down her
braid in a nervous gesture, eyes locked on his face.
"Sometimes that's when we're the loneliest."

He rolled up and onto his feet. Strode away from
the fire, though there was nowhere for him to go. Hell,
he wasn't even wearing a shirt. But leaving ended the
conversation, or at least this conversation. He didn't
want to talk about it. Didn't want to think about what
he'd lost, only what he'd found.

"David?"

She had come up silently behind him. Or rather, he'd been so deep in thought and hazy with gin fumes, he'd not have heard a cannon going off in his ear.

"Come to bed."

"If I didn't know any better, Miss Hawthorne, I'd say you were trying to seduce me." He tried for scoundrel, but it came out sounding more like wronged virgin.

She backed up a step, though her gaze never wavered. "You'll have a good sleep and things will look better in the morning."

Did she speak for him or for herself now? There was meaning hidden behind her expression. He couldn't put his finger on it. Couldn't read her eyes, but it was there. A shadow of trouble.

"A tried-and-true remedy. Unfortunately, it's never worked yet."

"There's a first for everything," she said with a brisk cheerfulness.

When he looked again, the shadow had vanished behind a teasing smile. Perhaps he'd imagined it. Perhaps seeing things was the first stage in going blind drunk.

"The first time we kissed, you jumped a mile and tried to clobber me," he said. "How far we've come in a few short weeks."

She linked arms with him, nudging him toward the wagon. "We have, haven't we?" she said, casting him a sideways glance that seemed to drag his heart right out of his chest.

Dark turned darker as they entered the wagon. He tripped over a trunk, a stool, and a bag before she wrestled him down onto the bunk, pulled off his boots, and upended him onto the mattress.

"You've done this before. I can tell," David said.

"Branston enjoys his grain-based pleasures too."

"Brilliant. You're comparing me to your horrid brother."

"If it's any consolation, you're heavier, but at least you don't sing."

"Thank you . . . I think."

She grabbed a blanket and a pillow.

"Where are you going?" he asked.

"I'll sleep by the fire tonight."

He shoved himself up against the head of the bed. "You can't do that. I can't take your bed and leave you to sleep on the cold, hard ground. What kind of gentleman do you take me for?"

"I hadn't taken you for a gentleman at all."

"Fair shot."

"I'll be all right, David. You forget, I lived this life before. It won't be the first time I've slept outdoors. I enjoy it actually. I'll watch the stars and listen to the breeze."

"And freeze your ass off. Sleeping outdoors is terribly romantic in theory, damned uncomfortable in practice."

"And how does one of London's most eligible know that?"

"Creature comforts were in short supply between Portugal and Paris. And humble army scouts rarely rated them."

"You've never been humble in your life."

"Sleep in here. I don't bite. I don't snore. And I'm housebroken." She continued to hesitate as he held an arm open for her to curl against. "This is only because you'll fall on the floor otherwise," he said. "This bed was built for pygmies. Trust me."

"You had me up until the last," she replied, but she joined him, curling into the crook of his shoulder, though other than that slight submission, she remained uncomfortably wooden.

David lay still, breathing through his nose in an effort to ease his discomfort and keep his hands from traveling. His cut hurt, but it was a dull pain, easily managed. The greater pain was the one burning along his nerve endings.

This was madness. Callista was no different from countless others—faceless, nameless strangers he'd pleasured and left behind. Why did he restrain himself? Why did he not use every persuasive weapon in his arsenal to peel away her proper exterior? Why did he lie here like a lad with his first hard-on and no idea what to do about it? Did it come back to that damn friend thing again? She was not a friend. Never would be.

He had never wanted to peel his friends' clothes off one delicious inch at a time. Nor had he had the insane urge to kiss his friends senseless. Friendship was definitely not making every drop of blood in his body flee southward, leaving him woozy and reckless . . . or rather, more reckless than usual.

Damn it, he was just about at the point of hating his new so-called friend when . . .

"It's funny, but the closer I get to Scotland and my aunt, the more I question if that's what I really want." Callista rolled over so that she faced him, her breasts pressed against his bare chest, her legs sliding long and lean against his own. So much for wooden and awkward. She must have taken him at his word and decided he was harmless.

He didn't feel harmless.

"A little late to be second-guessing your future, isn't it?" he said, though his voice sounded rough as if he'd been running hard.

"You once accused me of exchanging one prison for another, of hiding from life. But maybe that's only because I didn't see any other choice. I couldn't imagine any other future."

"What's happened to make you change your mind?" He felt himself holding his breath, terrified of her answer and yet willing her to say it just the same.

She motioned around her. "All this." Her expression softened while hesitation flickered in her eyes. "I've never known anyone like you, David."

"You mean a shapechanger?"

"I mean a brilliant, amazing man who makes me feel like anything is possible," she whispered, caressing his cheek, the taut line of his clamped jaw, "that I have choices and that my future is up to me."

So maybe she didn't like this friend designation any more than he did. Still, he found himself clasping her wrist before she could rouse him more fully. If that were possible. "I don't sport with maidens, Callista. Only women who understand the game."

But, oh, how he wanted to make an exception to that rule. He wanted to taste her on his tongue. Make her scream. Feel something besides tired and sore and frustrated and guilt-ridden and lonely and bitter. Wanted to fill his heart with an emotion other than rage.

"So it's just a game to you?" she asked.

"Up to now, yes. With you, I fear it would not be." And wasn't that the whole damn problem? The blasted dream that haunted him, offering the glimpse of a happiness that could be before a brutal end. Horrible and yet heartbreakingly tempting.

"I'm willing to risk it," she murmured, her words hardly more than a soft breath against his cheek.

But you're risking me as well, he wanted to say. Instead, he cocked her a practiced grin, turning his back on the last tattered vestiges of his principles. Friend? He'd show her his definition of *friend.* Hadn't he told Oakham that Callista was a grown woman who could make her own choices? A small, tired voice at the back of his head told him this was wrong, he was wrong. The louder, more demanding bits of him drowned it out.

David murmured in her ear as he drew her against him. "Who am I to refuse a lady?"

Laughter bubbled up inside her. Only a few short days ago, she had worried about the repercussions of visiting David's bedchamber. Now here she was poised to hand him her maidenhead without hesitation. And yet, rather than running, she pressed closer, her stomach tangled in a million knots and her skin prickling with lightning.

Maybe she was hysterical.

Or shamelessly wicked.

She wouldn't admit that it might be a result of her journey into death and the vision revealed there. That meant she had to face the truth, and she wasn't quite ready to do that yet. Facing it—rolling the possibilities around in her head—cemented it in reality, and she couldn't acknowledge that she might be running straight to her own death.

If only she'd seen the figure behind her, some hint of form or glimpse of a face. But the shadows had obscured him and she'd not learned to wield her powers well enough to illuminate the hazy half-seen images the spirits offered.

Corey? Branston? Eudo Beskin? Or some as-yet-unmet adversary?

Would it be tomorrow? Next week? Ten years from now? No way to know.

Questions that would keep. After all, death held no terrors for her. It was a landscape she knew too well. Tonight, it would be enough to feel the bone-melting heat of David's kisses and the strength in his arms as he held her close.

His heart beat steady beneath her palm, so different from her own wild fluttering. And why not? She knew his reputation. She'd seen Lady Fowler's greedy stare and Sally Sweet's bold advances. No doubt there were half a hundred women who could say they'd been pleasured by David St. Leger.

"I don't sport with maidens," he'd claimed.

But he would have her here in this cluttered, smelly wagon surrounded by Big Knox's spinning plates and juggling sticks. She felt as jumbled and topsy-turvy as any of them. Tossed upside-down until she was dizzy with stomach-plunging excitement.

His face was lost in the wagon's impenetrable gloom, but she could see the clean line of his jaw, and his eyes glowed like ice in the dim light. David was beautiful. The hard planes of his body, the muscled perfection of his chest, the strength in his arms and the sharply chiseled angel face. And for tonight, he belonged to her.

For an instant, he froze, his eyes cloudy with some indefinable emotion. "You play with fire, Fey-blood," he said, his voice shaky, almost angry.

"I thought you'd say I baited a wild animal," she answered, trying to sound worldly despite her dry mouth and clammy palms.

He gave a sharp snort that could almost have been laughter. "That too."

"No one need ever know." He was so warm. The cool air raised gooseflesh on her arms, while he wore naught but a pair of breeches and still sweat damped his skin. "It will be our secret."

"You've traveled alone with me over hill and dale unaccompanied but for a rabble of traveling carnival players, that's all the knowing anyone will need."

He was right, but by now she didn't care. Aunt Deirdre herself could have stood over them with an accusatory glare and Callista wouldn't have been able to stop herself. An ungovernable desire sizzled through her like wildfire, casting aside rational thought. She had known as soon as she'd awakened with him sliding in beside her that this was what she wanted. If this were her one and only chance, she would not let it pass her by.

"If I'm to be found guilty of a crime, I may as well commit it." Her hand moved across his muscular shoulder and down over the puckered, burn-scarred skin of his broad back. Feminine instinct took over, making up for her lack of experience.

His teeth flashed in a grim smile. "I think my wicked ways have rubbed off on you," he murmured just before he lowered his mouth to hers for another of those mouthwatering kisses that left her head spinning. His lips moved over hers, his tongue darting out to tease until she opened for him.

Her body went lax, her arms tightening around him as if she could draw him ever closer. Still he kissed her, long and deep and thoroughly, until a whimper rose soft from her throat and she arched into him, her body knowing what it wanted, her brain along for the ride.

He pulled her gown from her shoulders, taking a breast in his mouth, tonguing her flesh until her nipples puckered, and she moaned, wet and aching; any lingering reservations swept under by the torrent of her racing desires.

"I could get used to being wicked," she whispered, fumbling with his breeches, impatient for sinful and sweet and scorching hot. For David in all his ruthless, heartbreaking splendor. "If you'd let me."

"My pleasure, sweet Callista."

His hand stole beneath her shift to caress a thigh, raising shivers as it passed. A brush of his fingers at the junction of her legs quickened her blood to boiling, and she gasped, eyes locked on his face. His expression bore a dangerous intensity as his hand teased and caressed. Tears pricked her eyes.

She needed him. Needed skin and sweat and fiery kisses and bone-melting caresses. She needed to feel him inside her, moving slow and steady. This was what the songs and stories spoke of; this wild forbidden exhilaration as her heart pounded in her chest, and complete bliss was a kiss, a stroke, a thrust away.

"Callista . . . are you . . . ?"

"Yes, gods yes," she gasped, guiding him within her.

He filled her as muscles yielded, nerves jumped, and her pulse roared in her ears. A stinging pain shot from her womb to her brain, and she caught back a quick breath, but then it was gone and there was only sweet coiling heat and a fierce, unrelenting urgency. He withdrew only to plunge deep once more, but this time she met his assault with her own, lifting her hips, the raw friction of their joining sending stars flashing across her vision and scorching every vessel in her body.

David gasped, his muscles hardening to granite, sweat sheening his face. She felt the moment he surrendered, as he drove into her in a final rush of release. She tightened around him, his explosion dragging her into the same spiraling ecstasy. She cried out, and felt herself falling, the steel in his eyes rushing to meet her.

The sky brightened from slate to pearl as dawn approached. Already, David smelled the smoke from Lettice's cookfire and heard the first stirrings of early risers. Soon the sun would rise, Oakham and the others would wake, life would resume as if nothing had changed.

David knew different.

Everything had changed.

Callista murmured in her sleep, snuggling at his side, a half-smile curving her lips, a leg slung seductively across his thighs. He'd gone against every principle when he bedded her last night. He should feel ashamed, guilt-ridden, and lower than low for taking advantage of an innocent under his protection. Instead he felt horny as an old goat and hard as a pikestaff.

Damn, but he wanted to take her again. To feel the soft, milky flesh beneath the ugly gown she wore. To caress the curves and bury himself between her thighs. A thousand times he'd played the rake and a thousand times he'd come away unscathed and uncaring. Women had moved in and out of his life as passions waxed and waned on either side. No strings. No regrets.

But then, he'd never actually lingered long enough to know any of those women. Never allowed himself know them.

Not their favorite book—Callista's was *Secret Avengers*, a torrid romance by Anne of Swansea.

Not how they liked their tea—Callista took milk and a revolting amount of sugar.

Not even their middle names—Callista's was Annelle, for some obscure reason having to do with second cousins and an inheritance that never materialized.

This knowledge transformed the spontaneous interlude. It made him see more clearly, feel more intently, enjoy more fully. It made him want to be the hero she saw when she looked into his eyes. Somehow, without his quite realizing it was happening, Callista had burrowed her way into his heart. Her likes and dislikes took up space in his brain. The smell and taste of her, her quiet reserve and dry sense of humor, the tiny crooked gap between her front teeth and the way she had of wrinkling her forehead when she was concentrating. All these things had become endearingly familiar. She'd become someone he cared about.

Someone he could love.

It made the laughter brighter. The passion steamier. And the idea of losing her devastating.

David understood now why Mac hadn't confessed the severity of his condition to Bianca. He might wrap it in altruism, but David knew better. It was a purely self-centered urge to keep the lie going despite all evidence to the contrary. To hold to normal for as long as possible, until fate stripped it away.

David had once sobbed and begged for death.

His pleas were finally being answered when at last he had found something to live for.

Someone out there had a lousy sense of humor.

11

Callista checked her appearance in the chipped mirror hanging on the back of the wagon door. She cocked her head one way; hair braided and pinned, shawl draped demurely over her shoulders, and color pinched into her cheeks. Then the other; was that a blemish on her neck? Were her lips a bit too swollen? Her eyes a little too bright?

There must be some telltale sign that she had spent the last night in sinfully delicious congress with a man, but she didn't see a noticeable difference other than a slight ache in her legs and a tingly thrill sweeping through her veins. Oh, and the smile that wouldn't quite leave her face.

She could attempt to justify her actions as necessary to maintain their masquerade. Could excuse her wantonness as a last-ditch effort to disgust Corey enough that he would abandon his plans to marry her. But no matter how she sought to justify her wantonness, the reality of her decision smacked her in the face.

She had wanted David more than she'd wanted anything in her life, and nothing else had mattered in those heart-pounding, jaw-dropping minutes of raw physicality. Not society's condemnation or Sam's jealousy. Not Corey's pursuit or Branston's hatred. Not even the spirit's dark prophecy.

It had been desire in its purest form, brought on by the thrill of sharing a joke, the comfort of feeling protected, and the joy of finding someone who understood her loneliness. How long had it been since she'd been able to open up to someone? How long since she'd felt appreciated not for what she was but for who she was?

Had her mother and father felt that same sense of discovery? That same uncontrollable need? The topic of her parents' scandalous affair and marriage had been a taboo subject in their house. Callista had known only what she'd gleaned from overheard conversations and street gossip. Mother had come from wealth and was destined for a brilliant match. Father had been a poor lawyer whose wife had just died, leaving him a young, unruly son. They met by chance. Fell in love and ran away to wed.

It sounded blissfully romantic, but Callista remembered only the aftermath of their reckless affair; the leaky old houses, the washing Mother took in when Father grew too ill to work, and Mother's wretched weeping after he'd died, a pile of returned letters from her family scattered across the floor.

If there had been wild, unruly passion to start, it had been quickly consumed by the tedium of everyday difficulties.

Callista rummaged among a cupboard, shoving

aside a pile of spinning plates, three wooden batons, and David's saddlebag to reach her satchel. Opening the traveling bag, she removed the mahogany box with its carved scrollwork and brass hinges and set it beside her. With a practiced flick of the lock's tumblers, she opened the lid. Ran a finger gently over each of the three bells before resting her hand on the packet of letters. A dubious inheritance, to be sure; the ability to walk in death and ten years of unanswered pleas for forgiveness.

Mother had never given up hope that someday her family would relent and invite her home. Not for her sake, but for Callista's, whose gift marked her as a daughter of their house despite their refusal to recognize her as such.

It had been a hope unrealized, but never forgotten.

Aunt Deirdre was Callista's last chance to make her mother's dream come true, and Dunsgathaic represented her last chance to escape Branston's manipulations and Corey's malice.

David had grown incredibly dear to her: a companion, a friend, and now a lover. And while she refused to regret last night, she would do well to keep a tight hold on both her heart and her head. Common sense warned her that whatever she might think she felt this morning, forever was more than kisses in the dark. It was sacrifice and pain and finding your way hand in hand through life's heartbreaks. David had promised her nothing beyond those few blissful hours. She wanted nothing more.

A knock at the door jolted her back into herself.

"Cally? Are you feeling all right?"

"Coming." She placed the letters back in the box,

closed the lid with a roll of the tumblers, and stuffed it back in the heavy satchel. Casting one last glance in the mirror, she stuck her tongue out at her flushed, sparkle-eyed reflection. Cautions aside, heart, head, and every other cell in her body were in serious danger.

The door opened, and Nancy stuck her head in the gap, brows arched in question. "Are you feeling all right? You've been closeted in here for over an hour."

"I was just . . . tidying up," Callista explained, scurrying around, flinging bits of clothing into a pile, straightening the tiny bunk, banging her head on the low-hanging lamp. "You know how messy men are. Like pigs in a barnyard."

Despite Callista's furious bustling, Nancy stepped inside, closing the door behind her. "I know this is none of my business, but do you know what you're doing?"

Callista looked up, a pair of stockings in her hand, an expression of bland innocence plastered on her face. "Cleaning?"

"I mean with St. Leger? Are you sure he's"—Nancy huffed an angry breath—"are you sure you want to continue on with him to Scotland?"

For one life-flashing moment, Callista was certain Nancy could read every one of last night's sinful acts on her forehead. Her guilt blossomed in hot splotchy blushes all over face. "Of course. I mean, I love him. Madly. Desperately. Don't I look breathtakingly happy? And . . . and thoroughly content . . . if you know what I mean."

Nancy regarded her as if she'd lost her mind, which, if she were being completely honest with herself, she would have to admit was probably true. "If you change your mind, you can stay on with us. There's room, and we can always use you at the fairs. I watched you read Sally's future last night. You'd earn more money in a week than Polly and her silly crystals could in a month."

A shiver of cold slid up Callista's spine, but she easily shook it off. What she'd told David was true: a bright morning was the best medicine for a black night. And this morning was particularly fabulous. Birds singing, flowers blooming. Even the breeze had warmed from the earlier chill that misted the valleys and glazed the high meadows with frost, as if the troupe had brought spring with them from London.

Callista continued to bundle stockings, three pairs of gloves, and a petticoat into a ball, looked around for somewhere to stuff them, and finally shoved them under a pillow. "If I stayed on, what would David do? He's not exactly suited to the life of a packman."

Nancy blushed but didn't back down. "No, but Sam is."

Callista swallowed. She really didn't want to have this conversation. Nancy had always been kind to her. It was hard to dash her hopes, but dash them she must.

Nancy didn't give her the opportunity before laying out her case. "I know Sam's a bit moody and scruffy as a bear, but he's a hard worker, he's respected, he's got a little money saved, and he has plans."

"I know, but—"

"He wants to set up a school in London. Teach boxing like Gentleman Jackson or give lessons in pistol play. All the wealthy nobs would come to him."

"A fine idea, if only—"

"You'd be a respectable married lady with a home and a housekeeper and a cook and maybe even a footman to carry your packages. How does that sound?"

"It sounds lovely, Nancy, except for one very big hitch. I don't love Sam."

"No," Nancy answered tartly, "you love David St. Leger. Is that right?"

"I'm running away with him, aren't I?"

Nancy merely offered her a sterner stare. "Or are you running *from* your brother? Big difference."

Out of clothing to fold or refold, Callista sank down on the narrow bunk. "What do you want me to say, Nancy? I can't make my heart obey common sense. It doesn't work that way and you of all people should know as much."

She sucked in a breath. Had she really just said that out loud?

If Nancy's needle-sharp gaze was an indication, the answer would be yes. Callista had an overwhelming wish for a hole to open up beneath her feet before the other woman tore her into itty-bitty pieces.

Instead Nancy nodded as if she knew Callista would say this and was prepared for it. "I wasn't going to say anything, not until I talked to you, but I think you need to see this before you make a huge mistake." She handed Callista a piece of heavy paper folded and refolded again. "I saw it on a signboard in the last village."

Callista unfolded the broadsheet to find herself staring at a crude penciled likeness of David. She scanned the paragraph beneath with a sinking stomach. "It's not true," she said firmly.

"Which? The murder, the kidnapping, or the embezzlement?"

"These are lies spread by Branston. He's hoping someone will turn us in for the reward offered."

"Why does he want you back so badly? I thought he hated you."

"He did . . . he does."

"That money's enough to keep our troupe in funds for a year."

Callista crushed the notice in her hand. "Then what are you waiting for?"

Nancy shrugged. "I wanted to talk to you first. See if I could get you to come to your senses and realize St. Leger's not the man for you. But he's dazzled you stupid. Just remember"—she waved a hand over her stomach—"this is what life looks like after he's deserted you for greener pastures." She wrenched open the door.

"Wait!"

Nancy turned back.

"Give me time to think about what you've said before you make a decision about turning him in. Just pretend you don't know anything and haven't seen the notice. Can you do that?"

"I'll give you a day, but then I'm going to Sam to tell him what I know," Nancy said before departing with a hard slam of the wagon door.

Callista dropped her head in her hands, as drained as if she'd fought a battle. Just when she thought she'd slipped his grasp and was finally free of him, Branston managed once again to cast his sinister shadow. It had always been this way. She'd escaped three times and never reached farther than a few streets from home before he pulled her back into his seedy and scheming world. David's arrival had changed that. His arrival had changed so many things.

And now he was in danger because of her.

Should she show him the notice? Should she hide it while she decided whether or not to accept Nancy's offer? Should she tear it into bits, in the hope that it was the only one of its kind?

A knock brought her head up. "I'll be out in a minute, Nancy."

But it wasn't Nancy who opened the door.

It was David.

"Nancy said you needed to speak to me." He looked as sheepishly ill at ease as any man could.

She sighed. "You might want to see this."

"The Fealla Mhòr is starting all over again. The war between Imnada and Other. And this time, if the lot of you have your way, you'll finish what you started. There won't be anyone left or anywhere to run." He didn't even try to keep the bitterness from his voice as he gripped the broadsheet. "Mac and Gray were fools to ever think they could create a new peace between us."

Callista bristled. "You make us sound like inhuman monsters."

He flung the notice on the bunk beside her. "I'm simply returning the compliment."

"This is Branston and Victor Corey. It has nothing to do with Fey-bloods and shapechangers."

"Doesn't it? Then why aren't you even mentioned? They're not searching for a man and a woman traveling together. They're searching for me, the savage killer and seducer of innocent maidens."

Scarlet crept up her neck and across her cheeks, but

her gaze remained steady, as if she were daring him to refer to last night. He wanted to, knew he should, but for the first time, all his practiced polish failed him. This was not a high-priced whore to be bought off with an expensive bauble nor a wayward wife in search of a few hours' pleasure outside of the marriage bed. He'd stepped beyond boundaries he'd marked out long ago and straight into a mess of his own making.

Callista was courageous and commonsensical, vulnerable and vibrant. She was the complete antithesis of his usual bedmate. Perhaps that's why he had absolutely no idea what to say to her or where they went from here. For all his simmering rage, he could almost thank Corey for the diversion.

"Nancy has given me a day to decide."

"Good. That gives us twenty-four hours to make arrangements." A horrible thought occurred to him. "Unless you've chosen to accept Sam's suit."

"I don't love Sam Oakham."

"Marriages are rarely about love. The Imnada have their mates chosen for them by the Ossine, who match man and wife based on bloodlines and clan requirements."

"How callous."

"No more so than the aristocracy who base their marriages on property and political connections."

"Both sound heartless and horrid."

"What would sway *you* to wed?"

"My parents wedded because they loved one another more than they feared what people would say. They defied family and friends in their desire to be together, and you couldn't help but feel the electricity between them. That's the kind of marriage I'm looking for."

"That's a rare treasure few ever find."

"Captain Flannery and his wife found it."

"They did, but it will be a short-lived joy. The curse will destroy Mac like it's destroying me. Bianca will be a widow—again. But this time she'll have lost her soul mate."

"She'll have their child, though. A living tribute to that love."

"Will it be enough? When her bed is empty and she cries herself to sleep thinking of the barren years ahead, will she still believe that loving Mac was the right choice, or will she rue the day she laid eyes on him?"

Golden sparks surfaced in Callista's eyes. "My father died when I was ten. My mother gave up everything for the promise of an eternity with the man she adored and instead was left with a headstrong daughter, a stepson who despised her, and barely money to keep a roof over our heads. But she told me once she never regretted her decision to risk everything for love."

She rose to her feet, trapped between the bunk and his body with only inches to spare. "She said it had all been worth it for the memory of perfection."

He inhaled a shuddering breath, his chest tight against the ache in his heart. He caressed her cheek where a loose curl brushed against his skin, and then the slender column of her throat.

She closed her eyes, a tear leaking from beneath her lashes to slide into the corner of her full pink lips. "I finally understand what she meant."

Somehow, without talking about it, both of them had known exactly what to say.

*   *   *

The crowded fairground teemed with activity: a cacophony of shouts, screams, bells, bands, growls, curses, drums, pistol shots, and fiddles running one into the other until there was naught but a constant, deafening roar.

Callista had hastily converted the wagon into a replica of Oriental bazaar meets Romany Gypsy fortune-teller—from under a cushion she pulled a rotten apple core wrapped in a dirty handkerchief—meets boys' public school dormitory. And while it was not exactly the overbearing cloying elegance of the house in Soho, its single candle and close-set chairs made for cozy intimacies, as if half of North Riding were not just beyond the door.

The fashionable young woman sitting across from Callista held a lace handkerchief to her nose, but no amount of expensive perfume could eradicate the odors of manure, sheep, fried food, smoke, privies, alcohol, and sweat blanketing the still air like a fog. Only time and familiarity could do that, and a mere twenty-four hours into the fair, Callista barely noticed the stench. Just as she barely noticed the uncomfortable endless hours traveling, the awkwardness of sharing close quarters with a half dozen strangers, or the press of seething humanity at every stop along the road north. The last week and a half living among Oakham's Follies and it was as if she'd never left.

She glanced down at the bells lined up on the table and then back to the sweet, innocent dewy-eyed face across from her. But it was the young woman's husband who spoke, a man of means by the cut of his coat and the cut of his vowels, but as pink-cheeked and naive as his wife. Dupes waiting to be fleeced.

"It sounds like madness, but she believes it, and that's all that counts, Miss . . ." He groped for a last name Callista didn't offer.

The woman leaned across the table, her fingers trembling. "He haunts me. He comes to me in the night. I hear him crying, but no matter how I search I can't find him." Dark circles smudged the flesh beneath her eyes. Her cheeks were sunken, the skin sallow.

A child. Callista should have known as soon as Sam beckoned them into the caravan. A young couple hand in hand. Grief etched in their faces and weighing heavy on their frames.

"Annwn is well guarded, but sometimes a spirit will find a way back into this world," Callista explained. "Most are harmless or, like your son, have lost their way and don't realize they've slipped back into life."

"Most?" The woman's voice dropped to a whisper.

The flicker of the candle cast a leaping shadow upon the walls as Callista leaned forward. "There are darker things in the underworld than spirits of the dead, Mrs. Stockton. Why do you think Arawn keeps such a close watch?"

The woman's big blue eyes widened to saucers. "I . . . I thought heaven was a nice place, a beautiful paradise. That's what the vicar says. Why would dark things live there?"

"Death is a single realm made up of countless paths leading to infinite places, both beautiful and terrible."

Mrs. Stockton nodded as if Callista had imparted

a wisdom for the age. Her husband's expression, however, was one of indignation rather than belief. "I don't need a theology lesson. All I want is an end to these episodes. My wife won't sleep. She barely eats. I worry for her mind if you can't relieve her suffering."

"I'll do my best."

"Can you let him know I love him, Miss? Can you tell him his mama will always love him?" Mrs. Stockton pleaded, her voice high and trembling.

"The man outside said it cost two shillings. Do I pay you?" Mr. Stockton pulled out a change purse.

Callista felt her insides tighten. She hated handling the money. It made her feel no better than the charlatans hawking love philters or magic elixirs to eradicate the French disease.

Is this what her life would be should she choose to accept Nancy's ultimatum and join the troupe? An endless stream of bereft parents and heartbroken lovers hoping for a final communion with their loved ones? Giggling, blushing maidens wanting to know if the spirits could tell them who they would wed and swaggering, ruddy-faced farmers' sons looking for next season's Derby winner? All accomplished to the tuneless background cacophony of a fair's mad delights?

She shuddered to think. Yet if she refused, Nancy would turn David over to Corey's men.

An impossible choice.

David had spoken of a noose tightening about his neck. Was this what it felt like? This inability to catch her breath, a hard knot lodged in her throat, and a pounding headache?

When the man held out his coins, she swallowed

back her distaste and took them, dropping them into her apron pocket.

"Let's begin."

"For the third and final time, where's Callista?" David demanded. Oakham's pugnacious attitude was wearing at the best of times. After a morning spent haggling over two mounts even a knacker would shun and another interminable hour attempting to maneuver through the crush of humanity blocking the roads, David found it damned irritating.

Oakham scoured him with a belligerent glare. "Working."

"I need to speak with her."

"You'll have to wait. While you've been gadding about town, she's been earning the bread you eat and the bed you sleep on. I'd be grateful if I were you."

That was the last fucking straw. David's fist clenched, his stance braced for battle, and only a hand upon his forearm kept him from laying Oakham flat on his back in the dust. Nancy playing peacemaker again. She dragged David away before he could satisfy his urge to send Oakham into next week.

"She's with someone. Is it important?"

Of course it was bloody important. And the reason stood looking at him like he was some sort of butterfly-crushing, puppy-drowning fiend. Corey had accomplished what he'd set out to do—flush his quarry out of hiding. Once they left the troupe, it would be a race to Addershiels, one step ahead of every blighter in hopes of a fifty-pound reward. With the two knock-kneed nags he'd purchased, his odds were as long as

Rosemary Lane to a ragshop that they'd make it there unscathed.

"I'll wait." He spun on his heel, pushing his way through the crowd. His first thought was whisky. His second thought, hard on its heels, was Callista. His thirst died with a sick roll of his stomach.

For some reason, Nancy Oakham decided to follow. She kept pace, her condition in no way impairing her ground-eating stride. She eyed him like a disease with her too-shrewd gaze. "I don't begin to understand who you are or why you've dragged Cally into your mess, but she deserves better. She deserves someone who'll care for her. Who'll protect her and be good to her."

"Someone like your brother?"

"Why not? He's not rich or elegant and he doesn't act all high in the instep, but he's got a good heart and he'd make Cally a good husband. If you cared at all for her, you'd see that."

Was Nancy right? Marriage to Oakham would definitely thwart Hawthorne's and Corey's plans, and if anyone could defend his wife against all comers, the burly showman could. David had witnessed the man's crack ability with knife and pistol during the few shows he'd performed on the road, and David knew the weight of his fists firsthand. Besides, if he left Callista behind, his odds on reaching Addershiels alive grew exponentially. She would be better off here, among people who cared about her. She would have a home. She wouldn't be alone anymore.

"You and your brother love each other very much," he said.

Nancy's eyes widened, but she gave a jerk of a nod.

"Course we do. We're family. Family take care of one another no matter what."

He'd had a family once. And a clan. People who loved him. People who were there when he needed them.

He thought of Mac and his steadfast courage against the impossible. He thought of Gray and his hope when all seemed hopeless. And his heart squeezed uncomfortably in his chest when he remembered Adam, dead almost a year now, and the terrible words David had spoken that he'd never had a chance to take back.

The three of them had irritated David and angered him and driven him mad at times, but they had never once deserted him. Could he do any less now when they needed him?

". . . and leave before things go any further."

His hand dug into his pockets, coming up against the torn and crumpled notice.

"Before things go any further."

Too late. They'd already moved far beyond Callista. It was personal now.

Someone wanted *him*.

Someone wanted the Imnada.

A scream threw his heart into his throat and sent his hand reaching for a nonexistent sword.

"That's Cally." Nancy took off at a half run, dodging some and thrusting others aside in her haste. David followed, fists clenched, nerves thrumming under his skin.

A pretty, blond woman stumbled out of the wagon, a handkerchief clutched to her mouth. A man followed, his gaze wildly scanning the crowd as if seeking assistance. He saw Nancy approaching with obvious relief. "Something's wrong. I touched her and she was . . . she was stone cold. I think she's dead . . ."

He babbled on, arms gesticulating, the woman by his side sobbing uncontrollably into her drippy handkerchief. David pushed past and into the wagon, leaving Nancy to handle her hysterical customers. Moving from bright light to darkness, he was blinded for a moment. He tripped and stumbled over an overturned chair, grabbing the table to steady himself. The candle flickered wildly while the bells set in a row before Callista clanked and rattled, one falling into her lap. She made no move to retrieve it. Instead she remained completely still, her lips tinged blue, her eyes a shimmering, iridescent gold, as if the heat of the sun boiled in her gaze.

"Callista?" He touched her hand where it rested on the handle of the largest bell. Not the cool moist give of death. Instead her flesh was as cold and white as marble, frost riming her hair and powdering her shoulders. He felt for a pulse, expelled a relieved breath to feel the flutter of her heart beneath his fingers.

"Callista, it's time to come back." He knelt beside her, cupping her face in his hands. "Look at me, Feyblood. Hear me."

Tears formed at the corners of her eyes, tracking slowly down her pale cheeks before freezing like diamonds at the corners of her mouth.

Frightened now, he shook her by the shoulders. "Damn it, Callista, wake up."

Nothing.

Again. More roughly this time, his fingers growing numb where they touched her bare flesh, his stomach curdling into a tight ball. He'd never seen a necromancer at work, but surely this shouldn't happen. This couldn't be normal. What if she never woke? What if she was trapped in death forever?

12

The path wound. Turned and turned again. Right or left? She couldn't remember. The thick trees obscured her view ahead and behind, and the landmarks she'd noted to guide her back had faded as if they'd never been.

The right path descended into a thick wood. The left rose to a high ridge before disappearing. Neither seemed familiar. She shouldn't have come so far. The landscape was foreign, the twining paths looping and circling back. She had wanted to lead the Stockton child's spirit deep into death, where it could not find its way back out. Now she was lost as well.

She chose the right-hand fork, hurrying down the slope and beneath the trees. Here within the deeper reaches, the paths were either strewn with rocks and exposed roots or sucking, quivering bogs one must traverse with care. The trees reached their black and skeletal branches to grab and harry, and there was always the threat of dangerous beings who would be drawn to her warmth and her light. She'd never en-

countered one, but Mother had described them all in
gory detail, making certain Callista understood the
danger—shambling, mindless grel and rotting, worm-
riddled dead-flesh, the ghostly, shrouded soul eaters
with their reaching bony hands, and phantasms whose
eerie wails sounded like the screams of a million condemned souls; the world's nightmares made real.

The path narrowed, the footing treacherous. Beneath the trees, even the dim gray light faded to darkness. A prickle teased its cold way up her spine as if
something watched from the undergrowth. She peered
through the gloom, here and there catching a glimmer
of light, a whisper in her ear. Spirits flickered like will-
o'-the-wisps to lure her from the trail. Tempting her to
new paths and untried roads as she struggled to find
her way back to life.

She ignored the pull of their call, keeping to the
rocky path, praying it led her somewhere recognizable
before the cold or the creatures found her. Rounding a
bend, she staggered to a halt, gazing out over a greasy
gray bog, the water slick and still. Had she come this
way? She couldn't remember. But there was no turning around. The spirits closed in behind her and every
now and then, she heard a fearsome growl or an inhuman shriek from the wood behind. Her presence had
been discovered. The creatures of Annwn closed in.

She stepped carefully into the thick, oozing mud,
sinking up to her ankles, her gown slapping against
her legs as she moved slowly out toward the far shore
where the trees gripped firmer earth. With the ash-
handled Blade in her hand, she felt her way a step at
a time despite the panic eating its way up through her
gullet.

A ripple slid across the surface to her right; a shape rising and falling into the mud. She increased her pace as much as she dared, but the bog clung, sticky and cold; her stomach cramped against the icy pain, and there was no feeling in her calves.

Twenty paces away from the shoreline. Ten. The ripples moved toward her like an arrow loosed from a bow. She cried out, shoving herself onward through the glutinous sludge. Five paces. She was lurching for a scaly green branch to drag herself up and out, when the surface peeled away to reveal a long, eel-like creature. Its limbs were jointed at odd places—no normal creature had four elbows and three knees. But it was the face that was truly horrifying. A human skull, though the features seemed oddly askew and drooping, as if the flesh had melted. Its mouth was a wide gash showing rows of needle-sharp teeth; it had two vertical slits for a nose, and eyes round and white though clearly focused on her as it rose up out of the bog with a high-pitched, glass-shattering scream.

Her mother had called them grel—no earthly spirit to be frightened with a banishment spell traced in sound from Blade, the bell clutched in her fist. This was a creature of darkness and murder and disease and pain; a foul denizen of the deepest pits of Annwn that hungered for life and human flesh. Safe in her bed, Callista had shivered with delight upon hearing her mother's tales of these creatures. Trapped within the tangled maze of Annwn's realm, her shivers turned to racking, pulse-racing shudders.

She swung around, her lungs burning, her legs clumsy and slow as she fought to escape. Trees scratched and clawed at her face, tugged at her gown. The grel lumbered behind her, its grasping arms reaching for her, claws long as scythes.

The path turned again. She knew this hedge. She'd passed that fallen log. The trees thinned, and she was back on familiar ground. The path broadened to a wide bricked track lined with stately limes. She was steps from the door that would take her back into the world of the living.

The grel broke from the woodland behind her, its bloody mouth drawn back from ear to ear as if someone had opened its skull with a sword, its screeching like claws down a slate, its breath an icy burn on her neck and arms.

It was joined by a second grel, and by one of the dead-flesh, shrouded in a black bloodstained cloak, a face half-pecked, an eye hanging loose from a socket, entrails spilling like greasy snakes from its belly. She stumbled and the closest grel stretched to lash her across the back with one of its long hooked claws, even as the dead-flesh reached with a hand, the skin sloughing away from the bone as it grabbed her around her wrist.

She sketched the signs that would call Key to her hand. Closed her fingers around the ebony handle and rang it once. Then twice more. The door opened. She slid through, slamming the passage closed behind her as agony ripped behind her eyes and wrenched a scream from her knotted throat.

"How do you feel?" David sat on a stool, knees drawn to his body, looking exceedingly uncomfortable. His face was carved with tired lines, a grayish cast to his skin. But his eyes shone like pewter seas.

"Sore," she replied.

The colorful, gauzy scarves festooning the caravan still drifted above her head, but the table had been shoved into a corner, cloth torn, candle wax smeared, and a long singeing burn near the hem. She lay on the bunk, a pillow beneath her head, the smell of un-washed sheets wrinkling her nose.

"No lasting damage? Broken bones? Internal bleeding?" he asked, his tone brisk and physician-like. She couldn't decide whether she was annoyed, relieved, or still reeling from a bad knock to the head.

She inhaled slowly, feeling nothing worse than a tightness in her chest and an ache low across her back. Bracing a hand against the edge of the pallet, she eased herself over, teeth clamped. "I don't think so."

"Good. I'm glad one of us is feeling all right, because my damned heart stopped. What the hell happened?"

She gripped her head lest her brains ooze slowly out her ears. "Don't yell at me."

"I'm not yelling. I'm asking . . . loudly."

"Sounds an awful lot like yelling to me," she grumbled.

"Is this better?" he asked quietly through grinding teeth.

"Not much."

He closed his eyes, took a deep breath, and opened them again with a questioning lift of his brows and a motion to continue.

"It needs work, but it'll do," she answered faintly.

"What happened, Callista?" he asked quietly, though no less intensely.

She rubbed her temples, trying to remember what she'd just as soon forget. "It was a stupid mistake. A beginner's error. I should have known better, but Mrs. Stockton seemed so bereft. I kept thinking it would be all right. That I could find my way out."

"What would be all right? Pretend I don't know anything about necromancy or Fey-born magic and speak slowly and clearly."

She started to sigh before catching it back, seeing the combined look of concern and concentration on his face. He wasn't just furious—despite the bulging vein in his temple. He cared. A flutter of something besides fear bounced around her stomach. "Annwn is a tangle of paths, sort of like a funnel. The farther and deeper you go, the more dangerous it becomes and the more difficult it is to retrace your steps. I went too far in and got lost."

"Then what?" David looked as if he chewed nails, but at least his volume had receded to an acceptable level.

"There were creatures." Even the memory was enough to send a freezing sweat between her shoulder blades. "I fled, but more caught my scent. I managed to open the door, but after that I don't remember anything until I woke to you yelling at me."

"And if I was? Damn it, I thought you were dead."

A bleak smile touched her lips. "It's nice having someone worried about me—noisy or otherwise."

He didn't return her smile. Instead he rose from his chair, arms folded across his chest, one hand on his chin as he pondered her words.

She didn't know what she'd hoped for. An emotional bedside confession of his eternal love seemed beyond the realm of possibility, but a few kind words would have gone a long way to ease the churning pit her stomach had become. Last night had been a turning point for her. A toe-curling, heart-stopping revelation. To David, it seemed to rate somewhere between ho-hum and Callista who? She knew she wasn't his first or even his hundred and first, but did he really have to make her feel like just one more in a long chain? Like she'd made a huge, embarrassing mistake?

He met her gaze, his expression holding nothing of the passionate desire she'd once seen there. Instead he looked on her as a particularly irritating problem he was solving. "If you hadn't sealed the door, could this creature have used the rift you opened to escape?"

Her stomach shriveled, her heart sank into her boots, but she let none of that show on her face. Not this time. She'd already revealed too much of herself. She'd not compound her mistake with embarrassing entreaties, like a dog begging for a pat from its master. He would see only what she wanted him to see; a quiet reserve, a calm professional serenity. "I don't know."

His face tightened and though he couldn't pace, it was obvious he desperately wanted to. "What do you mean you don't know, Callista? I would think setting demons free should be at the top of your instruction list."

"You're yelling again."

He pressed his lips together and breathed heavily through his nose.

"I have the skill to comfort people like the Stocktons, but there's so much more. It's there in my head.

I can feel the magic, but I can't focus it. I can't mold it to my will."

"How much does Corey know?"

"About my powers?" She shrugged. "He used to watch me when I walked the paths into death. He said he enjoyed my showmanship."

"Or was he already planning? Did he see your gift for moving between life and death as his ticket to ultimate power?"

His questions beat against her tender head while his indifference slammed against her vulnerable heart. She wanted to cry, but there was no way she would do that in front of him. "I can't conjure lightning or turn armies to stone or spill gold from every brush of my hair. I summon and banish spirits. I speak with those who've passed."

"You open a door. That is where your power lies. If demons like the ones you ran into are searching for a way out, you can offer it to them. Maybe even control them." His gaze sharpened with tension.

"I didn't control the grel. They almost killed me."

"Did they?"

She remembered the screaming, the lurching shambling run as they sought to catch her, but when they had the opportunity, the grel had not taken it. Those razored claws had never slashed her open. But that didn't signify anything. She'd been too quick. Surely they would have struck had they had the chance. Wouldn't they?

"What are you saying? That Victor Corey wants to marry me so I'll open the door into Annwn for him?"

"And control his own personal dead army. Yes."

"That's insane."

"Is it?" His stare seemed to drill into her skull. "What would have happened if these creatures had caught you?"

"They would have feasted on the life within me until I was cold and gray. I would become one of them, a being forever lost within Annwn."

"And the door would close."

"Of course. It takes a necromancer to unlock the many gates and spells. Death is well warded, to keep the beings trapped within from escaping."

"So, perhaps these things weren't trying to kill you. They were trying to pass through the door."

"This is madness. All of it."

"You're right. Which is why I've decided you should take Nancy up on her offer."

She straightened, head spinning at the sudden move. "What? Now I think you're the one whose insane. We've had this talk already. I can't marry Sam."

"Sam can protect you."

Her headache tripled in strength until it seeped down her neck and into her spine. She wanted to be sick. "Marry Sam. Marry Corey. Why is it that the solution to every problem ends in my marriage to a man I don't love?"

"You could finally have the family you always wanted. A place where you're cared for and . . . and loved. It's the perfect solution."

"Perfect for whom?" Anger added to the feverish heat simmering beneath her skin. "I'll have all the family I can handle when I reach my aunt at Dunsgathaic."

"Or you'll be dismissed and tossed aside like a beggar at a miser's feast. Do you want to risk traveling all that way to be rejected out of hand? Or worse, handed back to your brother?"

She straightened, chin up. "A risk I'm willing to take. Besides, we made a deal."

"No, I said what I needed to get you to cut those damned ropes," he argued, a sour twist to his mouth. "I would have promised you a trip to the bloody moon."

"I don't believe you. If that was the case, why didn't you just shove me into a mail coach in London?"

Her question was met with a dry, angry bark of laughter. "I've asked myself that same question every day over the last two hundred miles."

"Why are you saying these things, David? What happened to this morning and the words we spoke to one another?"

"Words don't change anything. You imagine I'm a chivalrous hero carrying you off into the sunset. I'm not that man, Callista. I never have been. I'm an arrogant, self-absorbed bastard, and the sooner you realize that, the better off you'll be. I'm no hero and there is no happy-ever-after at the end of this story, only death."

The woman kneeling on the cold, stone-flagged floor. The flash of a blade. A figure she now recognized. She folded her hands into her skirts to hide their trembling, but she met David's gaze head-on. "My death or yours?"

He froze, a grim and dangerous light in his eye. Nothing of the teasing cynicism or the bitter loneliness was left. Only a white-hot fury that scalded her and made her drop her eyes to her lap, seeing her hands clutching the heavy fabric, a small tear in her hem, the dust shimmering in the afternoon air. She heard the

scrape of his boots on the floor, the squeak of hinges
as he opened the wagon door.

"Last night was a mistake, Callista. It should never
have happened."

"Too late," she snapped.

"To undo the past, yes. But not to change the
future—your future at any rate. Mine is writ in stone.
I'll not take you down with me."

She lifted her eyes, unable to keep the pain from
her gaze. "You know what you are, David St. Leger?
You're a coward. So afraid of being hurt, you've forgotten how to love."

"Or this might be the most courageous thing I've
ever done," he said, slamming the door behind him.

Callista pulled the crumpled broadsheet from beneath the bunk's mattress. Smoothed it out, staring
at the artist's crude sketch as if she might read the
thoughts behind the curled lip and carved jaw. She
wished things were different. She wished she could
feel for Sam what he felt for her. It would have made
her life so simple, her problems solved with the slide
of his ring upon her finger.

But she couldn't make her heart obey.

Not to love Sam. Not to hate David.

Both were impossible.

My death or yours? The question reverberated like a
loosed arrow as he shoved his way through the growing crowds. He repeated to himself, *A dream. It's only
a dream*, until the worst passed. Callista's last shouted
accusation was harder to escape.

The truth always was.

If only she knew how hard it was to stand aside and let Sam Oakham ply his claim. Somehow Callista had woven her way into his blood. His need for her was as destructive as the draught. He would walk away. Leave tonight. There would be no need for another conversation. And no, that was not cowardly. It was selfless, noble, and damned decent. So, take that, Callista Hawthorne!

He'd not even finished congratulating himself on his sacrifice before he slammed to a halt midway between a trio of enthusiastic fiddlers that made his head ache and a stall selling fried sausages piled with onions and mushrooms, which made his stomach growl.

The book.

In his haste to leave before he confessed more than was wise, he'd left his saddlebag behind in the wagon. Perfect. He'd have to skulk back with his tail between his legs and submit himself to another painful round of thunderous looks and finger-pointing. He wasn't sure whether he didn't prefer the Callista who kept her thoughts close to the vest and hid her feelings behind eyes as opaque as a leaf-clogged stream.

He spun on his heel, quickly retracing his steps, though with dusk approaching, the crowds that had been thick were fast becoming impenetrable. The stout farmers and apple-cheeked goodwives were replaced by quick-fingered cutpurses and shrill-voiced doxies. Torches guttered and smoked and the scents of roasting meat and sour wine warred with the stench of urine, sweat, and vomit.

As he shoved his way back toward the cluster of gaudily painted wagons, he fought off groping hands and pointed elbows, staggering shoves in the back and gin-heavy laughter blown in his face. Rounding a corner between a booth selling secondhand clothes and a stall offering gingerbread, two men stepped in front of him. A third closed in from behind. Within the space of a few pounding heartbeats before they rushed him, David detected the rancid odors of grease and cheap spirits, noted the lack of prickling along his nerves that would have signaled the presence of a Fey-blood among them, and caught the slide of steel from the corner of his eye.

He bested the first easily enough with a sidestep and a thrust of his elbow hard against the side of the man's skull, a second crushing punch to his stomach that dropped the bastard retching and gasping into the dirt. The second attacker dodged David's fist, spinning under his guard with his knife raised to strike. David caught his wrist, the bones snapping beneath his fingers. The man's screams were drowned out by the chaos swirling around them. David grabbed up the fallen knife and slammed it hilt-deep into the man's neck. The screams died to gurgling moans and then silence. The third man never saw the blow that killed him, a smashing close-fisted punch that shattered his nose and drove the bone shards into his brain.

"Hold, St. Leger or . . . or I'll shoot."

David straightened from where he crouched above the body, blood spattering hot across his face and leaking sticky and dark over his hand. Sam Oakham aimed a pistol at David's chest, his eyes cold and hard and undaunted. His hand shook only slightly.

"The broadsheet said you need me alive else you'll receive nothing," David said calmly, though his nerves thrummed and his muscles twitched just as they'd always done when he was faced with an enemy on the field of battle . . . or, more recently, in the cramped alleys and mean back ways of London's stews.

"Did I say I'd kill you?" Oakham answered. "Oh no. I can put a bullet in you that will deaden your legs. Alive, if not lively."

"Do you intend to split the fifty pounds with Sally or keep it for yourself?"

David lunged, grabbing the woman lurking at the edge of his vision, dragging her in front of him, deaf to her curses and shrieks, though her heavy cheap perfume burned his nose and turned his stomach. Sally's hair fell draggled and loose down her back as she wrestled with him, but his grip was firm, and a forearm across her tender throat quieted her quick enough.

"How skilled are you, Oakham? How desperate to win Callista's heart? Do you think she'll welcome you with open arms when you come to her with the blood of her lover on your hands?"

The pistol wavered as Oakham fought his temper. "You'll never escape. The law has men scouring every road for you. You're to be arrested and taken back to London in the name of the king."

"The king of the stews, perhaps. I've just rid the world of three black-hearted killers. If I go to London, it will be to be accept a knighthood for my valiant action."

Oakham steadied hand and voice. "Let Sally go."

"By all means." David leaned down, his lips almost brushing Sally's ear. "You'd have been better off with my coins. Your loss."

With a shove that sent her staggering into Oakham,

David threw himself behind the booth, rolling to his feet and into the mob thronging the wider alleyway. He braced for the gunshot that would take him in the back, but it never came, and Oakham was left behind. Still, he remained armed and dangerous. Add his pursuit to Corey's, who, once he realized his men had been killed, would send more and many to finish the job. The fair and Callista must be left behind now . . . this instant.

David's body simmered with a wild, driving power like a summer storm charge. The wolf smelled the blood on his skin and woke hungry.

The woodland was close. He would lose himself within the tangle of trees and thorny undergrowth. No swayback mount for him. He would run beneath the moon, follow the hidden ways used by badger and hare and fox, slink unseen past lighted villages and lonely farms, until he reached Gray and safety.

Where, before, the fair's crowds swarmed close, now they parted for him like waves breaking upon a rock. Fearful glances, hissed whispers, and shrinking bodies; he noted and dismissed them in the space of the same heartbeat. They might not know what prowled beside them, but they sensed his danger and his difference.

Even the sheep bleated and shuffled, huddling at the far side of the pens as he passed. A lamp hung outside the wagon he'd shared with Callista, but he dared not stop for the book. He'd return close to dawn. Or perhaps wait for word of his flight to spread and then come back to reclaim his possessions in a day or two. Time for Corey's men to leave the fairground for the roads and tracks nearby. Time for Callista to hate David for leaving her.

He couldn't help himself. He paused at the trees' edge. Opened his mind to the pathing, sending his last farewell upon a ribbon of thought, though it came with the sting of mocking amusement. *So much for twenty-four hours.*

Callista lifted her hand to knock at the door to Sam's wagon. A lamp shone from inside, men's voices too low to hear over the fair's nighttime revels.

". . . three men . . . dead . . . killer . . . should be sixty pounds . . ."

". . . let him escape . . . girl . . . want them both . . ."

Gorge rising, she couldn't breathe, couldn't swallow. She backed away from the wagon, nearly stumbling over Nancy, who'd come up quietly behind her.

"What's wrong? You're shaking."

"You gave me a day. That's what you said. A day to make my decision."

"I haven't given St. Leger away."

"Then who is Sam talking to? Why has he betrayed us?"

Nancy steered her unresisting away from the wagon. "You're mistaken. Let me go and find out what's—"

"No. You mustn't. They'll know you warned me. I'll gather my things and slip away. Now, before they come looking."

"Sam would never turn you over to Branston. Not for any amount of money." Nancy followed Callista as she stumbled up the steps into the wagon, shutting the door and bolting it as if a wooden latch might protect her. Mind racketing from thought to thought, she hastily snatched up her few meager possessions and stuffed them into the satchel. She paused, noting the carved box at the bottom of the bag. Someone had gathered her bells. Someone had carefully replaced them. Had it been David? Her mother's letters were just as she'd left them, but for one, which had slid free of the ribbon. Or had it been taken out on purpose? Had David read it?

"Sam loves you, Cally," Nancy argued. "You must have heard wrong. He wouldn't betray you."

Callista shook her head as she hefted the satchel onto her shoulder. Already she could barely catch her breath and the muscles in her back ached and pulled.

A knock at the door punched the breath from her lungs. "Nancy? Are you in there? Let me in. I need to speak with Cally."

"You wait and see. There's bound to be a simple explanation." Nancy offered what was supposed to be a reassuring smile, though Callista saw the doubts in the woman's eyes.

"Nan! Open the door," Sam hissed.

Nancy unlocked the latch and turned the handle. Sam pushed inside, the wagon creaking at the added weight, the air within seeming to grow stuffy and unbearably hot, but perhaps it was only Callista's fear making her dizzy and slightly nauseated.

Sam looked different. His eyes flickered dark and uncertain in a taut, pale face. His clothes were dirty, a long grimy smear across his coat, neckcloth untied, and dark brown mud edging a sleeve. She peered closer. Not mud . . . blood. But whose? His own? David's?

"What's this?" Sam's eyes widened to see Callista dressed for travel, her bag clutched to her chest. "I expected you to be in bed."

"I'm fine. Much better."

His gaze traveled around the wagon as if he thought David might be hiding under a blanket or in a cupboard. "Where's St. Leger? Did he come here? Have you seen him?"

Nancy and Callista exchanged a look before she replied, "I've not seen him for hours." Though she'd spoken to him. At least, it was speech of a kind. David's voice had rumbled up in her mind, closer than a whisper, the words clear and sharp and tinged with resentment.

Sam made one more raking look around, obviously stymied at this unexpected hitch in his plans, while his meaty hands opened and closed, showing the same dark brown stain clinging to his palms and caught beneath his fingernails.

"I know what you did," Callista said, anger trembling her voice. "Did you manage to haggle the price up to sixty pounds?"

"I never—"

Nancy stepped between them. "Tell her she's wrong, Sam. Tell her it's a mistake."

He stared over his sister's shoulder, bullish and unwavering. "I saved you, Cally. The man was a criminal . . . a fugitive from the law. They're taking him back to London to answer for his crimes. Hanging's too good for the likes of him. Drawing and quartering might be better."

"Is that what they told you? That he was a murderer?"

"Saw it for myself. The savage killed the three who tried to take him. Lucky for me and Sally, I had a pistol to keep him from adding us to his total."

"Sally? What was she . . . I don't believe it. You're lying."

But the blood didn't lie. Nor did the drawn and frightened look on Sam's face. He'd taken David for a London dandy, strong, perhaps, and trained in fighting but easily cowed and swift to surrender if he met with any real resistance. David's quick cunning and vicious brutality had shocked Sam and perhaps even made him realize what he'd unleashed in his unthinking jealousy.

"You always were a trusting soul, Cally. But this time you placed your trust in a murderous scoundrel."

"I'll not go back to Branston. I'd rather die."

Sam smiled in triumph. "That's where you wrong me. I never said nothing about you to the blokes what came after St. Leger. When they asked, I said you must have separated on the road between here and the city. That I'd never seen you."

"Branston won't believe you. He'll know I would have stayed with David."

"I'm not as stupid as I look. Sally backed me up. Told them how she and St. Leger were pillow mates. How he boasted of taking your maidenhead and then abandoning you. The men were angry but convinced. Sally's a good actress when there's money to be made."

"I have to get away before they realize you duped them."

Sam planted himself in front of the door. "You'll stay here where it's safe. And if you're right and these chaps suspect they've been lied to and come nosing about, I'll send them packing with a few broken ribs for their trouble."

"Please, Sam! You must—"

"Enough! I'll take care of you, Cally. And when that

St. Leger chap is gone, it'll be like it was before you left. I'll make you happy." He motioned to Nancy. "Come on, Nan. Cally needs her rest." Nancy offered a quick backward glance just before the door closed behind them.

The scrape of the key turned Callista's stomach. She was caught like a mouse in a cage. She perched on the narrow bunk as she sought to calm her mind enough to think logically. She needed to escape and she needed to find David. She tried the door, rattling the latch, slamming a shoulder into the jamb, but the wood held, the lock remained unmovable. She sank back down on the bunk. Closed her eyes as she conjured and discarded impossible plans. *Where are you, David? I need you. You can't just leave me here, no matter how much you think it's for my own good . . .*

Like the brush of a feather or the bite of cold when a snowflake touches one's skin, a glimmer of thought moved across her mind. Instinctively, she reached out as if to catch the sensation and hold on to it. But it receded, and she was left feeling emptier and lonelier than ever.

She opened her eyes, her gaze settling on a long woolen greatcoat hanging from a peg—David's. He'd left it behind. Perhaps . . . if she was very lucky . . .

She rose to search his pockets, hoping for a tool she might use to jimmy the door. Her fingers touched and then curled around a crumpled piece of paper. She scanned the few words scrawled there with a sick feeling in her gut. He'd hired horses. He was probably already in the village. She needed to leave now if she had any hope of catching him before he departed. But how?

Her hands shook and fear curled up her spine into her head as she sought to hold complete panic at bay.

The turn of a key had her on her feet, poised to flee. She'd get one chance. She would be ready. She snatched up her satchel, prepared to swing it full force at whoever appeared in the doorway.

"Cally, it's me!" Nancy shouted, putting up an arm to ward off the blow.

Callista slumped back, the bag a deadweight against her trembling arms. "What do you want?"

"Sam's gone in to the fair. I think he's still hoping to find St. Leger. If you want to leave, now's your chance."

Callista offered her a wary frown. "Why?"

"Because I saw the way St. Leger looked when he thought you were in trouble." Her hand smoothed down over her stomach, eyes dark with hidden emotion. "And because I saw the way you looked tonight when you thought St. Leger had come to harm. Sam doesn't stand a chance against a bond like that."

Callista squeezed Nancy's hand with a tremulous smile. "Thank you."

Nancy shrugged her off with a snort of irritation. "Just go before I come to my senses. He is still my brother, you know."

Callista nodded and, wrapping herself in David's muffling greatcoat and cradling her bag as she might a child, hurried out into the wild chaos of the night, dodging fairgoers as she slipped past the crowded sheep pens.

"Excuse me," she stammered as a figure loomed up out of the dark, hands gripping her roughly.

"Where you headed, little bit?" the man sneered.

She wrenched away, hurrying for the safety of the wooded track that would take her to town. Looked back over her shoulder to find him still watching her.

13

Night slid like a ghost over the land. One moment, the air hung gray and heavy, trees naught but purple and black silhouettes, birds quiet in the bushes, and a few lazy swallows circling homeward. The next moment, stars glimmered pale and high among streamers of cloud, and the moon rose up through their branches red as the blood he'd spilled.

The wood stretched all around him. He lifted his muzzle to the wind, feeling the scents burst like pictures in his head. The tang of pine and oak and elm, the soft, grandmotherly smell of moss and fern, and overall the bitter slightly sweet scent of the decaying deadfall stirred with each lift of a paw as he moved deeper into the trees. Ahead, a whiff of hot blood as a squirrel or rabbit darted across his path, and a passing breeze from the fairgrounds carried the fuggy warm aromas of manure and sheep and man.

He welcomed his shift to aspect like a freeing breath. He needed the easing stretch of taut muscles as he ran under the growing moon, the welcome of the spring night to wrap around him like a balm. The simplicity of instinct where every moment exploded into being with the immediacy of battle and then fell away, quickly forgotten.

A crow swooped down from a great sycamore, wings spread on the wind, beak sharp as a dagger. He snapped at it, but it fluttered away and dove once more before settling on a dead branch nearby, watching him with cocked head and ruffled feathers. It was half again larger than any normal crow, with a sharp intelligence in its jet gaze and talons tipped in silver. David recognized the creature from Mac's description.

Worry uncoiled from a deep part of his soul.

"This is fortunate. We were sent to find you, child of the wolf. And here you are, come to us."

So focused was he on the crow, David was unaware of the man's presence until he stepped from the long twilight shadows, the power moving over and through him like a storm wave buffeting the senses, dragging him under.

Imnada.

Yet not.

Human.

But much more.

He was large. Amend that—he was colossal. David, who looked up to few men, knew that in human form he'd be craning his neck to stare into this man's dark impenetrable eyes. And he was old. Despite the lack of gray in his hair or lines on his face, wisdom burned in his eyes and age hung upon him like a cloak.

What do you want with me? Did Mac send you? Has something happened to . . .

He couldn't complete the sentence. If Mac had been hurt or killed, it would be a nail through his heart.

If Beskin has harmed a hair on his head, I'll rip him to shreds and gnaw on his bones. A growl rolled up the back of his throat, pulling his lips back in a show of long, deadly fangs, his fury lifting the hair all along his spine. *And then I'll do the same to any damned enforcer that crosses my path.*

"The little dog owns a nasty bite."

Where the crow had been now stood a woman. It would have been easy to mistake her for a boy, with her short cap of black curls, sharp-boned face, and imp's grin. But as she glided across the grass, her cloak of ebony feathers billowed aside to reveal small upthrust breasts and rounded womanly hips, her skin glowing pearlescent in the gloom of the wood. She turned her rainbow eyes upon him and the fur along his back bristled, despite himself. He recognized her immediately: Badb, one of the true Fey. He'd never stood in the presence of one before. They didn't bother themselves with the shapechangers. Never had. Not even in the days before the Fealla Mhòr, when the walls between the worlds held many gates and it was easy to find the right path to cross over and back.

Perhaps this was because the true Fey knew in their hearts that the Imnada were different—their magic unlike any they had seen or understood. Even with all the Fey's powers, they held no real sway over the shapechangers. The Fey were not their gods, nor were the Imnada beholden to them as the Other were for their very existence. How it must have galled them.

Here to pick at the corpse, carrion crow? You'll have to wait. I'm still breathing, no thanks to you.

"Fine words from a hunter of cutpurses and a stalker of whoremongers," Badb mocked, her crimson lips widening, but the giant of a man laid a hand upon her shoulder, and she retreated.

Interesting. What kind of man could control one of the Fey? A man with enormous power, was the answer that shivered up from the base of David's brain.

"Can you put Mr. St. Leger's fears to rest, Badb?" the man asked.

The girl closed her eyes for a brief moment. "Flannery lives. More than that, I cannot see. The shifters cloud my vision and all is hazy."

David relaxed a fraction of an inch. *I've been warned about her, but who are you?*

The man shrugged. "A traveler . . . a friend . . ."

Friends are a danger. They make you care. I prefer enemies.

"Those you seem to acquire with ease," Badb snipped, tossing her cap of curls.

"Gray sent me to bring you to him," the man said. "And the book."

It remains within the fair, but it's not safe to return. There are men searching for me.

"Ossine?"

Men in service to Victor Corey, a gang lord. A man with half of London in his pocket.

"And why would this lord of gangs be searching for you? Does he also desire to study Zwanis Xhelho's *Book of Seven Forgotten Stars*?" the man asked.

Corey hunts a girl.

"The woman you take north to Dunsgathaic."

That's no concern of yours. Who are you? What are you?

"You sense the answer, but you fight it. I can feel your resistance."

David reached out once more, his mind pressing, searching. *You're Imnada, but you don't bear any signum I recognize. It's no clan or holding I know, which is impossible. As younglings, we're taught them all by the Ossine as part of our learning.*

"The Lythene died out long ago. I am all that is left."

A thought niggled at the base of David's brain. Some story heard at his grandmother's knee. A legend only half remembered.

The Ossine would never have allowed an entire clan to just die out without working to save it. That's one of their jobs—to chart the bloodlines and to keep the aspects feasible in new generations."

"The Ossine have the power over life . . . and death," the man answered. "They have grown in importance since I knew them last."

David had no answer, but more than enough questions.

He'd no time to ask any of them. Badb stepped forward, her cloak trailing over the ground with a soft rustle. She placed a hand on his head, ignoring the tension stringing his muscles, his lips drawn in a silent growl.

"You are dying, shapechanger. The curse and the draught working in harmony threaten to kill you. It is only a matter of time."

And whose fault is that, Fey? It was you and your companion who offered us this devil's solution.

"Enough," the dark-haired giant said. "If there are enemies in these woods, we must be swift away to Addershiels. Take us to retrieve the book. We cannot leave without . . ."

But David was gone. He tore away from them, losing himself in the deeper trees, muzzle lifted to the air, his body alive with fear and anger. She was in the woods . . . somewhere. He smelled the panic on her skin, he felt the mad gallop of her heart, heard her shout in his head.

Callista was in danger.

Through the thick tangle of ancient trees, light filtered weakly from above to lie green and gray upon old moss-covered trunks and sheened the pale leaves of ash and oak. He leapt over a rotten stump, slid on his belly beneath a web of bindweed as snaring as a spider's trap. There. He veered free of the thick, grasping undergrowth to find himself on a beaten-earth track. Up ahead, the chase came closer. He heard the crack and snap of bracken as it was shoved aside in haste, a cry quickly stifled as she fell roughly.

I'm here. You're safe. I'll not let them harm you.

Callista broke through the trees, her hair falling free of its pins and speckled with leaves, his greatcoat dragging half off her shoulders, her satchel banging against her thighs. She skidded to a halt as she caught sight of him emerging from the night.

"David!" she gasped.

It's me. What's wrong?

"They've found us. He's just behind . . ."

She stumbled forward, the satchel dragging her shoulder. David heard the twang of a broken wire and the squeak of a pivot, his body in flight before the spark hit the flint.

Spring gun.

A roar shook his blood, pain shot through his side, and he fell hard to the ground, the wind crushed out of him and every new breath shooting fire along his nerves, the trees swirling as if a great wind shook them. He heard a scream and felt a hand upon his neck, clutching at his fur.

"David! Please. Look at me. Don't close your eyes."

A roaring like the rush of a waterfall filled his head . . . the trees swept into a hurricane of color and sound . . . a great tear opening within a sky of sparkling cloud.

Don't follow the path. Stay with me here.

Callista's voice echoed in his head. He tried to answer, tried to hold to this world by his fingertips, the hole pulling him toward it, but his thoughts grew foggy and finally, he let go.

The wolf was David. The wolf was David and he'd saved her life. The wolf was David, he'd saved her life, and he was not dead. He wasn't. He couldn't be. She wouldn't allow it, and if anyone could fight death tooth and claw, she could. If not, what good was her power of necromancy, anyway?

Magic seeped up from the ground like mist. It crackled the air and tingled along her skin as it wrapped itself around the wolf's body. Then the drifting swirl of magic retreated, and David lay sprawled on his side, legs drawn up, one arm bent underneath him, another flung out, fingers dug into the soil. His ribs expanded ever so slowly, each breath dragged free of him in a painful sucking wet wheeze.

The door to Annwn cracked open and a bitter cold rushed to meet the hot wind, the violent mixture lifting leaves and bending branches. The pressure beneath her breastbone increased as if her ribs might crack wide, and she pressed a hand to her chest, unable to breathe.

A figure came up behind her. "I'd say good riddance and may he burn in hell, but Corey'll have my head if he dies."

She flinched but was too numb to care and too tired to run. She could hardly work up the energy to turn and face him.

"Here"—he tossed her a flask—"scoop up what blood you can. There's enough leaking out of him, should be easy. If we're lucky, Corey will be happy enough at having his bride returned that he'll overlook the shifter's death. And I'll still get my fifty pounds."

She gripped the flask, disgust rolling her belly. A crow circled, alighting on a nearby branch. A scavenger waiting its chance to feast.

"He's dying," she sobbed. "Just leave him to pass through the doorway in peace."

He struck her a hard blow to the side of the head, leaving her ears ringing, jaw sore. "The creature killed three of my men. As long as Corey wants the thing's blood to sell and so long as it's my skin if he don't get what he wants, you'll do as I say. Now, get busy."

Sell his blood? David had accused Corey of madness. Perhaps he was right. She could think of no other reason for such a gruesome desire. She bent closer to David, gently rolling him over, in the hope that his injuries would not be as bad as they appeared.

She closed her eyes

They were so much worse. She turned aside long enough to retch, wiping her mouth on her greatcoat, smelling the spicy musky scent of him in the heavy wool. "I can't. I won't."

The man dragged her to her feet by her arm. "Fine. Leave him. I'll tell Corey I got here too late. He was already dead. Half pay is better than none."

She dug her heels in, fighting him with all her strength as he tried to drag her away, but he struck her again. And again, until her teeth felt loose in her skull and her jaw throbbed. "He said he wants you. He didn't say in what shape."

"David!" she cried, though she knew it was useless.

"You think the shifter will save you? He couldn't even save himself."

She looked back over her shoulder, straining to see through the dark. Was that a hand moving? Did he lift his head?

She couldn't be certain, and then the trees closed around him and he was lost from view.

You claim friendship? Help her.

The thought burst in her brain. She frowned in confusion. What did he mean? Who was he speaking to?

"That shifter can't save her." A towering black shape stepped into the path ahead of them, head scraping the sky, arms folded over his chest, face hard as stone. "But this one can."

He needed to remember. It was vitally important. He grappled with his scrambled thoughts, but they slid like sand through a sieve. He tried speaking, but his throat was raw and his tongue wouldn't respond.

He swam through a red haze of pain before the black swallowed him once more, every sense jumbled up inside his head and then amplified a thousand-fold. He smelled the putrid musk of a battlefield, the charred burn of torn muscles, and the powdery snap of broken ribs with every shallow breath he inhaled. He saw the scarlet shock of blood behind his eyes with every rapid thud of his heart as, back arched, he bit down on the inside of his cheek to stop from screaming. He tasted the bitter tang of iron from a kiss laid upon his lips amid a swirl of soft black feathers and a narrow, pointed face. He heard the Fey magic as it coiled around him, passed through him, slid within the darkest parts of his soul, and burst out of his hair and fingertips, a song like a million voices twining and rippling in infinite shades of sapphire and plum, emerald and crimson, topaz and opal.

And, last, an endless series of bells ringing. Over and over. Pounding against his skull. Vibrating along his bones.

He sought to close his mind to the battering of sensations, but they followed him down into the dark, where hands reached for him and Adam's face swam up out of the gloom. His features blurred in David's memory until Adam smiled and reached out a hand. *Not yet, old friend.*

He woke.

Then he screamed.

Callista's hands shook. Her knees trembled. And bile rose into her throat at the memory of the . . . she could not call it a fight. The man had merely been alive one minute and dead the next, his head toppling from his neck after a single deadly blow from a blade she'd only seen as a blur of steel.

But where there was one dog, a pack was sure to follow.

There was no time to lose. They must flee before more followed the trail laid by Sam and his jealous plotting.

Lights shone throughout the fairground, cookfires and bonfires, the steady glow of lanterns and the flickering flash of rush dips. Shouts and calls interspersed with an occasional scream while fiddles, drums and the bellowing wheeze of a squeeze-box acted as orchestration to the more primal rhythmic grunting and moaning from a nearby tent that had Callista blushing.

She hoped the confusion would mask her movements, and that the night's amusements had drawn the players away from the wagons. She crossed the trampled dirt of the clearing at a half run, set a foot upon the wagon step and prayed none had even noticed her absence. Hoped they assumed that she was resting in Nancy's wagon.

As she opened the door, Sally emerged from a pavilion strung between the last caravan and a tree, dropping her skirts into place as she pecked a greasy-looking chap in a striped waistcoat on the cheek. He murmured something in her ear and she gave a girlish giggle, taking his arm to lead him back in for another round. Before she disappeared, she met Callista's stare, her expression gloatingly hostile before she dropped the flap back in place. Another few moments and the grunts began anew.

Callista swallowed back her repugnance. Who was she to condemn Sally's profession? Was she any better with her velvet draperies and flickering candles?

They both sold a dream.

Gripping the latch with slippery fingers, she opened the door. All was as she'd left it. Just as if the last hours had never occurred. She dropped to her knees to rummage in the cupboard for David's saddle-bag and the book he carried north.

Callista had agreed to fetch it. She was the only one with a reason to be among the wagons. The only one who wouldn't arouse suspicion if challenged. And the least needed while David hovered between life and death. With her breastbone vibrating as the door to Annwn swung wide, she'd fled, heart slamming in her ears, breath short and sharp. The toppling head, gushing blood, and sprawled body had replayed themselves over and over in her mind while she hurried through the wood toward the fairground.

Moving Big Knox's plates and batons, sticks and hoops, she pulled the saddlebag out, smiling at her success.

Now, to leave as unobtrusively as she arrived.

Slinging the bag over her shoulder, she rose to dust off her skirts. Cracked the door, peering into the night. The way was clear. No one to stop her or ask questions. With a hasty prayer and a held breath, she stepped outside. Went three paces and froze.

"Where do you think you're going?"

Sally had emerged once more from the canvas pavilion, lips pursed in an ugly frown, eyes hard as flint. Her blouse gaped open to reveal the swell of her breasts, and her hair hung in a wild tangle down her back.

"I'm leaving," Callista said, tightening her grip on the saddlebag.

"If you think to run off looking for St. Leger, I wouldn't bother." Sally raked Callista with a dismissive glare.

"You're the one who told Sam?"

"Course I did. You should thank me. St. Leger didn't care about you. He was just using you, same as he used all of us."

"Or maybe you told because David *wasn't* using you? That's closer to the truth, isn't it? You've been making sheep's eyes at him for a hundred miles and he's barely glanced in your direction. So you got even by turning him over to the men hunting him."

"They're Runners."

"They're killers."

Sally sniffed, her disdain obvious. "What do you care? St. Leger's like all the rest. He wants what's between your legs and nothing else. He'll toss you aside as quick as that fancy bloke who abandoned Nancy. You'll come crawling back fat with his bastard, and you think Sam will have you then? You'll be spreading your legs for any man with pennies to buy you and not so high and mighty."

Callista thought of the night she and David had shared. She had wanted him so badly. Had cast propriety to the spring-scented breeze, had done all but beg him for his touch. Could she . . . She lay a hand upon her stomach. Shook off the worry with a shudder. Clutching the saddlebag to her shoulder, she ran for the wood, Sally's voice following her like a caution.

"You're a fool, Cally. Neither man nor beast ever changes his nature."

A shiver raced up Callista's spine. *But what if they were one and the same?*

*　　　*　　　*

The knife shook in his hand. Every shuddering breath he took burned his ice-encrusted lungs, yet sweat damped his skin. Blood steamed in the frigid air as it poured in a crimson wash over her throat, over her gown, over the snow. Afterward, he cradled her in his arms, her hair trailing over his chest, eyes closed as if in sleep and her fingers linked with his . . .

He jerked and gasped and came awake to naught but the scrape of branches and the quiet hoot of an owl. He lay back, blinking up into the darkness, letting the nightmare fade back into the corners of his mind. Harder to do the longer he remained with Callista. As hard as resisting the urge to claim her as his own, or ignoring the need to mark her body and soul now.

"The Fey-blood woman is a courageous and capable soul. Any man would be proud to claim her as his mate." The man from the wood spoke, his ancient gaze dark and impenetrable. "Yet you hold back. Perhaps had I done the same in your place . . . but that is over an age past. My blood is colder now and I understand caution."

David's gaze narrowed and another queasy oath singed his brain.

The man smiled, though no light reached his eyes and sorrow still etched itself into the bones of his face. "Try not to throw yourself in front of a bullet for a few weeks."

David tested his strength. Raised an arm. Made a fist. Easy enough. Then he drew a deep breath and nearly passed out from the ache torching his lungs. Fuck all, that bloody hurt.

"By rights, you should be dead. Annwn was open. Your soul ready to flee."

"Who are you?" David whispered.

"I'm called Lucan."

The teasing half-remembered thought clung. Lucan of the Lythene; a clan extinct ages ago. A man with eyes vast and deep as centuries. A leader who commanded true Fey as if they were baseborn peasants. David's grandmother had told him the stories often enough. She'd passed along her love for such tales of passion and treachery. But it couldn't be. This man looked no cruel traitor or brutal monster who would condemn a race. Just sorrowful and stern and hard as the rock they'd lifted above his tomb.

"Not a tomb—a prison," Lucan said quietly.

"You can read my mind?"

"If I concentrate," Lucan answered. "Once upon a time, it was a common talent among our kind."

"Where's Callista?"

"She is well. The man who threatened her? Dead."

"You saved her as I asked."

"I helped a friend."

Adam had been a friend but Adam was dead. His face had been one of those looming up from the dark of shadowed paths. *Not yet*, he'd warned as he sent David back into life. But it wouldn't be long before he joined him there. He'd seen the end. Witnessed its form. Felt its horror. It still shuddered along his bones like winter. Callista was a friend. More than a friend, but he would betray her. The way of her death changed with every dreaming. The outcome never did.

"You saved her—this time. But what of the next?" David answered. "I should never . . . I'll only . . . fucking hell, I've cocked things up." His voice broke. He was closer to the edge than he thought, teetering as the nightmare swam once more before his eyes as the pain crushed his lungs and seized his muscles with every shift of his body.

"Is something amiss?" Lucan asked.

"Callista trusts me."

"Is that wrong?"

"She shouldn't trust me. She should run like hell."

"Why?"

"Because I'm going to kill her."

14

Callista stepped down from the coach with a nervous glance, her damp hands gripping her satchel. A man and woman stood upon the front steps of an enormous house, elegant wings of tawny stone spread to either side of a tall, columned main block. Light spilled onto the gravel from rows of tall windows, and from somewhere within the house, the haunting song of a violin played. The woman had wild ginger hair twisted up in a loose bun at the nape of her neck. The man was handsome, with straight dark brows and a strong chin, a pale slash of scar near his left eye. They both regarded her with the gold-flecked eyes of the Other.

"Welcome to Addershiels, Miss Hawthorne. I'm Lord Duncallan. This is my wife. We've been expecting you."

"I thought this was the home of Gray de Coursy."

"The Earl of Halvossa is"—he seemed to search for the proper word—"indisposed this evening. He'll meet you tomorrow."

"Earl of . . . do you mean the Ghost Earl?" Callista had heard the stories in London. The estranged heir to a dukedom, a mysterious battlefield hero who'd barely shown his face since returning home from war. He was the most sought-after guest at every party and the bachelor every unmarried woman desired. She wondered how those same matchmaking mamas and social-climbing hostesses would react if they discovered he was an Imnada shapechanger.

That he was cursed.

That he was dying.

The dinner was lavish and the wine flowed freely, but Callista picked at her plate and barely tasted what she swallowed. Her thoughts remained on David, who had been bundled upstairs as soon as they'd arrived, Lady Duncallan shouting orders to maidservants and footmen as she followed after. Callista had sought to attend him, but Lucan restrained her.

"He is Imnada, my lady. And the shapechangers have always been stronger and more able to withstand injury than normal humans, but it will not be easy or pretty to watch. Best leave him to Badb and Lady Duncallan for now."

Her Ladyship had soon returned to assure her of David's comfort, but the hours dragged and Callista's thoughts remained scattered and afraid.

"Faster. More agile. Quicker to respond to danger. Quicker to heal," David had boasted.

She prayed he'd not been wrong.

By rights, she should have been the one lying blooded and feverish upstairs. She had tripped the wire. The bullet had been meant for her. Only David's speed and animal instincts had saved her from the poacher's trap. He'd saved her life. She prayed it was not at the cost of his own.

As footmen offered and removed courses, she tried to listen as Lady Duncallan chatted and tried to answer when Lord Duncallan asked her questions, but mostly she choked down food she never tasted and sipped from a wineglass that seemed never to empty. By the time the last footman cleared the last plate and closed the door behind him, leaving the three of them alone, she was exhausted, dizzy with drink, and her stomach was more full of knots than of dinner.

"We're traveling to Skye," she said in answer to His Lordship's latest question. "My aunt is a priestess there."

"Mr. St. Leger is taking you?" he asked. He watched Callista from the head of the table, spinning his cane idly between ink-stained fingers. "He agreed to accompany you to Dunsgathaic?"

"I would have promised you a trip to the bloody moon," David had confessed. He had never meant to take her to Skye. Those had been empty words. A promise built on air. "We made a deal. He vowed he would see it through to the end."

"If only he offered us such devotion, eh, Katie love?" Lord Duncallan smiled, his eyes softening whenever they turned to his wife.

"Poor Gray," she answered. "He's been certain all it would take was the right sort of nudge and David would be won over to the cause."

"Are you the right sort of nudge, Miss Hawthorne?" Duncallan asked, turning his gold-flecked brown eyes to her.

"I don't know what you're talking about. And I doubt I'm the right sort of anything," she replied, fatigue and disillusion taking her over.

Lady Duncallan sipped at her wine while His Lordship leaned back in his chair, left leg stretched awkwardly in front of him. Unlike Corey, who used his walking stick as a gentlemanly affectation, the baron seemed to truly need it. He favored his right leg, and from time to time as he walked, his face would blanch with pain. Callista had not dared to ask, but he'd seen her noticing.

"An accident a few years ago left me crippled. Lucan saved my life," he explained.

"Mr. St. Leger must love you very much," Lady Duncallan broke in, her smile friendly, though there was a decided twinkle in her eyes.

"What?" Callista nearly choked on her wine. "No, it isn't like that. We have a business arrangement. That's all. We only pretended to be lovers fleeing north to explain why we traveled together."

"Truly?" Lady Duncallan's smile faded, a small downturn at the corners of her mouth, a crease between her brows. "From all I know of the shapechangers, it would take more than a handshake to persuade one to walk into Scathach's fortress, the heart of Amhas-draoi power."

But then, David hadn't been persuaded. And Callista had never for a moment believed he loved her.

David opened his eyes, but this time the pain did not come ripping up angrily from the same deep well where the wolf slept, waiting. It snaked along limbs thick and sluggish, as if his blood congealed within his veins and curled hard within his chest.

"Shhh, be still." A hand touched his brow, cool against his sweat-soaked skin. "Your fever's broken. The worst is over."

He should have known she'd be here. She'd been here every time he'd waked. When the agony left him drenched in sweat and raving. When he swam up from the haze of his darkest dreams, shuddering and racked with tears. The Mother knew he'd tried to leave her behind. Yet circumstances worked to keep them together as if the dream fought to become truth.

"Where are we?" he asked with a tongue thick and dry.

"Addershiels. Lucan and Badb brought us."

"Lucan?" His heart cramped, his lungs caught on a ragged breath.

"He claims you know him."

David closed his eyes, his theory fantastic but unshakeable. "Know *of* him, but . . ." He shook his head. "It can't be real."

"Has anything been real since you landed in that Soho alley like a hero out of a nightmare?" Shadows flickered across her drawn and careworn face.

"What of the book, Callista? Where is it?" He sought to sit up and nearly passed out as spots danced before his eyes. He flopped back on his pillows with a frustrated breath. "Shit, I left it behind. It's still with Oakham. Mac's going to fucking kill me."

"Calm down. It's safe with His Lordship."

"His Lordship? Who the hell is . . . oh, you mean de Coursy."

"I've seen him only once and very briefly. Since

then he's been closeted with Lucan and Lord and Lady Duncallan."

"The Duncallans? They're mixed up in this madness as well?" David ran a hand over the tight seam of the bandage stretching around his torso and up over one shoulder. His wits returned, though too slowly for his liking. "Secret meetings. Fey-bloods crawling all over the castle. A mysterious shapechanger wandering the halls in company with one of the true Fey. Damn it, I feel as tightly wound as an Egyptian mummy and about as useful. How long have I been lying here like a lump?"

"Two days."

"Shit. No doubt raving like a lunatic."

Sorrow glimmered in her eyes. "Only a little."

He didn't ask what secrets he'd revealed. He could well imagine.

"Lucan said as long as the wound doesn't sicken, you'll be back on your feet soon enough. Though he did warn that you'll have quite the scar to show off."

"I'll add it to my collection," he huffed. Inaction never set well. He needed to be moving, planning, running. It gave him less time to brood.

"David, you were delirious. The burn on your back—"

"For a man who shouldn't exist, Lucan's full of conversation," he interrupted before she could finish. That Callista knew of his shame was bad enough; he didn't need to add degrading humiliation to the stabbing pain already in his chest or the scars on his body. "Did he tell you where he came from? How he survived? What the hell is going on?

Her expression closed tight as a fist, but she took

the hint. She knew as well as he that the hurts of the past were best left in the grave. "What do you mean Lucan 'shouldn't exist'?"

David closed his eyes, letting his thoughts coalesce. It didn't make his conclusions any better, but his head didn't pound quite so much. "This will sound like madness . . . but I think he's the Imnada warlord who betrayed King Arthur. Lucan Kingkiller. The Traitor Lord."

"It can't be. The Lost Days were over a thousand years ago. Lucan was slaughtered during the battle."

"I know the stories as well as you do. When you're around him, do you feel anything"—he placed a hand against his bandaged chest—"here?"

She shook her head. "There's no feeling of death surrounding him. He's alive—or at least not dead."

"Is there a difference?"

Her face hardened. "Very much so."

"But how? Why does he travel in company with one of the true Fey? What's in that book that's so important to Gray he'd send men to their deaths over it?" He glanced at the scars crisscrossing his palm before closing his hand into a frustrated fist. "Questions but no answers and me flat on my back."

"Better that than six feet under, sewn into a shroud."

Callista rose in a fluster of skirts to wander the room, a hand trailing across a table, a cabinet, picking up and putting down a china figurine, a row of porcelain boxes, a Wedgwood urn. She glanced at the fire in the hearth but then turned her steps to the window to draw back the heavy drapes. The moon washed the park in silver and outlined her face and hair like a halo.

"Why did you do it, David?" she asked gently, her

gaze still upon the lawn and the far horizon where the hills dipped down toward the sea. "Why did you take that bullet?"

Another question with no good answer. Or at least one he dare not speak aloud. Not if he wanted to keep the dark future he dreamed from coming to pass. Instead, he offered her a flippant—and very painful— shrug. "It seemed like a good idea at the time."

She glanced back over her shoulder, her hair shimmering in the ghost light, her expression giving nothing away. "You used that as an excuse before."

"You'll find it's my answer to a great many questions."

She gripped the drapes in both hands, head bowed. "You were right about the Fey-bloods and about Corey. He wants you not because of me but for your blood. He wants to sell it. I don't know why, but he—"

Shock jerked him up against his pillows, pain wrung a gasp of air from his lungs as if he'd been punched. "There's only one reason to want to milk me for my blood and that's the *afailth luinan*. But how could Corey know? It's a legend. A faery tale."

Callista returned to the chair, brows furrowed. "What's the *afailth luinan*?"

"Translated, it means roughly 'blood heal.' My gram told me the tale of the Imnada chieftain Rinaci Hammerclaw who saved the life of Edern, his Fey-blood bride. It was too full of kisses and romance for me, but if I listened without complaining, she'd tell another story with enough battles and bloodshed to keep me happy for weeks."

"Imnada blood is a medicine?"

"It's said to contain properties that heal any hurt,

close any wound. I never believed it and most Imnada discount the ancient stories as myth, but my grandmother believed. She said all myths contain a shred of truth."

"That truth being that your blood holds the power to close the door into death? It's impossible."

"Corey believes. Enough that he wants to cellar me like a fine vintage. St. Leger 1817. Good oaky notes and a light, fruity finish."

A log fell in the fireplace, shooting sparks, throwing light across her face, and he realized that what he'd taken for tears and fear was actually anger, a fury as red and hot as his own.

"How can you joke?"

"What else can I do, Callista?"

"You can fight back. You can make him pay for treating you like dirt. You can show him you're not going to let him hurt you or humiliate you or . . . or . . ."

"Do we talk of me . . . or of you, Fey-blood?"

"I spent years trying to please my brother," she said softly, though still her voice shook with rage. "Trying to show him I was worth his attention and his love. It didn't matter. He sold me to Victor Corey as if I were a dog or a horse or a stick of furniture." She fairly quivered with unspent fury.

He knew the fire that churned her belly and coursed like lava through her veins. He understood her feelings of futility and powerlessness. Hadn't he experienced the same for the last two years?

"If I see him again, I'll kill him myself," she whispered. "And should Corey's threats come to pass, he'd better sleep with eyes wide open lest he find a knife through his heart."

David ignored the pain and sat up, swinging his feet onto the floor. The room swam in and out of focus, but he refused to swoon. Instead, he clamped his jaw and met her dark gaze.

"You walk the paths of the dead, Fey-blood." He levered himself up on his feet. "You do not send others down that road." He took a few shaky steps toward her. "Take it from someone who's sent many a man to Arawn's realm," He skimmed her sides before pulling her close. "Once you start killing, it becomes very hard to stop."

She stayed with him even after he slept—peacefully this time. His breathing deep and even, his body no longer racked with chills, his skin no longer burning like an inferno. It was a sleep without the moaning whimpers and short jagged cries that turned her stomach and made her want to place her hands over her ears. Such pain he'd endured, such horrific suffering at the hands of his own people. No wonder he would not speak of it. No wonder he carried such rage within his heart. But she'd heard other things as well. Darker secrets and shadowy dreams. And these were what kept her awake even as the hours ticked by and the earth turned toward dawn.

When the clock struck four and the first birds called in the fields, Callista rose. Pulled her gown across her shoulders, struggled with the buttons as best she could, and grabbed up a shawl.

The corridor was unlit, but she felt her way past rows of closed doors, through a long gallery where centuries of de Coursys held sway, and slipped down the stairs. Perhaps a novel or maybe even a shot of brandy. Anything to dull her mind and slow her pulse.

The castle was immense. Room after room, all threaded by a maze of corridors, passages, and stairways. She found her way back to the entrance hall by sheer luck, the great double doors barred for the night, a lamp left burning upon a table. But the salon where she'd spent a few awkward hours before arguing her way to David's side proved elusive. Behind one door, a paneled lounge. Behind another, a billiard room, a cue left abandoned upon the table. A third turned out to be the dining room, silent and empty, the sideboard cleared for breakfast. She descended a staircase and passed through a long hall populated by suits of armor and enough weaponry to outfit an army. Just when she'd lost hope of ever finding her way, she rounded a corner and there it was.

The door stood ajar. A light flickered within.

She peeked around the jamb to find a man seated in a chair by the fire, a whisky glass in hand, a crumbling old book open in his lap. From his tall, lean physique and his clothing—a sober coat of brown and a pair of well-worn boots—Callista would have mistaken him for the local vicar or a servant taking advantage of his master's absence, except for the aura of command that shimmered off him like a halo, even at rest. This was a man who wore control like armor. Even his stark, chiseled face registered nothing but mild surprise at her arrival, though his eyes glittered like blue ice, and when he turned his full gaze upon her, a shiver raced up her spine.

"I'm sorry to intrude, my lord. I didn't think anyone would be awake this time of night," she said.

Gray de Coursy rose from his chair. "I don't sleep well, either. Perhaps we can keep each other company."

A shadow rippled across the carpet like water, and Callista's heart fluttered before sinking into her toes as a voice croaked and scraped across the surface of her brain. *Death. Death. Death.*

Badb stepped from behind the door, holding out a hand to draw her into the room. "Your novel and your brandy can wait, Callista Hawthorne. Your questions cannot."

He woke alone. Air tickled over his bare skin, cool and scented with dust and old leather, steel and smoke. His chest hurt, but it was a bearable ache. He mended, slow and frustrating though it might be, and he would live to fight. To kill.

Callista had retired to her own room, hopefully to rest. She'd earned it, looking after him like a damned nursemaid. Another reason, if he still needed one, to forget the crazy ideas flitting through his head. It wouldn't be long before he'd be a full-time invalid. He'd not trap Callista into the role of drudge. He might be selfish, but he wasn't cruel. And Callista deserved more than to spend her days watching him disintegrate before her eyes. David had thought there was nothing worse than the hell the Fey-blood's black spell had wrought. He'd been wrong.

Worse than death was having what you desired as close as a mingled breath and being forced to walk away. It was looking at Callista and seeing what could be, perhaps even should be, while knowing it would never happen. And worst of all, it was knowing that even the brief time remaining was tainted with prophecies of death.

His enemies gathered.

The danger mounted.

The sooner Callista departed Addershiels for the Isle of Skye, the better. She would be safe there, beyond Corey's reach.

She would be safe there, beyond *his* reach.

He couldn't change his fate, but he might . . . just might . . . be able to change hers.

That would have to be enough.

15

From the window of his room within the comfortable hotel, Corey looked down on the busy square and noted every coach and carriage, as well as the throng of busy pedestrians out on a rare sunny day after a week of rain and sullen skies. He scanned the passersby, not because he thought he might spy the towering figure of David St. Leger cutting his way through the crowd or Callista's trim shape and dowdy attire moving in and out of the shops in nearby Catherine Street, but simply out of habit after a week on the road north in search of the elusive runaways.

Only the phlegmy clearing of a throat broke him from his scrutiny of a suspicious gentleman standing head and shoulders above those around him on a nearby corner. Corey swung around to face the weasely slump-backed cutpurse, his mutilated hand half hidden in the wide pocket of a greasy smock.

He continued to utilize gallows bait like this one when necessary, but his lip curled in repugnance at the stench of gin and defeat.

"I paid you your pennies. Is there a reason you're still here?"

"You said a shilling," the thug growled, his yellow teeth showing, in what Corey supposed was meant to be a threatening leer. "This ain't even half that."

"Bring me a shilling's worth of information next time. What you've given me is tavern gossip and whores' whispers," he answered before turning back to watch the gentleman across the square.

He hadn't moved, and the swarm of afternoon strollers and street vendors with their baskets and sacks had to joggle round him in consternation, yet, oddly, none confronted the man. Instead, they seemed to avoid him, heads down as they scurried past. As Corey continued to watch, the gentleman looked up at the window, his face shadowed by a broad-brimmed hat, but Corey had the sensation of the man's stare drilling down into his brain.

A crow settled on the ledge just outside the window, its great black wings spread, its beak wide as it croaked and squawked. A wash of cold splashed over Corey's shoulders and down his spine. He shooed the bird away, but the feeling of menace remained.

"You're trying to cheat me, you is," the thief-taker complained. "It's him just like in them drawings. I seen him with my own eyes not thirty miles from here."

Corey rubbed a hand over the knob of his cane, his patience fraying. "Then where's the woman? He's traveling with a woman." He rounded on his informer, cane raised. "Did your pox-ridden slatterns mention *her*? I want them both, you grimy, flea-ridden sewer rat."

The man's back rounded as if he'd been struck, but

he held his ground, coughing wetly into a large soiled handkerchief. "Next time, I'll take my news to the other fella. He'll pay what's owed me," he grumbled.

Corey visibly relaxed his face into a smile, though inside every alarm was ringing. "Other fellow?"

"You're not the only one out there asking about that St. Leger bloke. And he pays twice as much. I only come to you 'cause we had a deal. Not no more. Not when I see how you pay honest chaps for honest work."

"Honest, my ass," Corey replied. "You probably stole your mother's liver as you were being squeezed out between her legs. Give me a name. Who is he? Who is this champion of the rights of honest thieves everywhere?"

The man's expression grew petulant, arms folded over his chest. "We're to go to the Swan and Crown and tell 'em we've got news for Beskin. That's all I know."

It didn't matter. Let this Beskin son of a bitch play seek-and-find up and down the Great North Road; Corey knew where the two of them were headed. He would be there in a few days more. Then all he had to do was wait for St. Leger and Callista to come to him.

Corey smiled and flipped the cellar rat another penny. "And there's a half crown more if you tell this jack at the Swan and Crown that St. Leger's halfway to Cardiff with his doxy in tow."

As the man stretched to catch the coin, Corey's hand shot out, grabbing him around the throat, his fingers digging deep into his flesh. He leaned in, his voice low and almost pleasant. "Don't ever tell me I don't pay what's owing."

The penny hit the floor to roll away under a table.

The man hit the floor and lay unmoving.

David eased a shirt on over his head, stifling a groan as pain slashed up his chest and into his skull. The room wavered but did not spin. His body ached but did not collapse. And he'd be damned if he'd lay in that bed another minute. Still, he sat and breathed deeply for a moment before he dared attempt to pull on his breeches, glancing only briefly at the door.

"Come in and scold me in person," he called out. "Much easier than glaring at me through the keyhole."

The latch turned, and Gray de Coursy stood on the threshold, bearing a whisky bottle and two glasses. At least he assumed it was Gray. This gentleman bore the familiar rangy build and stark aristocratic features, but gone was the champagne shine and the cool, prideful gaze that had England's elite climbing over themselves to curry favor . . . and gain a husband for their daughters. Instead, he looked battle-toughened and forbidding in a way he never had before, even during the long years campaigning. Perhaps because this war was far more personal, the stakes much closer to home.

"How did you know I was there?" Gray asked, placing the glasses upon a cabinet. Filling them with whisky.

"You always were horrible at stealth. You have the tread of an elephant. I heard you halfway down the corridor." David sucked in a breath and resumed the laborious process of dressing. One leg . . . easy does it. "Stick to aerial surveillance and leave scouting enemy terrain to those familiar with the ground."

Now for his boots. When had his legs grown so damned long? His feet seemed bloody miles away. He squeezed his eyes shut, wishing for his valet. Wishing for any valet. Wishing for a room that didn't waver in and out of focus.

"Do you consider Addershiels in the hands of the enemy?" Gray turned around, a glass in each hand. David noted the bandage wrapped around his palm and his waxy complexion and silently cursed the draught's sinister destruction.

"The Duncallans, a Fey, and a dead traitor roam the halls. It's either enemy territory or a circus freak show, and I learned more than I care to about circuses in the past few weeks." David accepted the glass, though he did not taste. Somehow, the idea of alcohol at—he checked the clock—two in the afternoon didn't seem quite as appealing as it once had.

"An awful lot of people track your scent, St. Leger," Gray commented, sipping his drink.

If it had been David, he'd have downed the whole in one throat-burning swallow. Hell, he'd have tipped the bottle to his mouth and washed the world away. Or at one time he would have. Gray had always been a cold fish, passionless and prim as any maiden aunt and more severe than a Puritan. Gray was methodical, practical, and calculating. It drove David mad, but it had probably kept him alive through five years, three countries, and countless battles.

Not that he'd ever admit that to Gray. The man was as puffed up as a bloody rooster as it was.

"You can use the title, but that doesn't make me a soldier. Not anymore."

"The Ossine believe otherwise," Gray said.

"I wonder why. Maybe it has something to do with a stolen book and a dead Imnada courier, and a plot to suck me in that Machiavelli would have endorsed."

"The book came from the Deepings library and my grandfather's collection. It was Sir Dromon Pryor and the Ossine who stole it first. I merely reclaimed it."

"I doubt the semantics will make any difference to Kineally's family when they discover their kin has been buried with a stake through his heart, but I'll be sure to use it as my defense when the Ossine come to claim my head."

One boot on. He gritted his teeth. One to go.

"I wouldn't have risked Kineally or you if it weren't important."

"I don't want to hear about your insurrection or your new friends, Gray. This madness has cost too many lives already. You claim your efforts are to bring about peace and freedom. All I see is a trail of bodies."

"I'm offering the clans hope. We're dying, David. Not just you and me and Mac, but all of us. Every shapechanger in every holding. How long will our kind last? Our clans are fading, our powers dying out, and the Palings barely hold the world away from our lands anymore. We can't survive without allies, nor can we last more than a few generations without new blood added to the lines."

"I've seen plenty of blood. Unfortunately, most of it has been mine. Will it be yours next? Or Mac's? Perhaps Lord and Lady Duncallan's? Or will they be the ones wielding the blades alongside that feathered Fey and her trained shifter?"

"James and Katherine are good friends and loyal to the work of peace, David. James is a scholar of Imnada history and Katherine freed Lucan from a Fey prison. Surely that counts for something in your suspicious mind."

"Of course, though I'm not sure whether counting Lucan Kingkiller, the shapechangers' greatest traitor, among your associates is an advantage. This was the man whose lust and crimes instigated a mass slaughter."

"And he was also the commander who brokered a truce during the Viyachne Rebellion that spared thousands of lives. Lucan is as much an outcast as any *emnil*. And in as much danger. After all, he's a murderer to the Fey-bloods and a traitor to the Imnada."

"Sounds familiar. Is that why you're so chummy?"

Success. David straightened from pulling on his second boot, winded, nauseated, and dizzy, but fully dressed.

"I will use any edge I can to topple Pryor and his faction. Lucan is a weapon that can't be overlooked. He bears a power unheard-of among the Imnada these days. And his strength and his leadership are still talked of today."

"As are his lechery and his treason."

"Morgana used him. Her witchery ensorcelled him."

"Is that what he told you? I think it's his witchery that has ensorcelled you. Either that or his crow sidekick has cast a spell on you."

"They saved you, David. They protected Miss Hawthorne from Victor Corey's hired gun and they kept you alive when that bullet shaved a groove down your rib and ended against a lung. You owe them your life."

"Then the joke's on them. My life isn't worth tuppence."

"And Callista? How would she have felt had you died?"

"Don't talk to me about Callista. She's not your concern and you know nothing about it."

"I know she cares for you. And I know she fears for your future."

"She should fear *me*." He sat bent in his chair, elbows upon his knees, hands clasped together as if in prayer.

"Why?"

"It doesn't matter. Just send her to Skye, Gray. If you do nothing else for me ever, send her to Skye and safety. I'll be your man. I'll do whatever you ask."

"Whatever I ask?" Gray's gaze burned like ice.

"Anything."

"Very well. I'll send her to her aunt. But you're mine now, David St. Leger. Welcome to my war."

No matter how Callista stared at herself in the mirror, there was no transforming her serviceable gown into a ball dress of silver tissue and seed pearls. She tilted her head to the side and squinted. No, that didn't help, either. She huffed a curl from her face. She'd never cared about her appearance before. It had been Branston who'd chosen her elaborate velvets and expensive silks. He'd told her she must look as wealthy and elegant as her clients if she hoped to persuade them of her skills. But now . . . now she was the guest of a duke's heir. She ought to at least dress as if she hadn't fallen off the rat catcher's wagon.

And no, it had nothing to do with David. He'd seen her looking her worst. He'd seen her in nothing at all. It was not about impressing him.

She turned to inspect her back. Sized up the faded grass stain streaking the skirt. Dropped onto a chair.

So, perhaps it might be a little bit about David.

Katherine Duncallan was beautiful, with that fiery red hair and those golden eyes. She was graceful and stylish and the perfect baroness, and she made Callista feel a perfect frump.

She lifted her head at a tap on the door.

"May I come in, Miss Hawthorne?"

Speak of the devil.

"I hope you don't mind my intruding, but I thought you might need fresh clothes to wear. You didn't exactly arrive with a coach full of trunks and a lady's maid in tow."

"Did you?"

Lady Duncallan laid a floaty, tissue-thin gown in crimson and gold on the bed. "One trunk and Nellie, who's a magician with hair and wrinkles; fabric, not face, I'm afraid. I'm happy to send her to you."

"Thank you, my lady. I suppose a borrowed gown from you is better than a cloak of crow feathers from Badb."

"You'd look lovely in black, though I would recommend a garment underneath. Only one of the true Fey can carry off nudity without raising eyebrows. And please call me Katherine. When I hear 'my lady' I peer round in search of James's mother, who, thank heavens, is safely rooted in Tunbridge Wells."

Her friendly smile reminded Callista of Bianca Parrino, and she found herself relaxing despite her discomfiture. She took up the gown, holding it against her as she turned this way and that in front of the cheval mirror, the skirt floating around her ankles, the vibrant colors pulling color into her cheeks and sparkle to her eyes.

"Mr. St. Leger is very handsome, isn't he?" Katherine continued. "A bit like one would assume Apollo might look; all golden hair and flashing eyes and a face chiseled from Roman marble. He's not at all how I imagined he'd be. In London he always seems so charming and shallow. Laughing all the time. Always in the midst of some scandal. All the men want to be him and all the ladies want to bed him."

"He uses that golden smile like armor. It keeps people from looking too close and discovering the truth," Callista said, meeting the other woman's eyes in the mirror.

"You discovered it. You learned he's Imnada."

Death, came the thought, quickly suppressed, though she couldn't erase the memory of the scars on his back or the scars across his palm. Her hand trembled as she dropped the gown back on the bed.

"Yes, but that's not the truth he was hiding."

". . . silver disk of the Gylferion . . ."

David caught only every third word of Lord Duncallan's conversation. Enough to nod appropriately or make suitable noises when it was his turn to speak, but beyond that, his attention remained fixed upon the door and the woman framed there.

Was this the same woman who battled cutthroats in an alley with a broken plank? Who slammed Beskin to his knees with a bagful of bells? Who sat beside a cook-fire, her face a rosy glow, as she chatted with churls and laughed with charlatans, or shook the dust from her skirts as she gathered kindling or collected water?

It couldn't be. This vision carried herself like a queen, and when she moved into the room, her hips swayed and her skin shone as invitingly as any courtesan's. A complicated knot of dark curls exposed a long, graceful throat, while the cut of her gown revealed the rounded curve of her breasts.

". . . four of them placed in the obelisk . . ."

Then she met his gaze and her eyes contained a mix of shy pleasure and self-deprecating amusement, and the goddess turned back into Callista Hawthorne, the woman he knew. The woman he'd grown to love despite all his efforts to do otherwise.

". . . so I leapt on the table and skewered him with my butter knife . . ."

"You don't say," David mumbled, crossing the room toward her as if drawn by an invisible cord.

He shouldn't go to her. He should exchange gossip with Lady Duncallan or seek out Gray for another stern lecture. He should shed his skin and become the wolf, hunting along the wide empty coast and in the deep woods beside the brown, muddy river.

But while his mind screamed at him to run away, his body ached to be near her for as long as he could. To revel in these few precious days before reality kicked him in the gut. And why not? If Gray kept his word, the dream would die its own death. Callista would soon be beyond his reach, forever lost behind Dunsgathaic's high walls, shrouded in the gray of the *bandraoi* sisterhood.

Until then . . .

His steps came slower than normal, but she waited and her smile widened in welcome as he folded her hand in his.

"What did you say to Duncallan? He has the oddest grin on his face," she remarked.

"Honestly? I have no idea what the man was babbling on about. My attention was focused elsewhere."

"Do you like it?" she asked, her cheeks turning pink.

"I'd have thought my tongue on the floor would be answer enough."

"Dress a pig in pearls, she is still a pig."

"If you must compare yourself to an animal, rather call yourself the sleek and slender otter or the swan, whose beauty hides a lethal ferocity."

"Not the wolf?"

"Why *be* the wolf when you can possess one of your very own?"

"I'll wager you say that to all the girls."

"Yes, but they didn't get the joke."

"Who's there?" David whispered to the darkness. The bedchamber lay wrapped in gloomy shadows, the only light coming from the fire that smoked and guttered; the only sounds, rain smacking the windows, the shush of a curtain caught in a draft, and his heartbeat drumming in his ears. But something had woken him. Some sound that shouldn't have been. Some wisp of a scent.

A figure passed in front of the window, midnight blue against the black and stormy night beyond the glass. "It's me."

"Callista?"

"Were you expecting someone else?" She whispered the words that set flame to wick, the candle sputtering and crackling as it burst to life.

She still wore the crimson beaded satin, but where before she moved and spoke like a seductress, now she scowled at him and gripped the candlestick as if she might bash him over the head.

"When were you going to tell me?"

He rubbed the sleep from his eyes, scratched at his bandages, which itched like the very devil, and tried to decipher what in the hell she was talking about.

"Or were you going to tell me at all? After all, you've got Gray to do your dirty work. You can tease and charm all you like while behind your smile you're deciding my future for me. First you try to marry me off to Sam Oakham and now you're shoving me onto the Duncallans as if I were unclaimed luggage. I risked everything to escape people who were trying to live my life for me. I refuse to roll over and let you do the same."

He dragged himself out of bed, wincing only once or twice. The cool night air slapped him awake, and he was able to concentrate on the thunderous expression darkening her eyes and tightening her face. Of course, he was also able to focus on the way her gown dipped low and revealed the valley of her breasts, the perfume rising warm and fragrant off her heated skin, and the shapely curve of her hips.

He padded across the floor, combing a hand through his hair, noting the way her gaze traveled over his naked body before her chin lifted in a show of defiance and she stared only upon his face.

"I wish you wouldn't do that," she snapped. "Most men would at least don a dressing gown for propriety's sake."

"You came to my room in the middle of the night. Propriety was left behind long ago," he said calmly. Taking her hand, he threaded his fingers with hers, feeling the stiffness in her body, the way she held herself rigid and unwilling. "You must have had some reason for coming."

"Yes, to pummel you with a heavy object and tell you what a cowardly, backhanded, deceitful creature you are. Wolf? More like a rat."

He raised their linked hands for a kiss on her fingers, on the underside of her wrist. "Do you think I want you to leave? To put you on that coach and know I'll never see you again? But it's for the best. The Duncallans are highborn Fey-bloods. Your aunt will welcome them—and you—with open arms. Far different if you arrive escorted by an Imnada shapechanger who also happens to be a single gentleman of scandalous repute."

Bare inches separated them. Her perfume intoxicated him, her gaze was both endless and clear as a mountain stream. He knew what she wanted. He sensed it in every rise and fall of her chest, every sweep of her lashes across her cheeks, every expression rushing like wind across her face. His body would go up in flames if she kissed him.

"This is your chance to erase the weeks we spent together. No one need ever know."

"I'll know. Don't pretty this up by claiming you're doing it for me. You're doing it for yourself. You're running away like you've been running since the war ended. Since the curse was cast."

Her breath smelled of wine and cinnamon and oranges. Had he called her eyes muddy hazel? They shone with amber and glimmered with jade. Her lips were moist. He smelled desire and heat on her flesh. He closed the inches between them, his mouth hovering above her own as their breath mingled in the prelude to a kiss. Arousal damped his own skin and licked like honey along his nerves.

"I'm trying to save your blasted life," he whispered.

"You're trying to control it," she answered.

She stepped back, taking him with her. Step by slow step, she backed toward the bed, her gaze still hot, but now it contained as much passion as anger. His brain locked. He knew what he should do and what he wanted to do, but his legs just kept moving in pace with hers, his groin tightening as she pushed him down on the edge of the mattress and stood between his legs, her hands upon his shoulders.

"This is my life, David St. Leger. And I'm in control."

He closed his eyes, but every inch of her was etched upon his brain, the creamy skin, the round perfect breasts, nipples pebble hard, long slender legs, a brush of fine brown hair between them. He opened his eyes and she was there blazing in the crimson and gold of a flame or a comet. He was the moth, the dust pulled along in her wake. He couldn't break free, but he tried. Really, he tried.

"Damn it, Callista. You don't understand."

She kissed his chin, the corner of his mouth, his nose. "Then explain it to me. I'm not simple. I walk the tangled paths of death. I think I can fathom the inner workings of the male mind."

He rested his hands on her hips. His chest hurt, but it wasn't the bandages cutting off his breath or the blood flow to his brain. It was Callista, in front of him, within him. Waking and sleeping, she was there, offering him dreams of exquisite pleasure and horrific tragedy. Speaking of tangled. He throbbed with wanting her, every nerve strained and tense.

"Death. It's all death. I have a dream over and over. A dream of killing you, Callista. I don't know how or why, but I know it as well as I know my own name. I refuse to let this dream spill into waking."

She pushed him back upon the bed, climbing up beside him, her gown hiking up to reveal the silk of her stockings, the ribbons of her garters red against the white of her thighs. He was erect, his need evident, his surrender inevitable. She smiled, a dimple flashing in her otherwise solemn face.

"And if I know this dream?" she asked. "If I've seen this future and don't believe it?" She leaned close, her breath hot against his ear. "What's the use of visions if they can't serve as warnings? If you can't change the truths they reveal?"

He'd but to turn his head and her lips would be on his. Instead he held still. He could be strong. He could refuse the seduction. None would believe St. Leger the rakish bed-hopper would turn away a woman, but this wasn't just any woman. And this night would spell the beginning or the beginning of the end. "I won't hurt you, Callista. Not ever."

"Then that is the truth and the dream is just that—a dream."

She retreated, and for a moment, he thought she meant to leave him there, alone on the bed, his body shuddering with unspent desire. Instead she straddled him, the gown around her hips. She pulled the combs one by one from her hair, letting it fall like a cloud around her shoulders, then she reached behind her with one arm to slide loose a ribbon. A shoulder lay bare. Another ribbon and the bodice spilled open. Where the hell had this wanton come from? He'd known experienced mistresses with less tongue-tying pillow moves than this. She took his wrists, guiding his hands to her breasts. He couldn't help himself. His palms cupped them, his fingers traced the delicious curve of them, his thumbs grazed her nipples until they blossomed beneath his touch and she gasped.

"I don't want you to see me"—his voice shook and then broke—"see me fail under the draught and the curse. To wait and watch as I die."

"The truth at last. You're frightened. What happened to 'the wolf doesn't hide and the wolf doesn't run'?"

She rocked against him before sliding onto his shaft. Inch by inch, she took him within her tight, wet heat. It was his turn to gasp, his body jerking up as she arched, taking him deeper, harder, her muscles closing around him. Spasms of pleasure and fear and pain and desire hit him like a mountain storm, his body driving up into her over and over as he groaned his release.

"The wolf," he panted as he spilled his seed within her womb, "is a craven."

16

She'd asked for a quiet spot and a close-faced servant had showed her to this small summerhouse. Looking around, she wondered if he'd acted out of kindness or spite. The paint was peeling, the roof had more holes than a sieve, and weeds sprouted from between the floorboards. But it *was* quiet, with only birdsong and a constant breeze rustling the ivy that twined its way up the posts and over the railing.

The bells stood abandoned on a rickety, leaf-strewn table while Callista sat in drowsy contemplation of the wild expanse of lawn, populated only by a dozen sheep and a boy set to watch them.

She'd gotten as far as tracing the patterns, shattering the air with the ring of the first bell, and seeing the way open before her.

Then fear stopped her cold.

Fear and dread of what she might discover. Of what she might unleash.

"You say you mistrust what I have told you, and yet

you hesitate. Perhaps there is some small part of you that believes."

Callista had not heard Badb's approach. Hardly surprising, though after their last talk, she thought the Fey might have wreaked enough havoc for one lifetime.

Apparently not.

"The Fey are known to speak in riddles and half-truths when it suits them," Callista answered. "The old stories are full of examples. You could have some hidden reason for making me doubt myself and my ability."

Badb shone pale as milk in the sunlight, but for the dusky rose of her nipples beneath her cloak of feathers and the snapping black of her eyes. "I've lived among your kind long enough that I've learned to speak plainly and in words of few syllables lest I be misunderstood. St. Leger is right to worry over the man Corey's intentions. Lord Arawn in his arrogance has always believed his realm impregnable. He has never understood the threat the daughters of his seed could be, should they choose to wield their true power over the shadows. The grel are not the worst of Annwn's creatures that would rise up at the chance to hunt among the living."

"I would never offer Victor Corey such a weapon. I would die first and the door would be closed to him forever." The kneeling woman and the upraised knife.

"What is it about you humans?" Badb's pearly white teeth were bared in an angry grimace, the feathers of her cloak upright and rustling. "You are so gallant and so childish with your noble vows of sacrifice. Do you truly know what it means to swear such a vow? Or to live with the folly of it ever after?"

"Do not take your impatience out on her, Badb. She is not to blame for your plight."

Another visitor. So much for quiet and out of the way. Callista's solitary summerhouse was busy as a London thoroughfare. Lucan pushed through the overgrown shrubs, his steps oddly silent for such a large man. He offered her a bow as if he were a knight and she a great lady. She supposed at least the knight part might be true, but she was no lady. David had made sure of that.

"No, she is not to blame. You are," Badb snapped, her cloak aswirl, the black feathers purple and indigo and silver in the morning sun.

"I did not force you to honor your oath," Lucan answered gently.

High spots of color flashed in Badb's cheeks. "You did not force me to keep my promise, but you knew I would. I had no choice."

"You are more worthy than you know, Badb." His unfathomable gaze passed over Callista's bells to rest on her face. "There is always a choice, my lady."

"Corey would have me unlock the gates of hell," Callista answered. "The world would be helpless against Arawn's creatures."

"It cannot happen once you are among the *bandraoi* on Skye. None can scale those walls."

"And what happens to David when I leave?"

"He stays here," Lucan said. "He works to make peace between the shapechangers and the Fey-bloods. He dies. As you have your path, he has his."

She had been walking the path marked out for her

by others her whole life. First as her mother's acolyte in the ways of necromancy. Then as Branston's mummer's monkey, dancing to his tune. And in death, paths were her lifeline, where she risked losing herself forever with one stray step. When would she ever have the chance to forge a trail of her own?

"What if I choose to stay with David and not travel on to Skye and my aunt?" Callista asked.

"As paths have forks, so, too, can you make the choice to take a different turning," Lucan replied. "But there are always consequences to our decisions. Joining the sisters of High Danu would offer you protection, instruction, and a chance to heal the rift within your house. You could rise in the ranks of *bandraoi*, in time perhaps become Ard-siur and rule Dunsgathaic yourself. Death would be as easy as stepping between rooms in a house, and the creatures there no more dangerous to you than biting fleas at your ankles."

"And if I don't choose to go?"

"Danger, treachery, and a heart's greatest sorrow," Badb said. "I have seen it. You have seen it."

"That doesn't mean I believe. My gift is one of necromancy. The only knowledge of the future I have is that offered by the dead. Snatches of moments handed to me like crumbs."

"It is well known that Fey magic works in uncharted ways when it comes in contact with the shapechangers," Badb replied. "The Imnada are not of this world, perhaps not even of this plane of being. This disparity has always been their greatest strength as well as their greatest vulnerability. Perhaps St. Leger is affecting the mage energy within you and this gift of prophecy is a product of this strange warping and shifting." She shrugged with a ruffle of feathers. "Or perhaps it is as you say and there is nothing to these dreams but cobweb and moonlight and you have nothing to fear in what you see." Her black eyes crackled. "But dare you take that risk?"

"You will go to Skye, my lady," Lucan interrupted, his voice never rising, but still the command was unmistakable. "You will lose yourself in study. You will become a true daughter of death. In time, the memory of these few brief weeks will fade, and you will learn to be content."

Knots twisted her stomach, her skin cold as she met his black gaze. "Content? You were imprisoned out of time for a thousand years and more. Did you grow content? Did your memories fade?"

He bowed his head, his look contrite. "Nay. They shone pure as eldritch steel and trapped me tighter than the silver chains the Fey bound me with as they sent me to my doom. And no passing of years ever dulled them."

Callista touched each bell in turn: Key, Summoner, Blade. Within the curved and polished silver bowl of the metal, she saw the distorted reflection of her face, the columns of the summerhouse, the shimmering green of the trees. She opened her heart, seeing deeper, using her mind to push into the power running and rippling under her skin. A daughter of death, Lucan called her. And so she was. Her powers were inherited from Arawn and passed down through his human lover and the daughter she bore him; diluted over the centuries but never disappearing. Power that offered her life, death, and the answers found within both worlds.

She saw those generations of women, faces melding and merging through time, down to her, clear, bright, and startling. But she also sensed the shades of those not yet born—dimmer, faded, and ragged as an old cloak. Daughters not yet conceived. Seed not yet spilled. She was the linchpin between these two lines. She was the hinge upon which her house's fading hopes rested.

Callista squared her shoulders, placing a hand back upon Key, as if anchoring herself among women past and future.

"I've made my choice."

David found Callista in the Addershiels library, curled in a chair by the window, head buried in an enormous book. He didn't enter at first. Instead he leaned against the doorframe and regarded this surprising, miraculous woman who'd burst into his life like cannon fire, turning him upside down. Making him feel again. Making him love as he'd never loved before. As he watched, she licked a finger and turned the page, her brows scrunched in thought . . . or confusion. Hard to decide which.

He cocked his head, hoping to read the spine, but her skirts were in the way and all he managed was Th . . . Nur . . . oire. Hardly helpful. This much *was* obvious. It was no romantic novel or swashbuckling adventure, not unless the hero had just died or the heroine had run off with the cabin boy. Callista wore a three-furrow frown, and he could almost hear her teeth grinding. Beyond that, she seemed relaxed, her hair bundled hastily up in a bun, one foot bare, the other dangling a slipper.

"Do I have a carrot sprouting from my ear or a boil on my neck?"

He smiled. "What gave me away?"

Her eyes met his over the top of the book, glimmering with laughter. "You're not exactly unobtrusive when you enter a room, and your stare is like being struck by lightning or smashed by a falling piano."

Straightening from his post at the door, he took a seat on a nearby couch. "I'm not sure whether to be pleased or offended by that comparison."

"Pleased, I think. It had the women of London fawning over you." Her glimmer brightened to a giggle, which she quickly smothered. "Poor Lady Fowler with her etchings. I almost feel sorry for her."

"You needn't. Hearts never entered into it. It was a game to her . . . a quick thrill . . . a way to relieve the tedium of her days and the loneliness of her nights."

Her gaze dimmed. "For both of you."

He didn't respond. There was no need anymore. Callista understood the depths he'd reached and had not shrunk from him in revulsion or fear. His horrors had been laid bare and she'd not run. Her courage and compassion still shocked him, but it was the laughter they shared and their comfortable familiarity that bowled him over. He nodded toward the book in her lap, letting the moment slip away.

"Is this what you've been up to while I've been laid out like Egypt's last pharaoh? Raiding Gray's bookshelves?"

"All your stories about the Imnada intrigued me, and I was curious about Rinaci and Edern. Did you know he took the shape of a boar twenty-five feet tall with teeth as long as daggers?"

"Yes, and when he roared in anger, the trees bowed before him and the skies cracked with lightning. There are a thousand tales of Rinaci. Each more unbelievable than the last."

"Do you believe the *afailth luinan* a legend with no truth behind it?"

"It sounds like madness . . . my blood able to save a life? To close a wound? I can only wish I possessed such a power. Do you know how many friends and comrades I lost to French guns on the battlefield? Loyal soldiers I could have saved?"

"You said your grandmother believed that every legend bore a grain of truth."

"My grandmother was a dreamer. She believed the ancient sagas of the ships that rode the stars on waves of light and fire, bringing the clans to earth. She honored the N'thuil, voice and vessel to the crystal Jai Idrish. She respected the wisdom and the guidance of the shamans of the Ossine. And, thank the Mother, she didn't live to see the splintering of her people and the ultimate shaming of her grandson before the Gather."

"But the way you speak of her, it's clear she loved you. Surely she would have stood by you. She wouldn't have turned away when you needed her most."

"The *avaklos*, those shapechangers who reside outside the Palings, are always suspect, their allegiance to the clans always under question. It would have pained her, but Gram would have done what was necessary to uphold the family's honor. She would have obeyed the laws, no matter the cost."

"The laws are wrong, then, and should be changed."

"You sound like an arrogant lordling I know who

thinks just because he wants something badly enough he can make it happen."

"And why not? That's how dreams are realized."

"Because it's as much a fantasy as Rinaci and Edern. Wanting isn't enough."

"That's when you have to work and fight for it."

"Has Gray been whispering in your ear? I feel as if I've had this conversation before." He rubbed a hand over his face and the back of his neck. "You ask me what my grandmother would have done had she been faced with my crimes. Gray lived that situation. His grandfather is leader of the Imnada, but he spoke not one word as his grandson was handed over to the Ossine. The years of war hardened Gray, but it was the Duke of Morieux's denunciation that transformed him."

Her gaze drifted to his shoulder and the scarred flesh she knew lay beneath his shirt. "How"—she ran an agitated finger up and down the edge of the book— "how did you survive such an atrocity?"

A question with no easy or comforting answer. His muscles tightened to knots, his back twitching with a ghost pain as real as the red-hot iron that burned his mark away. "Survival *was* the punishment, Callista."

"Lord Duncallan says that if Beskin catches you, it could be the death of the Imnada rebels. That you know too much."

He laughed. "It's rare that I've been accused of too much intelligence, but I suppose it's true. The answer is simple; don't get caught." His smile faded. "Or kill Beskin first."

"You barely survived . . ." Her words faded, but David was well aware of his shortcomings during his last confrontation with the Ossine.

He would not make the same mistakes again. He would not flinch. He would rip that damned silver sword from the bastard's hand and bury it in his chest hilt-deep.

"Eudo Beskin has been a blight on my soul for two years. It's time I repaid him for his tender mercies."

Her gaze wandered over his face as if seeking some answer; her breath quick, her body trembling. "And Corey? My brother? You can't face them all alone. "

"The wolf doesn't hide, Callista. It hunts or it dies."

"But it's impossible. How can there be peace when so many on both sides are unwilling to look beyond a hatred going back millennia?"

"Simple," he answered, meeting her steady gaze. "One person at a time."

That night, when sleep refused to come and the dark seemed fraught with restless shades, she knew exactly where she was going. Rising from their shared bed, she tugged on a heavy, quilted robe. It dragged the floor and the sleeves fell down over her hands, but it was warm and smelled of David. She cast one last glance at his sleeping form twined within the blankets. The dying fire illuminated his muscled frame, brightened the gold of his hair, carved deep lines into his face. His normal sun-bronzed skin seemed faded and washed-out, but just looking at him sent butterflies banging around her insides and squeezed her heart. Turning abruptly, she left his room for hers.

This bedchamber was twice as large and three times as elegant, but devoid of the memories of love-damped skin and soft, shuddering moans. There was nothing here but fine furniture, expensive curios, and her own uncertainties. Before she could change her mind, she took down the box from the top of a high cabinet, lit a single candle, arranged the bells before her, and then, among the flickering, crawling shadows, she read each and every letter from her mother to her lost family, beginning with the first effusive explosion of excitement and hope through the years that followed until the last few notes, just as crammed with anecdotes and news about her life, but the happiness had faded. Nothing left but grief and resignation.

"She loved you. Surely she would have stood by you. She wouldn't have turned away when you needed her most."

Her words to David echoed back at her from the high ceilings and dark windows. When she spoke, had she been referring to his grandmother or to the Armstrong family, who'd cut off their wayward daughter as completely as if she'd died? How could her aunt have done this to her only sister? How could she have abandoned her with nothing? Not a word? Not a hope?

Callista folded the last letter and traced the first symbol. The notes of Key rang pure, shattering the gloom, cracking the barriers between one world and the other. An icy wind rushed forth, riming the tabletop, frosting her breath, and curling against her bare toes. She wrapped the robe more tightly around her, touched each bell in quick turn, and stepped into death.

The tree-lined brick path stretched out before her, but this time the statues depicted writhing limbs and arched backs, erect members and open mouths; each pose more erotic than the last.

Callista looked away, ice melting off her flaming face, even as she felt a throbbing between her legs and a tingling in her breasts. She gripped her bell tighter in the bone-chilling cold, but she would not go back through the door. Instead, she headed for the house on the hill and the dimly lit windows that seemed always out of reach.

Inhaling a breath of icy air, she stepped off the path and struck out across the lawn. The grass crunched like glass beneath her feet and a snow-scented wind buffeted her, tearing at her robe, freezing the very breath in her lungs. The path had gotten her nowhere, the house had remained always in the distance.

Not tonight.

The way grew more perilous, but Callista pressed on. The steep, rocky hill cut her hands and feet to ribbons, seeping the gray earth with black blood. Bent and crooked trees sprouted from crevices in the rock, their leaves rattling like bones. Now and then she caught sight of a spirit among the colorless landscape, but when she turned her head, the spark would flit out of sight and she was left once more alone. She paused on a narrow lip of rock, her hand ready to sketch the symbol that would bring Blade to her hand, but the sounds faded and she could not linger long lest the cold sap her strength before she accomplished the task she'd come for.

It might have been miles she walked as her feet burned, then throbbed, then went numb and ice crusted her robe and hair. It might have been weeks or years she traveled, no way to know within this starless landscape, but suddenly the hill broadened into a wide, sloping lawn. The house loomed gray and silent before her.

Windows stared like empty eyes and a doorway gaped like a wound. She climbed the steps and crossed the threshold into a dim entryway. Candles burned pale blue in sconces and on tabletops while blue flames danced in a marble hearth. As she passed from room to room, upstairs and down, she recognized the arched doorways, the antlered stair, the oriel window above the landing, from her mother's descriptions. Killedge Hall, the seat of the Armstrong family.

She called Summoner to her, the blood from her injured hands leaking onto the carved faces like tears. The world was silent but for her own heavy breathing. With a swing, she rang the bell, the chime vibrating along her bones, pushing against her lungs, heating her blood. She whispered the words of the spell as she traced the symbols that would call the spirit to her.

A gossamer mist rose up before her, thin as vapor, and slid toward the doorway to the empty garden. Callista rang Summoner once more and painted more symbols in the air, binding the spirit. It struggled, the mist darkening and twisting like smoke in a drafty chimney, but Callista had been trained well, if not thoroughly, and the bell's chime held it fast.

"What do you want with me?" The voice shimmered high and frightened as a figure took shape within the mist: a round face with a permanently soft and vulnerable expression, a body that in youth had been willowy but with age had grown gaunt and then skeletal, and arms that Callista ached to have embrace her.

"I wish to see what you see . . . Mother."

The spirit's expression never changed, never

warmed, but she nodded before sliding into Callista's skin and taking her over. She blinked, seeing the house, not as it was in death, but as it had been in life; golden stone in a long summer-afternoon light, a green lawn, and a sparkling stream. A girl raced before her; hair in pigtails, hand fisted on a kite string. A shout came from her lips. "Wait, Dee! My kite's caught in the bush!"

The girl kept running and laughing, her scarlet kite fluttering above her.

"Aunt Deirdre," Callista whispered.

The image gave way to another. It was night now and the house rose dark upon its hill. A carriage stood on the lane by the spinney; a tall, thin man with eyes sharp and clear blue as marbles smiled and took her shaking hand as he helped her into a carriage. He called her a name and kissed her lips as the house grew smaller behind them.

Faster the images appeared and vanished.

An ugly boy, his face ruddy, his lip jutting out in a pout, a swaddled bundle, a room drafty and cold with mold crawling like seaweed across the ceiling. A creaking bed where she and the man laughed and made love, a windswept cemetery by the sea. Stooped and ill and bent over, she wept, a letter falling unheeded in her lap.

"This is the past," Callista said. "I wish to see the future. What happens to me? Is there hope for David? I wish to see what you see."

The spirit seemed to harden within her. Callista couldn't breathe, her throat tightened as if she would choke and the air turned gray and murky, but the images continued.

A dead man with a blade in his throat; David, bent and shaking as he slid a silver blade across his palm; a wolf running across an empty hilltop as a crow dove like a shadow before it; Corey's scarred face flushed and twisted with excitement; a crowd of gray figures beneath an enormous stone wall; a woman kneeling; a knife falling; and the twisting unending paths of death stretching on forever.

It took all Callista's effort to lift her arm and ring the notes that would sever the bond and release the spirit. Her mother's form hovered before her, ghostly and pale, her expression sorrowful.

"But what of David? You didn't show me his future."

"I see nothing beyond death," came the spirit's voice, whispery as the rush of leaves or the slide of a snake along the ground.

Callista knew she shouldn't. Knew the pain it would cause. But she couldn't stop the words from coming or her voice from breaking as she asked, "Mother?"

Her mother's spirit seemed to shine brighter, her form almost solid as she opened her arms and took her daughter to her heart. For the first time ever in all her journeys within this frozen merciless realm, Callista was warm and she was happy.

David watched as she took her first quick breath and the sheen of ice cracked upon her cheeks to melt and slide onto her robe like tears. As she focused her empty gaze upon the candle's flame, the pinprick orange gleam reflected in her dilated pupils. As she lifted her blue-nailed hand from the largest of the bells, the ring banging like the clash of swords in his aching head.

She turned her heartbroken gaze to him.

"Now you understand why you have to leave with the Duncallans. Why you can't stay here with me," he said, though this was a rare moment when he took no joy in being right.

"I won't believe it. There is no one future, David. Life is too messy. Humans are too unpredictable. I saw one, but there are hundreds, thousands, an infinite number of ways in which this fate can be changed."

"It doesn't matter. Even if my dream is false, there's nothing for us. That's the true curse. The draught is killing me. That is my future. That is my fate. And you can't change that."

She seemed to sag as if the air and her hopes had finally been extinguished.

"I don't fear my death, Callista. There are worse things than dying. I know. I've survived them." He leaned across the table, cupped her chin, looked into her eyes, and cast her a scapegrace grin. "Nancy Oakham's cooking, for a start. That woman could ruin boiled water."

And with the quick eruption of her teary laughter, his heart turned over, and he finally knew what love was.

Then he showed her.

17

~~~~~~~~~~

She'd been gone a mere two days. Forty-eight quick hours and already he missed her.

"She's probably in Glasgow by now. Do you think Duncallan took rooms in the Black Bull or the Star Inn?"

"I think you need to stop staring at that bloody guidebook as if it were the holy grail and start listening to me."

David looked up from his edition of *Cary's New Itinerary*, but his finger held the page. The two of them were closeted in Gray's study.

"That's better," Gray said. "Now, according to Mac, Beskin's not been seen in London for the past two weeks. There was a report of a man matching his description in the area around Jedburgh, but nothing since."

"That's only about fifty miles from here. Do you think he suspects your involvement?"

"I'd be surprised if he didn't."

David knew he not only looked confused, he *was* confused.

"Pryor's not stupid," Gray pointed out. "He knows I'm involved. Hell, he probably knows I'm leading the charge, but he can't touch me. He can't lay a damn finger on me."

David was struck anew at the ice in Gray's gaze and the steel in his smile. He'd arrived in Portugal a coddled prince. Battle and betrayal had since honed him like a sword, polished but lethal.

"Counting on your grandfather to keep you safe? He didn't show you any favoritism before. Why would he stop Pryor and the Ossine now if they chose to make an example of the exiled heir to the clans?"

"Grandfather won't stop him, though I wonder if his intervention would matter," Gray answered. "As duke, he may be the hereditary leader of the clans, but it's Pryor who calls the shots these days. No, it's something else keeping Pryor from sending his legions of enforcers after me."

"There's a gentleman to see you, Gray. He's waiting in the hall."

Gray motioned with a hand. "And there is my best weapon against Pryor."

The Kingkiller stood at the door, his face grim. Or grimmer than normal. Which was hard to achieve. David wondered if the man ever smiled. Had it been David released from prison after a thousand years and more, he'd be dancing a damn jig.

"Lucan is your protection?" David asked. "How the hell did you meet up with him anyway? How does one approach a legendary Imnada traitor and ask if he'd like to betray his people a second time?"

"He approached me, actually. This past winter. I was . . . wary at first."

David gave a snort of suppressed humorless laughter. *Oh, to be a fly on that wall.*

"But I soon came to the conclusion that our alliance could be mutually beneficial. Lucan is a powerful ally. A seasoned leader of men and a skilled strategist whose powers the Imnada haven't seen in generations. Pryor knows he's returned. He knows and he's scared shitless. He dare not touch me until he's sure he has a plan to handle Lucan."

"And what does the Kingkiller get from this devil's bargain?"

"A chance to redeem myself." The answer came from Lucan himself, who remained at rest within the doorway—or as at rest as he probably ever managed. His body seemed coiled to spring, his face hard as granite but for a tic in his chiseled jaw.

"Fine. So we skulk and we plot while men and women die."

"I don't have time to wait, David. Mac doesn't. You don't." Gray leveled a cold blue stare in his direction.

"De Coursy?" Lucan interrupted. "There is a man to see you."

David opened his palm to the crisscross of scars, old and new. "The power of the draught wanes."

"Like the power of the clans," Gray said. "But just as I plan to bring the Imnada back, so, too, am I determined to break the curse . . . once and for all."

"Break the curse?" David forgot himself enough to let the guidebook fall from his fingers onto the floor with a thump.

Gray smiled. "I haven't been hiding away like a hermit because I fear the Ossine or Fey-blood rumors."

"No? Maybe you should."

"I've discovered a clue. A hint. It's a long shot. I give us less than a one-in-ten-thousand chance, but it's more hope than we've had since Gilles d'Espe laid his black spell upon us."

"Lord Halvossa." Lucan's voice punched the air like the fall of the lash, his simultaneous mental shout almost making David stagger to his knees. "Come. Now."

Lucan's dark empty eyes were aglow with a pale light, with power, and with something else shimmering off him in waves. Something feral and dangerous and wild. David saw now why Pryor might tread carefully around this man. He carried the blood of the ancients in his veins. Hell, he *was* an ancient. The Mother only knew what he could do.

"Royne from the mill caught an intruder slipping over the wall below the stream. He carried a paper bearing St. Leger's likeness, a blade of silver, and a flask of"—his face wrinkled in disgust—"blood."

The prisoner lay bound on the stone cellar floor. A gash on his scalp bled into his hair and streaked his badly bruised face. Royne had not been a gentle jailer. Magic tingled along David's bones as he circled the interloper, but it was weak, barely a ripple along his spine. The man might not even realize he carried the blood of the Fey.

Gray had questioned him and come away with answers, but none that satisfied David. The prince held to his honor. David did not.

The prisoner opened his eyes, his mouth curled into a broken-toothed snarl. "Dirty shifter. I can smell your kind like vomit and shit and maggoty flesh."

So, he was either aware of his Fey blood or had been indoctrinated by their hate. Either way, he was dangerous.

David knelt by the man, his eyes barely flicking over the knife and the broadsheet before coming to rest upon the flask. The pungent scent of blood filled David's nostrils. He picked the flask up and tipped it to his lips for a taste. "You said your name was Edrik."

"Some call me that," the man said, suspicion and fear battling his gutsy bravado.

"Should we punch a knife into your gut, Edrik? Offer you a sip or two and see what happens?" David asked.

Edrik's eyes widened and he struggled against his bonds.

"Not so sure of the power of the *afailth luinan*? Afraid Corey might be chasing a fantasy that doesn't exist?" He licked the blood from his lips, the heavy taste lingering on his tongue. "Sheep." He gave a bark of angry laughter. "Did you really think Corey would be fooled by such a fraud?"

"I'd have my money and be gone afore he found out."

"More likely he'd test it on you before he paid you a penny."

Edrik shuddered. "I survived ten years in Newgate and know a thing or two. He'd not find me easy."

"He'd find you as easily as you found me." David paced the cold cell. "How did you track me here?"

"There are stories about this place. Whispers. A man like me hears things and understands where other folk might not."

"If you're so bloody clever, why the sheep's blood? My veins are full of the real stuff." He toed the cord on the floor with the tip of his boot. "All you had to do was bind me with this silver and I'd have been powerless."

"That blood was just in case. Once I had you, I'd not need it. Corey'd have paid me what he owed. Fifty pounds."

"Fifty pounds for you. Untold wealth for him. Hardly fair."

"It's fair enough for me. I don't need more than my share."

"An honest murderer. A rare thing. So, catch me, bind me, and off to London to claim your prize."

Knowledge flickered in the man's eyes. David's breath stilled, his hand tightening. "Not London? The king of the stews has left his throne empty? Where is he, then? Where would you and I be headed had you managed to capture the wolf in your net?"

Edrik shut his mouth.

"No? Loyal to Victor Corey or still believe you can escape and take your chances?" David picked up the silver dagger. Immediately, he sensed the poison sapping into his skin. His flesh crawled and a chill shuddered through him. But he clamped his hand tighter and, like a painter with a brush, drew the blade across Edrik's arm.

The man struggled, his mouth clamped against a scream.

"You're in the bowels of the shapechangers' stronghold," David snarled. "None will care or come to your aid. Shout all you want."

"You're a monster."

"No, just curious." David drew another line curved parallel to the first.

It took another sting of the blade to loosen the man's tongue and a last deep gash to make sense of his babblings. "Skye," he gasped. "Corey's on Skye."

Mother of All! Callista was riding into a trap.

David rose to his feet, shaky and sickened, dropped the bloody blade, his heart like ice, leaving the bastard where he lay, with the crescent mark of the Imnada carved deep into his bloated flesh.

The coach rattled over the narrow track, the horses straining at the harness as the mountains rose steeply on either side, covered in gray-green stands of pine and birch, the highest peaks shrouded in mist and low-hanging clouds. They had hoped to make Fort William by nightfall, but delays upon the road had slowed their progress. The sun sank red and bloody behind them, the landscape barren of life except for a few remote homesteads nestled within the glens, smoke curling white into the fading sky.

Still, if the weather stayed dry and the tracks passable, they would be crossing over to the island in a day, perhaps two.

She should be relieved. Ecstatic. Awash with anticipation and excitement. She would finally be beyond Corey's grasp. She would finally meet her aunt, the only real family she had left. She would gain a new life with the priestesses where her gifts were more than a circus act.

She would never see David again.

At one time, the prospect would have been easy. He

was arrogant, stubborn, vain, and reckless. He hopped from bed to bed and woman to woman with the ease of a born scoundrel. He was an Imnada, the sworn enemy of her people. And yet none of that mattered when she measured his would-be faults against his honor, his loyalty, and his courage. When she watched him fight to chain the rage that burned white-hot behind his gray eyes. When she felt him shudder in her arms as the weight of the Fey-blood's curse crushed him and despair was a breath away.

No, she reminded herself. Skye was her destination. She owed it to her mother to try to mend the rift between sisters. She owed it to herself to understand the family she belonged to, even if they never acknowledged her. David was her past. He'd said so himself. He'd sent her away. Had he wanted her, truly wanted her, he would have begged her to stay. He would have given her that much of himself, surely. So, perhaps he did not care as much as she hoped.

Or perhaps, a small voice whispered, he cares more than you know and this is his final sacrifice.

She stiffened, lips pressed tight, a knot choking off her breath, the broad, windswept hills and dark mysterious lakes blurred as her eyes burned with unshed tears. She wiped a hand across her cheeks and stared hard at the wide silver sky, where clouds spread and broke and spread again. A bird rode the drafts, its wings outstretched. As she watched, it dove close to earth and she saw it was a crow, black and sleek as a missile.

Badb? One of her sisters?

She shielded her eyes. "You're one of the true Fey," she whispered. "You must know how to help him. If a curse can be cast, then a curse can be broken."

The crow soared high, beating its wings before dropping like a stone toward the trees. *Death. Death. Death.*

The word filled Callista's head and broke against her heart. The sun slid behind a cloud, and she dragged her shawl close around her shoulders.

"I'll warn you now, divine intervention can bring unwanted consequences." Lord Duncallan had awakened. He sat across from her, his hand gripping his cane, his eyes bleak. "And Badb is clever and cunning. Causing trouble is one of her few real pleasures."

"I ask again and again, but I only ever receive the same answer."

"I assume by your glum expression that it's not the answer you want."

"David can't die. He's so strong, so full of life. He's like a human lightning bolt, all fire and energy. How can he just . . . not be?"

"Death takes us all in the end."

"Don't preach to me of death. I know the place intimately. I've trod its paths and seen the flickering shades of countless men as vital as David, but I refuse to let him just give up without a fight."

"Is it your decision to make?"

His words stung, and she turned back to the window to watch the passing country. If David wasn't hers to lose in the first place, then why was she fighting so hard to keep him alive?

The sting became a hollow feeling that dropped into her stomach and tightened her throat. The answer was simple. Because she didn't want to look up at the moon one day from within the cold stone walls of Dunsgathaic and know that he was gone forever. That she had missed her chance to have a life with him. As long as David lived, so, too, lived her hope.

The coach crested a hill. The sky seemed to stretch forever before disappearing into a gray horizon. The crow had vanished and the clouds moved slowly east, darkening the long, winding lake below.

Somewhere up ahead lay Dunsgathaic, a seat of Other power, a source of Other wisdom. She blinked, heart turning over in her chest, lip caught between her teeth in sudden inspiration. Other wisdom . . . Other power . . .

If an Other cast the spell on David, could an Other possibly . . . maybe . . . perhaps . . . conceivably lift it?

Her stomach knotted with excitement.

Perhaps it wasn't death that awaited David on Skye . . . but life.

"Lord Duncallan, we have to turn around."

"Was violence necessary?" Gray leaned, arms folded, against the doorframe to David's bedchamber, his eyes hard as steel.

David shrugged. "I don't know if it was necessary, but the bastard deserved it."

"And what of our bid to win hearts and change minds?"

"Do you really think if I'd treated him with kindness and dignity that the slimy, worm-ridden sack of shit would suddenly change his opinion and love and trust a demon shifter? There are some people you can't win over, Gray. Not with all your pretty words of alliance and common cause. They hate you because you're not them. The end." David's rage turned in his chest like a blade, his mind aflame.

Gray pushed off the doorway, coming into the room, and eyed the maps spread out on a nearby desk. "Where are you going?"

"Where do you think?"

"Duncallan can take care of Miss Hawthorne. No harm will come to her."

"You're right about that. I'll be there to make sure of it."

"And if Corey's men are as thick and as close as we suspect? You'll never win through to Skye undetected."

"They're looking for the man on that broadsheet." David jerked his head at the wrinkled piece of parchment on the bed. The wolf scented blood and the thrill of the hunt. Fangs extended, skin prickled and burned, and his heart drummed in his ears, but this time it was in anticipation of the shift. "I'll win my way through."

"And what then? What of your vision of her slaying and your death? Can you dismiss that so easily?"

Always reasonable. Always cool, calm, and collected. Gray was bloodless. Heartless. As remote as his godforsaken castle.

"Do you think this is easy?" David seethed. "What awaits me chills me to the bone, but doing nothing is a hundred times worse." He looked to the window where twilight bleached the color from the far hills and transformed the trees to black shifting shapes against the gray sky. But above, the Mother hung fat and golden in the sky, her light spilling through the curtains to bathe him in her power. It was Silmith, the night of the full moon, and there would be no greater time to face Corey than when the wolf ran strongest. "Callista is my responsibility."

"Liability, more like. She makes you vulnerable, David. She sidetracks you from your ultimate duty, which is to the clans."

"Fuck the damn clans!" David wheeled on Gray. "Ever since Charleroi, ever since Beskin took his red-hot iron to my back and ripped my very mind apart with his weapons, I've been devoured by hate and rage and bitterness. Then I met Callista." He tried dragging in a breath, but it was as if steel bands clamped his chest. His hands shook. "I won't go back to that, Gray. Not for you or the clans. If you want me after, I'm yours. But I have to see her safe within Dunsgathaic first. A week is all I need."

"You don't have a week. You'll need to dose yourself again or suffer for it before long."

David closed his hands around the scars on his palm. As always, Gray was right. The first stirrings of illness tightened David's muscles, and the lick of blue and silver flames hovered at the edges of his sight. The curse strengthened as the medicine ebbed from his weakened system. "The draught must wait. Callista cannot."

"And what of your promise? You swore that if I did as you asked and sent her away, you would follow my orders."

"I made a promise to her as well."

"No, you lied to get what you wanted, which is all you've ever done, David. But no longer. You're mine. I'll send Lucan if that will ease your worry, but you stay here. I need you, Captain."

David closed his eyes in silent apology before spinning on his heel, his fist catching Gray clean on the jaw with enough power behind the blow to crush a normal human's skull. Caught off guard, Gray reeled backward, unable to stop the second punch that dropped him to the floor unconscious.

David dragged his friend into a chair and poured him a whisky for the pain that would come when he woke.

"Sorry, Major. You know I never took orders well."

18

The inn consisted of one large drafty room downstairs and a few damp chambers above, while their grizzled, one-armed landlord MacDonald more closely resembled a sheep-stealing reaver than a jolly innkeeper, but the place was relatively dry and comparatively warm, attributes that couldn't be overlooked as the weather turned foul and the roads vanished beneath an icy layer of white.

Callista could only stare out the window in disbelief, nerves jumping with impatience. Snow in June? Really?

"And here I thought Wales in January was frigid," Lady Duncallan said, dragging her cloak around her shoulders and scooting her chair closer to the fire. "Scotland in June is ten times worse."

"Do you suppose the roads will be clear by tomorrow?" Callista asked, peering through the swirl of snow beyond the glass.

"This is just a wee dusting, miss." If MacDonald had been intimidating in a loud vulgar way, his wife's honeyed smiles and flattering words were downright frightening. A gaunt, beak-nosed woman with a shock of white hair beneath a dirty mobcap, she smiled broadly enough to show her broken and blackened teeth. "Naught to worry your head over."

"My father once told me Dunsgathaic was built over hot springs, and there are pools where one can bathe in water that never cools," Katherine said, in an obvious attempt to draw Callista's attention from the gale outside and the tension within. "I can't wait until we reach the place. I'll soak in one for at least a week."

"You travel to the fortress of the Shadowy One?" Mrs. MacDonald asked with a simpering leer. "Now, what would such comely maids be seeking in such an unnatural place as that?"

"Miss Hawthorne has family among the holy sisters there," Lady Duncallan offered.

"Does she? A strange and haunted place is the fortress there. Not safe for such pretty things. Full of spirits and devilry and old magic." Her voice lowered, her eyes snapping as she warmed to her story. "The islanders steer clear of the place and even the fishermen avoid the coves below the cliffs for fear of the beautiful roanes and sinister kelpies, both able to drag a man down into the deep waters and send back only bones. Here." The woman handed Callista a mug. "Have a cup of warm cider to calm your nerves. You're white as the snow, lass." She leaned in close. "White as death."

Callista's hand jerked, cider slopping onto her hand, hot against her skin. "What do you mean by that?"

Mrs. MacDonald tilted her head and rounded her shoulders in an obsequious simper. "I meant no offense, child. I've three daughters of my own and ten granddaughters. I know a body heartsick and a mind full of worry when I see one." She offered another secret smile. "My cider will give you sweet dreams and when you wake, all will look better."

"Or you'll wake with a head like a bass drum and a stomach weak as jelly," Lady Duncallan commented, a teasing twinkle in her eye as she sipped from her own drink.

"There, now. Rest yourself by the fire, and I'll see to supper. I've some stew simmering and there's cheese and ham and a bit of bread." With a last darting look, the innkeeper's wife passed into the kitchens.

"She reminds me of a maid I once employed," Katherine whispered to Callista with a smile.

Callista took another swallow. The heavy sweet cinnamon and clove taste coated her tongue, but the heat loosened the hard press of worry in her gut. She made a turn about the room, sat, and picked up her book, but read only three words before she was up and back at the window.

Flakes fell from a dingy, washed-out sky, mixing with a pelting ice that sheeted the ground and made walking from the inn to the stables treacherous. She sighed and made another turn around the room, the walls seeming to close around her. And these were walls of mud and brick. How much worse would it be when the walls were stone, thirty feet high and twelve feet thick, and guarded by warriors of Scathach's brotherhood?

Katherine eyed Callista with kind apprehension. "Naught will happen to him in a fortnight. He's well and out of harm's way at Addershiels. Gray will make sure of that."

"You don't know David. He doesn't just seek trouble, he hunts it down."

"We'll send word as soon as we reach Dunsgathaic. As soon as we speak with the sisters."

Callista knew this was the sensible course, the proper course, but she itched to be doing. Not sitting and waiting. She'd spent her life in such patient desperation and garnered nothing by it. Only after she'd taken charge and taken off had her life truly felt her own.

"What if it's too late? What if the sisters refuse to help? What if David refuses to answer my letter?" So much for the cider's restorative properties. Frustration banded Callista's shoulders and pounded in her temples.

"What if there's nothing the sisters can offer?" Katherine answered sensibly. "Bringing him to Dunsgathaic will only raise his hopes. Could you stand by while they were dashed . . . again? It's better this way."

"And if it were your husband in trouble and you were stuck in the middle of a snowstorm unable to do anything but watch and wait?"

Katherine turned her eyes to the flames in the hearth, hands clenched white on her cloak. Her memories were obviously painful, though at least she had the comfort of the present. Lord Duncallan was just outside with the horses. He was safe. He was whole. He was hers.

Callista had no such comfort.

"Is it like that between you and David?" Katherine asked. "Circumstances must have changed while you were at Addershiels. You weren't so certain when we spoke last."

"I'm still not certain, but how can I live knowing I didn't try? That I might have had everything and gave up? That I let the dream . . . and David . . . die."

"James and I lost five precious years because of mistakes and misunderstandings." Katherine shivered, though Callista wasn't sure this time it was from cold. "If you truly believe there's a chance for David on Dunsgathaic, I'll help you convince James to go back for him. Five years was an eternity. I can't imagine living a lifetime without the man I love."

As if cued from the wings, the door banged open, and Lord Duncallan shook the snow from his coat and dusted it off his dark hair. "The horses are settled."

"Where's MacDonald?" Katherine asked. "Lost in a drift?"

He rubbed his hands before the fire as the old woman brought him a heaping plate of stew and a mug of frothy beer. "Attending to another guest."

"Caught out in this weather? Poor man, he must be half frozen."

The door opened again, MacDonald stamping off his boots. "A right blow out there, but I'd say it'll be over by dawn. Winds are shifting from the south and the snow smells warm."

A second man followed him in, bundled in greatcoat and muffler, his hat dusted with flakes. He carried his saddlebags over his shoulder, but it was the scabbard at his side that drew Callista's eye before she lifted her gaze to his face. He returned her stare, his lipless mouth curling into a cold, dead smile. "I almost rode past without stopping. How fortunate I didn't."

*　　　*　　　*

The snow blanketed the uplands, glittering like crystal under a high, cold sun or shining soft and blue beneath the goddess moon, frosting the bent and broken trees, shriveling and blackening their spring leaves with cold. It drifted thick and treacherous over ditches and ponds and swirled in the cutting crystalline wind. Tracks dotted the fields and forests; hare, fox, stag, and stoat. Once or twice he scented the trail of a lynx or caught a glimpse of the cat sliding gray and brown against the monochromatic landscape. He opened his mind and lifted his head in lonely song, but there was no mental touch of minds, no brush of a signum he recognized. These were not the lynx of the Sorothos, these cats wore only one shape. They would not assist him, but they would not name him *emnil* and offer him a rogue's death, either.

He padded silently beneath the bowed trees and slithered through the snow-weighted bracken. Caught a squirrel and ate it, the flesh hot and steaming as he pulled it from the bones. Drank in a stream so cold the water torched his throat and sat in his stomach like a rock. The day melted into night and the moon rode high through long streamers of cloud, the snow glowing blue and white as the dark curse's flames.

He'd glimpsed no sign of Victor Corey or his men since the snow began and the roads ended. But that didn't mean his enemies weren't out there. Only that the wolf proved more elusive. But he could not be the wolf forever. The draught's potency faded as the sickness increased. First it was the cramping of his muscles and a fever's burning heat. Then it was the jaw-clamping tremors that racked him hour after endless hour, until he curled tail to nose in the shelter of a rocky outcropping and dreamt of evil words spilling like snakes from a dying Fey-blood's mouth, waking only when dawn kissed the snow pink.

It was then that he rejoined the road, standing on a high ridge and looking down upon the muddy snow-crusted trail as it wound its way around the edge of the loch, the water an oily pewter beneath the gray sky. Behind him, three blue-veined stones stood sentinel over the valley below. The potent magic within their borders raised a ridge of fur down his back and buzzed against his brain. A chill breeze tasted of game and the sharp aromas of pine and elder and hard fern. Nothing moved below him, either east or west, but a horse's prints left a wide, plowed trail ending in a churned muddy patch where a man had dismounted and walked into the wood to relieve himself.

A shadow passed over the snow. He looked up to see a bird high against the clouds, an eagle by the size of it. It circled and headed west. A small flock of chittering black wheeled and rippled and wheeled again, then dove for the loch.

The wind changed direction even as a horse's soft whicker twitched the wolf's ears. There, half hidden by a fold in the earth and a trick of the drifting snow, was a stand of four or five trees. Enough to conceal a horse and rider, a figure wrapped in a heavy woolen cloak though it was drenched from hood to hem, snow-draggled and caked with ice.

He froze as the stranger scanned the ridgeline where he hid, her scent twisting in his chest until the pain was an agony of desire and fear, relief and danger. He dare not path to her. He dare not even move, for he scented another—faint but present, like a swirl of ice across the snow.

She lifted her face to him, the hood falling from her hair. Her features were bone-white, her mouth open on a scream of warning: "Behind you!"

David leapt to the side, his paws breaking through the crust of heavy snow, his breath steaming the air. A sword, silver and glittering as ice, swept down where his head had been an instant before.

He danced away from a second strike and a third, his mind aflame with past horrors and paralyzing fear.

"Your blood is as black and tainted as your heart, St. Leger. Did the pretty little Fey-blood whore spread her legs for you? Did you take her as man or beast . . . or both? Perhaps I'll do the same before I drive a dagger through her heart."

David drove the past from his mind, refused its power and its pain. He would not bow to Beskin's slimy threats. No fetters held him fast. No hostile crowds eyed him with loathing. He would not cringe and cower. He would bury his shame and his memories in the same grave as the enforcer's body.

St. Leger sprang for the throat. Beskin parried with a slam of his sword. The snow muffled the sounds of battle while blood spattered scarlet across the white ground.

Tied hand and foot to the horse, Callista struggled with her bonds, the ropes digging into her wrists, blood leaking down over her fingers. Luckily, her extremities had gone numb hours ago. There was no pain, only a sense of impending doom with every growl and curse blowing down off the ridge, bringing with it showers of blood-speckled snow.

A swarm of crows gathered overhead, their raucous squawks and croaks scraping against her brain like nails on a slate. They must have had the same effect on Beskin's horse. It shifted and backed and tossed its head. She clamped her knees tighter against its sides in an attempt to keep her seat on the slippery saddle. Fettered as she was by a length of cord running ankle to ankle beneath the horse's belly, a fall would trap her between the nervous gelding's legs.

She gritted her teeth and struggled once more, in and out, back and forth as the blood slicked hot over her hands and she forced her mind from dwelling on the Duncallans' fate. Had Beskin killed them before he'd stolen her away in the middle of the night? Had he decided the only good Fey-blood was a dead one? Or had they managed to escape? Were they looking for her? Was help on the way?

A shelf of snow broke free and spilled in a thick cascade off the ridge, bringing with it the tumbling and rolling gray shape of an enormous wolf. The horse lifted its head in a frightened whinny, its hooves pawing at the ground as Callista tried desperately to hang on.

The wolf lay panting, a long, jagged gash upon its shoulder, blood and slaver dripping from its jaws. Beskin's shadow speared the snow above it, his silver sword flashing against the slate-gray sky.

"David!" she screamed. "Look out!"

Just as the sword descended, the wolf rolled up and away, its jaws clamping on Beskin's leg, tearing through flesh and muscle, ripping in a frenzy of animal brutality, though the beast's eyes shone pale with human hate and human desperation.

The enforcer screamed in agony, the sword falling from his hand as he grappled with the wolf, the snow a churned mess of blood and earth. A dagger aimed for the wolf's throat was turned aside at the last minute, glancing off bone and rib instead. The animal yelped and sprang free, sides heaving, blood streaming from half a dozen wounds. It took a few shaky steps before sinking lifeless against a tree.

Callista fought the ropes, tears streaming frozen from her eyes as she cursed her helplessness. Just a bit more. A little farther.

A hot wind buffeted her face as the air around the wolf shimmered and blurred like rain streaming down a pane of glass. Raw, unfamiliar magic sizzled along her skin and flip-flopped her empty stomach. She blinked away her tears to see David lying wounded and dazed on the snow. A shimmer of light rippled across his broad shoulders and down his long legs before dispersing to mingle with the rivulets of blood sliding in ribbons and curls down the hill.

"David?" she whispered.

He rolled up and onto his feet. Eyed Beskin with revulsion. The enforcer's leg below the knee was a mess of pulpy cartilage and bone, his face an ugly mask of horrified agony as he struggled to crawl across the snow toward his abandoned sword, dragging his mangled limb behind him. The crows thickened and wheeled, diving down to pluck at Beskin's flesh, grabbing up gobbets of blood.

A little more. A little closer. She could feel her right wrist sliding free. The horse shimmied to one side, agitated at the scent of blood and animal and the growing cloud of crows and ravens drawn by the blood-soaked snow.

David crossed the few yards and plucked up the enforcer's sword with a smile as cold and cruel as death. He stood over Beskin, his expression grim, his jaw jumping, muscles taut. It was like watching a stranger. The man she knew and loved had vanished behind a brutal and merciless mask of vengeance. She wanted to call out to him, speak words to pull him back from the brink of madness, but her voice caught in her lungs, her breath naught but a frosty cloud. Bending low and awkward across the horse's shoulder, she turned her efforts to the icy-hard knots at her ankles.

"This is for Kineally and the others you've slaughtered."

"Kill me, more will follow," Beskin groaned through lips drawn back from long sharpened teeth. "Pryor's power grows. The Duke's time is past. The Ossine rule"—his hand whipped out to latch on David's ankle—"now!"

He dragged David off-balance and hard into the ground, his fist driving up into his jaw with bone-crunching strength. "The curse tainted your blood. The Fey-blood polluted your mind. You're weak."

David struggled for the sword, but the hilt had tumbled just out of reach and Beskin's hold was like iron. His face seemed to warp and lengthen, the shades of man and beast flickering beneath his skin as he sought to shift. As David scrabbled to reach the fallen sword, Beskin reached to his left boot. Drew free a needle-thin blade. Let it sail.

Callista shouted as her right ankle came loose,

while the blade whistled past her ear to land hilt-deep in the horse's neck. It screamed and reared before falling to the ground in a tangle of churning legs. Callista tried rolling clear of the dying gelding, left, then right, until her head exploded in a burst of red and black, and darkness took her.

David kicked and twisted free of Beskin's grip and scrambled over the snow to where Callista lay curled at the base of a tree, the snow from its heavy branches half burying her, the dying horse thrashing as it pumped its blood onto the churned ground. He pulled her clear and felt the lump at the back of her skull. She'd survive, but he needed to get her out of the weather. Somewhere warm. Somewhere safe. A shadow speared the air above him. He looked up into the maddened eyes of an enormous bear dragging the grisly ruin of its leg behind it. Small advantage when David still faced razor claws and fangs long as daggers.

He threw himself sideways as the bear swung one giant paw down in a blow that would have scissored through flesh like a knife through butter.

He spun and darted, luring Beskin away from Callista, drawing ever closer to the fallen sword. Beskin followed, roaring his rage and pain. His breath blew hot on David's neck as he swiped at him. Claws tore into David's calf, dropping him to the ground. Rising up on his hind legs, the bear bellowed in triumph. Lurching with one last gasp toward the sword, David braced for the crushing, gut-ripping, claw-tipped strike. Instead, a rush of wind and feathers brushed his face.

The bear roared and reeled backward, deep gouges

slashed across its snout. The crow dove again, raking and clawing. David snatched up the fallen sword, and before he could breathe or think or regret one more ghost to haunt his dreams, he drove the blade through the enforcer's chest. Pulled it free with a sucking yank and slashed downward, slicing deep into the bear's shoulder and neck.

Blood gushed from the bear's throat and it slumped to the ground, its eyes glazing as death approached, its great hairy body fading in a rush of shimmering air back into the naked pallor of a man. Beskin stared up into the hard sky and the girl in her cloak of crow feathers. Blood spilled from his mouth and his chest as his life ebbed. "It's true. Lucan lives."

Badb returned his black stare. "He never died."

Crumpling to his knees, David retched his stomach empty. His body shook with tremors, his head crawling with voices, dry and crackling, smooth and silky sweet, hard as a smithy's anvil. Fey magic sizzled the air, and he gripped his skull as if his brain might leak out his ears.

"The enforcer is dead. They will see you the rest of the way to Dunsgathaic," Badb said, her voice coming from far away and yet echoing through his shattered skull.

David looked up to see a group of gray-robed women surrounding them. Old, seamed faces and gnarled fingers; plump, young cheeks and curious stares. One stepped forward. Small as a child, she walked with the grace of a dancer. Her golden eyes shone like the sun. Her potent Fey-blood magic nearly doubled him over. "The stones will see us home," she said.

"I can't," he tried to explain. "I mustn't."

"It is for us to maintain the path between. You must bear her body."

"The dream . . . you don't understand. I'll kill her. Badb, tell her . . ." But the Fey had flown, the crow no more than a black speck in the sky.

"Child of the clans, bring her or leave her, but *you* will come with us to Dunsgathaic. *You*, the Ard-siur wishes to see."

Weak from illness and blood loss, he couldn't fight. Besides, there was no point. He knew a superior force when he saw one. And these, for all their soft words and slender figures, were as single-minded as any of Napoleon's officers. Marshaling his last ounce of strength, he scooped Callista up in his arms as they tied a rope threaded with golden and pearlescent strands to his wrist, the other end knotted around the wrist of the young priestess.

"The connection will carry us together through the void of between. Do not fear the dark. Do not heed the cries. Do not speak to those who would lure you from the path. And whatever happens, do not loosen the knot binding us together."

"What lies within the between?"

"The abyss where the Unseelie dwell, the soulless and the damned and the forgotten."

He limped with his precious burden behind them up the hill to the ridge and the stone circle. Stepped into the waves and wash of Fey magic captured there. The midnight black took them where none of his Imnada senses worked. He was blind and deaf to the emptiness around him. He felt only the weight of Callista's body in his arms. Only the heat of the rope taut against his wrist. The force of magic tore his words away, then his breath, drove his stomach into his throat, clawed at his mind with a thousand screaming voices.

But at least in the emptiness of the abyss, none could hear his painful screams and he might weep without being seen.

19

⚜━━━━━⚜

Warmth woke her. Blankets tucked to her chin, a hot brick wrapped in flannel against her feet, and a cheerful fire dancing in the hearth combined to ease the throb of thawing tired limbs. Then memory flooded her sluggish brain and she sat up with a cry. A hand, spotted and knobbed with age, but deceptively strong, pressed her back against the pillows. A face swam into view above her, but it was not the one she yearned for. Instead wrinkles lined a pleasant countenance and crouched in the corners of two pale blue eyes. "Easy, lass. 'Tis all right. You're out of the wicked snow and warm as toast within the walls of Dunsgathaic. None will harm you."

She'd arrived on Skye? But how? Callista remembered nothing after falling beneath the horse's flailing hooves. Her memories were all of snow and ice and blood and death. And a red-hot slash of pain in her head before the black swallowed her.

"Where's David? Is he here? Did he . . ." She couldn't bring herself to ask the question.

"The shapechanger lives," the woman answered, though her gaze grew serious, and the smile fled from her face. "Rest now. I'll return when you're summoned before the head of our order, the Ard-siur."

She wanted to argue. Wanted to wrestle the sister aside and search for David, but her body refused to cooperate. Her brain was as muddled as her memories, and her legs and arms seemed weighted to the soft mattress.

She slept and woke again. The shadows had moved, and the sky beyond the window was a crisp blue. She gazed around at the room for the first time noticing the scattered rugs upon the floor and the comfortable chairs drawn up to a tiled hearth. A cabinet contained a pitcher and washstand. Another table was scattered with curios and curiosities. A bird's nest. A bowl of sea-washed pebbles. A vase of celadon holding skeletal winter branches.

And, set upon a far cabinet by the door, a familiar mahogany box, the carved lid worn smooth with generations of hands running over it, the round brass lock and hinges as shiny as if new forged.

She rose from bed to take up the box. Set it back on the coverlet beside her, positioning the tumblers and springing the lock. Key, Summoner, and Blade; all as she'd left them. Her mother's letters still nestled in the corner. Callista pulled them from their resting place. Felt the crinkle of the thin paper under her fingers, the faded ink, the frayed ribbon.

"I'm finally here, Mother," she whispered to no one. "I'm in Dunsgathaic."

Wind rattled the casement and moaned round the door, a lonely sound that sent worry curdling unbidden up through her. She swallowed back a hard knot of fear. The sisters wouldn't harm David. But what of the Amhas-draoi? They lived within these walls as well. The battle-queen Scathach's army of warriors and mages were sworn to protect and defend. Would they see David as a threat? Would they recall the story of Lucan Kingkiller and take their revenge?

Bypassing the robe hanging over a chair, she scrambled into her own discarded gown drying upon a rack before the fire and wound her hair up into a knot. The mirror over the mantel showed her a peaked face of drawn skin and dark hollows. It also revealed the tremble in her fingers as she buttoned the last button and the nervous pulling at her lip with her bottom teeth.

In a moment of childish longing, she slid the packet of old letters into her pocket as a reassuring talisman against nervous uncertainty. These were all she had left of her mother, a last link to the heartbroken woman, forever torn between love for the family into which she'd been born and the family she'd built together with the man of her dreams. A last link to the last true home Callista had ever known. These, even more than the bells, were the true treasure kept safe in that box.

The door opened, a draft chilling the back of her neck and guttering the sconces. The priestess didn't even lift an eyebrow when she saw her charge up and dressed. She merely motioned for Callista to follow. "Ard-siur is ready for you now."

"What of Mr. St. Leger? I refuse to budge a step until you tell me where he is."

"All your questions will be answered when you see the Ard-siur."

"I want them answered now." Callista folded her arms over her chest.

The priestess's pose of serenity cracked and an irritated frown passed over her face. "The shifter is safe and in one piece, which is more than you'll be if you keep the head of our order waiting."

Without another word, she led the way through a long stone passage and down a steep winding flight of steps. Callista had no choice but to follow. She stared with wide eyes as they crossed a broad, muddy courtyard. A group of sisters stood in conversation. A heavy-set priestess in a dirty apron carried a basket on her shoulder. Another trailed a tail of four young girls like ducklings. Two *bandraoi* mounted on mules waited among a knot of laborers with shouldered picks and shovels and a man leading a bullock.

This would be her home from now on. These women would replace the family she had lost.

Why did the idea not fill her with the joy and anticipation she had thought it would? Why did the walls seem higher, the sky seem grayer, and her heart feel weighted with lead?

A set of tall double doors opened onto an enormous chamber of streaming blue and gold and ruby light from rows of high stained-glass windows. The priestess gestured Callista in with an impatient wave of her hand. "Miss Hawthorne, Ard-siur."

"Thank you, Sister Brida." A woman stood at a table, her gray robe edged in royal blue, her expression hard and unyielding as flint, but it hadn't always been that way. Callista had seen it young and unlined and bright with laughter as a girl gripped a kite string and raced across a green lawn toward a house of golden stone.

"Aunt Deirdre?"

David felt the priestess's hard gaze like a blade, her disapproval evident in her stiff posture and her clenched arms. She did everything but curl her lip in a superior sneer. He flashed her a winning smile that usually had London's mothers queuing up with daughters in tow.

She scowled harder.

"You're fortunate in your allies, Mr. St. Leger. The sisters do not bestir themselves for every traveler plagued by difficulties. Without Lord Duncallan's persuasive urging, you would have found yourself without our aid. You owe His Lordship your life."

"With that and a penny, he'd have enough for a beggar's bowl," David quipped.

She eyed him down her long hawkish nose. "Just so."

"Always good for the convent coffers to help a peer of the realm, but that wasn't what really brought you scurrying to our rescue, was it?"

She pursed her thin lips tight, her hands in her long sleeves tighter.

Callista stepped forward, face flushed, dark hair spilling free from a hasty chignon to curl against her cheeks. Just seeing her clenched his stomach and heated his skin.

"Please, Aunt Deirdre. I've told you everything. Can you help him? Can you lift the curse?"

If the woman sneered at him, she fairly glowered at Callista. Not exactly the hearts-and-flowers reunion with her aunt that she had been hoping for. The head priestess had been as sour as a lemon, unbending as an oak.

"A curse is the darkest of magics," the Ard-siur said sagely. "A foul twisting of the mage energy. It would take much to unravel such a confusion of evil intent."

"Is that your way of saying no?" David asked, hoping to turn her wrath from Callista back onto him. It wouldn't be the first time he'd been brought before a superior to answer for his transgressions. And after the Ossine's savage punishments, it took more than a brittle, stick-up-her-back old snob to frighten him.

Even so, if she could shoot flames from her eyes, he'd be dead a thousand times over. "It's my way of telling you and Miss Hawthorne that we do not take orders for magic like a village dressmaker with a new gown. There is much to consider."

"Like whether you want to save the life of an Imnada rather than kill me now."

"The sisters of High Danu do not commit murder, Mr. St. Leger."

"What about the Amhas-draoi? They're known for stopping at nothing in defense of you Fey-bloods."

"The brotherhood has heard the rumors of the Imnada's astounding survival, but there was no proof. No evidence the shifters were more than a drunkard's tale."

David spread his arms. "Here I am. In the flesh . . . or the fur, as you like."

"Yes," she said, her eyes raking his attire, a borrowed pair of breeches and a scrounged shirt that barely fit across his shoulders. "That's more than clear. We'll have to consider all this carefully."

"My current existence or my future health?"

"Both," she snapped.

Callista stepped in front of him like a martyr before the pyre. Her chin tilted defiantly, her shoulders squared. "He'll die without your help, Aunt Deirdre. I've heard the voices on the wind and seen his future through the eyes of those whose spirits wander the paths of the dead."

The Ard-siur grimaced, her hands lying knobbed and crooked on her desk. "Your mother should never have taught you such things. She gave up that privilege when she chose that man over her birthright."

"That *man* was my father."

"That man," Ard-siur snipped, "was a cunning social climber who thought he could seduce himself a fortune. He was mistaken. The Armstrongs of Killedge Hall do not pay blood money, as he found to his cost."

"No, they don't. They hurt and insult and ignore." Callista pulled a packet of letters from her pocket. Tossed them on the desk in front of her aunt. "She wrote to you over and over. Begging for forgiveness. Wanting only to know you cared, that you loved her. You gave her nothing."

"Not really the way to persuade her to help," David whispered in Callista's ear.

Ard-siur stared at the battered cache of letters tied with a faded blue ribbon. Her face was as white as bone, the skin drawn and smooth as old leather.

"What did your mother give us? Shame, disgrace, and lowly connections. Roberta Armstrong had everything a girl could want. A good home, parents who doted upon her every wish, and a glorious match with a man of wealth and prestige. What did she do?

She threw it away on a charming smile and a pleasing word." She shot David a contemptuous look. "Like mother, like daughter, it would appear. St. Leger's handsome enough and, no doubt, he knows the words that will flatter you, but what is he beneath it all? A beast wearing the skin of a man. A treacherous creature who would rip your heart out as soon as look at you."

"So, that would be a no on the cure?" David quipped, choking on his dagger-sharp fury. It would do him no good and only worsen Callista's situation.

"You're right, Aunt. David St. Leger has ripped my heart out and claimed it for his own. I love him. An emotion unknown to you."

Color splotched ugly across Aunt Deirdre's sunken cheeks while David simply boggled. Fury forgotten, he put a hand against the small of Callista's back, and let her warmth ease his jangled nerves and relax muscles tight as wires.

"I was wrong to come here," she said, her voice calm and carrying. Only David, feeling the tremors underpinning her words, knew how much she was really hurting. "Wrong to think I could ever find a family among you. Family isn't about blood. It's about love and compassion and the unselfish giving of yourself. I had more of that with Nancy, Captain Flannery and his wife, the Duncallans. Even Lucan Kingkiller and Badb. They cared about me and worried over me, and when I was lost or sad or upset, they stood by me. Can you say you would ever do the same?"

Ard-siur's face was expressionless, her eyes flat, but her hand clenched the letters in a white-knuckled fist. "You're welcome to stay as a guest of the convent until your strength returns, but I do not think a life among the *bandraoi* is suitable for someone so volatile and capricious. As for you . . ." She turned her attention to David. "You will remain with us for the nonce. There are many questions and much to discuss."

"Is that your subtle way of telling me I'm your prisoner?"

"It wasn't meant to be subtle."

"It's not exactly how we would have planned such a meeting, but it's past time the sisters of High Danu knew the truth about the Imnada," Katherine said as she curled in an armchair, a blanket drawn across her legs.

Just as old the innkeeper's wife had predicted, the sun had returned and with it, warmth enough to melt the snow to slick black mud, the icicles dripping long and thin from every eave.

"James is with David, and despite your aunt's unfortunate opinion, there are plenty who feel differently upon hearing the clans survive. We'll win our way out of this mess, wait and see."

"I think it's brilliant," Sister Clara piped up.

The young priestess had arrived with dinner and stayed for conversation. Her cheerful chatter as much as her tray of food had done much to restore Callista's equilibrium, though nothing could erase her last look at David as they led her from her aunt's office while he remained behind. His grin was cocky as ever, but she saw the careful way he held himself and the caution in his gaze.

"I had an old auntie that used to tell me stories of

the shifters," Sister Clara said, drawing Callista back to the conversation. "Hair-raising they were, sent shivers right up my spine, but I loved them."

"See?" Katherine said confidently.

Still, Callista couldn't shake the sense these high walls she'd run to for refuge were closing around her like the jaws of a poacher's trap. She kicked herself for being such a dim-witted optimist. She'd been foolish to believe her aunt would welcome a niece she never knew and stupid to think the order would overlook the fact that David was Imnada and help him break the curse.

". . . baths, milady? Aye, they're still here. Hardly used anymore, though. Ard-siur discourages it. I've only been down there once since I arrived as a novice."

Dreams of a lifetime lay shattered around her, but Callista refused to give in to the heartbreak. She refused to sit and weep over a pile of old letters and useless regrets. Her mother had done that, finally surrendering to grief and loss and loneliness.

Callista was made of sterner stuff.

". . . mum lives on the southern shore near Kinloch. Sister Walda's not supposed to, but she lets me visit her each morning and take a bit of soup and bread from the kitchens."

"Can you get a note to Mr. St. Leger for me?" Callista asked.

Sister Clara and Katherine looked up as one.

The priestess's eyes lit up. "You mean a secret love letter? That kind of note?"

"Can you do it?" Callista repeated.

The girl bit the tip of her finger as she thought. "I heard whispers he's being held in the north tower.

That's usually Sister Lissa's domain, but I can manage easy enough."

"Callista, what are you planning?" Katherine asked, an uneasy look on her face.

"I can't allow David to be locked away forever because of me. I need to see him. Need to let him know . . ." She shook her head. "I need him. That's all. I need him."

Sister Clara jumped to her feet. "You write the note, miss. I'll deliver it."

Callista sat down at the desk. Stared long and hard out the narrow window onto the busy yard below, where sisters in gray moved about their daily chores, a herd of cows was being shepherded by a girl in a kirtle and apron, and a boy was riding a mule with a dog at his side. Riders streamed in through the fortress gate, with nothing about them to signal who they were but for the swords at their hips, the daggers at their belts, and the stern looks in their hard faces—Amhas-draoi. Scathach's warriors. Guardians of the divide between human and Fey. Was this the beginning of the war Gray and the Duncallans feared?

With a shiver, she bent pen to paper in a frightened scribble and prayed David would come.

"Callista? Are you down here?" David's footsteps and voice echoed against the brick walls as he stepped off into a long room lit only by high slitted vents, a welcome breeze riffling down to stir the hairs at the back of his neck. Otherwise, the air hung heavy and damp against his skin. Stone benches ran the perimeter of the room, rounded and softened by thousands of years of use. High buttresses of intricately carved marble rose and then were lost in the dark of the ceiling, while steps to his left descended into a murky green pool.

He knelt and dipped his hand in the water. Pleasantly hot. Horribly stinky. And bitter on his tongue. He splashed it on his face to relieve his faint dizziness; let it trickle under his collar to ease the fever heat and the tightening and cramping of his muscles. Too much magic. Too small a space. It was like having every nerve plucked and every breath laced with needles. His brain hummed while his flesh crawled. He doused his head with another handful. Slapped his wet hair off his face with a flick of his neck and closed his eyes until the worst passed. Felt a hand on his shoulder.

He wheeled around, reaching for the dagger that wasn't there, his body a live fuse.

"David, it's me."

He breathed a silent prayer to the Mother. Callista. Whole. Unharmed. A few shadows that hadn't been there before. A strain in her face and around her eyes, but otherwise untouched. He could take solace knowing that whatever else happened, Corey had failed. The door to death would not swing open. Callista would not be the key to the king of the stews becoming the king of the world.

"*Orneai aimara*," he said in the language of the ancients. "My beautiful." He cupped her face in his hands and drank in a deep thirst-quenching kiss, his body alive now with more than sickness.

"You're ill. And burning with fever."

"It's nothing."

She gave a small shake of her head, but otherwise didn't argue. Instead she gripped his arms, her gaze clear, though he saw the fear lurking just beneath the surface. "I wasn't certain you'd get my note . . . or if you'd be able to come."

"I've offered my parole. I'm free to move about the fortress as long as I don't attempt to leave. Your aunt is playing nice for the moment."

"For the moment is well and good, but you need to escape before they change their minds. Sister Clara can smuggle you out when she goes to visit her mother tomorrow at dawn. She thinks you're brilliant and our story's a romantic adventure straight out of Sir Walter Scott."

"Did any of those stories end well?"

"Don't joke, David. The Amhas-draoi will never let you go. They'll hold you captive until they pull every last secret of the Imnada out of you. Then they'll go after the clans. You have to run while you can."

"I thought you didn't want me running."

"It's different now. Didn't you say this place was the heart of the enemy? That you'd never be caught within its walls?"

He took her hands. Brushed a kiss upon her forehead. "Don't fear for me, Callista. As long as I'm their only connection to the Imnada, they'll treat me with respect."

She opened her mouth to argue, but he placed a finger on her lips. "To show their good faith, the commander of the garrison sent men to search for Corey and your brother. An army of dead ravaging Great Britain is in no one's interest, shapechanger or Fey-blood."

She molded herself against him, the leap of her pulse in her throat and the catch of her breath making his own body respond.

"You're finally free, my love. No longer forced to

hide. You can find a life anywhere and be anyone you wish to be."

"With you?" she asked.

He couldn't keep the sorrow from his gaze. It reflected back to him in the dark of her eyes.

"I meant what I said to my aunt, David. Every syllable. I love you."

"Then unsay it. Take it back and never think on it again."

"Love doesn't work that way."

"I did what I set out to do, Callista. The book is safe with Gray. You're safe from Corey. And Beskin is a frozen corpse. I can die a happy man."

She frowned. "Stop it. Stop talking that way. There are other convents and other priestesses. We'll search them out. Scour their libraries and their archives. Find a *bandraoi* more powerful than any living here and convince them to help, but you need to escape before it's too late."

"Is this what the spirits have shown you? Is this my future?"

Anger flashed in her face. "The spirits know nothing."

"You saw my death, didn't you?" he asked. She did not deny it, but there was a stiffening of her body and she slid her gaze to the wall behind him. "You saw your death as well, didn't you?"

"Prophecies are not fact," she argued.

"Why ask the question if you won't believe the answer?"

"To change the answer. I've stepped from the path once. I can do it again."

He pushed a curl behind her ear, caressed the curve of her cheek. "You make me almost believe."

"I won't stop trying until you do." She pulled him down to her, her kiss sweet with sherry. Her tongue dipped to taste, her teeth nibbled at his lip. He drank her in, the scent of her hair and her skin, the honey warmth of her mouth. She answered with a rising passion, her back arching as she melted into his touch.

Then, just as suddenly, she stepped clear of his arms. Holding his gaze, she unbuttoned the ugly brown wool gown they had given her and let it fall to the bricks. Slowly, sensuously, she untied the prim ribbons of her chemise, drew one arm free and then the other, and the slip of cotton soon joined the gown as a puddle at her feet.

Her skin glowed pink and silver, golden and white as milk. The heat from the baths moistened her breasts, a trickle of sweat sliding into the valley between them. Her dark hair curled over her shoulders in the humid air, little ringlets damp against her forehead and temple.

She passed him, hips swaying with just a hint of come-hither sensuality, the earthy scents of sex mingling with the mineral tang of the baths. Stepped into the murky water, a slow step at a time. It lapped at her ankles, her knees, the junction between her legs.

A smile lit her face, and she slapped at the surface of the pool, sending spray to douse him. "Wake up!"

He answered her smile with an encouraging grin. "Minx." Shed his clothing, pausing upon the top step, his need for her evident. "Where's the shy maiden who knew nothing of kisses and shrank from my touch?

"I left part of her in a closet in Cumberland Place, another piece in a wagon between Grantham and

Newcastle, and finally shed her in a castle bed high above the North Sea."

He descended into the bath, dropped below the water, letting it wash away his last hesitation. He surfaced with a flick of water from his face to find her molten gaze devouring him as if he were a confection. "Much warmer than that creek."

She took his hands. "You didn't touch me then."

"I wanted to."

"Touch me now."

"Gladly."

He lapped at her skin, sucking the water from her shoulders, her collarbone, her breasts; took her nipples in his mouth and suckled until they hardened under his tongue. His hands moved in the water, gliding over hips and the flat of her stomach, touching the brush between her legs, the cleft of her mound. She gasped, the water moving with them, stirred by their desire.

She guided him inside her, the dark wrapping close around them, the damp air warm in their lungs, dripping down their cheeks, silvering their hair. He held her, feeling her close around him, sheathed tight inside her. He made no move. And then slowly . . . very slowly he withdrew and plunged deep again. Each stroke a torture. Each thrust dragging him closer to the edge. He locked his gaze with hers, dilated pupils and parted lips, clawing fingernails and wet skin. Her pleasure aroused him further until lightning licked along every raw nerve.

This was the end between them. He tried to console himself. She was not the first woman he had walked away from without a backward glance. Yet his heart ached as he pictured the future that might have been theirs, the family they might have had, the life they might have lived. And for the first time, David felt an irresistible urge to fight tooth and claw against his fate rather than resign himself to the inevitable. Because, for the first time, he had someone worth fighting for.

Callista wrapped her legs around David's waist, lifted her hips to take him deeper. Head thrown back, she groaned as the water sluiced over them and between them, as she felt her blood pouring volcanic through her body. She'd heard the act of love called the tiny death, but there was nothing of death in this giving and receiving of pleasure. Death was a cold and frigid place, a vast empty landscape, a gray forever where no sun burned or stars shone. This was light and heat and life and blazing, heart-stopping emotion. This was the promise of bliss shadowed by the fear of despair.

This was what she had told herself she would not and could not do.

Love.

She arched against the sweet friction of their joining as he kissed her in a sweeping, heated, toe-curling, stomach-knotting kiss. Felt the cresting wave of her bliss pull her under, and cried her climax into his mouth. His sending struck hard as a warrior's vow in her dizzy head.

I love you, Callista.

The groan of door hinges broke the spell, the splash of lantern light over the bricks tore them apart, and the soft shush of robes over the stone had David bracing for attack.

"Down here, Ard-siur." A grizzled priestess with a mole on her chin wobbled down the stairs. Two more followed, the last gripping the wrist of Sister Clara, who shot Callista a look of frightened apology.

The outraged group drew to a halt at the bottom of the steps, Aunt Deirdre close to boiling over as she took in the scene. "How dare you!" She fairly trembled with rage. "I offer you comfort and you repay me with lechery. I offer you aid and you pay me back with whore's gold. Mr. St. Leger, you're to return to your rooms. Tomorrow you'll be turned over to the Amhas-draoi. You can be their distraction. I hope they offer you the hospitality that one of your kind deserves."

Beneath the water, David squeezed Callista's hand. Touched her leg. "You can't keep him against his wishes, Aunt," she argued. "He only came with me because I asked it of him. He's only here because he worried about my safety."

"Perhaps it's best this way," David murmured, and she knew he recalled his dangerous dream. That the fear of what he might do to her still gripped him. She would not believe. She could not believe that so soon after such joy there would follow such pain.

Ard-siur dismissed Callista with a scowl. "You will leave Dunsgathaic at first light. I'm sorry you traveled so far with nothing to show for your journey."

David's hand froze, his breath caught in his throat.

Callista had been wrong. It could happen. She closed her eyes and refused the horrible, violent images assailing her.

"Don't be sorry, Aunt Deirdre," she answered, defying her aunt as much as the voices raking her skull with whispers of death. "I've gained far more from these past few weeks with David than I could have found closeted away here with you in a hundred lifetimes. Love."

20

The sun broke above the ocean's horizon, throwing diamonds across the water, while far to the north, clouds hung low across the distant hills and wide, brown moors of the Cuillin. Callista cast a final glance over her shoulder as Dunsgathaic disappeared from view, and tried not to imagine the worst that her dreams last night had shown her.

She sat back against the lumpy seat, hoping to empty her mind of the whirl of useless, plaguing thoughts. Hard to do in a coach that smelled of mildew and rattled like rocks in a pail, but sleep had been scarce in the long dark hours and her eyelids soon grew heavy as the coach crawled over the bumpy track toward the ferry crossing.

From there . . . who knew?

She'd no destination in mind, no schedule to which she must adhere. There was no one to tell her what to do or how to do it. Her future was finally her own. And she'd never felt lonelier.

Should she return to Gray de Coursy at Addershiels? He might not welcome her when he heard about David's capture by the Amhas-draoi, but she'd a notion to read more of those stories she'd found in his library, to discover the lost history of the Imnada among those dusty stacks.

She smiled. One Fey-blood at a time, David had once said.

The coach hit a rut, knocking her to the floor. As she clambered back onto the seat, she saw that they had turned off the road and onto a narrow track winding up into the rocky hills rather than down toward the nestled village and the ferry crossing. A slithering tendril of fear curled up from her stomach and snatched her breath.

The landscape grew wilder as long-haired cattle wandered the wide, barren uplands and the sea shone like glass away to the south. Off to her right, a thatched crofter's cottage stood alone in a narrow valley.

The track ducked beneath a rusted iron gate into a courtyard, drawing up in front of a tall stone house of turrets and towers with moss growing thick up the walls. Seabirds wheeled and dove from the cliffs into the pounding surf and the ever-present wind carried a salty spray.

The coach drew up on the gravel. The door opened. Callista's fear blossomed like an icy fist around her heart.

Victor Corey held out a hand, his twisted smile never reaching his hard glittering eyes. "And here's my blushing bride, just in time for our wedding."

David stood, hands braced on either side of the window, body thrumming with rage and an almost consuming panic.

". . . back from my ma's house . . . go every morning . . . she's not well and there's the cows to look after . . ." The young priestess gabbled her story in a frightened and breathless half whisper. "I tried telling Ard-siur, but she wouldn't listen . . . said it wasn't our concern . . ."

"You were right to come to us," Lady Duncallan said before looking to her husband. "Could you speak to them, James?"

"I could, but I doubt it would help. It took all my persuasive abilities just to keep David from being tossed in a cell to rot while they bicker over what to do with him."

"So we do nothing while Callista's in trouble?"

"Not nothing." Duncallan spoke a low string of indistinguishable words, the air shimmering gold and orange and green as he summoned the power of his kind, shaping it, manipulating it, training it to his hand.

The hair on David's neck rose at the confluence of such potent Fey-blood magic, and he turned, stomach churning, just as a wraithlike figure flickered into being in front of him. Tall, broad-shouldered, steel-gray eyes, and a jaw set like stone.

"You did this?" He touched his ringer, half expecting his hand to pass through the tangle of mage energy like drawing aside a curtain. Instead, he touched warm flesh, hard muscle. "It's like looking in a mirror."

"The illusion won't last long nor is it strong enough to fool the Amhas-draoi for more than a few minutes," Duncallan said, "but it should buy you the time you'll need to escape . . . if that's your plan."

"Damn Corey to hell." David closed his eyes, but

there was no blotting out the horrors imprinted upon his mind: Callista kneeling before him as he lifted his blade high. Her body limp in his arms as her life drained away. No matter how he'd run from it, this was the future awaiting him. Perhaps it was time to stop running and start fighting.

"You will go after her, won't you?" Duncallan asked.

David took a deep breath. Then another. But the wolf would not be denied. It boiled to the surface, every heartbeat twisting him into a creature of Feyblood nightmare. Every breath torching his body with the savagery and skill of the predator.

Corey had searched for David from one end of Great Britain to the other. Today he would find him.

Then the bastard would die.

That was the future David would focus on. That was the vision burned on his heart.

He opened his eyes to meet the Duncallans' gold-flecked, inquiring gaze. "Of course. What are friends for?"

She paced the room where they'd locked her, a bedchamber as ostentatious as it was uncomfortable: furniture polished to a mirror shine, a chimneypiece of rose marble veined in cream, enough bric-a-brac to keep maids dusting for years, and, in the middle of the spectacle, an enormous bed decked in purple damask and crimson tassels.

Corey watched her from a seat by the fire, his smile as twisted and harsh as his mind. "Anxious for your wedding night? I am, too, sweetling, but a few hours more and I'm all yours. Even better, you're all mine."

"You're mad."

"*Shrewd* is the word. Your beloved aunt was a mirage. She didn't want you. Nobody wants you . . . but me, my dear. I'll care for you like my finest treasure. I won't even punish you for running away from me in London. Instead, you'll be waited on by a dozen maids. You'll have a coach and four and be mistress of a house as big as Blenheim or Chatsworth or any of the nobs' finest. Duchesses will kneel for your favors, dukes will kiss your slippers, and maybe the prince regent himself will wipe your pretty ass. It's there for the taking."

"Branston was a fool to entangle himself with you."

"I'll agree the man had the business acumen of a brainless slug. It's best he's dead. You should be pleased I killed him. Left under his care, you'd never have amounted to anything more than a third-rate fortune-teller in a fourth-rate circus, but with me . . ." He rose from his chair to cross to her side. Lifted his hand to touch her hair, her cheek. "With me, you'll rise to the rank of queen."

She refused to flinch. Instead she raked him with every ounce of dripping contempt she could muster. "Queen of the stews," she spat. "I don't care how you pretty yourself up, you're still naught more than the stunted offspring of a hedge whore and a rat catcher."

The slap knocked her to the floor, her cheek on fire. He stood above her, his scar white against the red of his face. "Your brother wasn't wrong about one thing. He said you needed a strong whip hand." He grabbed her by the arm, wrenching her to her feet, his breath hot on her face. "What's a few words when we've a lifetime ahead of us?" He dragged her toward the bed. "I've a mind to shove myself between those sweet thighs. By the time I'm done, you'll be begging for my touch."

She dug in her heels, but he slapped her again before he shoved her down on the bed. Panic skittered cold across her skin. She couldn't swallow. Couldn't breathe. Her gaze locked on his white-lipped mouth, the hunger in his eyes.

"Take the gown off or I'll cut it off you," he hissed, pulling a blade from his waist.

She fumbled with clumsy fingers at the buttons and tapes. Slid free of the muslin, chin up and unashamed. Time, she needed time. If she closed her eyes and lay very still, perhaps he would finish with her quickly and leave. She would think of the friendly glow of a cookfire and laughter over a shared jest, quiet conversations and delicious kisses. Corey might have her body. He could not steal her memories.

He knelt over her to fondle a breast. Pinched her cruelly. Held her chin tight as he forced his tongue into her mouth, his breath sour. "Did St. Leger take you as man or beast? Did he mount you like a dog? Did he fuck you hard and fast like I will?" His face grew flushed with arousal as he shucked off his jacket and loosed his breeches. A rigid cock sprang purple from a thick bush of hair. "You do what I want when I want it or I'll make you hurt, Callista. If I can't have your respect, I'll have your fear."

Callista's expression hardened to marble, her blood as cold as ice water.

A knock at the door slammed her heart into her throat. "Corey, sir," a voice called through the crack. "All's ready."

"Right." Corey rolled away from her and out of bed. He fastened his breeches and pulled his coat back onto his shoulders. "Our pleasure will have to wait. Duty calls."

"You won't win, Victor. David will find me."

Corey's leer became a smile of wild-eyed triumph. "I'm counting on it."

He slipped free of the concealing shadows in a flash of speed, slaver dripping from his jaws, muscles wired taut as they ate the distance to his prey. A man guarded the main door armed with knife and musket, but his attention was all for the gathering storm clouds, their bellies slashed with green lightning.

It was an easy thing to take him unawares. A crouch, a leap, and the man dropped with a spine-snapping blow to his chest, his neck ripped wide. The wolf lifted his head to the wind, blood sliding hot down his throat. The doors opened, men tumbling like spillikins onto the gravel. They stank of sour wine and stale sweat. A silver dagger swiped down to tear into his shoulder. Another slashed at him with a blade of steel, its bite twice as sharp. It took David in the haunch. He yelped and danced away, leaving a blood trail behind.

He heard the cocking of the pistol before it exploded with smoke and flame, avoided the crush of a bullet into his skull with a wild leap that nearly pulled his shoulder from its socket. The man with the dagger was quick and cunning. He ducked beneath David's reach, the knife falling again. David twisted away before it could slice his stomach open, but all the time he felt his strength failing. Withdrawal from the draught had left him weak and feverish, and the curse's reemergence meant a slowing of his mind, a sickening of his body. Blue and silver flames rippled at the edges of his vision. The curse rose from the same well as the wolf. And every moment he delayed was a moment lost.

David growled, his fangs dripping with blood as he shook off the illness and surrendered himself completely to instinct and bloodlust and a savage brutality. Ignoring the jagged rake of the blade and the silver burning his flesh, he sprang. Felt the crunch of bones as he bit down, the screams and useless flailing as the man scrabbled to free himself, and the final wrench that left him armless and bleeding his life away. The wolf lunged again, his claws tearing into another man's stomach, spilling his entrails, shredding the man's face and then his chest. Corey's third hireling sought to run, but the wolf brought him down, snapping his neck, smashing his skull.

Were these all the protection Corey boasted, or did the house hold more of the same, the wretched refuse of every stew and thieves' den from London to Fort William?

David's stomach rolled while his head pounded as if a spike had been slammed between his eyes. Blue and silver flames leapt, crackled, torched him from the inside out. He took a step and then another, but the wolf's strength left him.

He fell to the gravel, the pain as intense as the ripping free of his signum, the curse infecting his mind, burning away his powers like acid on steel. A hot wind curled around him, the air beating like wings against his muzzle, his paws. He couldn't breathe lest it singe his lungs. He squeezed his eyes shut. And waited.

"Here's the little mouse now. Just in time for my big day," a voice sneered.

Rough hands gripped David. A heavy knobbed cane descended in a blur. A white light exploded behind his eyes.

Callista! he shouted.

She was wed.

A ring and a few mumbled words by a bought priest, and she'd chained herself to Corey forever. Anything to stop his men from hurting David. She'd been brought a lock of his guinea-gold hair first. Then a bloody fingernail. Finally a finger.

She'd surrendered, retching up her breakfast, dry gulping sobs tearing raggedly up her throat.

Corey had come to her, proud as a peacock, and the marriage had been performed. Thankfully, he'd left straight after, and she could only wait in half-panicked frustration as the hours ticked past.

Circling the bedchamber, she paused at the window. No escape there. Far too small for her to climb through, and the only way was down—far down, over the sheer, knife-edged cliffs to the gray-green sea below. And if they caught her attempting to leave, what would happen to David? Bile curdled her stomach. She knew all too well.

The door opened, and Corey entered, dressed as if he were preparing for war, with a pistol and a sheathed dirk at his waist. He motioned to a wiry man, his shaved head and stubbled jowls giving him the look of a belligerent mastiff. "Bring her."

They climbed two sets of stairs to a narrow wooden

door leading to a wide bricked parapet and a low, crenellated wall running the length of the house. The sea churned and growled below, the cliffs a tumble of jagged rocks and broken boulders. This morning's sun had given way to heavy clouds licked black with storm shadows. The wind flapped at Callista's skirts and tore the pins from her hair as it shoved her unwilling toward the wall. It wouldn't take but a quick wrench to escape her captor. A few steps to the edge and she'd be free.

She glanced down at the foaming surf and the wild spumes of icy spray and knew she'd never be able to do it. Not while David lived. Not while there was still a chance. Killing herself was the coward's way. And the weeks past had proved her no coward.

A table had been set in the middle of the walkway. Beside it rested her box. Upon it stood her bells. Corey's smirk grew.

"This is madness, Victor," she pleaded. "You've more wealth and power than half the nobility already. What more could you want?"

"I want those nose-in-the-air toffs with their high breeding and their ancient pedigrees to admit that I'm just as good as they are. After that, I want them to fear me and know their lives depend on my goodwill. A wrong word, an ill-thought whisper, and I'll make them wish they'd never been born." He motioned to the bells. "Open the door. Open the door and summon me an army."

"I won't."

"You will, my dear, or I'll slice off another finger. He has nine more he doesn't need."

She glanced to the door where her bribed coachman stood with a pistol to David's temple. He knelt upon the bricks, head bowed. Blood-spattered and shoulders hunched. She couldn't see his face. Afraid she wouldn't want to. Not after the hours he'd spent with Corey. Not after the sight of his finger laid on a bed of velvet as a bridal gift.

Don't fret, sweet Callista. I've been in tighter places than this. David's voice curled warm and protective against her heart.

This is my fault, she pathed.

He lifted his head for a moment, and she caught back an anguished gasp at the wreckage of his face. *There's only person to blame. And he's a fucking dead man.*

Callista scanned the hills for hope, praying to see the dark wings of a crow against the clouds. To catch sight of a troop of Amhas-draoi riding to the rescue.

Nothing. And no one.

She stepped to the table. Knelt. And laid her shaking hand upon Key.

Blood . . . pain . . . fire . . .

The only part of his dream yet unrealized was death. And that would be denied him as long as Corey believed him worth more alive. David focused on the pattern of the bricks on which he knelt, the mossy cracks, the ants crawling, the wind moving across his raw and broken flesh, the cold of the pistol's mouth against his skull. It kept him from dwelling on the agony of his maimed hand, the savage pain gnawing at his innards, the blue and silver flames tearing through his mind.

Nine fingers they would take. Ten toes. An eye. Or two. A nose. His tongue. The process had been recounted in gory detail in the hell of Corey's basements. But that was nothing compared to the threats the bastard had made toward Callista, the whispered promises that left David struggling against his bonds, every word a hurled curse.

Corey had laughed.

Corey wouldn't be laughing soon.

Back and forth. Over and over until blood and torn skin slickened his wrists, his jaw clamped against the agony of his smashed hand. He kept his head down as shadow and sun passed across the surface of the stone. Smiled, for none knew it yet, but freedom was almost his.

The path wound through a deep, silent wood. Even the stream sliding beside her moved slow and sluggish and without a sound. She had never been here before; the landscape was wild and black, with upthrust boulders like grasping hands and trees climbing forever into a flat gray sky.

Annwn's creatures watched her. She couldn't see them but she felt their eyes crawling over her skin and sensed their desire for the heat and the life she possessed. What would they do if freed of the realms of man? But how could she refuse when it meant David would suffer?

She had no choice.

Lucan would claim otherwise. "There is always a choice," he'd told her that long-ago afternoon in the Addershiels summerhouse.

She knew what her choice must be, no matter how it pained her.

She continued walking, and now snow dusted her shoulders and coated the path in white. The chill bit into her face and numbed her hands; her fingers upon Blade were cramped and throbbing. The gray light dimmed and the trees became sentinels, their branches reaching for her, their roots ensnaring her feet and twisting round her ankles. She fell, the bell clanging as it rolled from her hand. The creatures receded into the murky twilight with the crash and rumble of feet upon the packed earth and the screech and yowl of voices raised in frustration.

She drew her legs up to her chest, but the cold sapped her strength as it clawed her throat and raked her lungs. It wouldn't take long. All she need do was remain here, and if the snow and ice didn't claim her, something else would.

Corey would fail. The threat would end with her death.

She smiled, feeling the pinch of cold in her cheeks. If she died within, she would die without. She would have changed the dream. She would have outsmarted the fates.

The screeches grew in volume. The rumble of footsteps grew in number. She struggled to her feet with a moan of pain and failure.

Annwn's monsters did not flee her bell.

They raced for the door.

The wind stank of sulfur and sweat, the stench of sickness and rotting flesh, grave earth and wounds gone sour. Clouds rolled thick and green across the sky, spreading out across the rolling barren cliffs and crags. Magic crackled the air like a summer storm, electrifying the hair at the back of his neck, the pain in his head, and the illness churning his gut.

No breath stirred Callista's frozen lungs, and her flesh shone white as snow. Ice coated the three bells, and the table upon which they rested was slick and shiny. Around her, shadowy forms snaked over the stones of the parapet. Curled along the walls. Drifted up into the sky like slender wisps of smoke.

David ignored the hard, tight knot centered in his chest and the raging inferno tearing into his muscles as the curse and the draught warred for dominance. In one fluid move, he rose from his knees. With one hand, he swept the gun from his temple. With the other, he crushed the man's nose before snatching the cocked weapon free. A quick squeeze of the trigger, and the guard tumbled to the stones, blood pooling beneath his body.

Corey pulled a pistol from his coat. "You might be faster than a bullet, but she's not." He aimed the pistol at Callista. "And you'd do anything to save her life, wouldn't you? You'd even let me carve you into pieces as I sell you off an ounce at a time."

David eyed the distance. Ten yards. No more. But weakness slowed him, and Callista was an easy target. Dare he take the chance?

"What's a few fingers to save the woman you love? A scar or two?" Corey smiled viciously. "And you do love her, don't you? Why else would a shifter dare show his face within the stronghold of Scathach's brotherhood? Why else come chasing after her when you know what you'll face? You'd have to be mad or desperately in love."

"Maybe I'm both," David said, rage taking him over.

"You must be, to fall for a penniless nobody like Callista Hawthorne when you've had every highborn lady in London panting for your cock like bitches in heat."

David's first move caught Corey off guard. His second had the bastard pinned at the edge of the parapet, his wrist caught in David's steel grip as he slammed the pistol away to be lost in the foam below.

"Maybe because she's a necromancer and I'm a dead man," David snarled.

Corey's eyes grew round in fear as they flicked from David's grim stare to the deadly crags. "Here's a deal. You and me. Fifty-fifty. Think of the profits. You'd be wealthy beyond your dreams. Enough money to buy Scathach's army right out from under her. The Imnada would be safe. You'd be a bloody hero to your people. Adored and revered. Just a few drops. That's all it would take."

A hero. The savior of the Imnada. David could go home. Erase his family's shame. He would no longer be *emnil*. No longer be alone. David's hold loosened. "All you need is a few drops?" he asked.

A smile curved the edge of Corey's mouth. "Yes, of course. Eighty-twenty. I'll do all the work, make all the contacts. All I need from you is"—Corey pulled a knife. David twisted aside as the blade slammed along his ribs—"your blood."

David screamed in pain and rage as he shoved Corey backward over the wall. Arms and legs flailing, the king of the stews flapped at the air before disappearing into the mist clouding the spiked and jagged rocks below.

"The answer is no," David said, a hand pressed to his side. He tried straightening, but his side burned where Corey's dagger had gouged a deep score along his rib cage.

Shadows continued to slide free of the rift between death and life, rising like a flock of crows or vultures into the air with a shriek of jubilation. The most frightening passed into Callista herself to settle beneath her skin, see the world through her eyes.

One crow spun away from the screaming flock, diving earthward like an arrow. *End it, shapechanger. End it now before the world is overrun.*

Badb stood before him, her cloak of feathers black as the figures passing like shades into the world of men, ghosts tossed on the ill wind, moving outward from the rift. "The door to Annwn stands open and unguarded. Death escapes into life."

David shook Callista's shoulders. Stared deep into her eyes, which glowed yellow as the sun. "Come back to me. You must close the door. You must stop the dead from escaping."

"She is lost within Annwn. As long as she is trapped within the maze, she cannot pass back into life. She cannot close and seal the door. You must do it for her. You must end this now."

"How?" he asked, though he already knew the answer. He'd seen it happen a million times.

Badb picked up Corey's fallen knife.

"I won't kill her," David argued. "This is not a fate I choose."

"Look around you. Death gapes like an open wound and through it ride nightmares you can't hope to imagine."

"There has to be another way."

The Fey's gaze gleamed black as midnight in a face like bone. "You would trade the world for the life of one woman? Corey was right. You are mad."

"And in love."

"If you play the craven, it is left to me." Standing above Callista, Badb gripped the knife, lips drawn back on her pearly teeth, face carved in harsh lines. Raised her arm to strike, paused on a shuddering breath before completing the downstroke, the blade whistling as it descended.

David winced, sweat beading against his temple. A ragged smile broke over his face. "You couldn't kill her, either."

Badb swung around, the knife in her fist. "You think this will save her life? You are a fool, shifter. The woman kneeling before you is not Callista. It is her form, but the true woman is trapped within death. Without the soul, the body is naught but a shell. A shade. You have gained nothing."

"I'll find her. I'll bring her back."

"For this, you must go into death."

"How do I do that?"

Badb smiled, her face as cold and cruel as winter. "You die."

Snow swirled to crust Callista's shoulders and hair, dragged at her feet as drifts piled. By now the cold froze her lungs and every breath came laced with pain.

Each step was an effort as her feet turned blue, then white, then black. Her gown was soaked to her waist and she wanted only to sink into the deep, soft white and close her eyes.

Mother had tried to warn her. Don't stray from the paths. Keep your head or you'll lose your way. The cold and emptiness found in death are nothing compared to the frozen loneliness of heartbreak.

She'd been right about all of it.

Tears turned to ice against Callista's cheeks.

Wake up. You mustn't sleep. You mustn't close your eyes.

Callista lifted her head at the shimmery voice, but all that met her eye was the endless white snow, the endless black trees, and the infinitely circling and twining paths.

Focus. Concentrate on the path. One step at a time.

The voice sounded like the song of the dead, but deeper, almost cutting. And very familiar. But it couldn't be. She must be dreaming. Or hallucinating. David couldn't be here unless . . .

She peered through the blizzard until she glimpsed a wavery blue and silver form like frozen mist, moving toward her. Slowly the mist coalesced into the figure of a man. The sight of his body, tall and broad-shouldered, with a Greek god's rippled abdomen and corded muscles, pricked at her heart and tightened her hands to fists. But it was his face, hard-jawed and chiseled cheeks, that dragged a sob up through her scraped and frozen throat. Corey had not been kind.

"David," she whispered, unable to tear her gaze from his eyes, silver as mist, and hollowed with sorrow.

"I told you once I saw my end when I looked in your eyes, and it was not a gentle death."

"Corey . . ."

"Will never hurt you again." He reached for her, his touch like ice but the rasp of his fingers familiar enough to clench her heart. She could not bear to look at his other hand, to see the cost of her hesitation in the horrible damage. "You have to find your way back, Callista. Until you do, the door stands open. You're the only one who can close it."

She shook her head. "I tried to stop Corey, but the grel and the dead flesh, all of Arawn's creatures, ignored me in their flight toward the door. You were right. Life beckons them. Compared to the feast that awaits them on the other side, my tiny spark is a crumb. Not worth the trouble."

"A feast they can't be allowed to have. Come on. A little farther. Just to the next turning."

David guided her along the path, but the snow continued to fall, a white, windswept torrent stinging her face and stealing her breath. Her throat ached with every breath, and she groped for orientation within the wild swirl of white and gray. Up. Turn. Turn again. Back down. Left. Right.

"Which way?" he asked.

Nothing looked familiar. "I don't know," she replied. "I can't see. My mind . . . I'm too tired . . ."

"Damn it, Callista. Concentrate."

Shadows passed her, fleeing toward the open doorway and the heat and fire they would find in life. She struggled to follow, but they moved too fast. A slithering tentacle brushed her face. Another curled around her ankle. Cold breath at the back of her neck. Claws curling around her shoulder. Glowing red and yellow eyes. She froze, but soul feeder and grel, dead flesh and the wraithlike phantasm, none did more than offer her a token stare or a grimace of sharp teeth.

The snow piled to her ankles and her knees. "I . . . I can't . . ."

David shimmered silver as his eyes, his body hard as rock, cold as ice. He gripped her under her arm. "You must. Badb sent me here, but only you can bring me out."

The trees marched on like a twisted jungle. No way to pick the right path beneath their weighted limbs. No landmarks to bring her back to the house and the wide avenue lined with statues. And the door.

She sank to the ground. "You can do what the creatures will not. You can close the door."

David's jaw clenched in a face like stone. His hands curled to fists at his sides. "I won't."

She glanced at the blade he carried at his waist before meeting his stare. "You have no choice."

"There's always a choice. Isn't that what you told me? That we could fight our fate. We could change the future we saw."

"I was wrong!" she cried. "Look at me. I ran with my tail between my legs from London to Skye and still I ended wed to Victor Corey. I fought to get Aunt Deirdre to lift your curse, and she refused. I even tried to thwart the death the spirits showed me, and yet here you are. Fates are fixed. And this is the only way. I've seen the monsters that live down here in the dark corners. They can't be allowed to escape."

"I . . ."

"Please, David."

"If I kill you, the door closes?"

"It can only be opened from the outside. We'll not stop those that have already escaped, but no more will pass through into life."

A grim smile quirked his mouth. "I always said the dead were the only ones who might make a difference." He cupped her cheek with his mangled hand. His lips found hers in a kiss as warm as summer. "I would not have traded these few precious weeks for a lifetime without you in it," he murmured, his breath soft against her temple.

She cried, her tears freezing on her cheeks. "I've destroyed you just as you said I would."

"No, sweet Callista, you found me after I'd been lost for a long time. I love you. In life . . . and death." His smile curved those perfect lips as he bent to take her once more in his arms.

"Now, before it's too late." She knelt in the snow beneath a gray sky, her hair falling soft around her shoulders. "Before I lose my nerve."

She closed her eyes. He knelt to whisper in her ear, his words a murmur of Imnada and English. All of it a promise of love. She smiled even when he drew the blade across her throat, the first quick sting becoming a burn like fire and ice at once. Fog shrouded her vision, the snow falling faster until the world was a torrent with no up or down.

Her breastbone hummed and prickled as death yawned wide. Arms folded her close. She looked into eyes as silver and empty as the world around her.

The door closed.

*   *   *

David held Callista's body in his arms, her gown awash in crimson, his hands sticky with her blood. The snow had vanished and with it the silence of a dark forest blanketed in white. The paths now stretched away across a seething, smoking ridgeline. Some dipped down into sunken lanes where men struggled with swords and bayonets. Other tracks rode up and over the hills toward the far orchards and a village, a church spire pointing above the trees.

The sound of artillery rattled his ribs and pounded in his chest like a second heart. Above, the air burned hot and smoky, flames writhing up from a house into the cinder-lit sky. Twisted corpses littered the track, their faces masks of agony. Crows pecked at their wounds and ripped free their staring eyes. The wounded cried out for help, for water, for their mothers. A few merely wept or screamed or moaned. The stench made David gag, his stomach rolling, his nerves raw.

Waterloo. The last battle. All around him, men fought, muskets rattling, bayonets and swords ringing. A boy fell to David's left, his chest blown out. A scarred cuirassier with a bloody sleeve screamed as a bayonet skewered him to the ground. Beyond, three cavalry rode down an English soldier, crushing his body into the mud and offal near the courtyard. Out of the smoke, a wild-eyed Frenchman rose up with a cavalryman's saber, his face a rictus of battle madness. David threw himself across Callista's body, hoping to shield it from the descending sword, but no blade bit deep. The man passed through him as if he were a ghost or a dream, no more substantial than the pall of black, choking smoke billowing across the wood.

Then he understood. This was his death and his path forever to walk. He would not even have the solace of finding Callista within Annwn. He might cradle her body, but her spirit moved along other dark tracks within the tangled web that was Arawn's realm. With that realization, the cold overwhelmed him; a biting freeze slashed at his lungs with every breath. The aches in his body and the agony of his mutilated hand disappeared as the glow and glimmer of cinders became the pale light of a million spirits sliding in and out of the trees, over the writhing bodies, curling up from the ripped and bloody dead.

One turned and rolled and spun until it hung in the air above him. It grew in brightness until the sight burned David's eyes and he had to look away.

"I've sent you back once. She will send you back again. A third time and you will stay forever."

A voice in his head and in his ears. David lifted his face to the ghostly figure of a man. Handsome. Tall. A bit stocky, with broad, beefy shoulders and a stomach just the trim side of paunch. An icy fist clutched at his heart and stole his frozen breath. "Adam?"

The man smiled. "I am the spirit who is. Adam who was."

"I've come to join you," David said.

"No. This is not your time and this is not your death."

"Could have fooled me," he answered, trying for cocky and failing miserably. Exhaustion weighted his limbs and even the sounds of battle seemed faded and ragged, the colors and sounds and life drifting away like smoke. He tried focusing on Adam. He'd not seen him for over a year—not living, at any rate. And their last conversation had haunted David ever since. But even Adam grew indistinct and shimmery like the shine off a river at sunrise or the dew caught within a spider's web. "With death comes life, David. Live it well."

"Wait. I'm sorry, Adam. I never meant those things I said. The curse wasn't your fault. Nor any of the tragedy that came after. We needed one another, Adam . . . I needed the three of you . . ."

His breath felt trapped within his chest, throat burning as he struggled to draw in air, bones vibrating until he clamped his jaw against the sensation. Pressure built deep in his center as if he might fly apart at the merest touch.

Spots danced before his eyes as his vision narrowed to a pinprick.

"The blood, David," Adam called out. "It's in the blood."

David screamed out a final desperate sending into the abyss.

21

He woke to the hard scowl and white lips of Ard-siur bending over him, her gray gown billowing like the wings of a giant bird. Above, the sky shone hard and blue. Beneath, the stones of the parapet dug into his back and shoulders. The pain in his hand blazed a path all the way to his brain, and he bit back a groan. "Where . . ." His breath came in spasms, every swallow felt as if he'd inhaled glass, and he shuddered with a bone-deep chill. "Am I dead?"

"Do you *feel* dead?"

His head throbbed until he thought his brain might leak from his ears and even blinking hurt. "I feel like shit."

She winced, her eyes gleaming gold before shrugging away from him.

With a quick steadying breath, he rolled up onto his knees, the world tipping and spinning like the deck of a ship. In between the bursting fireworks shattering his vision, he made out Badb's feathered shape, a kneeling figure that might or might not be

Lord Duncallan, the table, the spilled bells. "Where's Callista?"

The Fey knelt by his side, her cap of black curls tousled in the wind, her cloak billowing loose to reveal her pearly skin. "You succeeded, child of the wolf. You sealed the door."

"Damn it, what's happened to her?"

Badb's gaze flickered, her lips pursing slightly.

"My niece chose death. She is a true daughter of Arawn now." The head of the *bandraoi* stepped aside, her skirts revealing Callista's still form laid upon a blanket. Her dark hair glimmered in the afternoon sun, but her face was white as chalk, white as the snows of Annwn.

No mark of his knife marred her throat. No blood stained the white of her muslin gown. She could be asleep, her hands placed upon her breast as if already prepared for her coffin. A death of earth and dust. No journey beyond the stars and through the Gateway.

"I killed her." David scrambled to her side, touching her, brushing her hair from her face. Waiting for the moment she opened her eyes, stuck out her tongue, and told him it was all a prank. All a dream.

But the dream had been real. His dream had unfolded as he'd seen it a million times. He'd failed.

"You were merely the weapon Callista turned upon herself. It was her choice," Badb said.

"Damn it, there was no choice about it. You forced her to close the door. You forced me to be her killer." He rubbed his sticky hands over his face, blood tasting of iron and salt on his lips. It mingled with the tears burning against his cheeks. He fisted his good hand against the rage. Opened it slowly, his gaze locked upon the silver scars interlacing his palm, the blood slicking his wrist. An idea formed in his weary head. A chance. A hope. All he had left.

He grabbed up a fallen knife, clumsy with only four fingers, but still adept enough to slide it over his opposite wrist. His blood oozed from the narrow gash. He placed his wrist against Callista's blue lips, letting his heart push the blood a drop at a time into her mouth. One . . . two . . . three . . . four . . .

"Come on, Callista. Open your damn eyes. Take a breath. Something."

"What are you doing?" The Ard-siur rushed to pull him away, her words snapping against his brain, her fingers wrenching his shoulder, but Lord Duncallan stopped her with a gentle word and a stern grip. "He offers her the *afailth luinan*. His blood for her life."

"Death cannot be undone," the old woman argued. "Arawn will not be cheated."

Lord Duncallan pulled her away, his words calm but allowing no resistance. "The Imnada owe no allegiance to the lord of the dead, and the ways of the shapechangers are not our ways. I've seen it work and felt its power. Let him be."

Ten . . . eleven . . . twelve . . .

David seemed to float above his body, his vision fading in and out as his injuries made themselves felt in every muscle.

Twenty . . . twenty-one . . .

Did her chest rise? Did her cheeks pink? He bent to lay his head upon her chest, and felt the curve of an arm come round to hold him close. A breath warm against his cheek. "David?" she murmured.

He gathered her up against him, her hair spilling over his arms, his kisses brushing her temple, her forehead, her cheek, her neck. "Callista. Edern, my beautiful Fey princess. *Orneai aimara*."

". . . reconsidered my initial and perhaps hasty assessment. I will allow you to stay on, but you can expect no special treatment due to our . . . familial connection. You will be taken in as the lowest novice and worked harder than you've ever worked before, but perhaps, if you have a tenth of your mother's promise . . . there might just be . . . hope for you as a necromancer."

It must have been like chewing worms to speak those words. Callista wanted to laugh at the pained expression chasing its way over her aunt's dour face. She wanted to, but her throat hurt and her chest felt prickly, as if bees had taken up residence under her ribs. Instead she closed her hands around the book she'd been reading and smiled her thanks.

"You can't know how much it means to me to hear you say that. But why? After all you said, why go into death after us? You could have simply let the door remain shut. It would have been simple."

Her aunt pulled the packet of letters from her pocket, the frayed blue ribbon replaced with a purple satin bow. She put them on the bed beside Callista. "No matter your unfortunate paternity, you and I share blood and birthright. I couldn't make up for the years I lost with my sister. I needed to try to make amends with her daughter."

How many momentous decisions in life hinge on a single moment in a single day?

Had her aunt spoken those words just one day earlier, all would have ended differently. Now Callista swallowed around a knot in her throat, dreading what she had to say. Her heart's desire lay spread before her, but despite her aunt's softening, Callista knew this was no longer the right path for her. "I appreciate your offer, Aunt Deirdre. But"—her aunt frowned—"I can't accept. You were right. I don't belong here. In my mind, I turned Dunsgathaic into the home I never had and you into the mother I lost. I thought I could make a place for myself here, but I can't. The home and family I truly want is still out there waiting for me." She glanced to the window, where sunset painted the sky red and gold, pink and orange, while the sea rippled dark as ink.

"If you speak of St. Leger, he's gone." Aunt Deirdre's hand clamped round the bedpost, her large knobby fingers white.

"Gone?"

"He disappeared last night. None know how, but the castle has been searched with no sign of him, and Lord Duncallan refuses to answer any questions. A disappointment, as I would have liked to interrogate the shifter further, but it is not to be helped."

Callista frowned, the bees settling to her stomach with a dull thud. "He can't have left. We . . . he called me Edern."

Aunt Deirdre sniffed, her gaze falling to the book. "The Fey-born princess married off to the monster to save the kingdom. A sentimental if affecting tale."

Callista's cheeks flushed hot even as the rest of her shivered with cold. "Rinaci Hammerclaw won Edern's heart. He loved her."

"As long as Mr. St. Leger's alive, you'll be wed to this ridiculous dream."

"No, the dream is past. We fought it and we won. I just didn't realize that winning the battle would be losing the war."

"So you will stay here with us. I will inform Sister Hosta, our mistress of novices, of your decision and—"

"I won't wall myself away, Aunt. I won't exchange one prison for another."

Aunt Deirdre's expression hardened as she straightened her gown with a twitch of a sleeve. A brush of the collar. "You say the shifter is doomed to die? Perhaps I should have left him in death. Perhaps that would have been the mercy . . . for both of you."

From her high window, Callista took a last look at the swiftly churning clouds, the flocks of feeding seabirds, and far sails upon the sea beyond Dunsgathaic's walls, but it was Rinaci Hammerclaw and Idrin the Traveler, Helene of the Rhaynor and Brune the Hairy, she saw out her bedchamber window. Lords and ladies, heroes and villains, daring battles and tragic romances. She knew all about those. She ran a hand over the book as if she might step within the pages before shoving it in her satchel beside her bells. The letters Aunt Deirdre had kept.

She turned her mind from thoughts of David. A week had passed with no sign of him beyond a hastily scribbled note, the handwriting sloppy, ink splattering the page. She tried not to imagine him fumbling with the pen, awkward with his mangled hand. Struggled to forget the deep slash on his cheek, the broken bloody nose, and the smashed and splintered wrist. Instead, she focused on the words he'd whispered, the way he'd held her, the depth of his fog-shrouded gaze. It was all she had left of him.

"Ahhh, *The Collected Tales of Moriaen Golden Tongue*, a classic." Lord Duncallan joined her at the window, ready for travel in a long coat, a stylish hat covering his dark hair.

"I'd never heard of the book until I found it among Gray's shelves. Now I'm hooked on stories about Swen of the Silver Ship and Morag the Rat Tail. How could the Other have discarded so much of a past rife with such majesty and magic? How could they have destroyed the Imnada in retribution for one man's crime?"

"There are a thousand more stories that never made it into the books, an oral tradition passed down from generation to generation but never written. Stories of brutality and fear and starvation and death. The Fealla Mhòr is the most frightening of these. It's spoken of as one might speak of the end of the world."

"It was the end of the world for them, though, wasn't it? Of all they'd known and everything they'd been."

Duncallan's gaze grew distant, almost forbidding. "It was. Villages razed, populations slaughtered. Any who bore a drop of shifter blood singled out for execution. 'We shall not suffer a demon to live among us any longer. They are deceitful, wicked, evil creatures.' Said as the Other were tearing babes from their mothers' arms, hacking the heads off young men, and butchering whole families together."

"After such savagery, how can you ever hope to bring about a peace between the races? Even after so long, the hate is still there on both sides." She closed her eyes against a sharp, painful breath.

"We'll never know unless we make the attempt," Duncallan responded. "If you're ready to go, the coach is waiting. It's a long journey to London."

"Are you certain this is a good idea? The Earl and Countess of Deane won't even know we're coming until we arrive on their doorstep, and I've learned to my cost, it's not wise to turn up unannounced."

He smiled. "Deane House has more rooms than I could count on hands and feet together and most of them depressingly empty since Seb's wedding to Sarah."

"I read about it in the papers. I saw Sarah Haye perform once in Bath as Lady Arabella. She was brilliant."

"Unfortunately not all her acting skill can mask her lowborn background. Society does not like an upstart. Sarah has few friends. You'll do each other a world of good. And it will only be until you're back on your feet."

"She's friends with Bianca Parrino . . . I mean, Bianca Flannery, isn't she?"

His gaze grew bleak. "Yes, the captain's wife and the countess are close. Sarah will be able to offer Bianca comfort when . . . when it's needed . . . but you'll understand her pain better than any."

Oh, she understood pain all right. It lived cold and hard in her chest. It woke her at night with wet cheeks and scratchy eyes and turned every dawn into a sentence to be served. She might have comforted herself with the knowledge that even if he was not with her, he was still out there somewhere. But even that solace was denied her. David was doomed. The curse ate him alive. There would come a day that she would look up at the moon and know he was gone forever.

She swung her satchel onto her shoulder, took one last look at the cozy tower chamber, and closed the door of Dunsgathaic behind her.

"Sir? Can I bring you a bit of supper? I've some mutton left from this morning and a bit of ham." A knock and a rustle of heavy skirts on the other side of the door. An eye pressed to a crack in the slats. He sensed Mrs. MacDonald watching him. She'd spent nearly every moment since he'd arrived at this sad excuse for a roadside inn attempting to wheedle information from him with simpering smiles and sweet words. Unfortunately, she only managed to give him the shivers.

"I'm not hungry, Mrs. MacDonald."

"Have it your way, young man."

He heard her muttering all the way down the creaking stairs. A few choice phrases about queerish rattle-pated gentlemen and moon madness.

She was half right.

He glanced out the window at the gathering dusk. The sun dropped beneath the horizon to the west while Piryeth's maiden moon, a yellow waxing crescent, scraped the trees in fast pursuit. He watched and waited for the blue and silver flames to engulf him, for the curse to tear at his muscles and warp the blood in his veins. The faint lines crisscrossing his palms seemed to shine in the weak light while the scar on his wrist burned as it did every night. He rubbed a hand over the healing gash, knowing the pain would always be with him, the connection he shared with Callista. A bond of love . . . and now blood.

He'd hated leaving her, but he couldn't remain within the walls of Dunsgathaic. Not once the *bandraoi* learned of the power of the *afailth luinan*. He would not exchange Corey's brutal captivity for the pampered ease of a softer confinement by the *bandraoi* as they picked him apart with needle precision until the secrets of the Imnada were laid bare upon their cutting board.

He told himself it was for the best. Callista had gained the family she'd always wanted and the life of a priestess, where her Fey-born powers could be honed for the good of her race, rather than the enhancement of her coin purse. She would forget him in time. He only hoped she could forgive him.

He glanced once more to the window to see that night had truly fallen, not even a glimmer of orange to brighten the purple, star-shot sky. Stared down at the table, flinching only slightly at the stump on his right hand. The maiming played havoc with his handwriting and his table manners would need some adjusting, but it wasn't the loss of a finger or the aches in his wrist or even the piratical scar down his cheek that gripped him immobile in his chair. It was the untouched cup of rancid Fey-born brew infused with his blood. A potent blend of Imnada power and Other magic; two forces wholly opposed and always at war. No wonder the draught killed him and saved him at the same time.

He'd not taken it in two weeks. By now he should be retching his guts up, his entire body one exposed nerve as the curse tore through him like shrapnel. Sunset. Sunrise. The days marked off by the forced shift as his body morphed from man to wolf against his will while he screamed.

Two weeks. Nothing. He remained healthy. He remained in control.

He remained completely and incurably confused.

He ran a hand through his hair. Rubbed at the back of his neck. "I don't understand."

"You died."

He peered over his shoulder at Badb, who'd materialized in the cheerless garret, her shift of feathers rustling as she crossed the floor, her naked body lithe as a willow.

"The MacDonalds should get a cat," he groused.

She laughed, her snapping black eyes alive with mischief. "You seek answers. I bring them. You died, St. Leger. You went into death. And death took you."

"Then spat me out again, no thanks to Deirdre Armstrong." He rose to pour himself a glass of wine. Only one. The rage had left him. And for some reason, loss left no room for drink.

Badb crossed to his side to lay a hand on his arm. "The necromancer pulled you free from the paths. You should be grateful. The door to death—"

"Only opens from the outside, I know. But what's that to do with the draught and the curse and why I feel . . . good."

She frowned, tossing her cap of curls. "So dense, you are. The answer stares you in the face. You died, and so, too, did the curse. It ended with your death as the spell was originally wrought. Though I doubt that the Other who cast it intended such a flouting of his purpose."

"So, that's it? The spell is broken just like that? No

more draught? No more shift? No more . . ." Wine forgotten, he dropped into a chair, staring unseeing in a
haze of amazement.

"You are not dying, shapechanger. You are reborn.
New. Cleansed of the curse. Free of its taint."

He held up his mangled hand. "Yet still missing a
finger."

"I see your dubious idea of wit remains intact as well."

"So, if Mac . . . if Gray . . ."

"No, shapechanger. This was your path. Theirs still
remain for them to follow."

The curse had been broken, his death sentence
lifted. Too late for him to make amends? To create
a future with the woman he loved? He dared not go
himself to find out.

"Can you deliver a letter for me?"

Fog hung in ghostly streamers across the valley, the
long narrow loch gleaming like polished steel beneath
the gray sky. Even the distant hills took on a soft blue
and purple patina in the damp air. From here, she
could look south and east across the endless mountains or turn her face to the north for a last glimpse of
the sea and the rocky shores of Skye far to the west. She
stood upon the brink; both paths still within reach. No
decision unchangeable . . . yet.

Below her, the coach waited, the Duncallans loung-
ing upon a blanket with a basket luncheon. As Callista
watched, Katherine leaned over to kiss her husband. His
arm wrapped round her waist. A quiet breathless giggle
carried on the breeze to where Callista walked alone.

She swallowed the hard ache in her throat and

scrambled farther up the slope, out of view of her companions. She didn't need a reminder of what she had almost had. What might have been hers but for a Fey-blood's black spell.

A fold in the hillside led her into a hidden meadow. Mist moved like water over the ground, but here and there, sheltered from the wind, star-shaped leaves grew in a burst of bright green from a craggy rockface and small purple flowers littered the long grass.

He stood at the far end of the meadow. A figure as gray and wraithlike as the mist-shrouded hillside. Only his gaze burned hot and startling in a face carved in harsh lines and grim angles. No longer the Adonis, he still paralyzed with a stomach-plunging intensity. A bolt of lightning. A sword cleaving the heart. "I don't blame you for wanting to get away from them," he said. "They make a sickening couple."

"They love one another. There's nothing appalling about that."

Heat crawled up her throat and into her cheeks, and she shivered imagining David's hands upon her body, his fingers combing out the heavy curling fall of her hair. Desire flooded her with a new and different ache, a throbbing between her legs, a tingling in her breasts. Their eyes met, and she knew he knew what she was thinking . . . and feeling. His mind was open to her touch, as her thoughts were clear for him to read. "Are you a ghost?"

He laughed. "What does your power tell you?"

"That you're real . . . you're alive."

"And mostly in one piece."

"What have you done, David?" she asked.

He approached, his body leaving a trail within the

dew-silvered grasses. "The blood I offered you connects us. I'm part of you . . . as you're a part of me."

As if he'd a map to her soul, she felt him inside her, a presence filling the hollow place in her heart. "You can't . . . I mean, you said you couldn't read my mind."

I still can't, Callista. Or not entirely. Thoughts sharp and loud, these I catch snatches of now and then. He switched to speaking out loud. "But no, you're safe from that trespass."

"Then what do you mean, 'we're connected'?"

"Honestly?" He gave a brittle laugh. "I have no idea. But Gram's stories always spoke of the bond between those who'd shared the *afailth luinan*. Souls connected. Destinies intertwined. It's the most powerful magic the Imnada possess and is not given lightly."

"Yet you left me."

"I fled Dunsgathaic. Your aunt saw me offer you the life from my veins. She would not have been satisfied until she drained me of every last drop."

"Aunt Deirdre is not Victor Corey."

"She may not have sold me off a vial at a time, but her brand of sucking me dry would have amounted to the same thing. The Imnada are under siege. I would not be the fuse to bring the walls tumbling down around them."

"Even after they tortured and banished you?"

"Once I would have said good riddance and run the other way. But someone I know told me to stop running and face my demons. The Imnada are still my people. I won't turn on them when they need me most."

"I'm returning to London," she said. "My aunt and I have come to an understanding of sorts, but the priestesses are not where I belong."

"Where do you belong, Callista?" he asked.

"I thought I knew. But that was a mirage, wasn't it? This is good-bye."

"What if I told you I never want to say good-bye? That I would hold you forever if I could—if you would only say yes? What then?"

Her mind grappled with this odd new awareness of him. The slow draw of his lungs as he breathed. The scent of him, musky and sharp and intensely masculine, the hard angles and planes of his face, and the jump of need that matched her own. She felt it sizzle the air between them. "I would take you for as long as the gods would give us."

"For a lifetime?"

Her eyes widened, her heart crashing against her chest. "Would, could, might, if . . . what are you trying to ask me, David?" she snapped.

He laughed, grabbing her around the waist, his grip nearly crushing her lungs. "The curse is broken. Your aunt saved my life in more ways than one, though I doubt she meant to, the old besom."

Callista lifted her face to the sky, where a bird floated high on an updraft. A small dark shape against the backdrop of wind-chased clouds. "I asked again and again. The answer was there all along."

His eyes glowed silver. "Marry me, my beautiful? I can't guarantee what the future will bring nor that the days ahead won't be dangerous. I only know that I love you and can't live without you. Not for a week nor the next fifty years."

She drew him down to her, hungry for his kisses, his touch, the hard vitality of his body against hers. "I will have you, Mr. St. Leger. Till death do us part."

Glossary of the Imnada

Afailth luinan. Also known as the blood cure. According to ancient legend, Imnada blood possesses great healing powers. It's said that a drop can heal most injuries or illness, though few believe the old stories anymore.

Berenth. The night of the last quarter moon. This begins the period when the Imnada's powers to shift at will begin to ebb and it becomes both more difficult and more dangerous.

Bloodline scrolls. The written history and genealogies created and maintained by the Ossine. These records are used to select mates for the Imnada from the five clans.

Clan mark. The crescent symbol tattooed on the upper backs of the male members of the Imnada, signifying their full acceptance into the clan upon their majority. Both males and females are also marked mentally with a signum identifying their clan affiliation and holding.

Dunsgathaic. A mighty fortress located on the Isle of Skye in Scotland that encompasses both the military headquarters of the brotherhood of Amhas-draoi and a convent of Sisters of High Danu.

Emnil. An exile who has been formally sentenced by the Gather and had his clan mark and signum removed and his name erased from the Ossine's bloodline scrolls. An *emnil* is considered dead to the clan and his life forfeit if he attempts any contact with a clan member or a return to clan lands.

Enforcer. The warrior arm of the Ossine whose job it is to track down and eliminate any potential threat to the Imnada.

Fealla Mhòr. The Great Betrayal: the betrayal and murder of the last king of Other, Arthur, by the Imnada warlord Lucan. This event triggered a vengeful purge of the Imnada by the Fey-bloods, who had always mistrusted and feared the shapechangers.

Fey-bloods. (Slang.) Also known as the Other. Men and women who possess the blood and magical powers of the Fey.

Gateway. The door between Earth and the galaxy where the Imnada first originated.

Gather. The ruling council of the Imnada, consisting of seven members: the clan leader from each of the five clans, the head of the Ossine, and the Duke of Morieux, who is hereditary leader over the five clans.

Idrin the Traveler. Among the first Imnada to come through the Gateway and settle on Earth. He is considered the father of their race and from his seed the five clans sprang.

Imnada. A race of shapechangers and telepaths divided into five clans overseen by the ruling Gather. They wield no magical powers, though they are sensitive to its presence and can identify those who possess magic. At first they existed peacefully with the magical race of Other but when the Imnada betrayed King Arthur to his death, they were hunted down in the wars and uprisings that followed. In the ensuing centuries, those who survived grew reclusive and fiercely suspicious of all outsiders to the point that most believe the Imnada no longer exist.

Krythos. Also known as a far-seeing disk. A notched glass disk about two and a half inches in diameter. It is used to augment and amplify the Imnada's natural telepathic abilities over long distances.

Lucan. Leader of the clans during King Arthur's reign. He conspired with Morgana, the king's half sister, to place her son Mordred upon the throne. His betrayal led to Arthur's murder. He was captured by the Fey for his treachery and imprisoned within the Bear's Stone for all eternity.

Morderoth. The night of the new moon, when the shift is impossible for the Imnada.

Mother Goddess. The moon from which the Imnada derive their magical powers.

Ossine. Shamans and spiritual advisers to the clans, they tend to be the strongest and most powerful of the Imnada. They maintain the bloodline scrolls used for selecting each Imnada mating pair and protect the Imnada from out-clan interference with their armed militia of enforcers.

Other. See Fey-blood.

Out-clan. Someone who is not a member of the five clans.

Palings. Magical mists conjured and maintained by the Ossine of each clan. They are used as a natural force field, disguising and shunting people away from the hidden holdings. In recent years, these warded fields have weakened as the clans' powers have weakened.

Pathing. Speaking mind to mind. Imnada can use this telepathy to speak to one another over short distances or when they are in their animal aspect. For longer distances, they use the amplifying power of the *krythos* to connect with each other mentally.

Realing. A magical servant bound to a specific person or place.

Rogue. An unmarked shapechanger without clan or hold affiliation.

Signum. The mental imprint set on every shapechanger's mind at birth by the Ossine. It identifies clan affiliation and rank. Those cast out of the clans have their signa stripped, denoting their outlaw status.

Silmith. The night of the full moon, when the shift comes easiest and the powers of the Imnada are at their height.

Sisters of High Danu. An order of Other priestesses, also known as *bandraoi*, devoted to a contemplative life in service to the gods.

Warriors of Scathach (Amhas-draoi). An Other brotherhood of warrior mages who serve as guardians between the Fey and human worlds.

Ynys Avalenn. Also known as the Summer Kingdom, this is the realm of the Fey.

Youngling. A child of the Imnada who has not yet reached maturity or been marked.

Keep reading for an excerpt from

WARRIOR'S CURSE

Book Three in the Imnada Brotherhood Series

by Alexa Egan

Available May 2014 from Pocket Books

Turn the page for
a preview of *Warrior's Curse* . . .

Prologue

DEEPINGS, CORNWALL—THE PRIMARY SEAT OF
THE DUKE OF MORIEUX

No matter what, they would not see him weep.

Instead Gray bit his lower lip until blood dripped hot down his chin to mix with the streaks already smearing his bruised and battered chest. He twisted against the silver fetters clamped around his wrists and ankles, his torn flesh mottled a sickly shade of green from the metal's poisonous touch, but the struggle only served to sap him of the little strength he had left.

"Just get it over with," he shouted, despising the weakness cracking his voice and the tremors shaking his knees.

The old man merely stared with milky pale eyes at his only surviving grandson. An air of disappointment carved long lines in the Duke's solemn aged face. His heir had let him down—again.

Gray's gaze widened to take in the Gather elders ringing the Duke like hounds round a carcass. The ruddy-faced corpulence of Lord Carteret down from his lonesome Highland holding. Owen Glynjohns from Wales, with his bold good looks and bard's clever tongue. The Skaarsgard, who'd traveled from the ocean-sprayed Orkney cliffs where the seals basking upon those rocky shores and the rugged fishermen plying their coracles on the cold northern seas considered each other kin. Each of the men looked on impassively, their duty done if not enjoyed.

The fourth elder watched the proceedings with a face pale as bone and eyes hollow with mute rage, his hands clamped against the arms of his chair like claws. No doubt Sir Desmond Flannery was imagining his own son's sentence, due to be carried out on the morrow. Mac would never snivel or flinch in fear. He was the consummate soldier, unlike Gray, his supposed senior officer.

Sir Desmond leaned forward, his mouth twisted in disgust. "Enough dallying. Let's have it done then. The sun'll be down in another wee bit and he'll"—he seemed to choke on his words—"he'll shift. The chains aren't intended to hold a bird on the wing."

The elder was right. Already Gray felt the queasy slide of Fey blood magic stealing over him, flames burning blue and silver at the edges of his vision. The sun would set soon, and the dying sorcerer's curse would take him over, twisting his unwilling body from man to beast for the hours of night. His eyes flashed wildly toward his grandfather before darting away again, his bowels churning ominously.

"Of course." A nondescript little gentleman with a clerk's fastidiousness stepped forward in response. The

Arch Ossine—Sir Dromon Pryor—had eyes that saw everything and a mouth trained for truth-twisting. "Mr. Copper. Whenever you're ready."

Gray tried meeting Pryor's triumphant stare but faltered when the enforcer stepped to the scaffold, a red-hot iron brand held in one brutish fist.

A restless audience whispered, feet shuffling against the benches, but no one called out or came to his defense. They knew the laws that had governed their existence for a hundred hundred generations. Understood the weak and the sick and those no longer able to serve the bloodlines must be excised like a cancer for fear the whole pack would be brought low. Lowest peasant or heir to the Morieux himself made no difference when it came to keeping the five clans of Imnada safe.

Gray found himself scanning the crowd for one particular face—though he knew she wouldn't be there. The Duke had sent her north months ago. Still, Gray found himself repeating her name in his head like a mantra, a way to hold himself together in these final horrific moments.

What would she have done had she been here to witness his sentence? Would she have turned her back like the rest of them? Or would she have leapt to his defense as she had so many times over the years? He'd never know, and for that he was almost glad.

The brand's heat could be felt from three feet away. Gray clamped his jaw lest he embarrass himself with last-minute pleas for mercy. Still, two broken rasping words leaked from his bloody mouth as he stood bowed and shaking beneath the weight of his fear.

"Grandfather. Please."

The Duke's chin lifted from the sagging folds of his neck while his hands fluttered for a moment as if he might speak. Then Sir Dromon leaned close to the aging leader of the five clans of Imnada, whispering his poison like silver into the old man's ear. The Duke nodded. His hands relaxed into his lap. His mouth pursed and his eyes hardened once more, pale and uncaring as stones in a pool.

The enforcer laid the brand to Gray's back, singeing away the skin to the muscles and tendons below. The charred stench of roasting flesh filled his nose. The screams ripped from his body tore up his throat and bounced off the stone circle of the Deepings Hall, echoing back to him in waves of anguish. His knees buckled as he arched away from the pain, every nerve aflame, every drop of blood in his veins on fire, his very soul being cleaved from his body.

Squeezing his eyes shut, he escaped to the darkest corner of his mind as a hunted creature burrows away from even the hope of light, but the desolate keening sounds of his disgrace followed him even there as his clan mark was burned away in a stripping of everything he was or would ever hope to be. He retched until his ribs cracked and piss leaked into his boots.

But not one tear fell.

They never saw him weep.

She never saw him weep.

1

The bells were ringing nine in the morning when Major Gray de Coursy stepped from the hackney at Tower Hill. Despite the hour, fog cloaked the streets in a thick, choking darkness. It swirled in the alleys and gathered in the parks, bringing with it the stench of dead fish, river mud, and chimney soot. Lanterns threw dim greasy pools of light over the cobbles while footsteps and voices echoed eerily in the green-gray miasma. A link boy offered Gray his services but was waved away. His keen vision cut the gloom like a knife, and he wanted no witnesses to his final destination.

He passed through a narrow, dingy lane, coming out near the disused water stairs south of the Tower and St. Katherine's, stopping finally in front of a door set deep into a stone wall—part of an ancient chapter-house, though the wall and yard beyond were all that remained. He knocked once, then twice more.

A key turned. A bolt slid clear and the door swung

open on the hunched figure of a man. "She awaits you, my lord."

"It's simply Major de Coursy, Breg. Lord Halvossa was my father's title and would have been my brother's after. Never mine."

"Yes, my lord . . . er . . . Major, sir. As you say." The porter bowed him in, throwing the bolt behind him. "I offered her breakfast but she refused."

"You did as you should." Gray approached a low columned outbuilding, Breg following. At the entrance, the old man paused, shuffling foot to foot.

"Out with it," Gray said sternly.

The porter licked his lips and gave a quick breath as if steeling himself. "It's an enforcer, my lord. Prowling the streets near Cheapside last night."

"How could you tell it was an Ossine?"

Breg huffed. "I may be rogue and cast from my holding, but I can still sense a member of the five clans right enough. And I know a shaman when I cast my peepers on one. They're different, ain't they?"

"What was he doing?"

"Asking questions, my lord. I was afraid to get too close. Didn't want him catching wind of me following. No clan member would sob to hear old Breg had ended as food for the grubs with a stake through his heart, that's for sure."

Gray's mouth curved in a faint smile. "This clan member would. If you see him again, send word. But don't go sniffing around on your own. I can't afford to lose you."

"They're growing bolder, ain't they, my lord . . . Major, sir? I heard tell of a rogue clansman near Clapham disappeared and turned up dead. Another one up north off Islington Road by the Quaker workhouse. It's not safe to be unmarked no more."

Gray's hand tightened around the head of his cane. "Things will change. They must, or the clans are doomed."

"Hope you're right, Major. I surely do."

Gray left Breg and entered the outbuilding, placing aside his worry over the man's revelations, to be mulled over later. This morning's meeting was too important for distractions.

A woman rose from her chair to meet him, the lamplight gilding her golden hair and flushing her rose and cream skin. "It's been a long time, Gray."

Lady Delia Swann's serene beauty hid many secrets, as Gray well knew; her Fey-blood magic, her alliance with his rebels, and her sexual activities with a prince of the realm, two generals, and an archbishop. She assumed she knew all his secrets as well, but there were some things he did not speak aloud. Some fears he refused to name.

"I've been busy." He bowed over the hand she held out, ignoring the glitter of conquest in her eyes.

"As have I, but that doesn't mean we can't be busy together from time to time." Her gaze traveled sensuously over him, lifting the hairs at the back of his neck. "By the looks of you, I'd guess you haven't been to bed yet. Was it that little Nicholls girl? She practically leapt in your arms last night at the Prater's ball. I wouldn't think virgins were to your taste, but then you've always been full of surprises. And she comes with an ample dowry."

"I'm old enough to be her father."

Lady Delia laughed. "Only if you'd sired her at the ripe old age of eleven."

"I should have said I *feel* old enough to be her father."

"That I would believe. But if it wasn't the Nicholls girl, it must have been Lady Bute." She laid a finger against her full lips, gold-flecked eyes lifted in thought. "Then there's that opera dancer they say tried to drown herself in the Thames for love of the mysterious Ghost Earl. Hmm . . . so many choices . . ."

"Whoever came up with that damned sobriquet should have their heads boiled in oil."

She crossed to his side. "You should be flattered. It makes you seem dashing and dangerous and passionately gallant. A hero in a swashbuckling romance." She cupped his face in her hands. "If they only knew the half of it, am I right?"

He stepped back, out of her reach. "Can we move on with the reason for this meeting?"

She gave a little half shrug. "Of course. Have you made the arrangements we spoke of? If I'm to disappear, I want to be sure all my affairs are in order and that includes the boy."

His hand tightened around the head of his cane, lips pinched tight. "It's been done just as you asked."

"And my personal payment for services rendered?"

Gray took a leather pouch from his coat and tossed it on a nearby table. "You can disappear quite thoroughly with what's in there. Make a new life on the Continent or the Americas. You'll be safe. You'll be free."

"I like the sound of that. I've already booked passage on the packet to Calais. From there, the world is my playground."

"You leave so soon?"

"You sound disappointed"—she offered him a sly smile, which he did not return—"but now that you've done as I asked there's nothing holding me here."

"The boy is here."

"He's a boy no longer. He'll miss me for a short while, but life will rectify that quickly enough." She shrugged, though he knew she cared more than she let on. "I've been asked politely by Lord Drummond to vacate my town house in favor of his latest *affaire de coeur*, and the family pile in Devonshire was never a home to me." She shivered. "Too full of ghosts for my taste. My sister is welcome to it." The leather pouch disappeared inside her voluminous cloak, and a narrow flat jeweler's box, designs etched into its surface with an artist's skill, was laid on the table in its place. "The last missing key of Gylferion, as promised. I believe you have the other three already?"

"I might." Gray opened the lid to reveal a notched copper disk, dulled green with age and bent at one corner. On one side, the crescent of the Imnada. On the other, two vertical opposing arrows within a diamond. "How did you get hold of it?"

"Best not to ask. You might not like the answer." She cocked her head, a frown drawing her lips into a pout. "You know, I could take your money and still sell you out to the highest bidder, Gray. The Ossine would be on your doorstep by nightfall. And if they didn't kill you, the Other would. Your enemies are mounting."

He closed the box and slid it into his coat pocket. "You could, but you won't."

"What makes you so certain? I'd sell my own mother if it gained me a profit."

This time it was he who reached out and touched her cheek. "You say these things, but I know you better."

"You always did." She sighed. "Probably why we never got along." Her eyes grew troubled. "Be careful, Gray. In my line of work, I hear the whispers. You're being watched by my kind as well as yours. There are wagers about who'll move first to eliminate you. Perhaps you should think of joining me in Calais."

He rubbed a thumb across his scarred palm, the myriad pale lines crisscrossing the roughened skin like a tangled skein of threads. Each day brought a new cut and a new scar as he worked the magic that kept him whole and the black curse at bay. A magic that had become an addiction. He could not stop. He could not continue. Either choice brought sickness and then death. "If I can't break the Fey-blood's curse, neither side will have to worry over me for long. I'll be dead and the Ghost Earl shall be ghost in truth."

The mouse squeezed its way into the narrow crack between street and foundation, glancing back once to make sure it had not been followed. No sign of pursuit. The way was clear. Wriggling through the maze of lathing and plaster, it followed its clever rodent nose past the kitchens, now quiet this late at night, and upward to the ground floor. The study was dark, the dining room empty, but the mouse expected that. It was the perfect time to explore unseen, and the perfect form to do so unnoticed. What was one mouse among a colony of such? A nuisance, but hardly worth more than a stiff whisk with a broom. Better that than a sword in the gut, which might be the reaction should Gray discover the real identity of the rodent creeping along his wainscoting.

Sliding under a broken slat, the mouse moved through the walls with purpose, assessing the town house's layout should quick escape be necessary, searching rooms as it went. No guests resided in the empty chambers. Only half a handful of servants lay sleeping in the attics. Of guards, she saw no sign. He was alone and unprotected. Didn't he understand the danger?

Reaching a small room at the back of the second floor, the mouse paused at the flicker of candlelight coming through a gap in the chair rail. Following the dim glow, it sniffed and pushed its beady-eyed head out through the hole. A bedchamber. *His* bedchamber, by the lived-in, cluttered look to it.

A shocking thought followed close upon this observation. A shocking, unnerving thought that had the mouse shoving its way out through the hole into the room to rise on its hind legs, whiskers twitching. Did that heap of blankets in the bed move? Was someone sleeping? Was it two someones and were they sleeping at all? What if they were in the middle of . . .

So focused was the little creature on determining whether the four-poster in the corner contained one or two people, it never saw the descending glass until the crystal walls surrounded it, held in place by an enormous hand.

A face leaned close, studying the mouse, searching for answers. Older now. Harder. The gentle rounded features and sweet innocence of youth had been stripped bare and scraped raw until it seemed honed like a knife blade, no softness to dull the glittering edge. No tenderness to moderate the harsh austerity. But the same icy blue eyes shone from beneath dark winged brows, the same tiny scar remained at the edge of a strong uncompromising mouth. The same long aristocratic nose flared now with suspicion and doubt.

Scooping up glass and mouse both, the man lifted them to eye level. "Eagles eat mice, you know."

*   *   *

Meeryn Munro was the last person Gray had expected to visit him—in his bedchamber—in the middle of the night . . . alone. Yet here she was, shed of her mouse's skin and seated on the edge of his bed in nothing but his borrowed robe. At this point, he would have preferred her covered in fur. It was far less revealing. Far less apt to make his thoughts wander away from what her unexpected arrival meant.

"You've changed—grown up." A trite and pointless comment. Of course she'd changed. It had been almost ten years since he'd seen her last.

"Age happens to the best of us, I'm told," she answered with a wry smile.

"Yes, but . . ." He waved a hand in her general direction. "The curls are gone"—replaced by soft waves of honey colored hair—"and your figure has matured"— the gawky flat-chested girl of his memories was now a woman of luscious, feminine curves and long elegant limbs—"and you used to have . . . I mean there were the . . . the . . ."

She wrinkled her nose. "Spots. I know, they were positively horrid, but thankfully long gone. Lemon juice and Gower's Lotion every evening before bed. But surely, I haven't changed that much."

"No, not exactly." His gaze traveled over her from head to foot and back. The ghost of the old Meeryn lingered in the narrow elfin face, pert chin, and full coral lips, but there was a shrewdness in her eyes and a severity to her jaw that had never been present in the laughing playmate of his youth. "And then again—yes."

"Well, you haven't. You look just as you always did."

His smile came laced with bitterness. "That's the first lie I've caught you in tonight."

"It's true. You do look the same. A bit longer in the

tooth and leaner in the face, of course, but that's to be expected after . . . well . . . after all you've been through."

She couldn't say the words. He didn't blame her. It had taken months before he could speak of his sentencing without vomiting his guts until his throat and stomach were raw. He rubbed his scarred palm without even thinking. Dropped his hand to his side when he caught her watching him.

"I heard rumors that you'd lifted the curse," she said.

"Contained . . . not lifted."

"But it's night"—her gaze cut to the window—"the sun is down and you're still . . . they said when the sun left the sky, you were forced to become your animal aspect. Forced from man to beast against your will. That's what I was told."

"There are ways to hold the spell at bay and keep to the form I choose, but it comes at a price." He poured and handed her a glass of restorative brandy from the decanter permanently set beside his bed for those nights he couldn't sleep.

"Things never change, do they, Professor Gray? Still got your nose caught in a dusty old book," she commented with a nod of her head toward his cluttered desk.

"That's where the answers are," he answered. Realizing he stared, he quickly busied himself with clearing away the various manuscripts he'd been studying, arranging his pencils in a row, pocketing the four ancient metal disks.

Laughter danced in her eyes. "Your response hasn't changed in ten years either."

Ten years—the blink of an eye. An eternity. They'd grown up together; Duke's grandson and Duke's ward. Close as siblings—closer even. His sibling had been seven years his senior and barely noticed Gray except as a nuisance to be shed at the first possible opportunity. Meeryn had filled that slot, becoming his boon companion in all things from illicit raids on the Deepings kitchens and nasty pranks on the string of tutors and governesses when they were young to illicit raids on the Deepings wine cellar and midnight forays beyond the protections of Deepings's walls as they grew older.

As a child, he'd foolishly imagined their friendship would last forever. Time, distance, and circumstance had ended that dream long ago. Yet she'd remained a bright memory among so much he'd tried to put behind him when he'd been condemned to exile. Was that memory, like so many other things in his life, about to be irrevocably shattered?

"What are you doing here, Meeryn? And why come sneaking in via mousehole? Was knocking at the front door too plebeian for your tastes?"

She offered him a flippant roll of her eyes. "Would you have welcomed me in if I had?"

"Not while Pryor and his enforcers scour London, hunting anyone they think might be in league with me." He poured himself a brandy.

"But, you see, it was Pryor who sent me."

He froze with the glass halfway to his lips, but there was no hint of mockery in her placid expression. She was dead serious. "Did he? This visit grows more interesting by the moment."

"I know what you're thinking, Gray, but you can relax. I'm not here to kill you. I'm here to bring you home."

"I *am* home," he replied just as solemnly, placing his still-full glass on a nearby table. This conversation called for stone cold sobriety.

"Don't be clever. You know what I mean—home to Deepings."

"And why would I want to do that? Despite what people might think, I'm not looking for a quick death, even less a slow and gruesome one."

"What if coming with me meant preventing more bloodshed among the clans? What if it meant saving the Imnada?"

"Dromon was clever in sending you as his emissary. Anyone else would have been shown the door . . . or the end of my sword. You have five minutes to explain, then you leave."

Defiance lit her unflinching stare. "The Duke is dying."

Gray closed his eyes briefly on a silent prayer, though for what he couldn't say. For some reason, he'd always just assumed the old man would live forever; a craggy irascible rock upon which the world crashed and broke. His presence solid and eternal as the cliffs below Deepings.

"He's been ill since you . . . since the summer you were sent away," Meeryn continued. "Then this past spring he took a turn for the worse. It's his heart. They don't expect him to last more than a few weeks."

"And if I said good riddance to the old bastard?"

Candlelight flickered over her face, glinting in her auburn hair, flames reflecting in her deep brown eyes. "You don't mean that. He's the only family you have left. When he dies, you'll be—"

"Duke of Morieux," he finished her sentence.

"Leader of the five clans," she amended.

Neither role had been his by birth—a fact his grandfather had never ceased to remind him of even as Gray struggled to fill his dead brother's shoes. He'd finally escaped into the military, unsure by then whether he hoped to win honor in battle or a quick death. There he'd found the praise he'd sought, in the letters that arrived from home. A pride that ended in the Gather's circle with the flames charring the clan mark from his back.

"Sir Dromon Pryor is leader in all but name." He stood at the hearth, a hand upon the mantel as he stared into the cold expanse, wishing he might glimpse the future, but seeing only the past.

"His grip on power isn't as secure as he wants you to believe and it will only worsen if the Duke dies without an heir in place," Meeryn explained. "Rumors spread as your rebellious Imnada grow in numbers. The Gather elders chafe under his heavy-handed authority and the brutality of his Ossine enforcers. Summary executions of clan members on the mere suspicion of sedition are becoming common. Even the Palings begin to fail, the mists thinning dangerously in some places. Now that the Fey-bloods know we've survived the Fealla Mhòr, it's only a matter of time before they discover a way through the wards and the slaughter begins in earnest."

"It doesn't have to be that way."

"So you say, but can you speak for all the Fey-bloods? Can you guarantee us our safety?"

"Can Pryor?"

"The clans won't survive an attack from without while they are beset from within. Pryor concedes this and wants to talk."

"Pryor's tongue is as crooked as his brain. Why should I trust him?" Gray asked coolly.

"Don't trust him. Trust me." She smiled, her eyes alight with mischief. "As N'thuil, I can guarantee you safe passage on holding lands. So long as you're with me, you're protected."

She spoke. He saw her lips move, but he heard nothing after the bit about Meeryn being named N'thuil. Voice of Jai Idrish. Living vessel of the Mother Goddess.

She dragged the robe from her shoulders and twisted around so her back faced him. There, high upon her back, was the crescent of the Imnada, a whorl of black against her golden skin. And just to the right of it, still pink at the edges, was the smaller circlet that signified her ascension to the seat of N'thuil.

Unthinking, his fingers traced the needle's narrow marking as it curved up over her shoulder blade to the base of her neck. She shivered and cast him an arch look, the laughter dying in her eyes to be replaced with something uncertain and almost shy. His finger became his hand. The skin of her back was like silk beneath his palm as he caressed downward along her spine to the point where her hips flared and the robe and his own ragged self-control stopped him from descending further. Her lips parted, and he sensed the suspension of her breath, the tremors running beneath her feverish skin. Her eyes darkened within the thick fringe of her lashes. Was it longing he saw? Excitement?

His heart thrashed against his ribs, and sweat splashed hot and cold over his skin. He wanted to tempt Meeryn further; an inch lower, a breath nearer. Then a breeze teased the candle's thin flame. Her look vanished as if it had never been, and he surfaced from the lecherous swirl of his desire just before he made an utter ass of himself.

"When did this happen?" Thankfully, his voice emerged only slightly raspy.

Meeryn yanked the robe up to her neck, her body rigid, her gaze fierce. "A month ago. I'm surprised you didn't hear." Her voice trembled, though the emotion behind it was difficult to decipher. "Sir Dromon accuses you of having spies in every household and knowing our secrets before we speak them."

"I'm flattered, but unfortunately, my network isn't quite that extensive or well informed."

She opened her mouth as if to respond, her gaze swimming with thoughts left unspoken. Gave an almost imperceptible shake of her head before continuing on. "Muncy Tidwell died unexpectedly a few weeks ago."

Somehow he doubted that was what she'd originally intended to say, but if she chose to ignore his boorish behavior, he sure as hell wasn't going to bring it up. And so the awkwardness dissipated ever so slowly.

"A more useless N'thuil the world has never seen," Gray replied.

"Granted, but Jai Idrish chose him . . . it must have seen something within his heart that spoke of promise."

"What did it see in you?"

She ducked her head, looking almost shy . . . or ashamed. "I don't know. It has yet to speak to me. Not since the night of my choosing has it woken from its slumber."

"Which must be a tale in itself. Jai Idrish has never chosen anyone not shaman-trained."

"Or male," she added. "So I've been told—repeatedly."

"Then how . . ."

"It wasn't my fault, Gray. Honestly. I woke one night as if someone had called to me. I walked out into the corridor, thinking I was being summoned; that the Duke needed me. I don't remember much after that, but the next thing I knew I was standing in the tower sanctuary, the sphere glowing warm beneath my fingers. It was as if a piece I never knew was missing had suddenly slotted itself into place and I was whole."

"Sir Dromon must have been furious.

"The Arch Ossine wasn't happy, but there was nothing he could do once the crystal had chosen its Voice.

The laws are clear, and if Sir Dromon is a stickler about anything, it's following clan law."

"Hoist with his own petard. He must have been furious after so many years of a compliant toady like Tidwell serving as mouthpiece and cover for his crimes." A smile quirked his lips as the implications of this news sank in. "Perhaps that's why you were chosen. You've never been compliant in your life."

A fact he now counted on.

A

and

Demon's Curse

"Complex world-building and compelling characters. Egan's creatures are sexy, soulful, and dangerous."

—Molly Harper, author of the Nice Girls series

"A luscious, well-told story."

—*New York Times* bestselling author Grace Burrowes

"Replete with dark, sensuous, and honorable characters and a fast-paced, intricate plot, this highly romantic and exciting story is a winner."

—*RT Reviews* (4½ stars)

"Sexy shifters, ancient blood feuds, and a heroine who won't quit her man. . . . I could not put it down."

—*USA Today* bestselling author Caridad Piñeiro

"Will leave readers eagerly anticipating future volumes."

—*Publishers Weekly*

"Alexa Egan promises to be a star of the genre."

—Kathryne Kennedy, author of the Elven Lords series

Also by ALEXA EGAN

Awaken the Curse
Demon's Curse

Available from Pocket Books